AW YEAH COMICS & ACTION LAB PRESENTS...

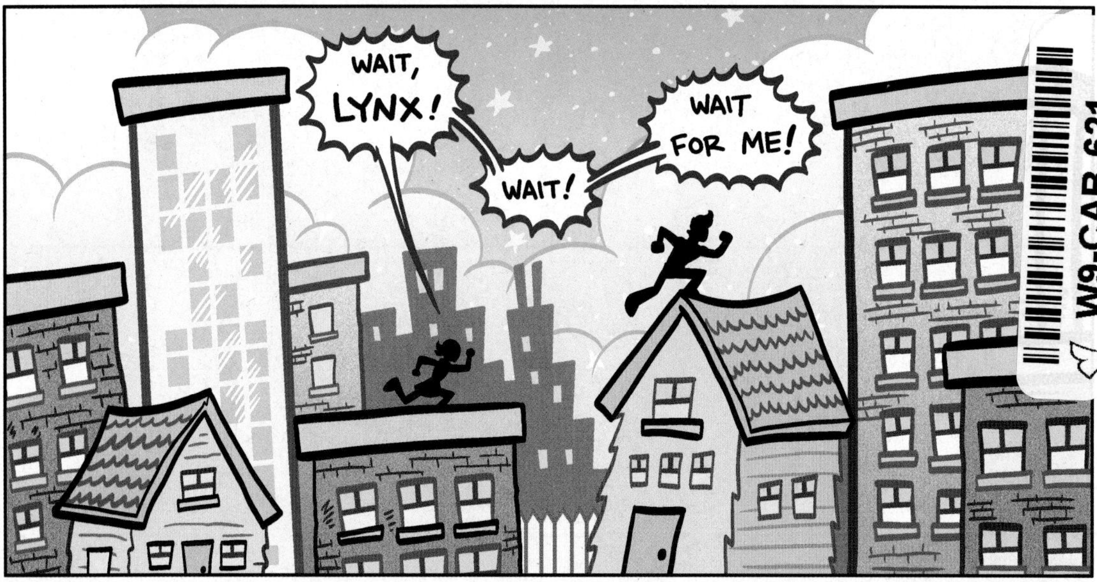

WAIT, LYNX!
WAIT!
WAIT FOR ME!

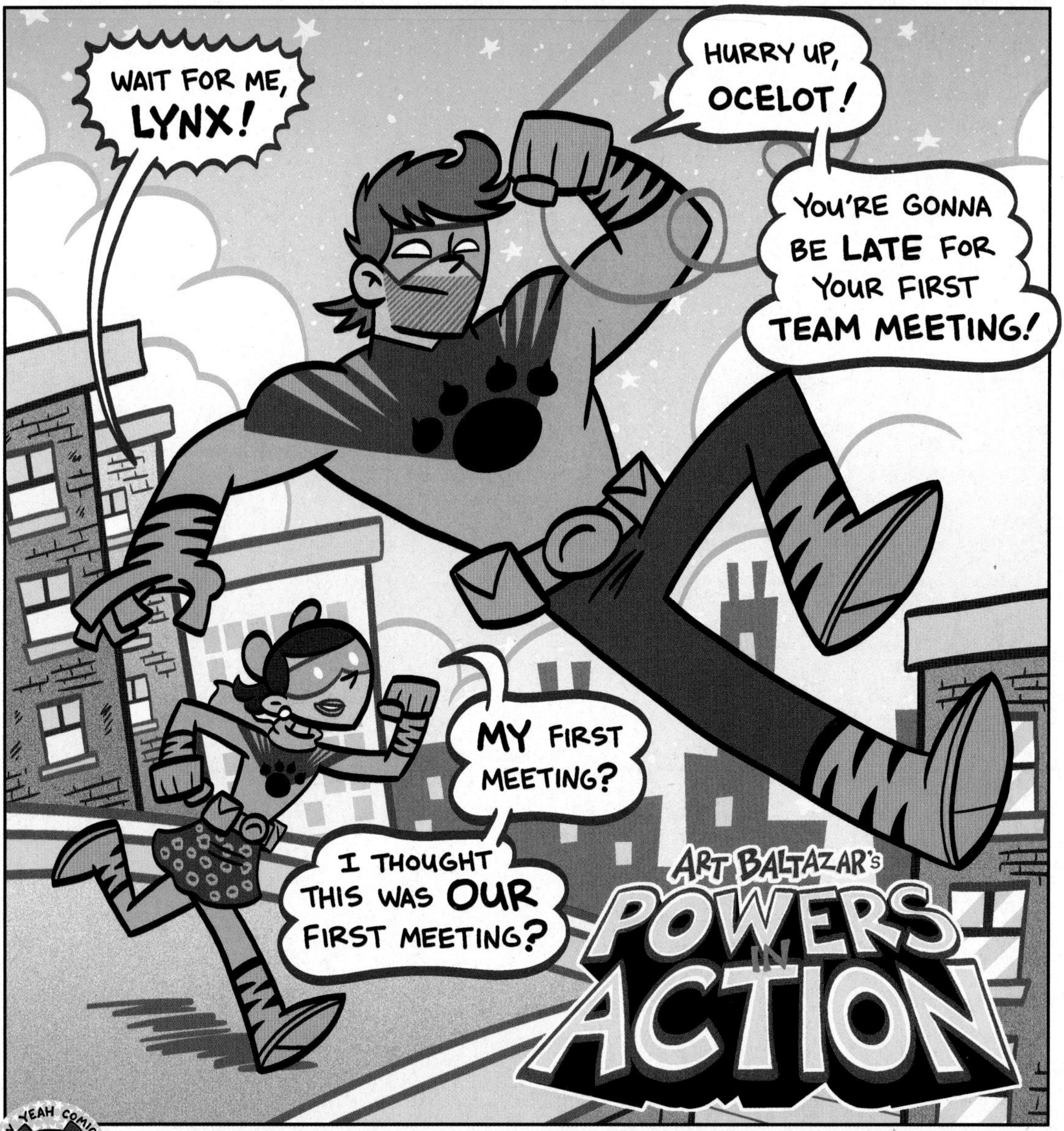

WAIT FOR ME, LYNX!
HURRY UP, OCELOT!
YOU'RE GONNA BE LATE FOR YOUR FIRST TEAM MEETING!
MY FIRST MEETING?
I THOUGHT THIS WAS OUR FIRST MEETING?
ART BALTAZAR'S POWERS IN ACTION

Bryan Seaton: Publisher/ CEO • Shawn Gabborin: Editor In Chief • Nicole D'Andria: Marketing Director/Editor
Danielle Davison: Executive Administrator • Chad Cicconi: Team Mascot • Shawn Pryor: President of Creator Relations

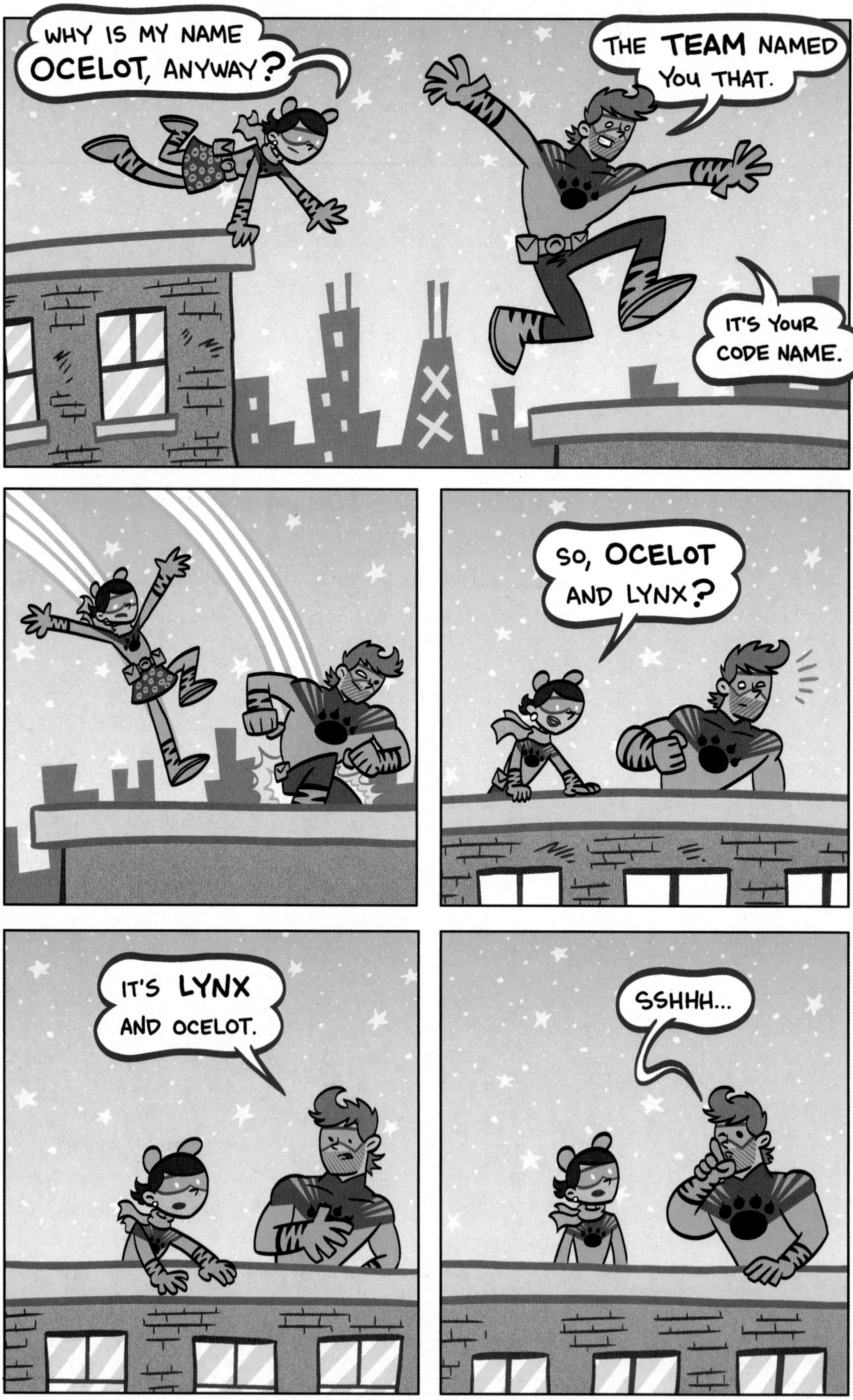

WHY IS MY NAME OCELOT, ANYWAY?
THE TEAM NAMED YOU THAT.
IT'S YOUR CODE NAME.
SO, OCELOT AND LYNX?
IT'S LYNX AND OCELOT.
SSHHH...

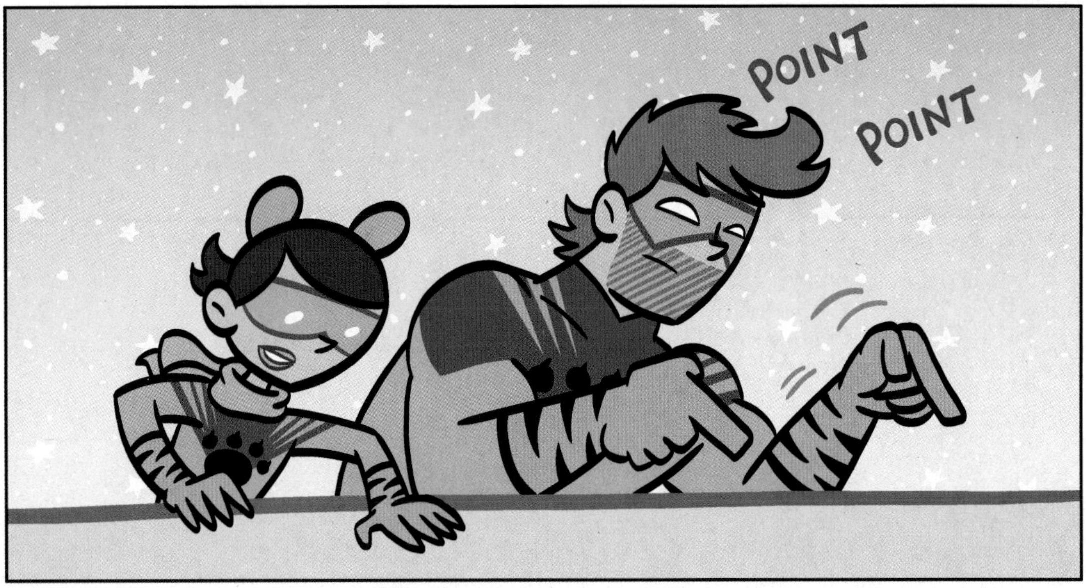
POINT
POINT

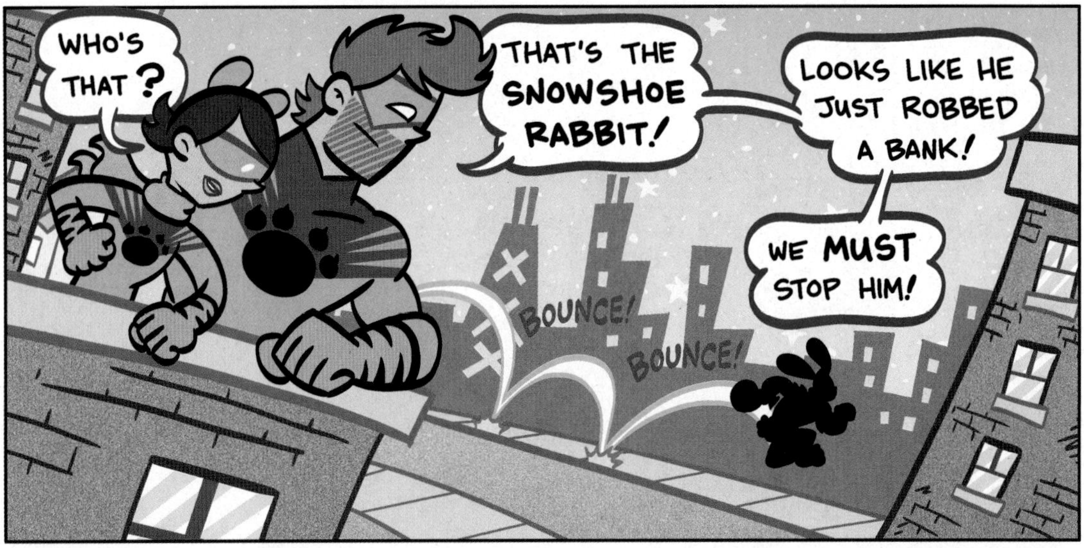
WHO'S THAT?
THAT'S THE SNOWSHOE RABBIT!
LOOKS LIKE HE JUST ROBBED A BANK!
WE MUST STOP HIM!
BOUNCE!
BOUNCE!

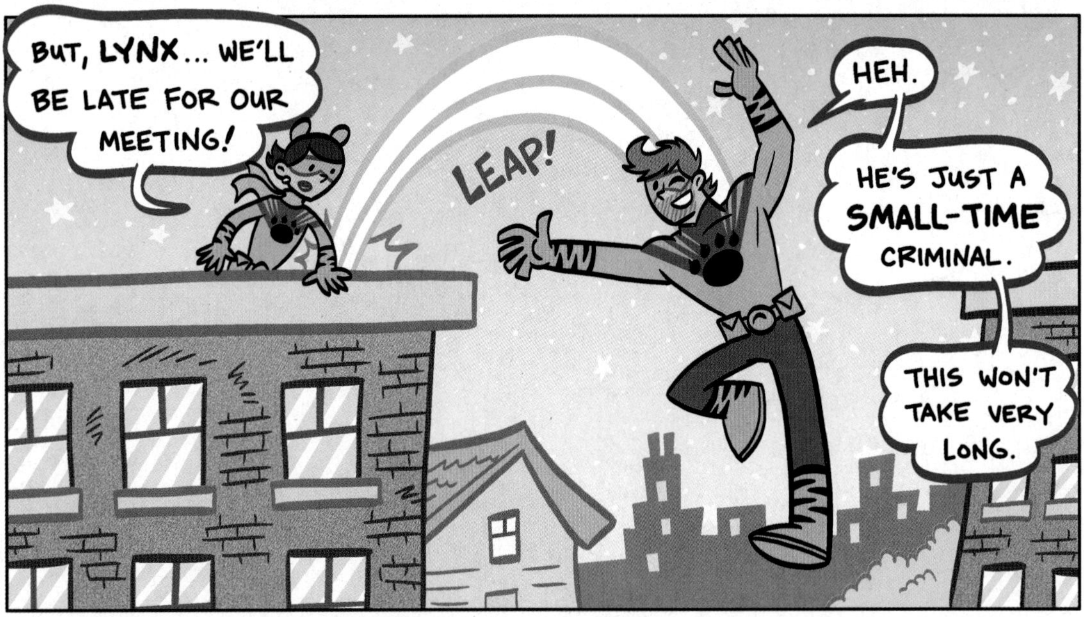
BUT, LYNX... WE'LL BE LATE FOR OUR MEETING!
LEAP!
HEH.
HE'S JUST A SMALL-TIME CRIMINAL.
THIS WON'T TAKE VERY LONG.

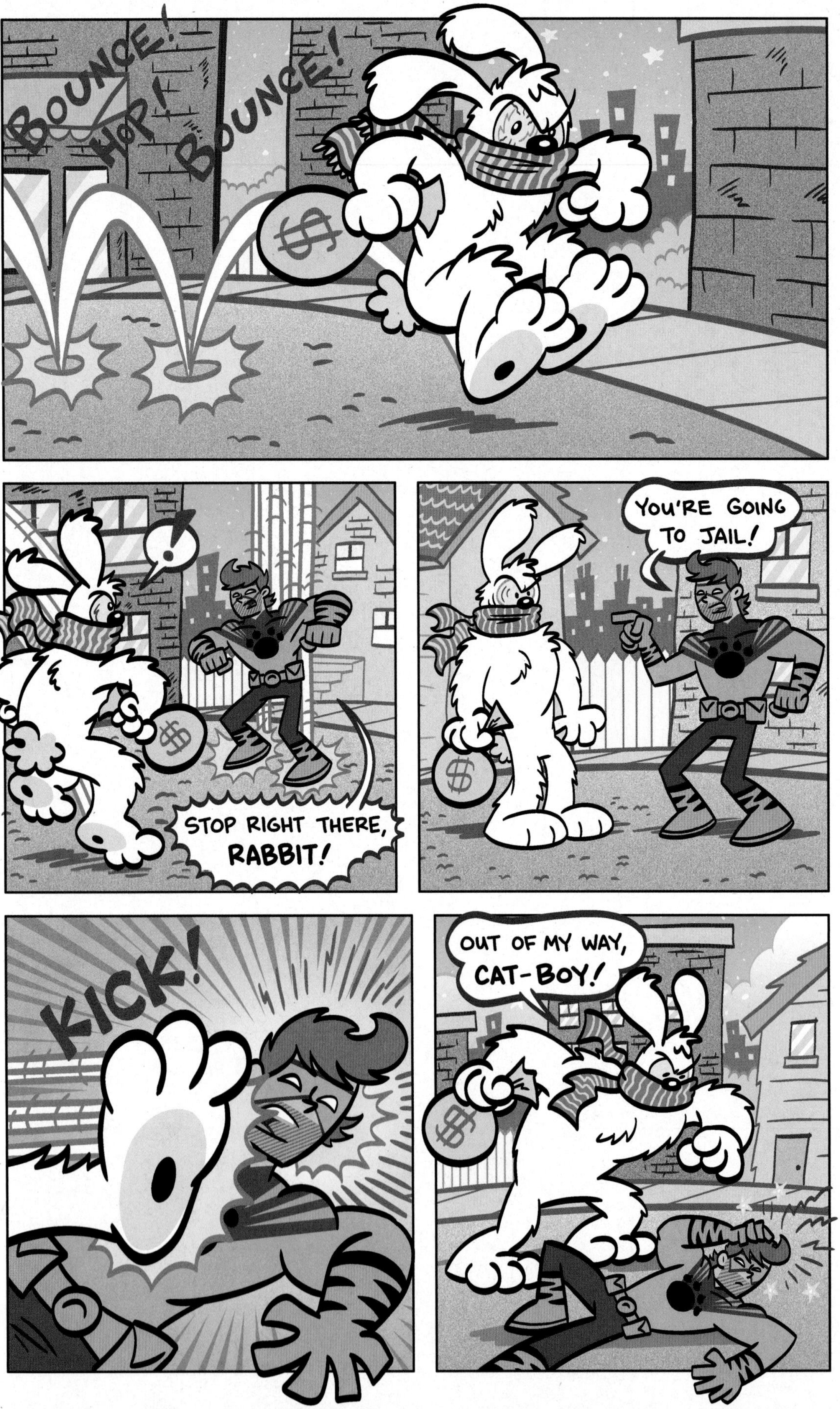
BOUNCE!
HOP!
BOUNCE!
STOP RIGHT THERE, RABBIT!
YOU'RE GOING TO JAIL!
KICK!
OUT OF MY WAY, CAT-BOY!

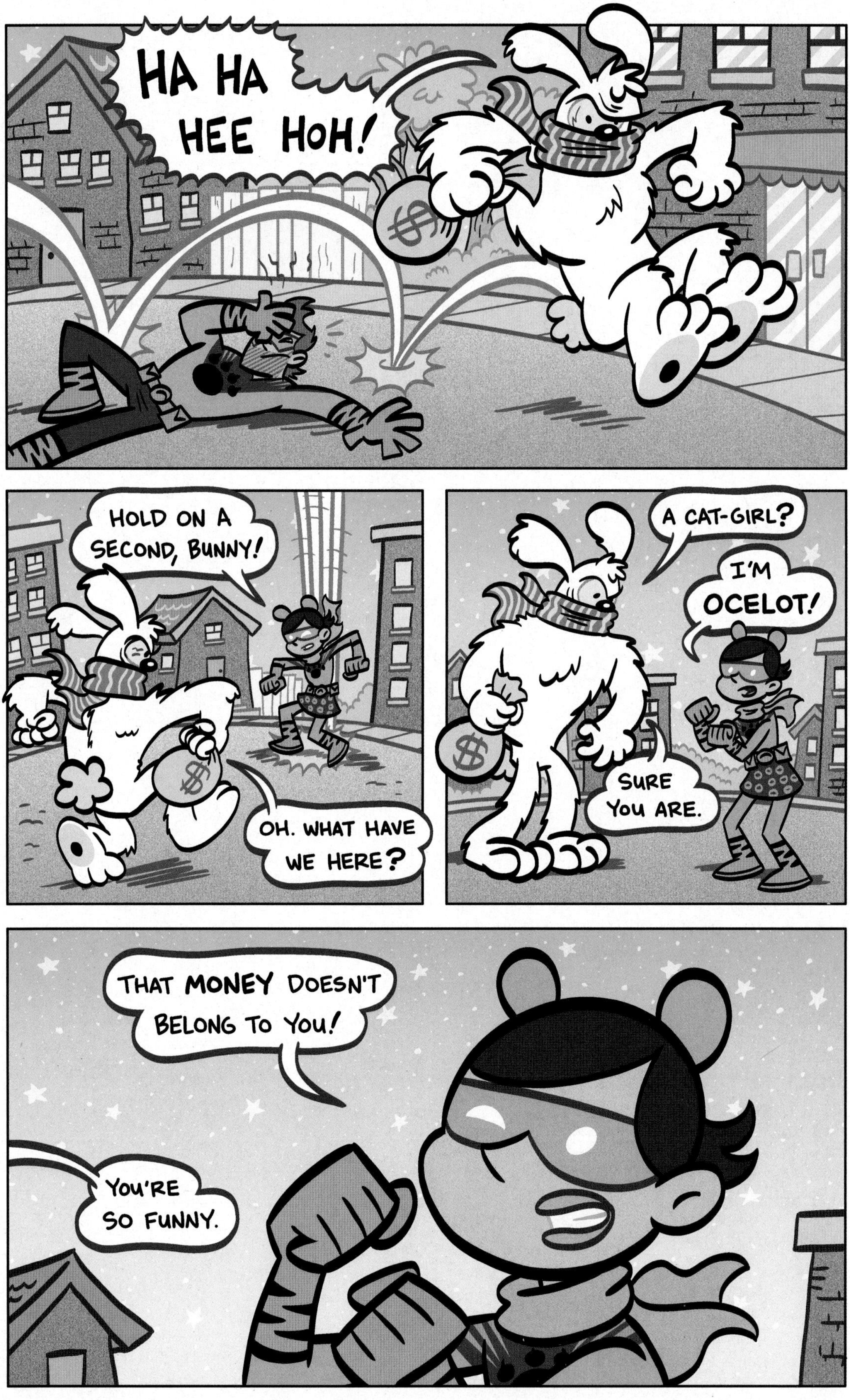
HA HA HEE HOH!
HOLD ON A SECOND, BUNNY!
OH. WHAT HAVE WE HERE?
A CAT-GIRL?
I'M OCELOT!
SURE YOU ARE.
THAT MONEY DOESN'T BELONG TO YOU!
YOU'RE SO FUNNY.

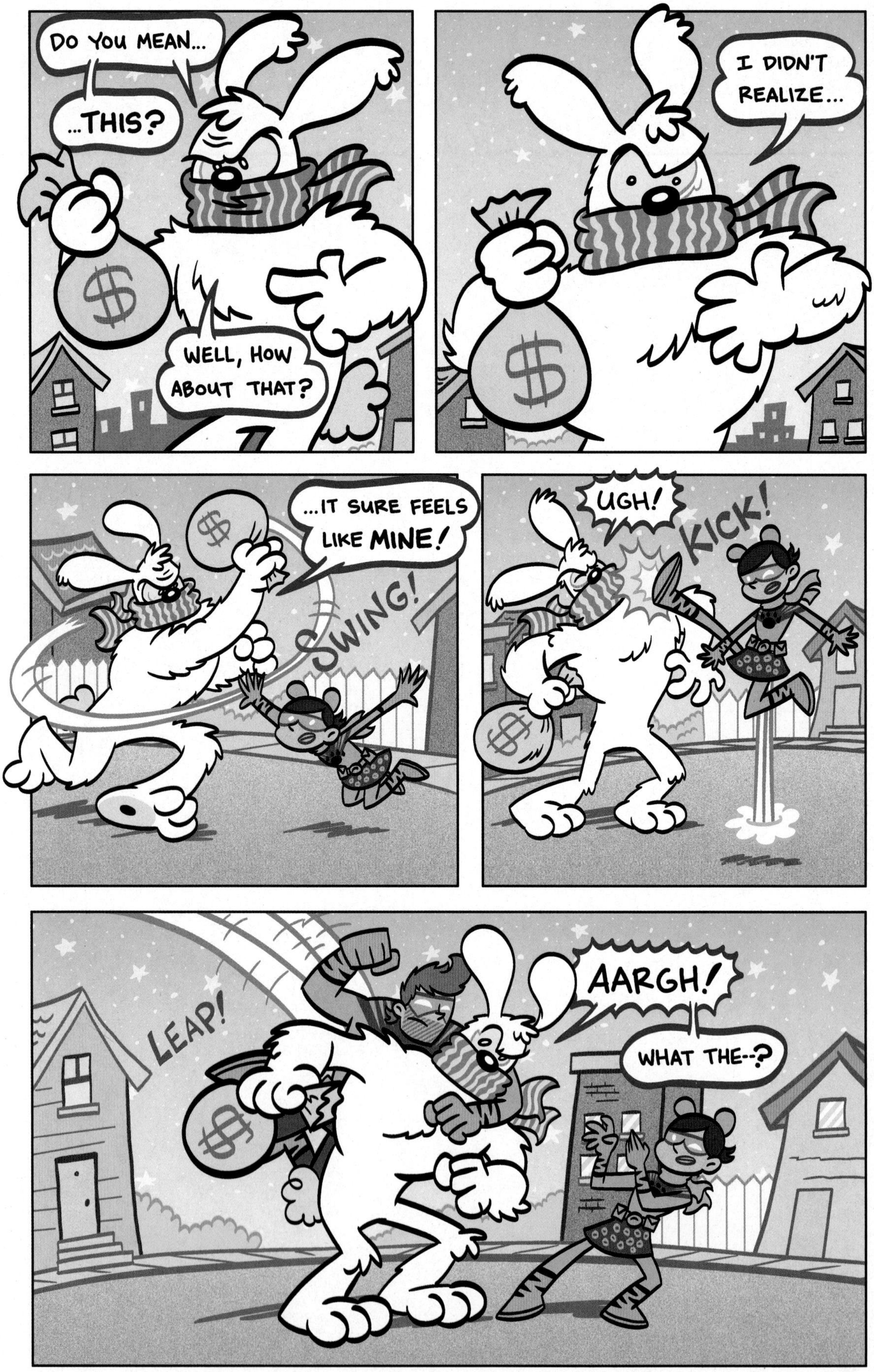
DO YOU MEAN...
...THIS?
WELL, HOW ABOUT THAT?
I DIDN'T REALIZE...
...IT SURE FEELS LIKE MINE!
SWING!
UGH!
KICK!
LEAP!
AARGH!
WHAT THE--?

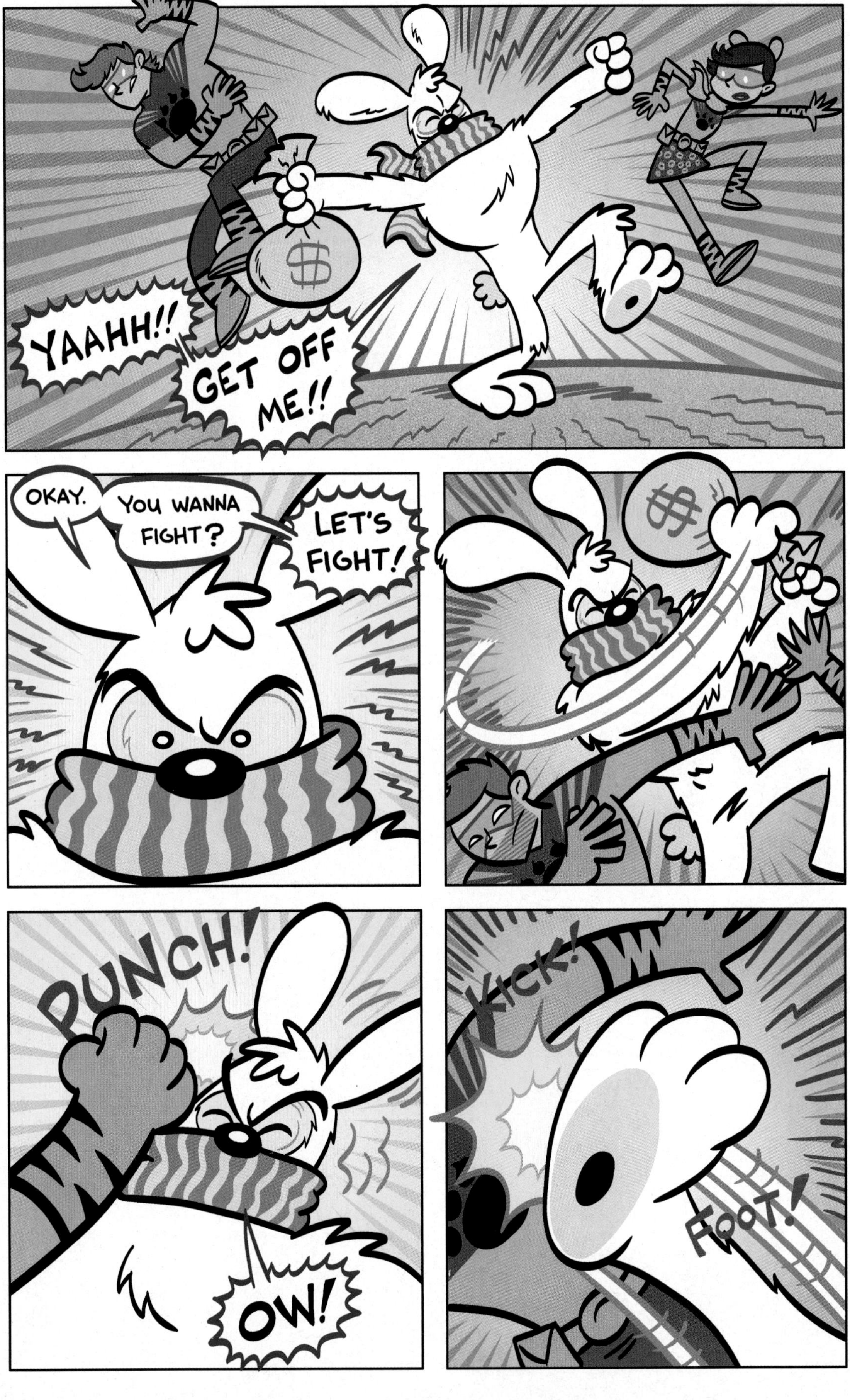
YAAHH!!
GET OFF ME!!
OKAY.
YOU WANNA FIGHT?
LET'S FIGHT!
PUNCH!
OW!
KICK!
FOOT!

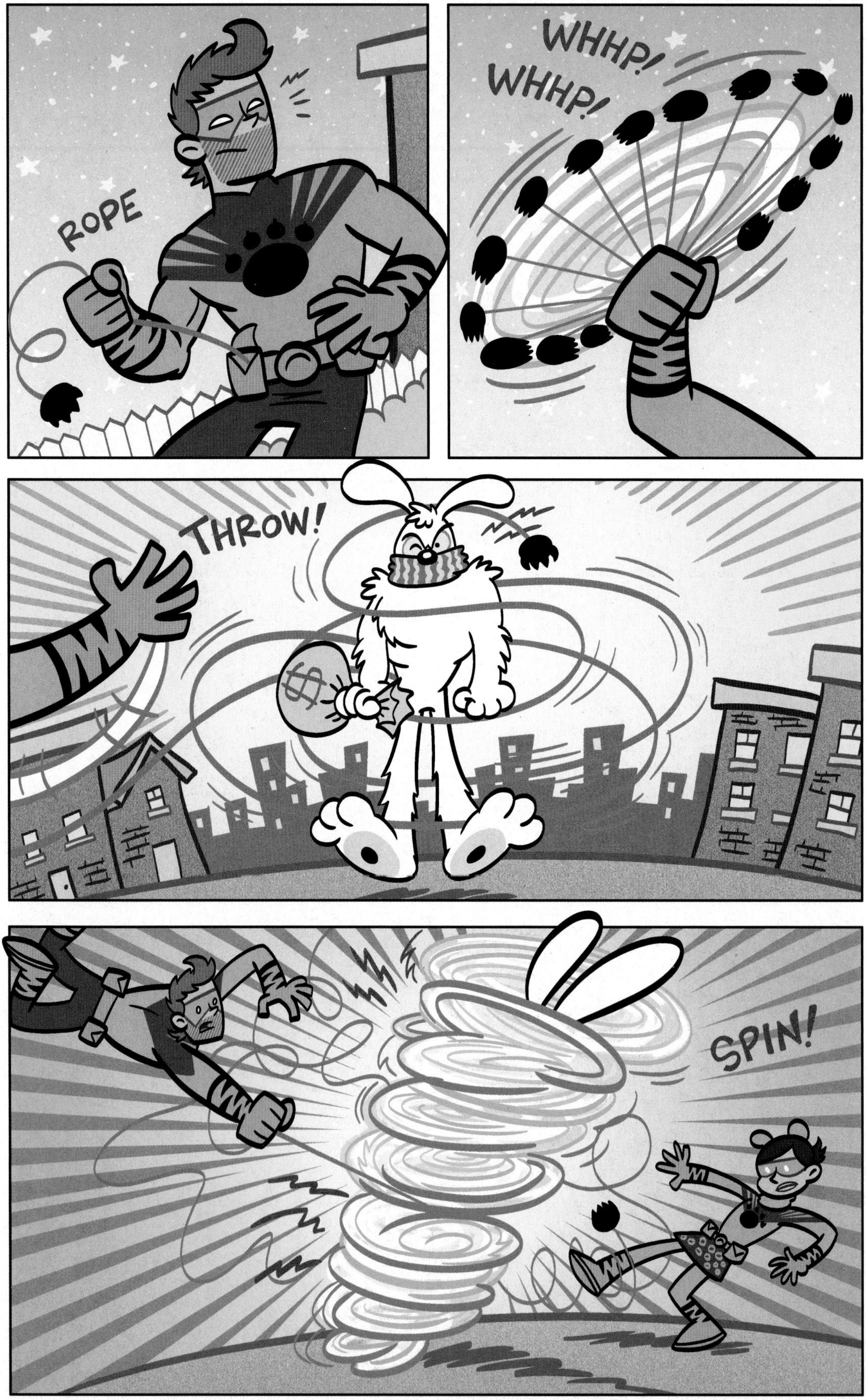
ROPE
WHHP!
WHHP!
THROW!
SPIN!

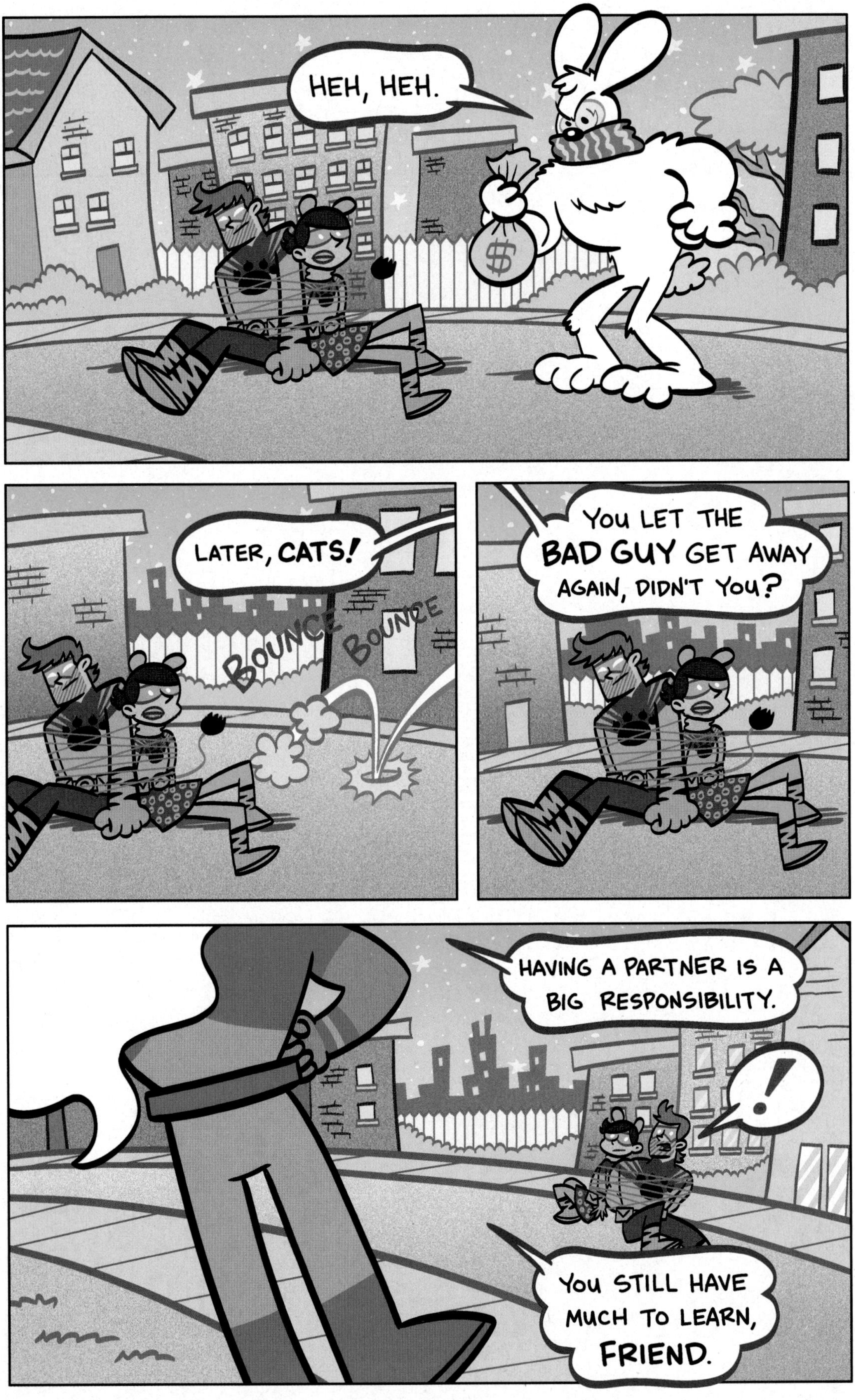
HEH, HEH.
LATER, CATS!
BOUNCE
BOUNCE
YOU LET THE BAD GUY GET AWAY AGAIN, DIDN'T YOU?
HAVING A PARTNER IS A BIG RESPONSIBILITY.
!
YOU STILL HAVE MUCH TO LEARN, FRIEND.

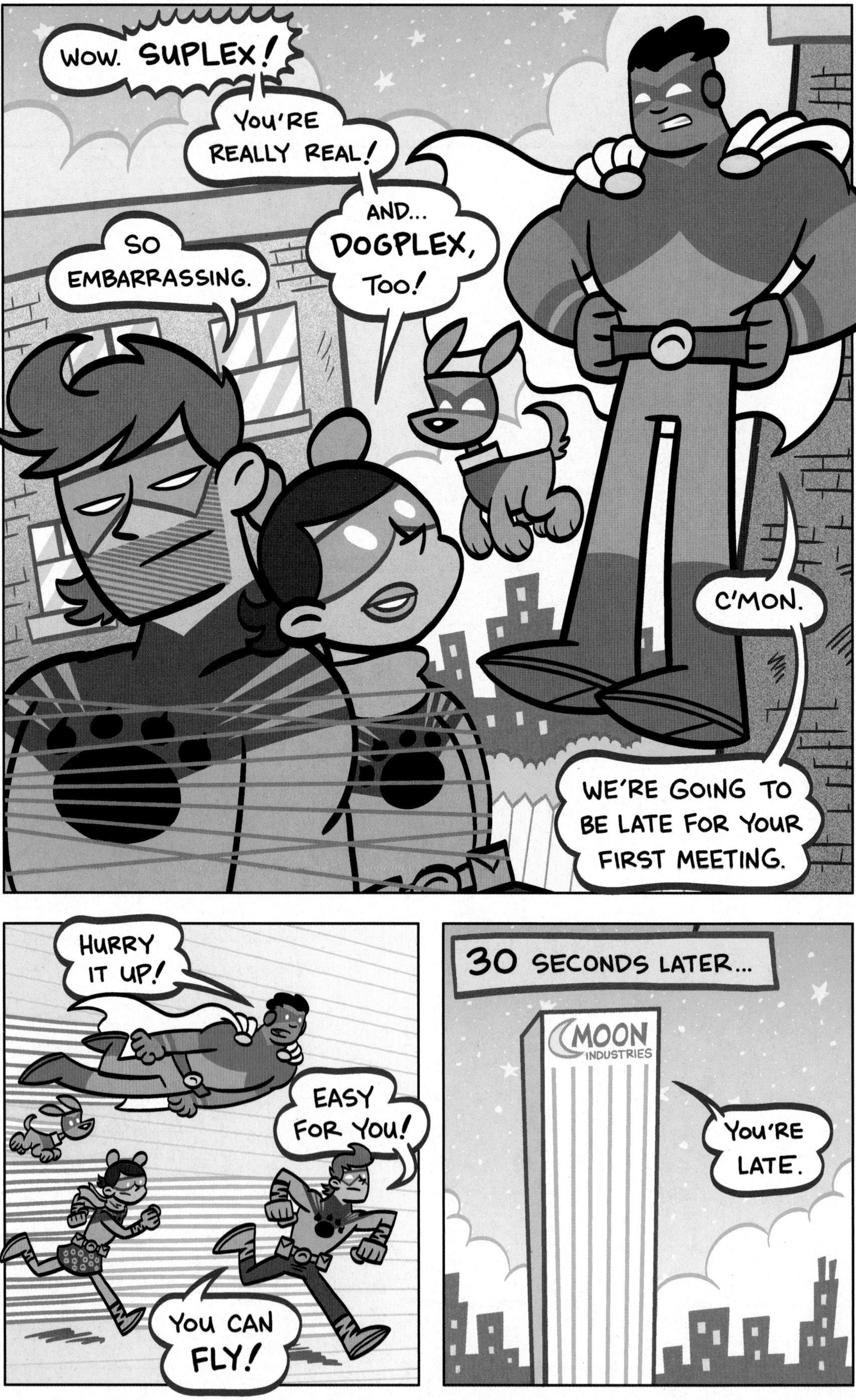
WOW. SUPLEX!
YOU'RE REALLY REAL!
AND... DOGPLEX, TOO!
SO EMBARRASSING.
C'MON.
WE'RE GOING TO BE LATE FOR YOUR FIRST MEETING.
HURRY IT UP!
EASY FOR YOU!
YOU CAN FLY!
30 SECONDS LATER...
MOON INDUSTRIES
YOU'RE LATE.

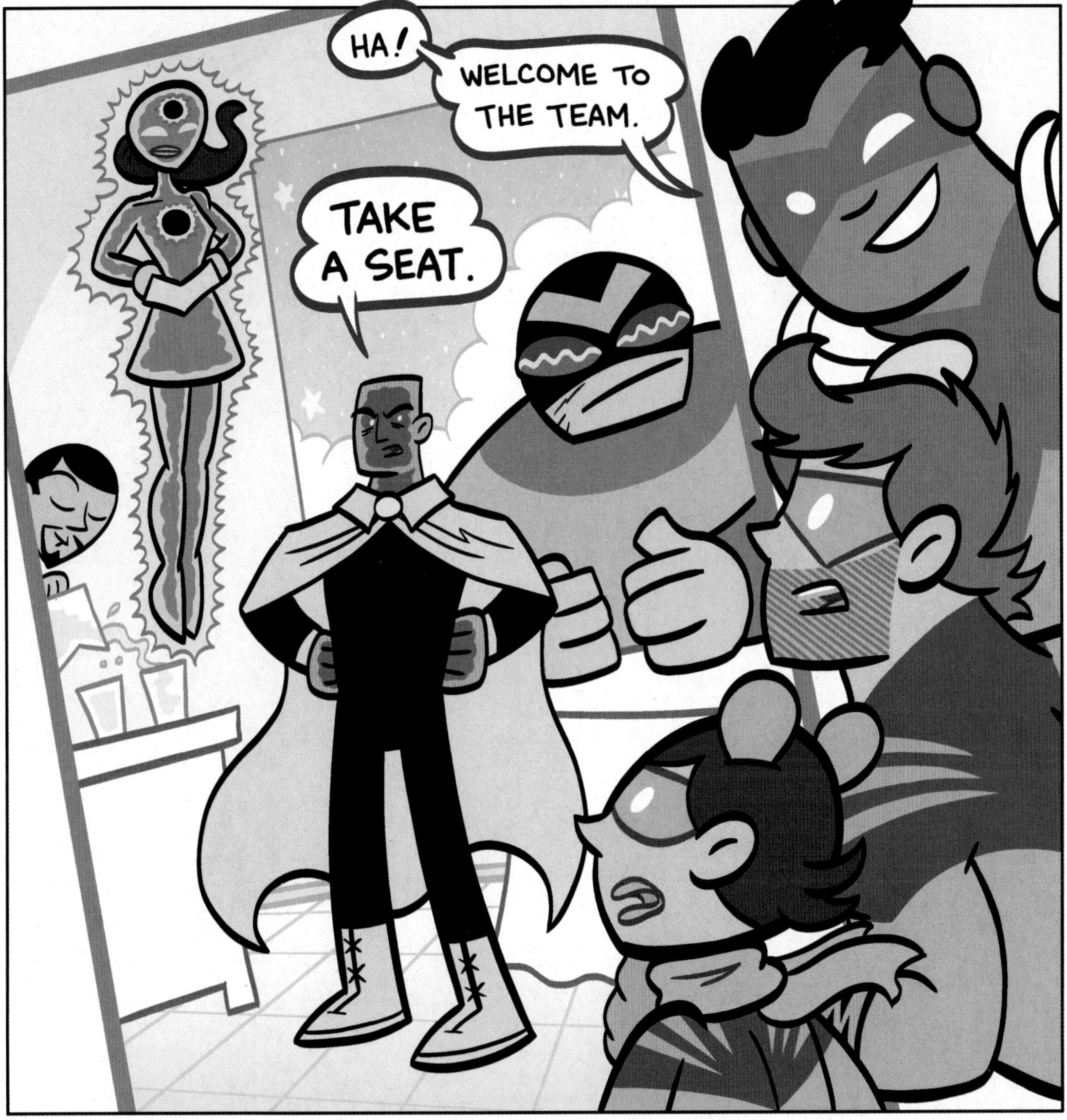
HA!
WELCOME TO THE TEAM.
TAKE A SEAT.

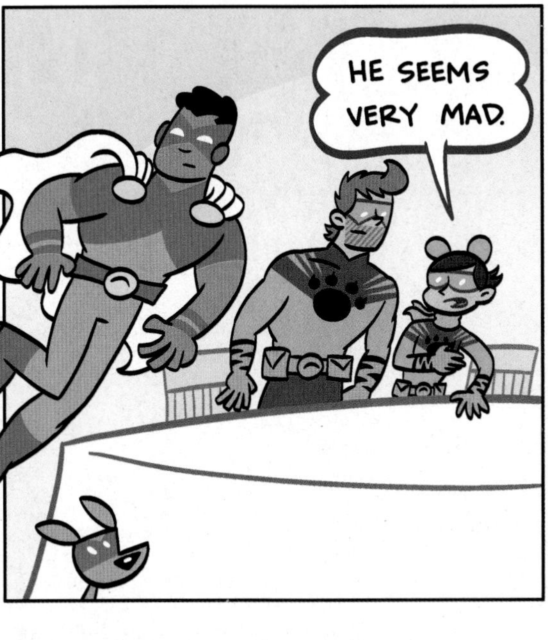
HE SEEMS VERY MAD.

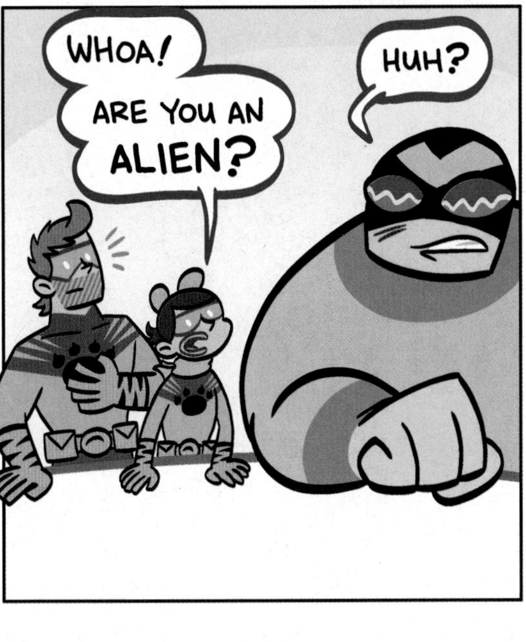
WHOA!
ARE YOU AN ALIEN?
HUH?

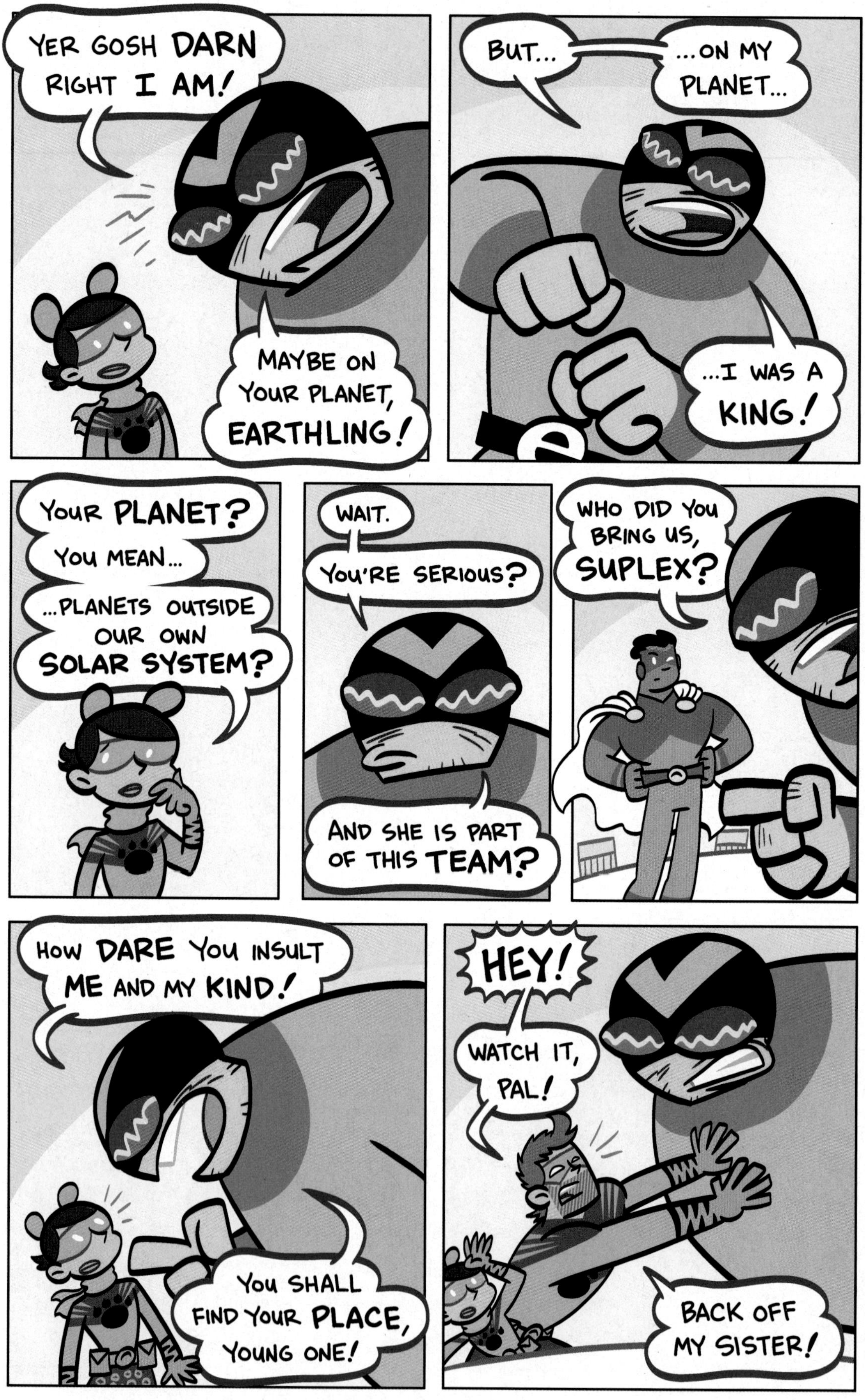

YER GOSH DARN RIGHT I AM!
MAYBE ON YOUR PLANET, EARTHLING!
BUT...
...ON MY PLANET...
...I WAS A KING!
YOUR PLANET?
YOU MEAN...
...PLANETS OUTSIDE OUR OWN SOLAR SYSTEM?
WAIT.
YOU'RE SERIOUS?
AND SHE IS PART OF THIS TEAM?
WHO DID YOU BRING US, SUPLEX?
HOW DARE YOU INSULT ME AND MY KIND!
YOU SHALL FIND YOUR PLACE, YOUNG ONE!
HEY!
WATCH IT, PAL!
BACK OFF MY SISTER!

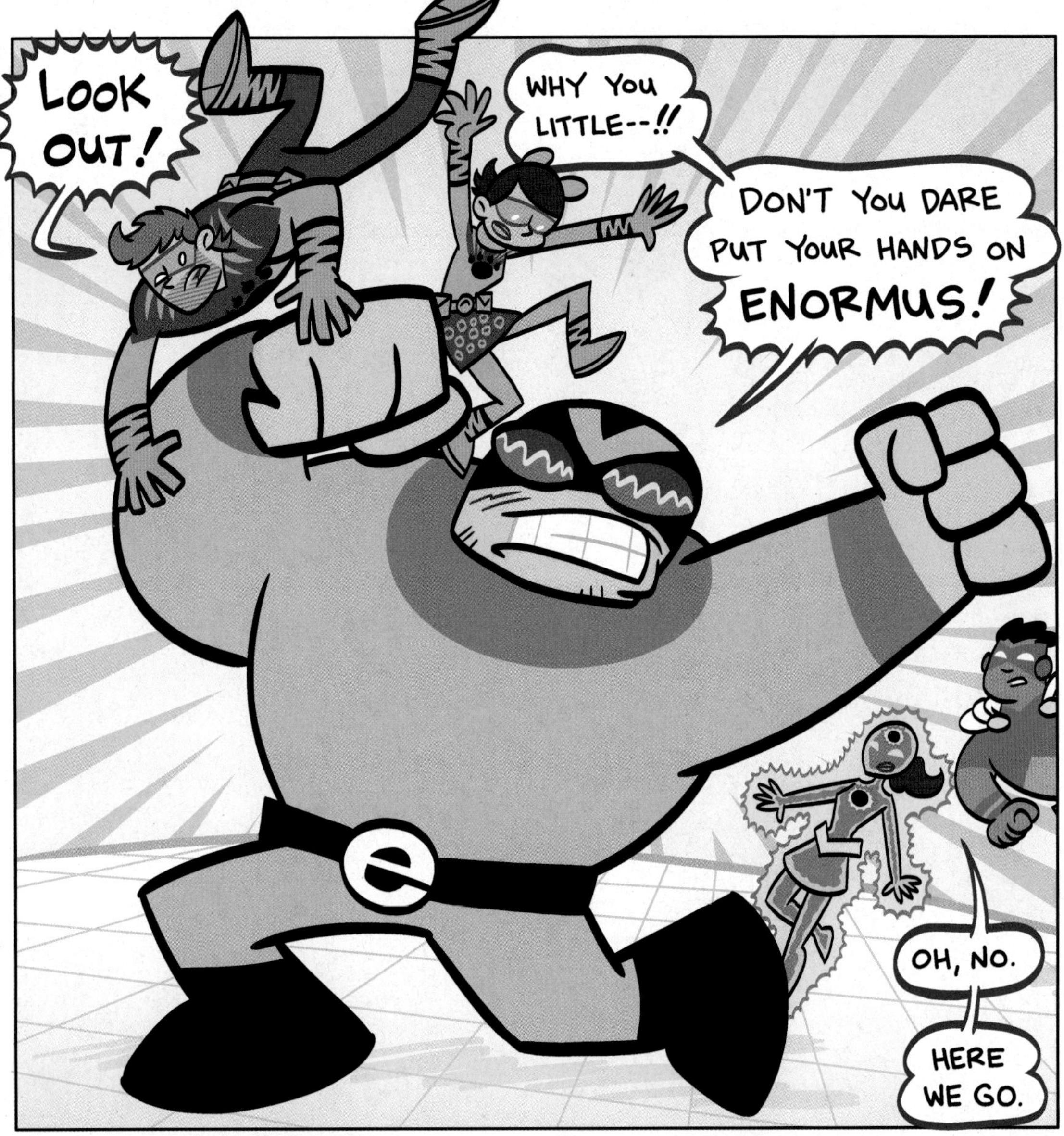
LOOK OUT!
WHY YOU LITTLE--!!
DON'T YOU DARE PUT YOUR HANDS ON ENORMUS!
OH, NO.
HERE WE GO.

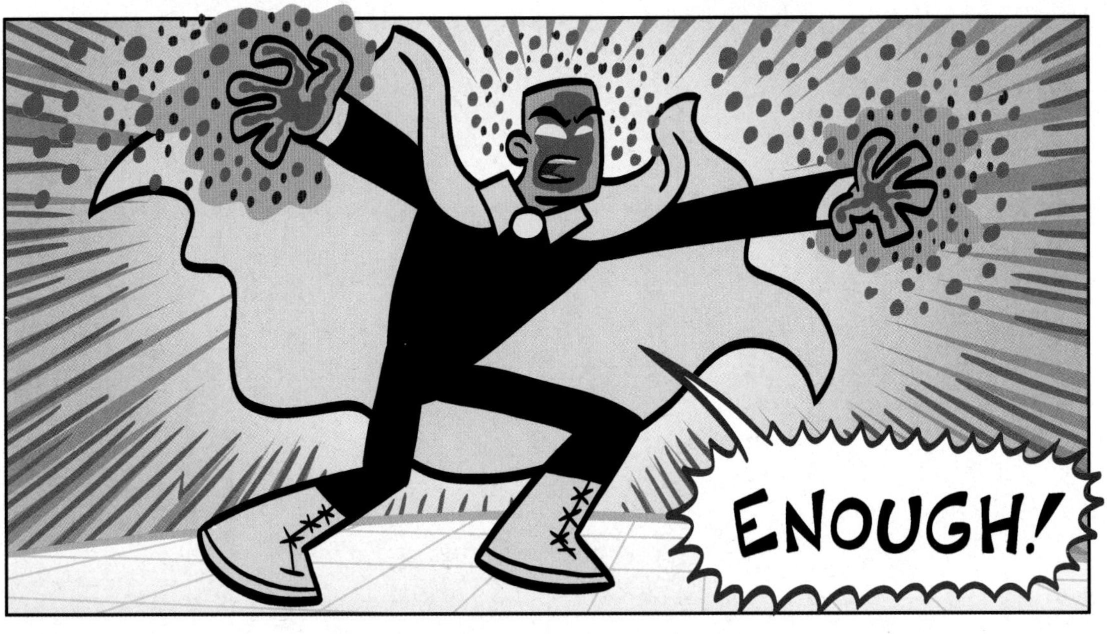
ENOUGH!

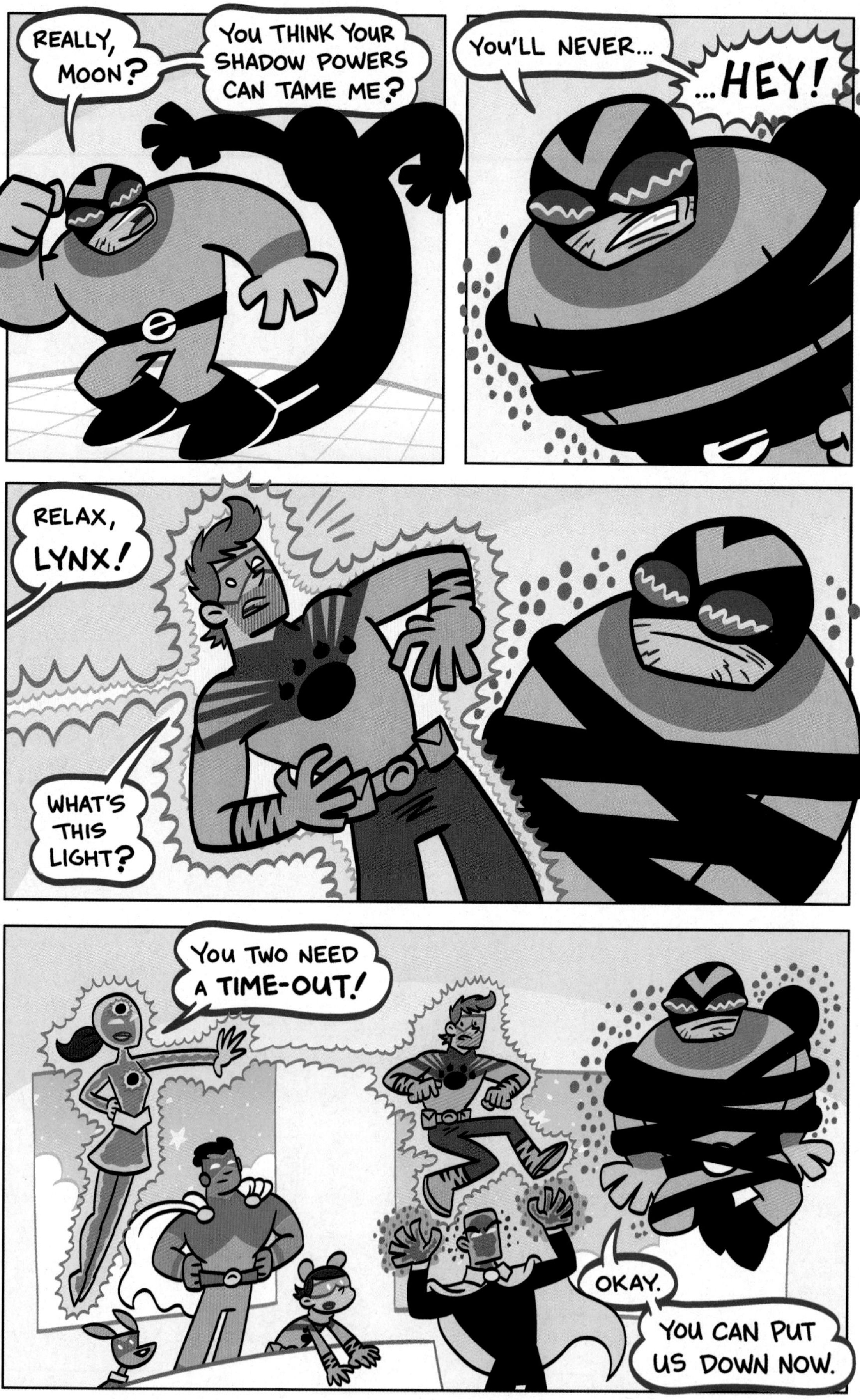
REALLY, MOON?
YOU THINK YOUR SHADOW POWERS CAN TAME ME?
YOU'LL NEVER...
...HEY!
RELAX, LYNX!
WHAT'S THIS LIGHT?
YOU TWO NEED A TIME-OUT!
OKAY.
YOU CAN PUT US DOWN NOW.

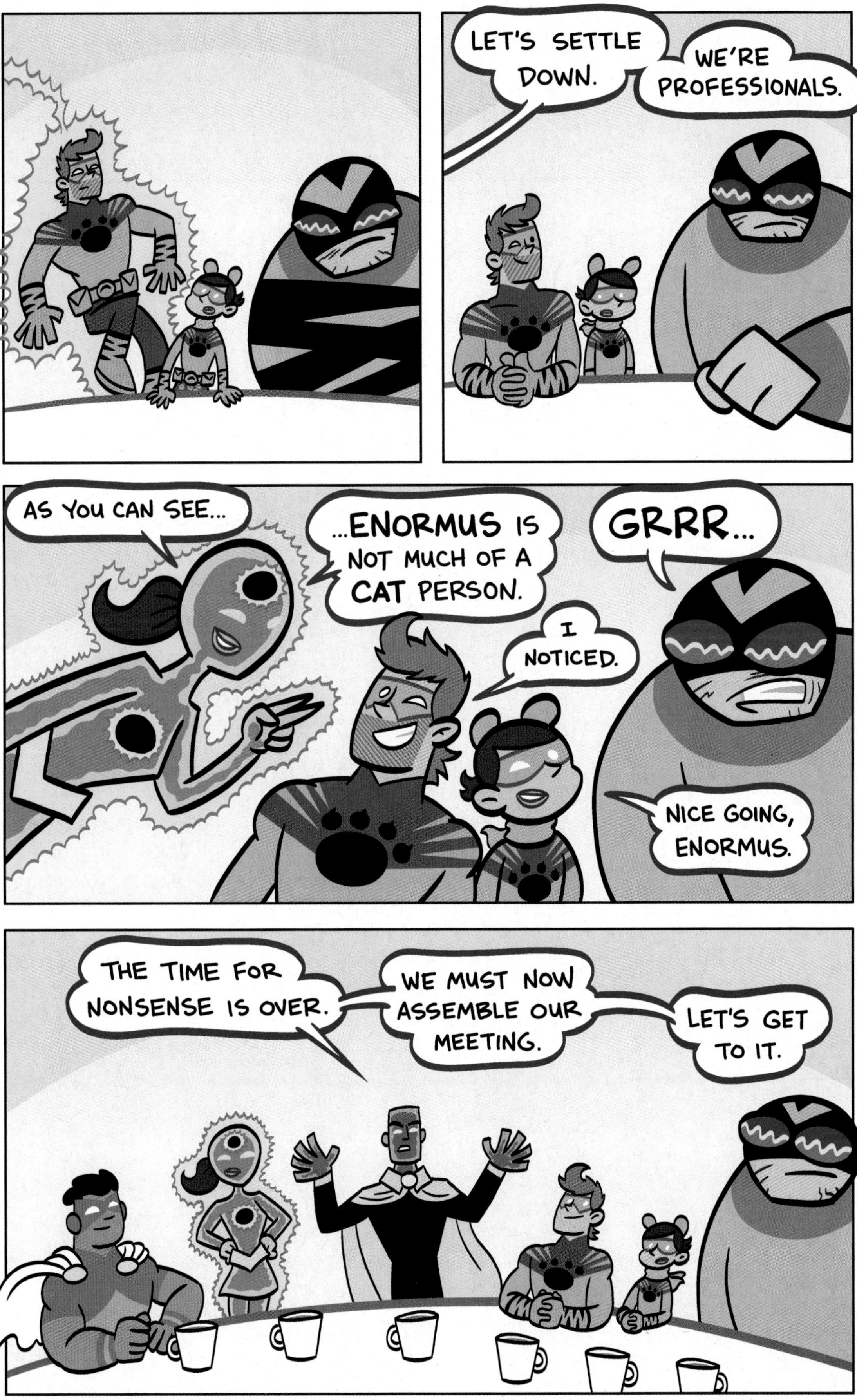
LET'S SETTLE DOWN.
WE'RE PROFESSIONALS.
AS YOU CAN SEE...
...ENORMUS IS NOT MUCH OF A CAT PERSON.
GRRR...
I NOTICED.
NICE GOING, ENORMUS.
THE TIME FOR NONSENSE IS OVER.
WE MUST NOW ASSEMBLE OUR MEETING.
LET'S GET TO IT.

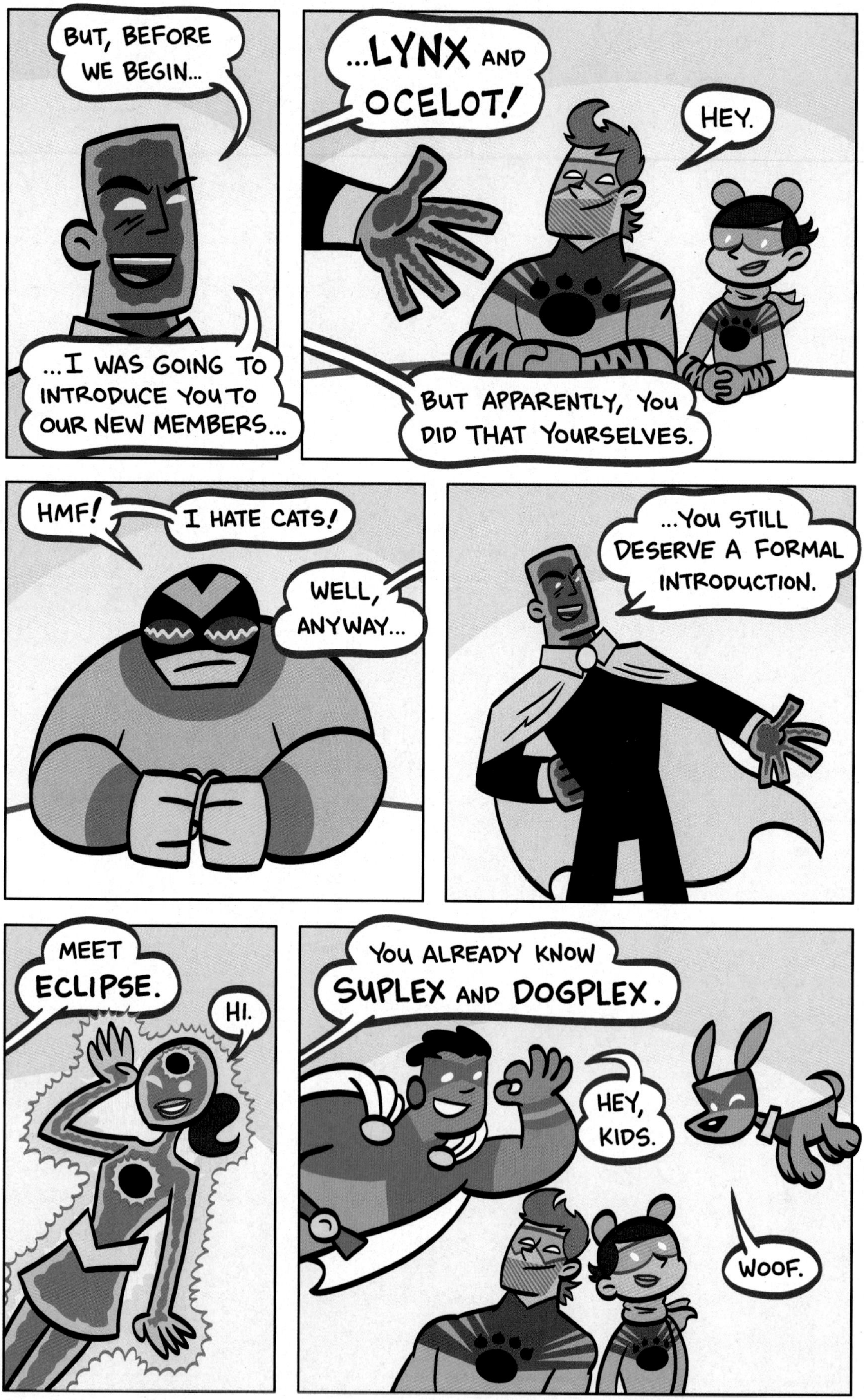
BUT, BEFORE WE BEGIN...
...I WAS GOING TO INTRODUCE YOU TO OUR NEW MEMBERS...
...LYNX AND OCELOT!
HEY.
BUT APPARENTLY, YOU DID THAT YOURSELVES.
HMF!
I HATE CATS!
WELL, ANYWAY...
...YOU STILL DESERVE A FORMAL INTRODUCTION.
MEET ECLIPSE.
HI.
YOU ALREADY KNOW SUPLEX AND DOGPLEX.
HEY, KIDS.
WOOF.

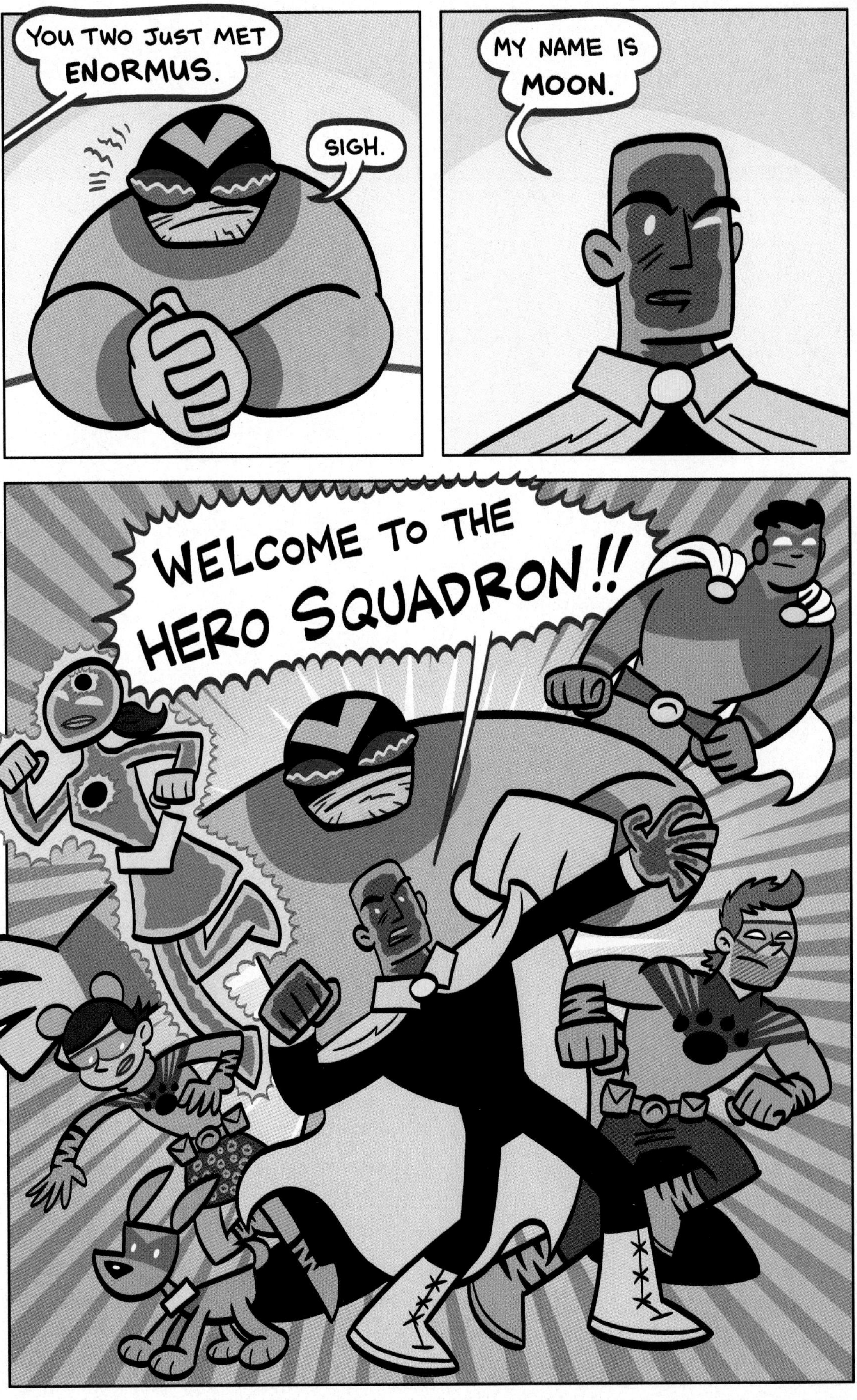
YOU TWO JUST MET ENORMUS.
SIGH.
MY NAME IS MOON.
WELCOME TO THE HERO SQUADRON!!

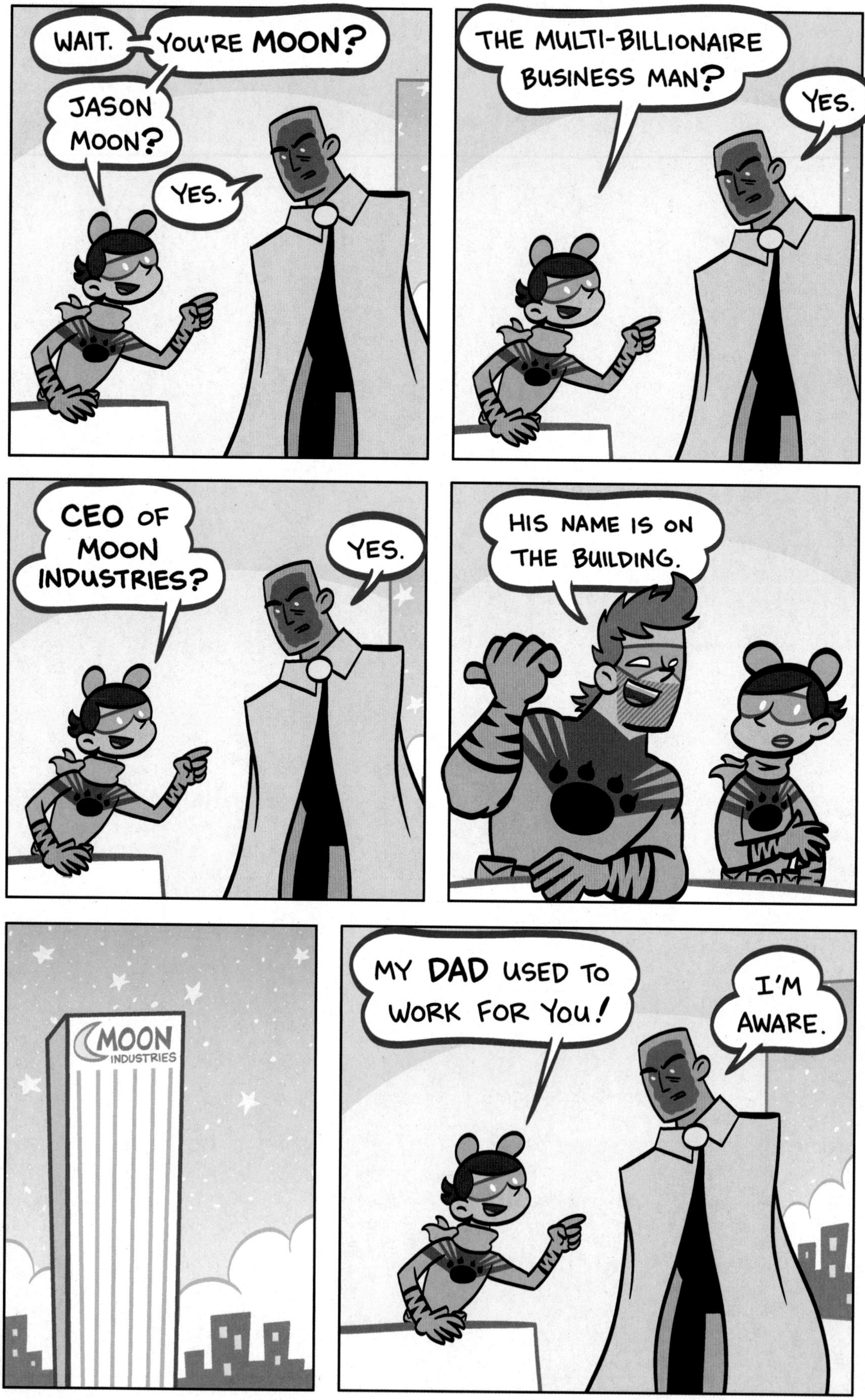
WAIT.
YOU'RE MOON?
JASON MOON?
YES.
THE MULTI-BILLIONAIRE BUSINESS MAN?
YES.
CEO OF MOON INDUSTRIES?
YES.
HIS NAME IS ON THE BUILDING.
MOON INDUSTRIES
MY DAD USED TO WORK FOR YOU!
I'M AWARE.

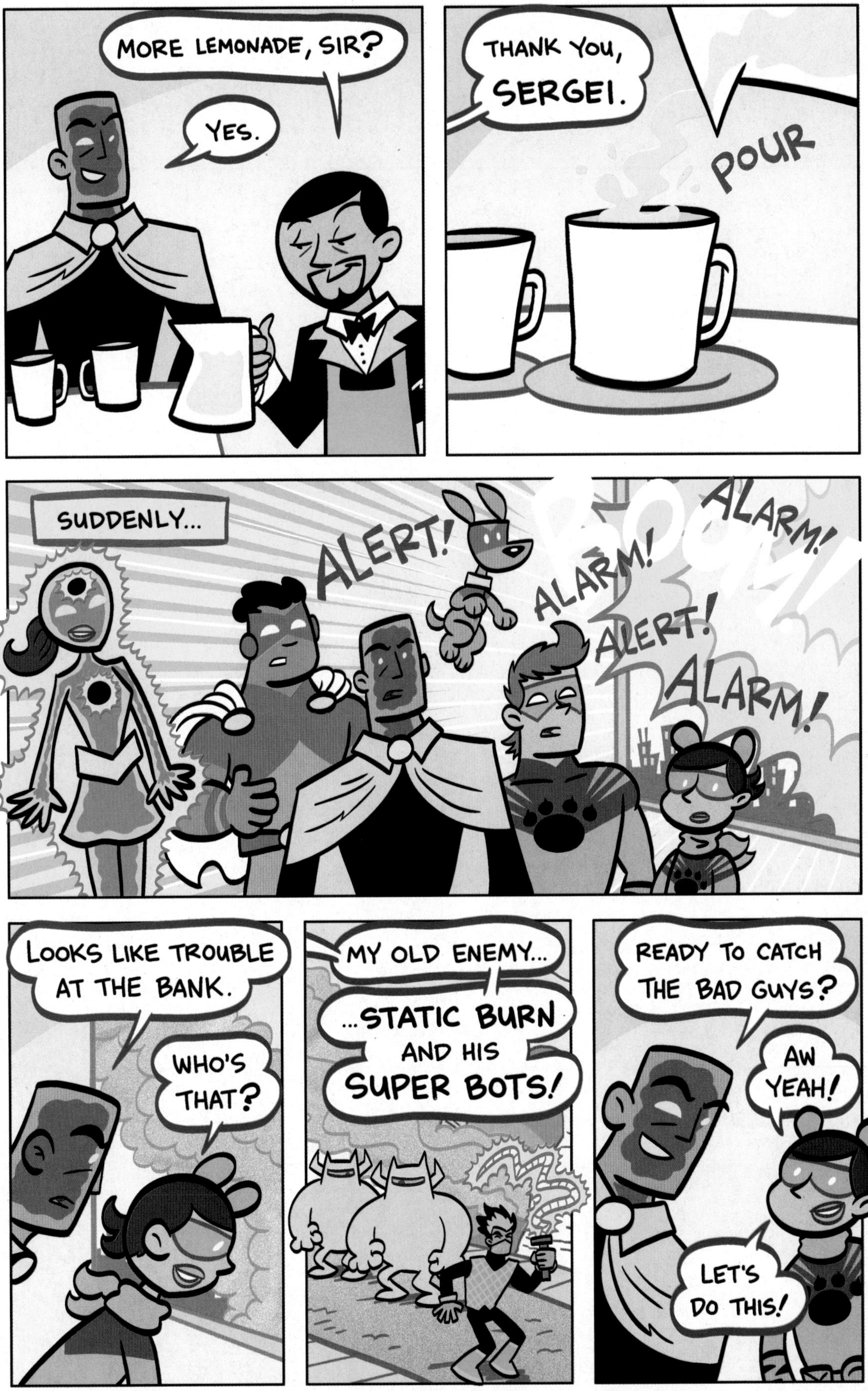

MORE LEMONADE, SIR?
YES.
THANK YOU, SERGEI.
POUR
SUDDENLY...
ALERT!
BOOM!
ALARM!
ALARM!
ALERT!
ALARM!
LOOKS LIKE TROUBLE AT THE BANK.
WHO'S THAT?
MY OLD ENEMY...
...STATIC BURN AND HIS SUPER BOTS!
READY TO CATCH THE BAD GUYS?
AW YEAH!
LET'S DO THIS!

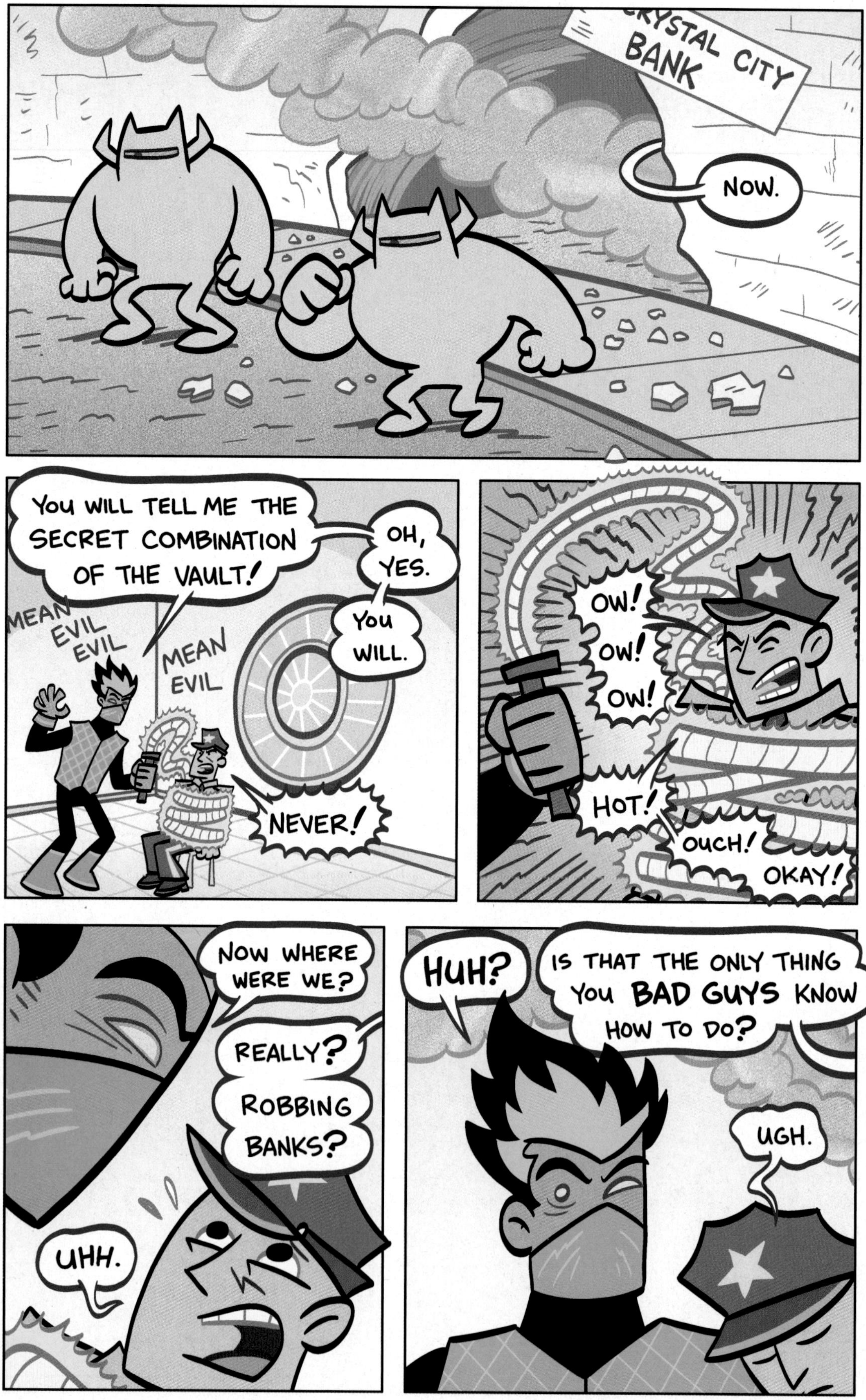
CRYSTAL CITY BANK
NOW.
YOU WILL TELL ME THE SECRET COMBINATION OF THE VAULT!
OH, YES.
YOU WILL.
MEAN EVIL EVIL
MEAN EVIL
NEVER!
OW!
OW!
OW!
HOT!
OUCH!
OKAY!
NOW WHERE WERE WE?
REALLY?
ROBBING BANKS?
UHH.
HUH?
IS THAT THE ONLY THING YOU BAD GUYS KNOW HOW TO DO?
UGH.

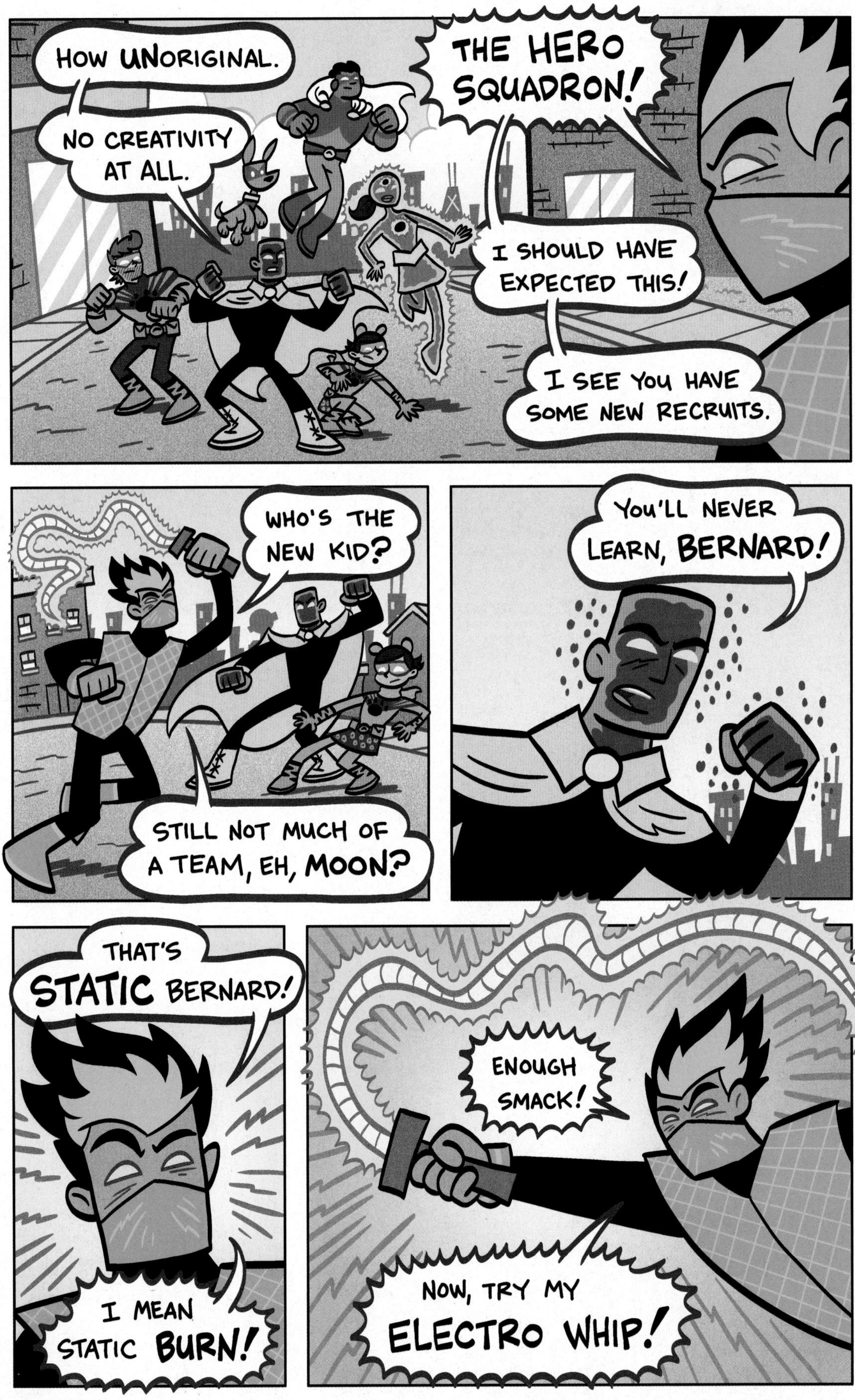
HOW UNORIGINAL.
NO CREATIVITY AT ALL.
THE HERO SQUADRON!
I SHOULD HAVE EXPECTED THIS!
I SEE YOU HAVE SOME NEW RECRUITS.
WHO'S THE NEW KID?
STILL NOT MUCH OF A TEAM, EH, MOON?
YOU'LL NEVER LEARN, BERNARD!
THAT'S STATIC BERNARD!
I MEAN STATIC BURN!
ENOUGH SMACK!
NOW, TRY MY ELECTRO WHIP!

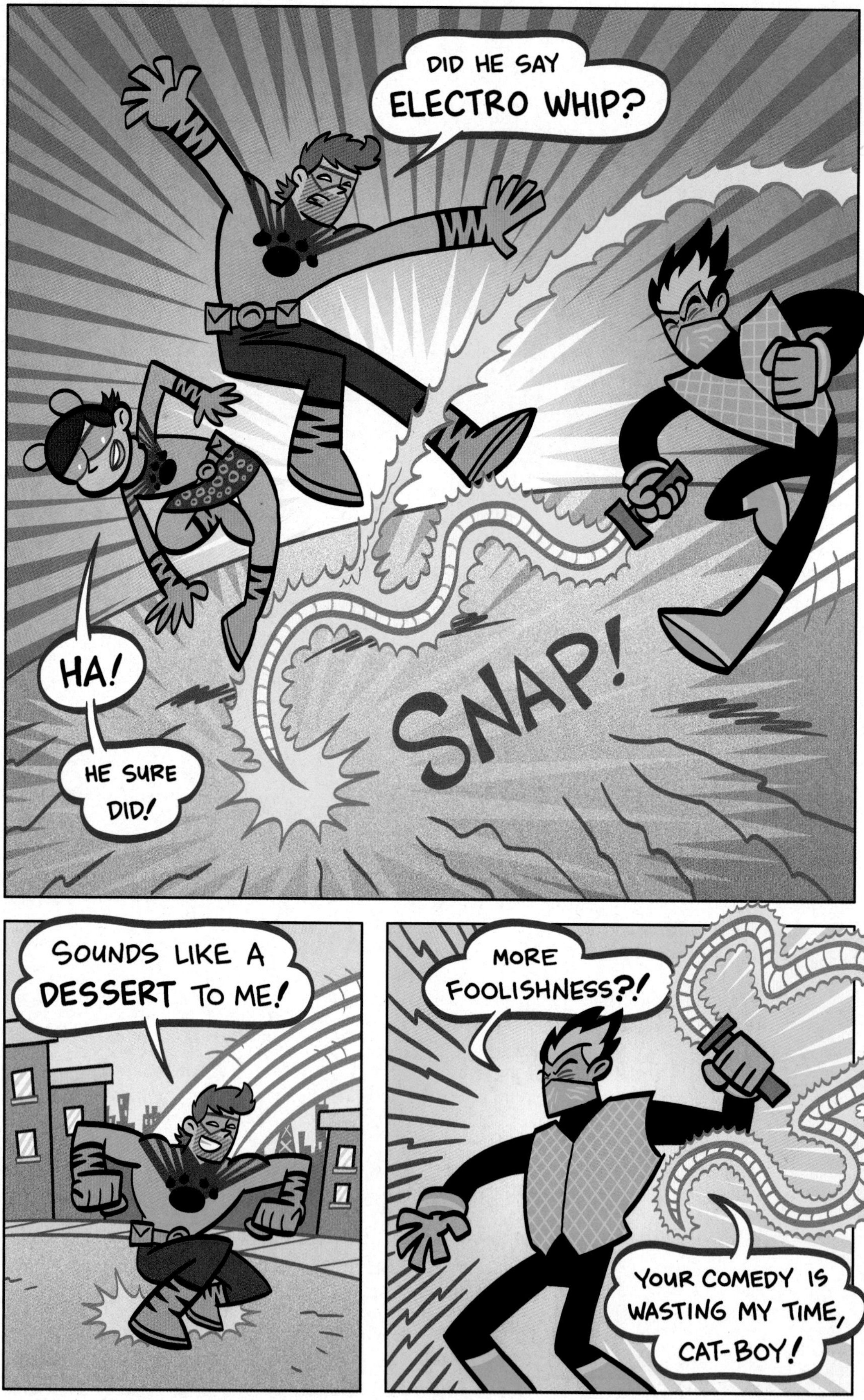
DID HE SAY ELECTRO WHIP?
HA!
HE SURE DID!
SNAP!
SOUNDS LIKE A DESSERT TO ME!
MORE FOOLISHNESS?!
YOUR COMEDY IS WASTING MY TIME, CAT-BOY!

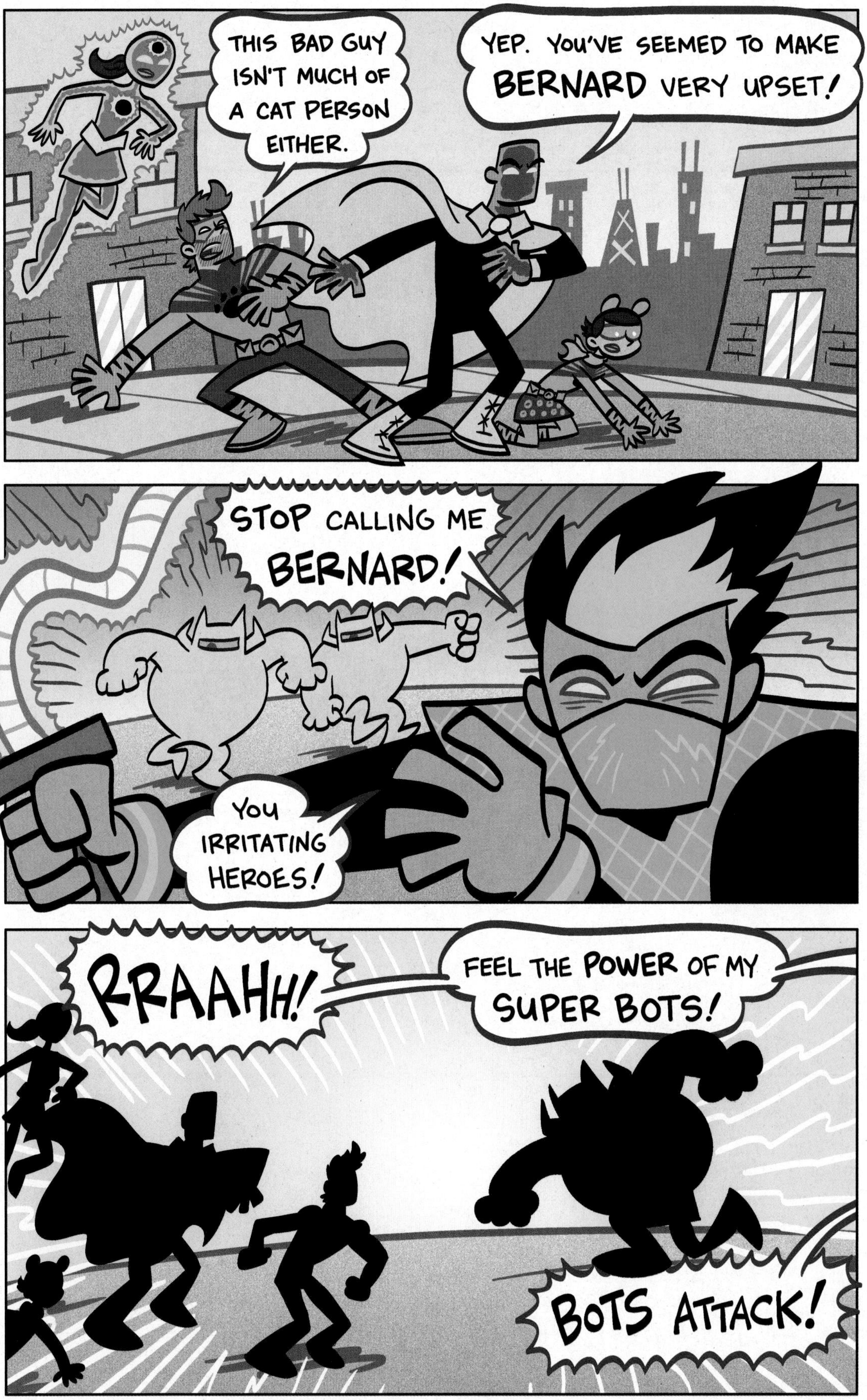
THIS BAD GUY ISN'T MUCH OF A CAT PERSON EITHER.
YEP. YOU'VE SEEMED TO MAKE BERNARD VERY UPSET!
STOP CALLING ME BERNARD!
YOU IRRITATING HEROES!
RRAAHH!
FEEL THE POWER OF MY SUPER BOTS!
BOTS ATTACK!

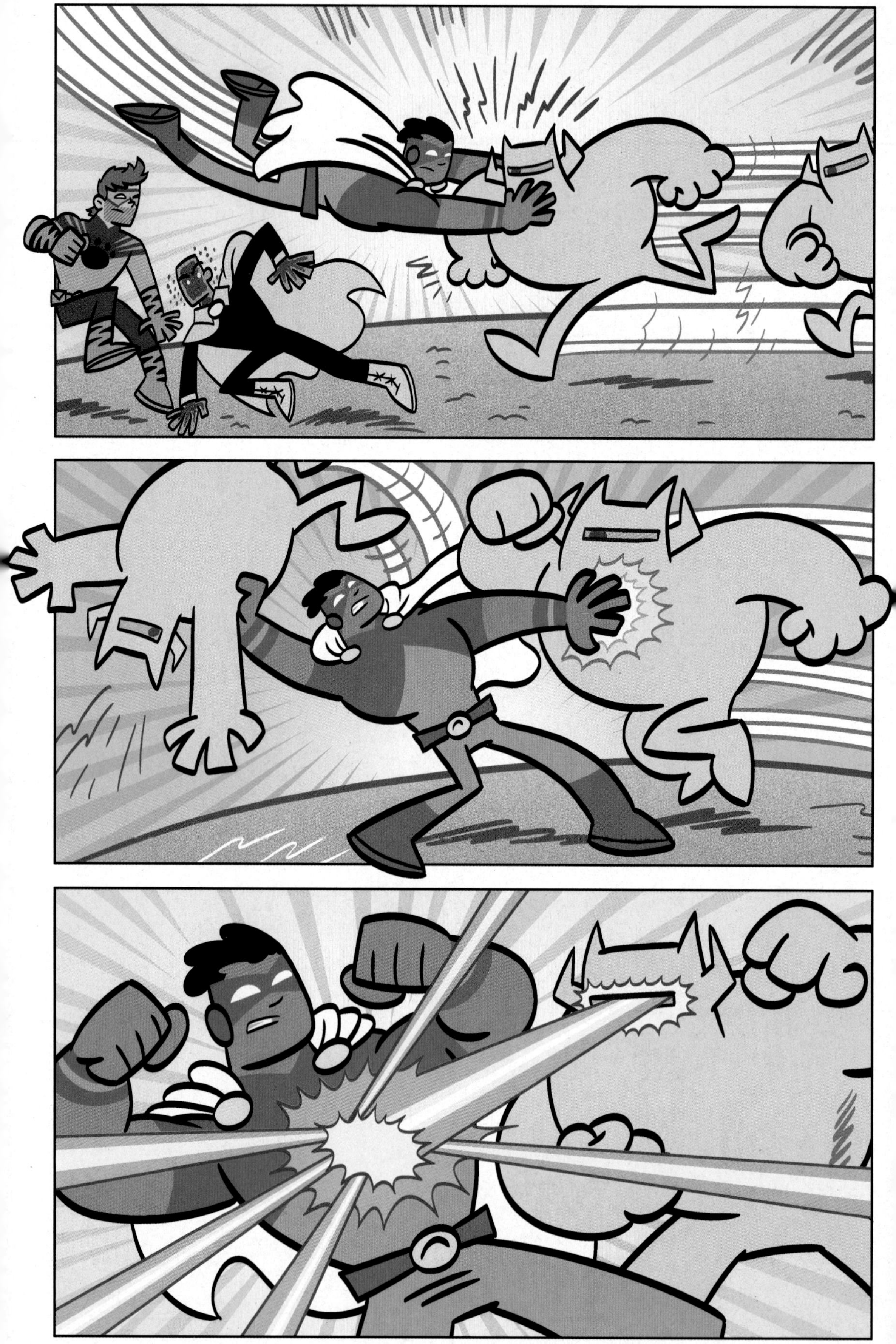

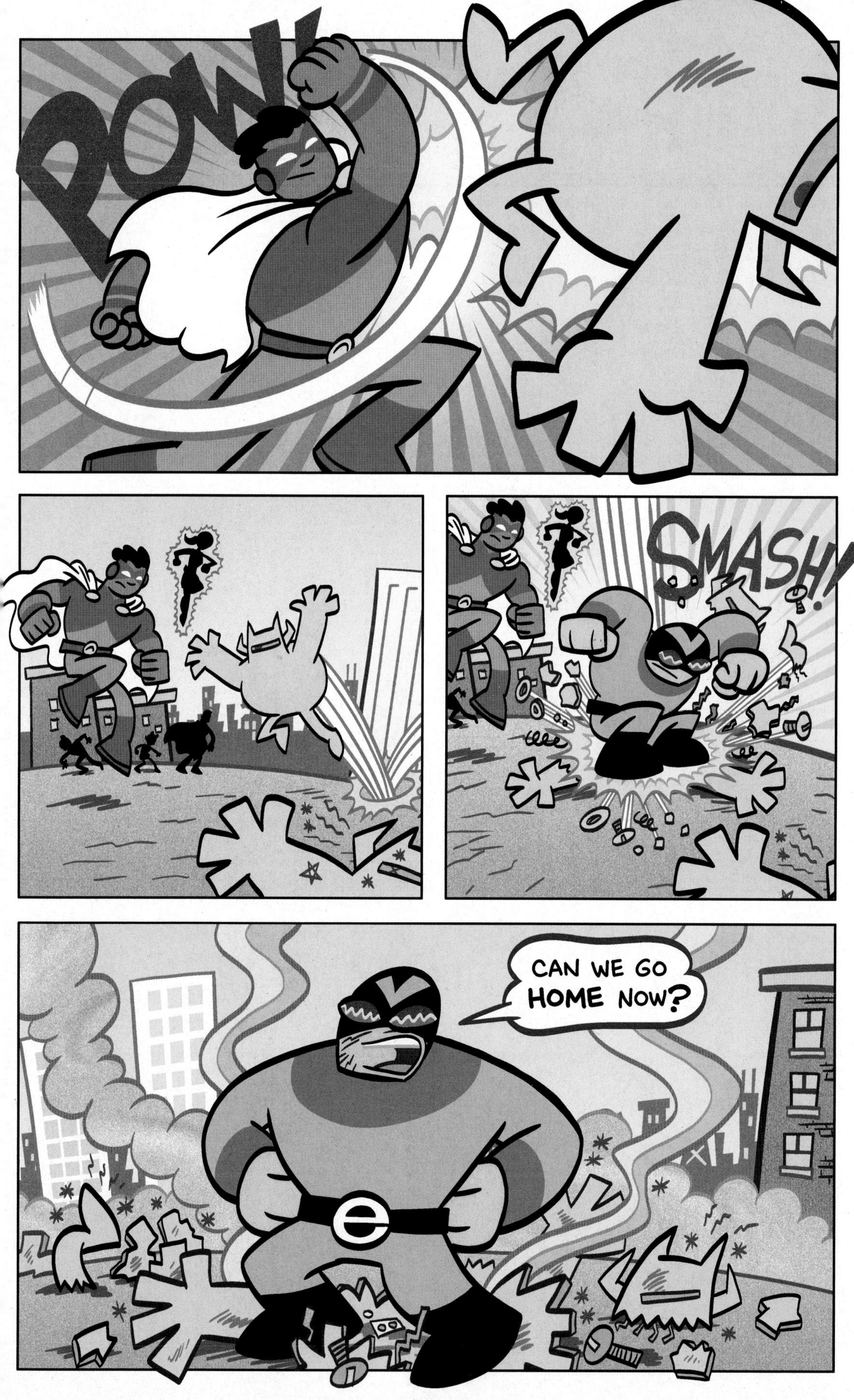
POW!
SMASH!
CAN WE GO HOME NOW?

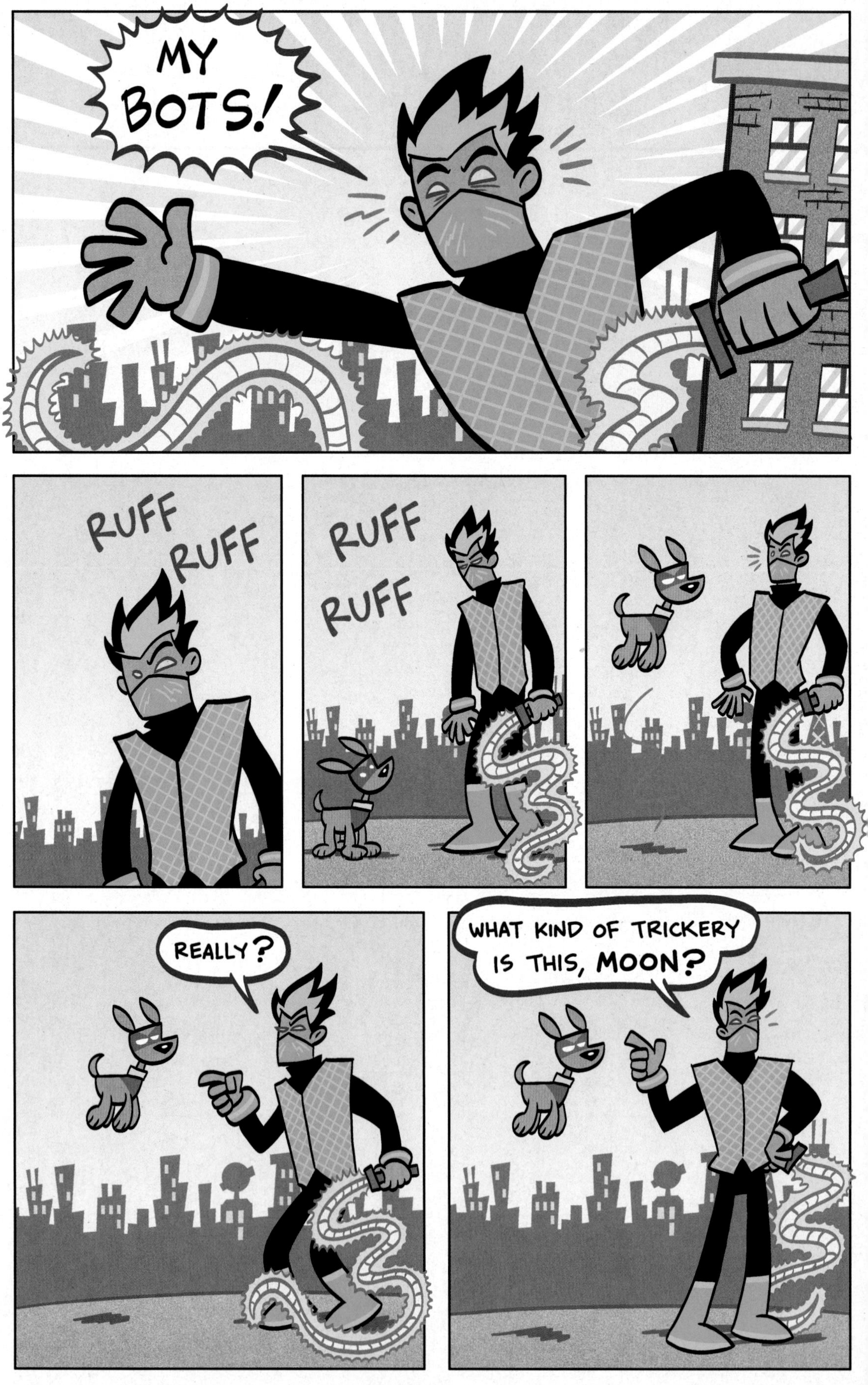
MY BOTS!
RUFF RUFF
RUFF RUFF
REALLY?
WHAT KIND OF TRICKERY IS THIS, MOON?

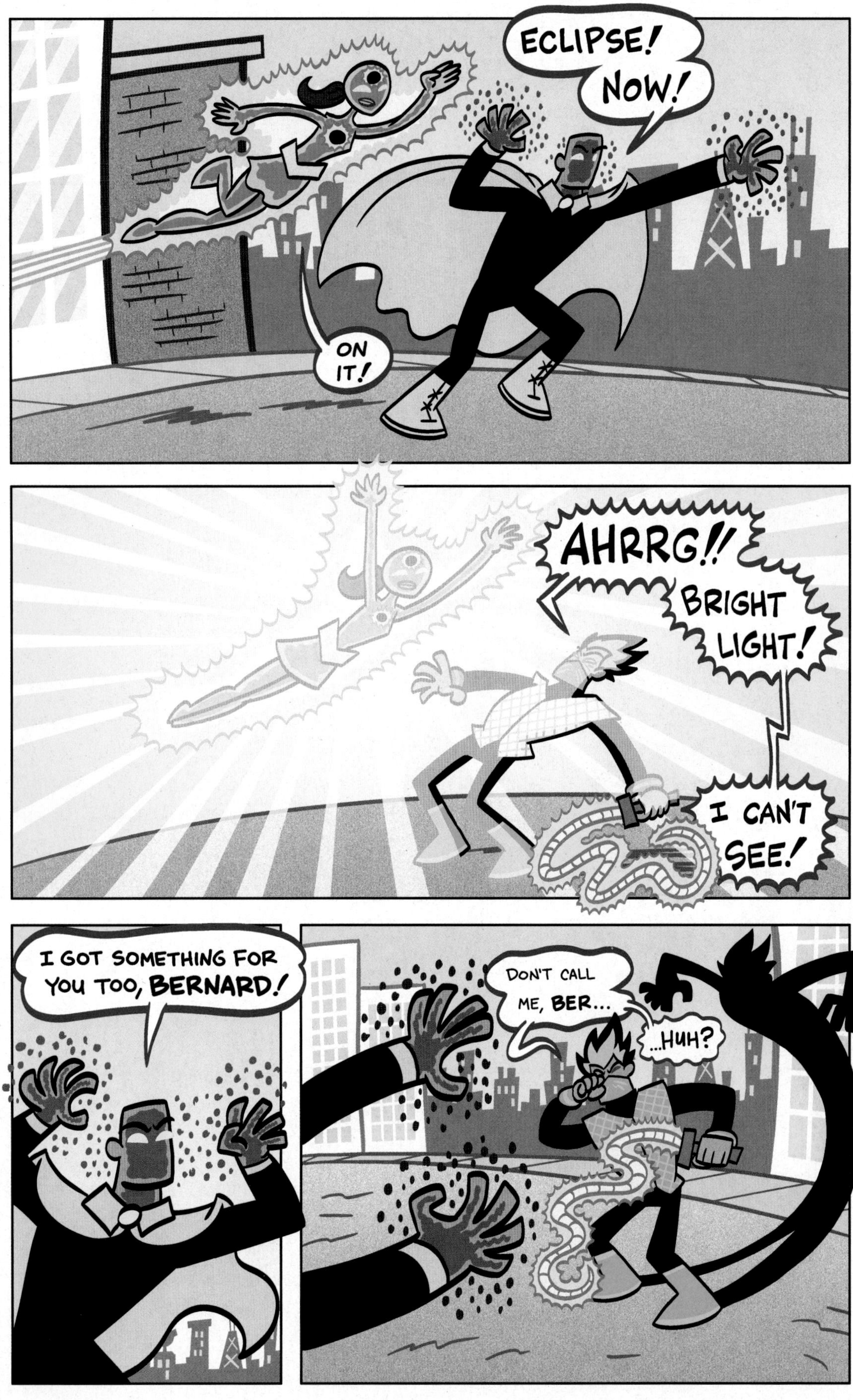
ECLIPSE! NOW!
ON IT!
AHRRG!! BRIGHT LIGHT!
I CAN'T SEE!
I GOT SOMETHING FOR YOU TOO, BERNARD!
DON'T CALL ME, BER...
...HUH?

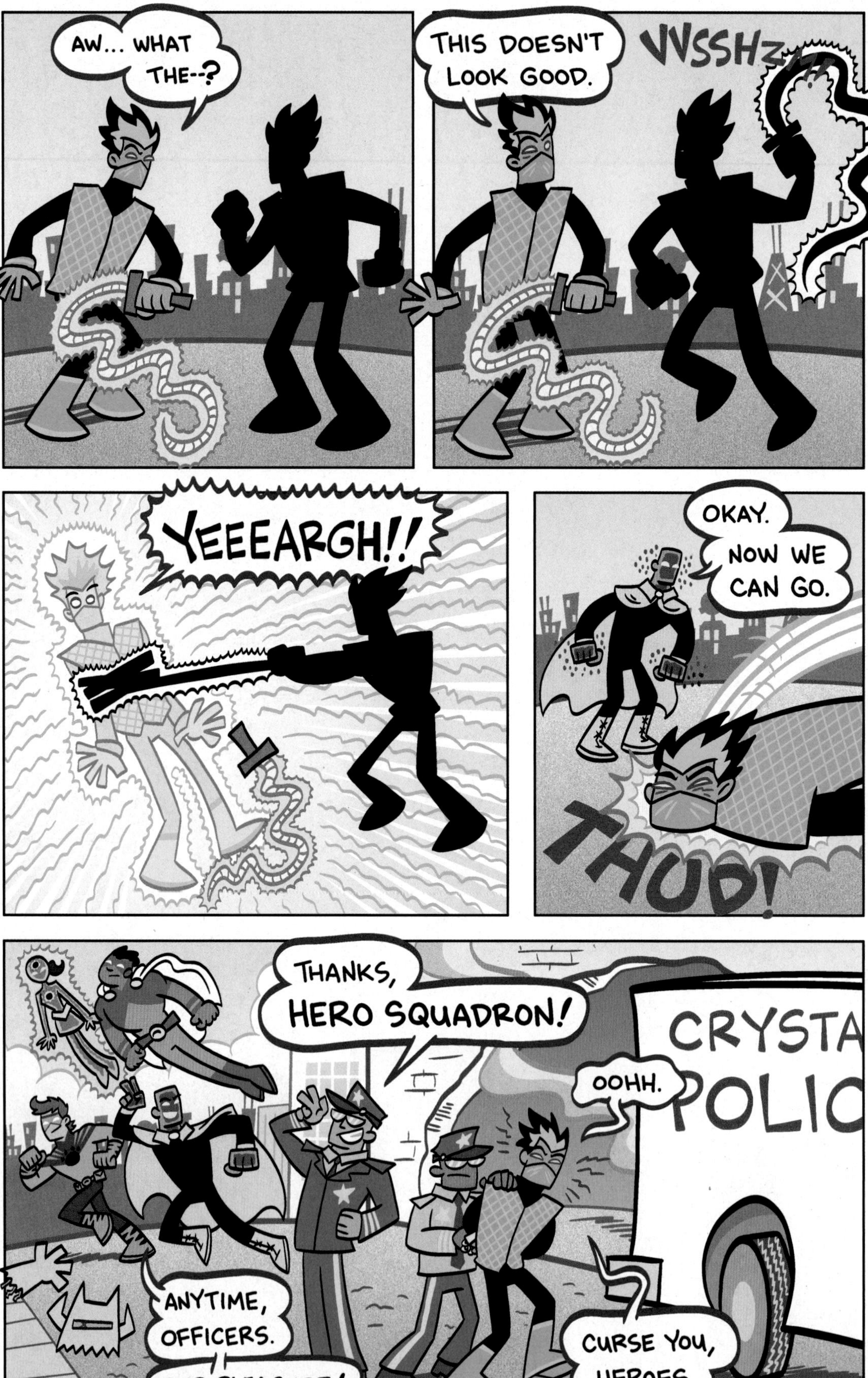
AW... WHAT THE--?
THIS DOESN'T LOOK GOOD.
YEEEARGH!!
OKAY. NOW WE CAN GO.
THUD!
THANKS, HERO SQUADRON!
CRYSTA
POLIC
OOHH.
ANYTIME, OFFICERS.
OUR PLEASURE!
CURSE YOU, HEROES.

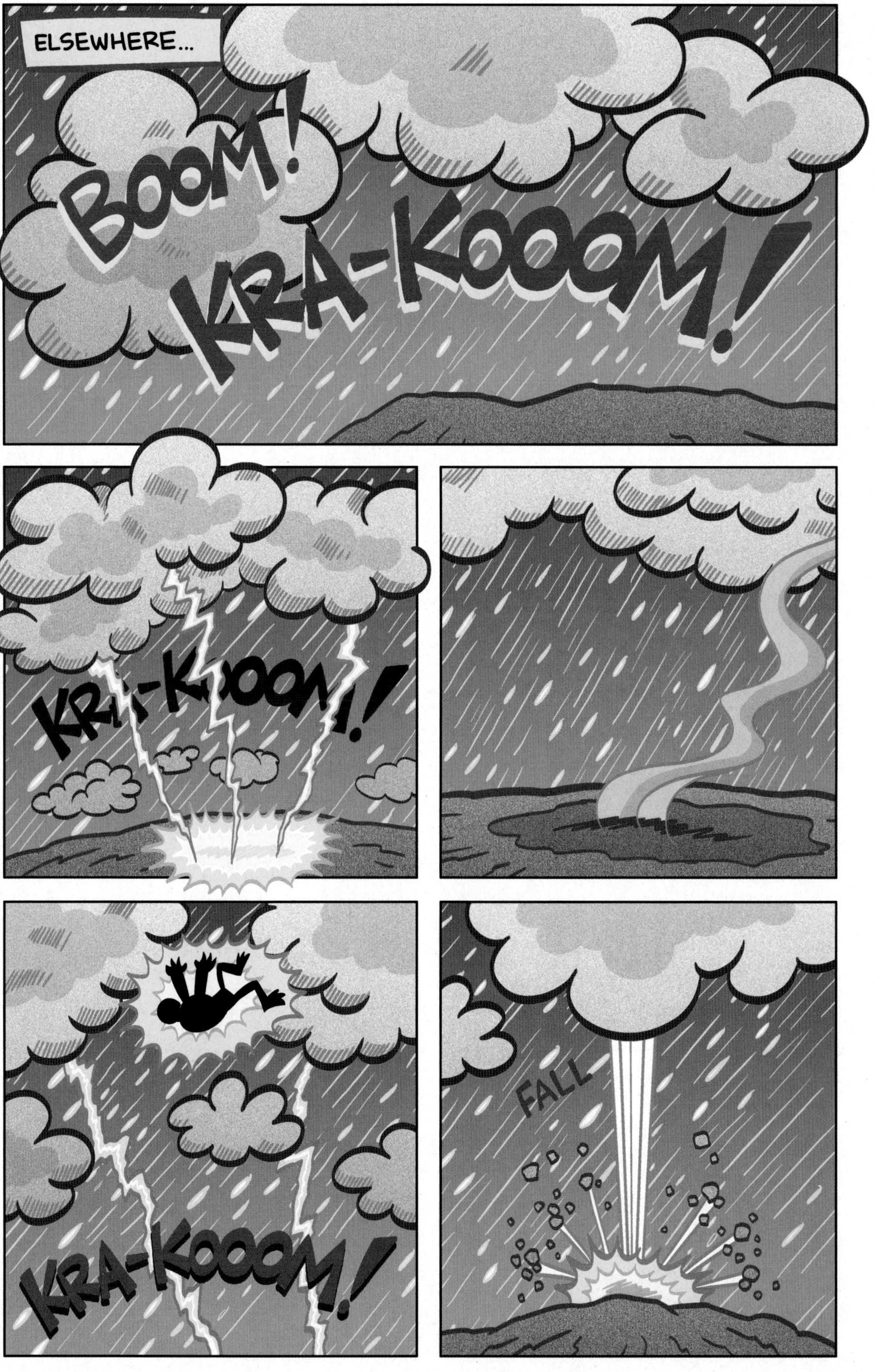
ELSEWHERE...
BOOM!
KRA-KOOOM!
KRA-KOOOM!
FALL

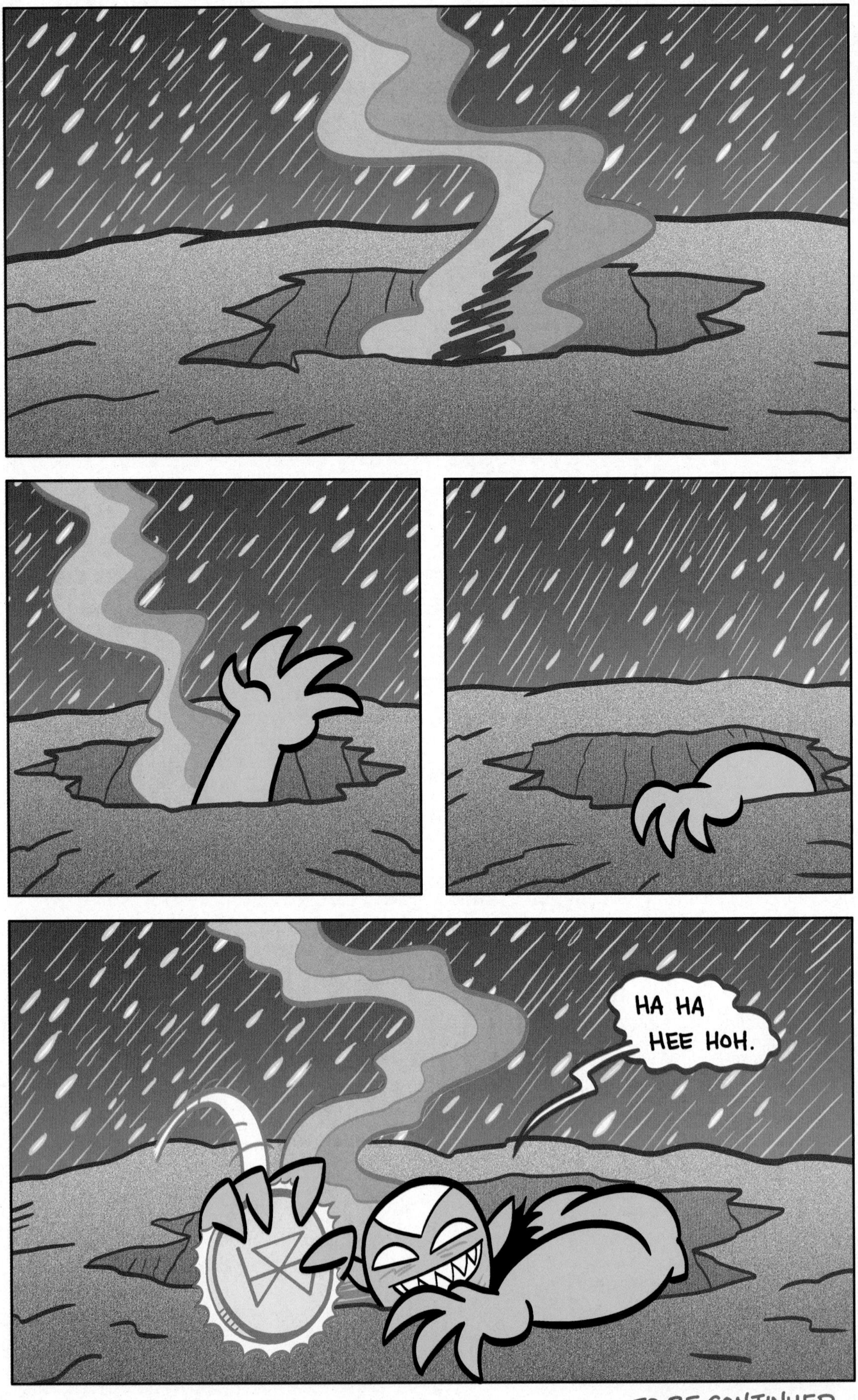
HA HA
HEE HOH.

-TO BE CONTINUED...

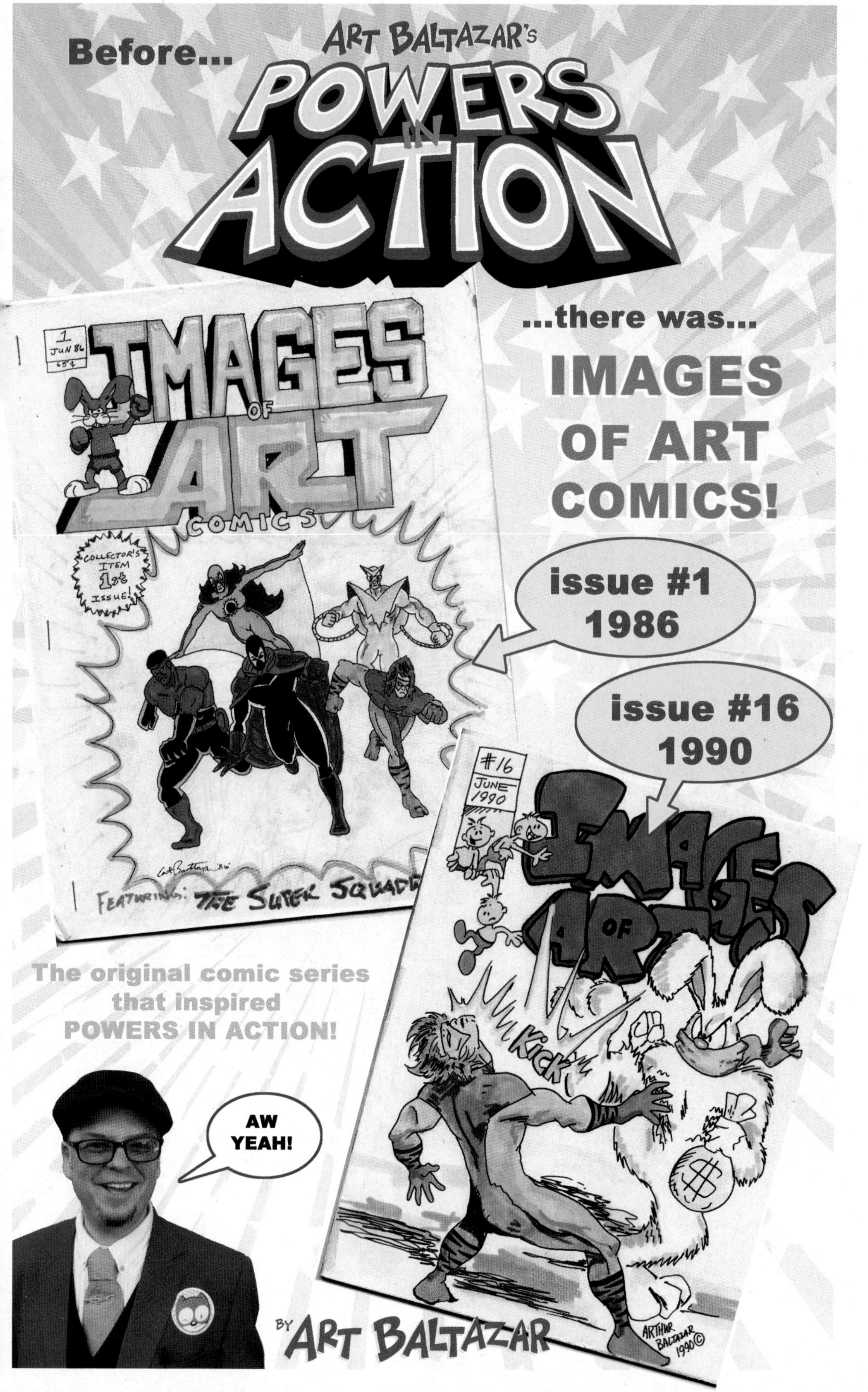
Before...
ART BALTAZAR's
POWERS IN ACTION
...there was...
IMAGES OF ART COMICS!
1 JUN 86 65¢
IMAGES OF ART COMICS
COLLECTOR'S ITEM 1st ISSUE!
FEATURING: THE SUPER SQUAD
issue #1 1986
issue #16 1990
#16 JUNE 1990
IMAGES OF ART
KICK
ARTHUR BALTAZAR 1990©
The original comic series that inspired POWERS IN ACTION!
AW YEAH!
BY ART BALTAZAR

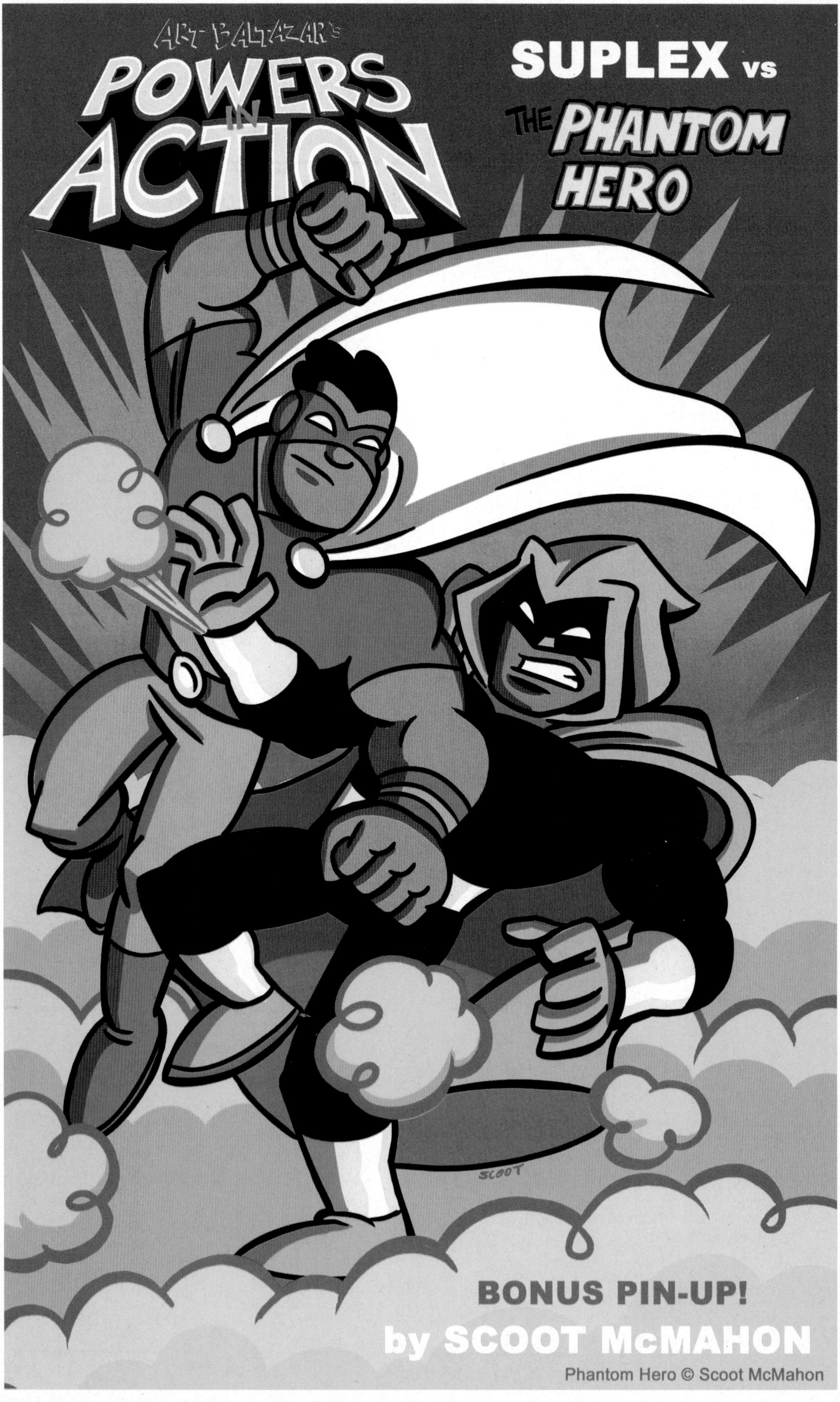
ART BALTAZAR'S
POWERS IN ACTION
SUPLEX vs
THE PHANTOM HERO
SCOOT
BONUS PIN-UP!
by SCOOT McMAHON
Phantom Hero © Scoot McMahon

AW YEAH COMICS & ACTION LAB PRESENTS...

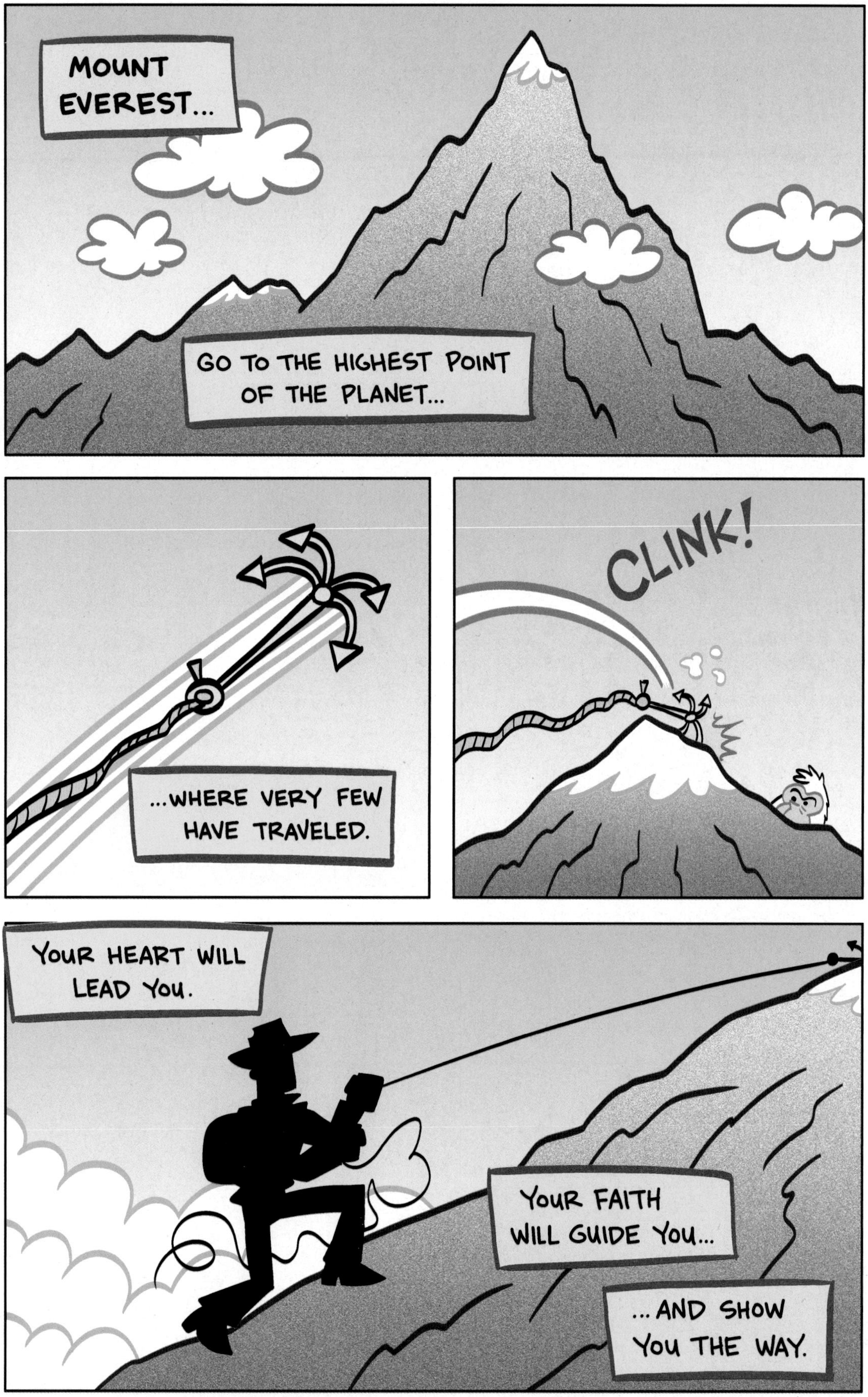
MOUNT EVEREST...
GO TO THE HIGHEST POINT OF THE PLANET...
...WHERE VERY FEW HAVE TRAVELED.
CLINK!
YOUR HEART WILL LEAD YOU.
YOUR FAITH WILL GUIDE YOU...
...AND SHOW YOU THE WAY.

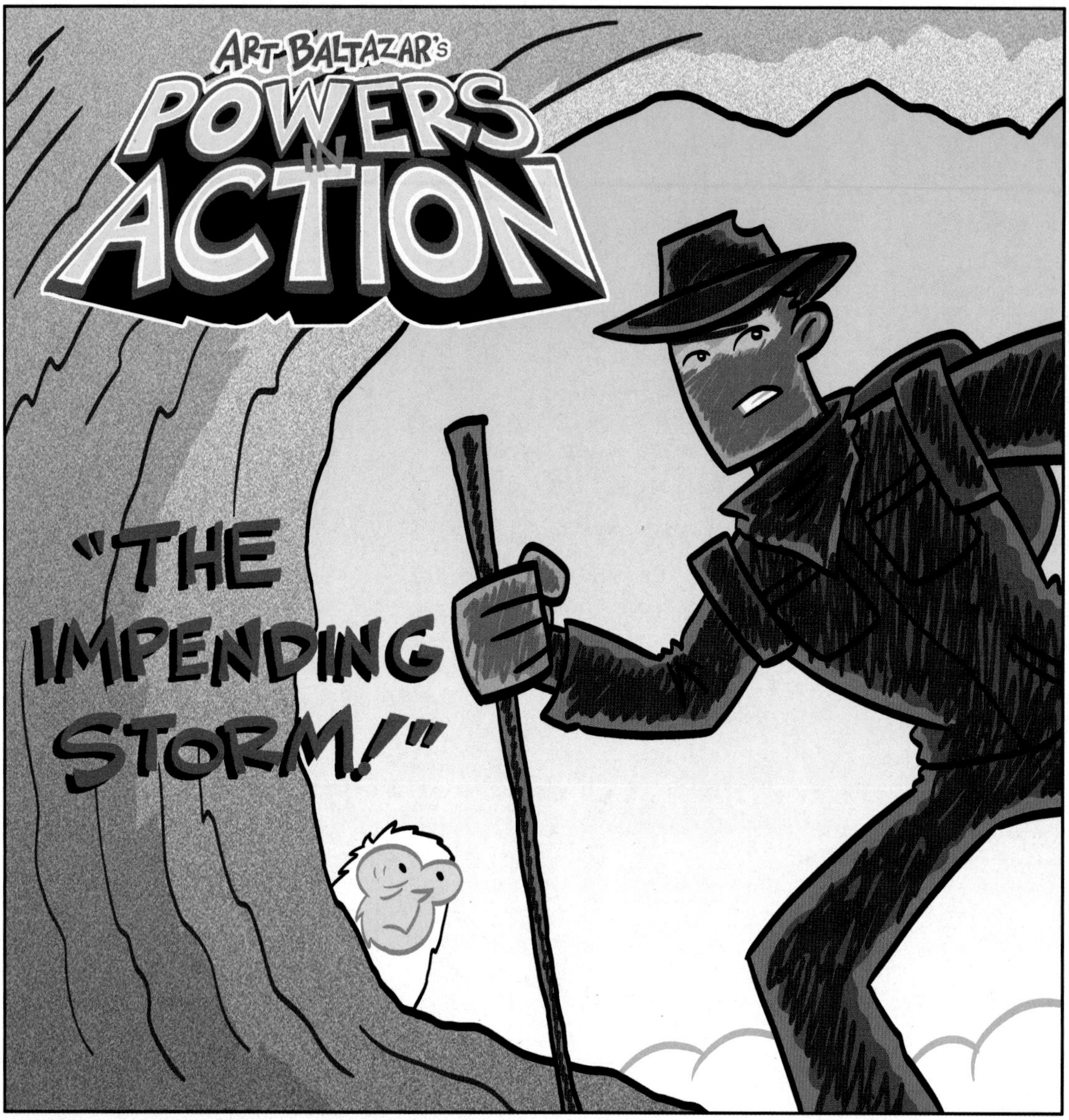
ART BALTAZAR'S
POWERS IN ACTION
"THE IMPENDING STORM!"

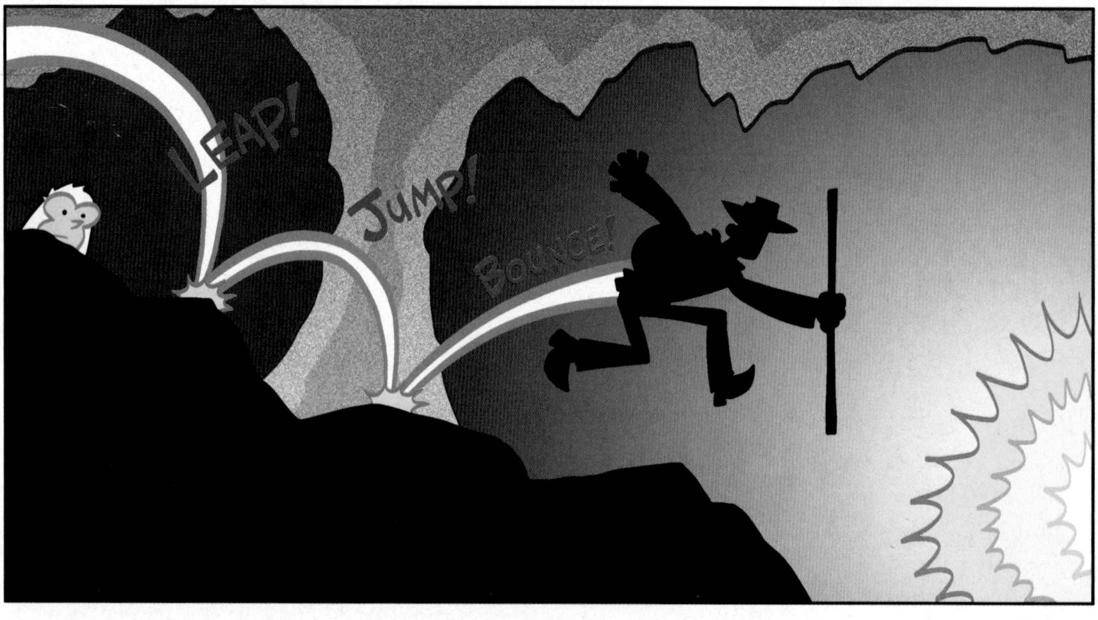
LEAP!
JUMP!
BOUNCE!

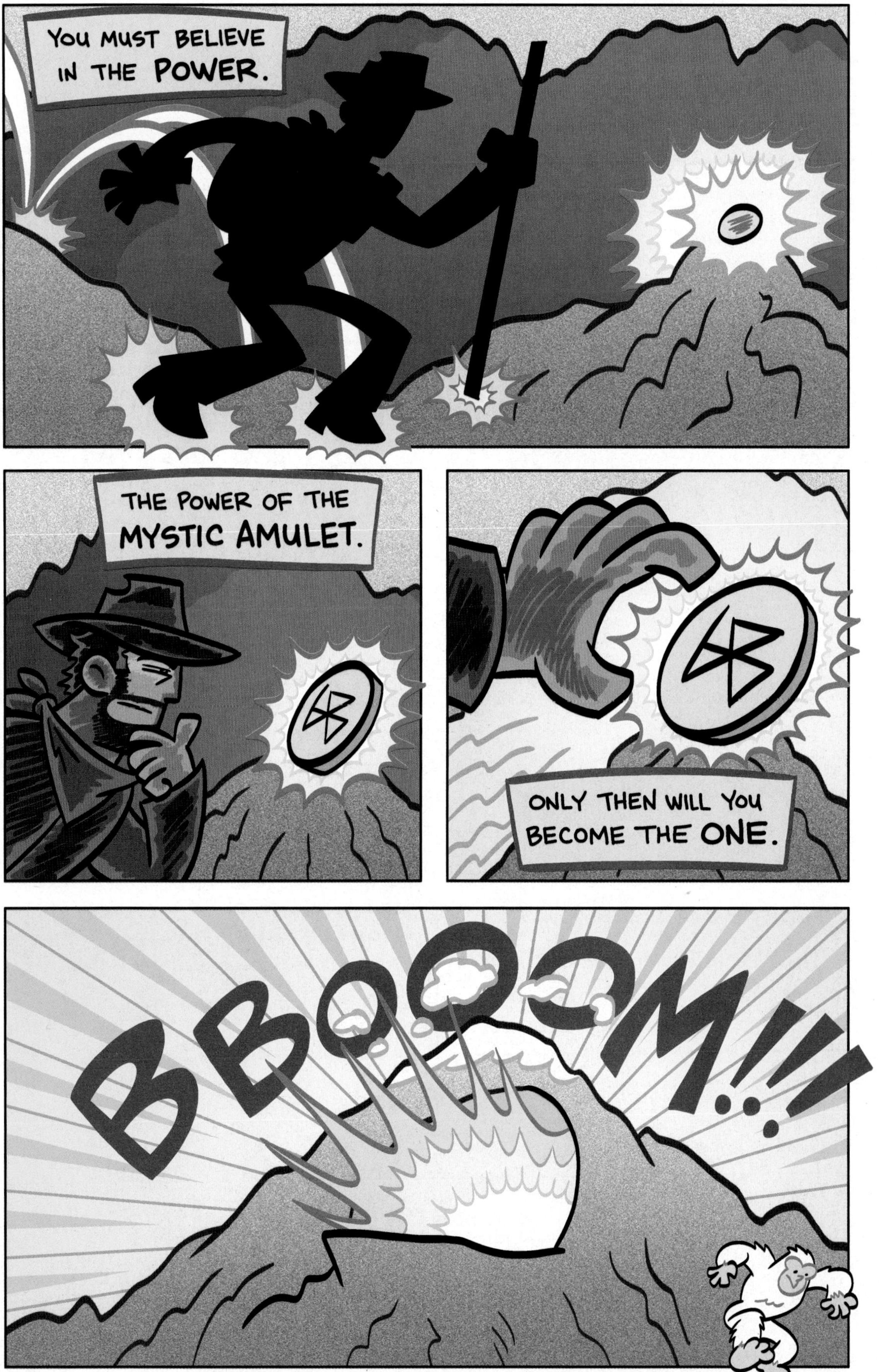
YOU MUST BELIEVE IN THE POWER.
THE POWER OF THE MYSTIC AMULET.
ONLY THEN WILL YOU BECOME THE ONE.
BBOOOOM!!!

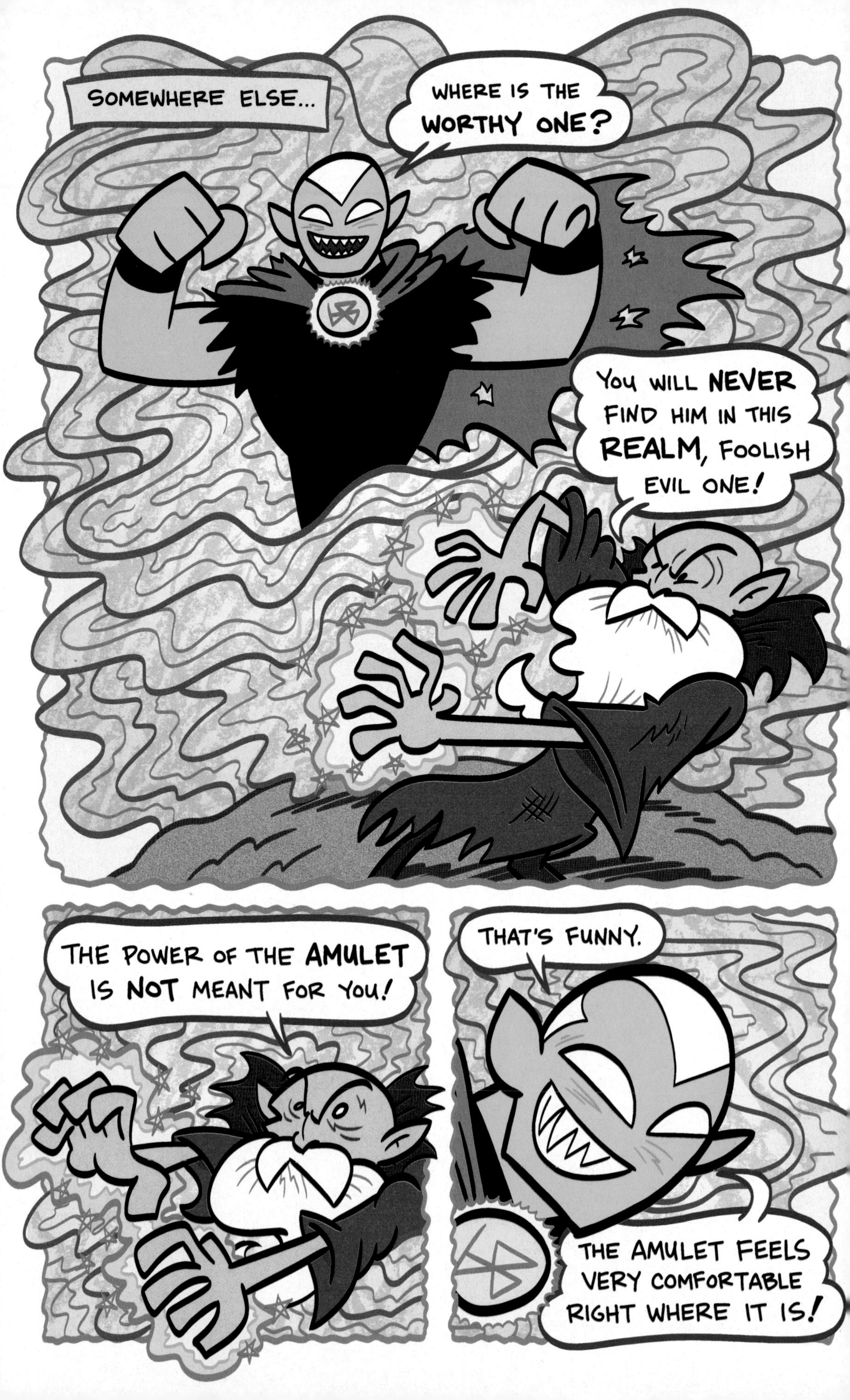
SOMEWHERE ELSE...
WHERE IS THE WORTHY ONE?
YOU WILL NEVER FIND HIM IN THIS REALM, FOOLISH EVIL ONE!
THE POWER OF THE AMULET IS NOT MEANT FOR YOU!
THAT'S FUNNY.
THE AMULET FEELS VERY COMFORTABLE RIGHT WHERE IT IS!

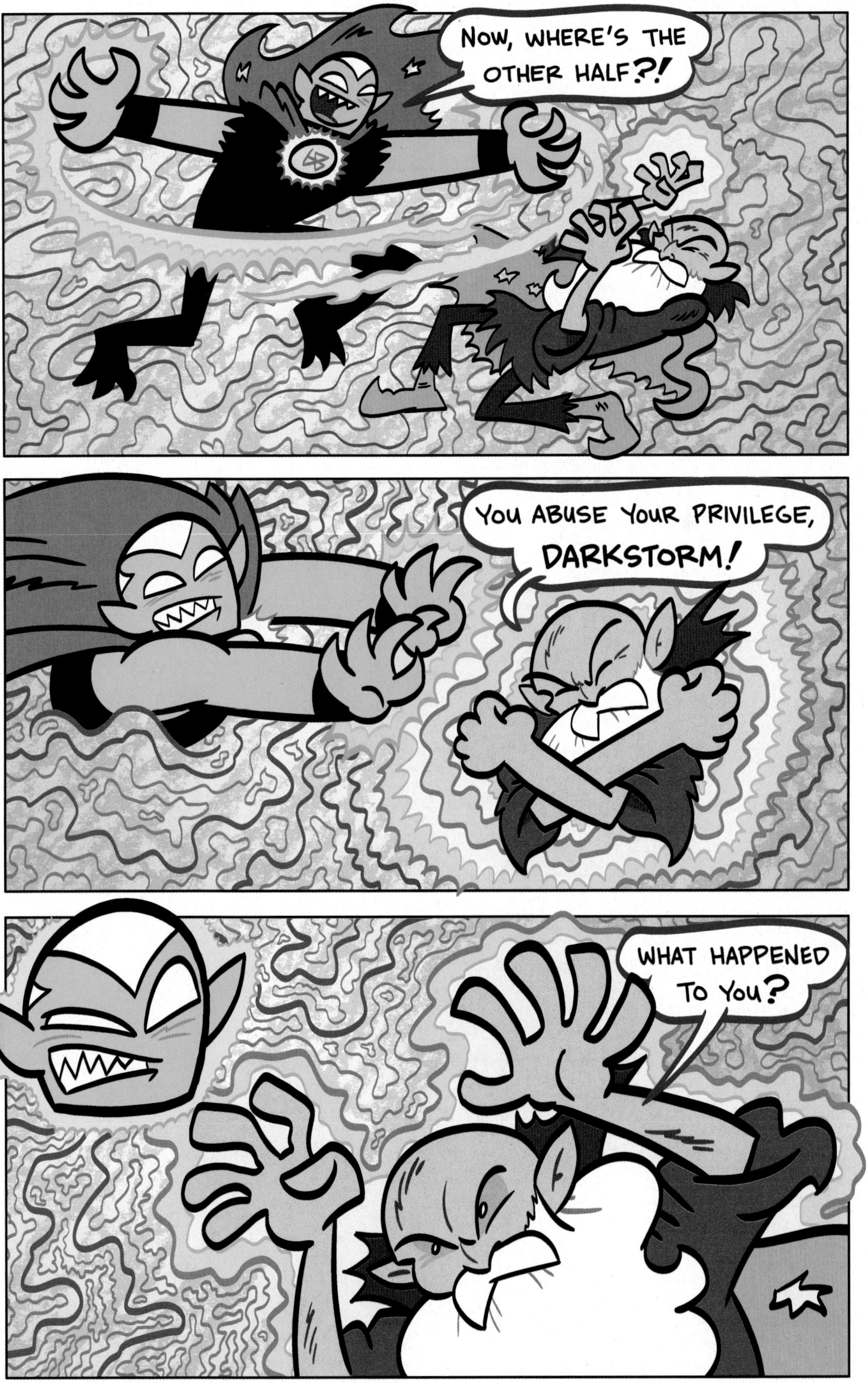
NOW, WHERE'S THE OTHER HALF?!
YOU ABUSE YOUR PRIVILEGE, DARKSTORM!
WHAT HAPPENED TO YOU?

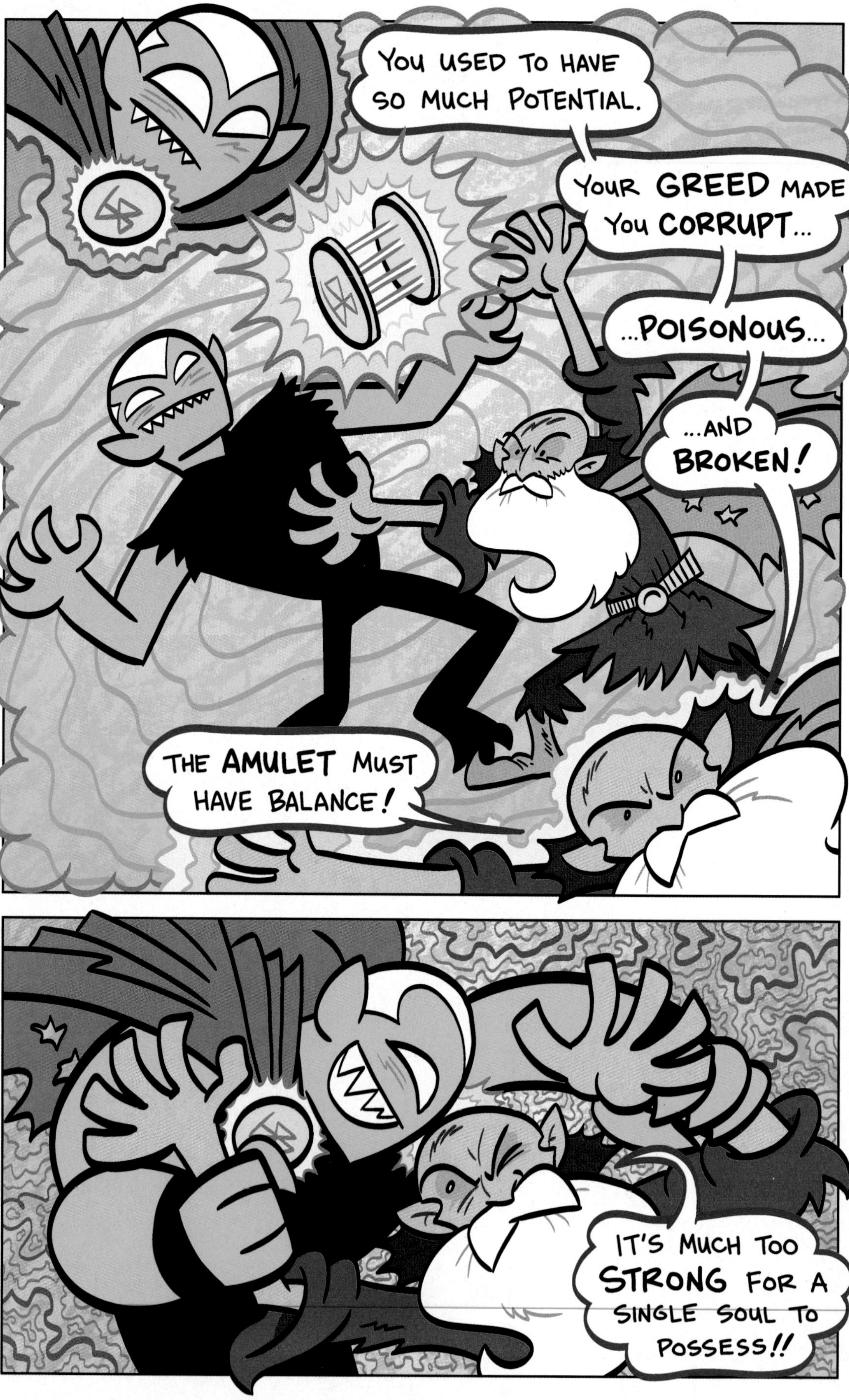
YOU USED TO HAVE SO MUCH POTENTIAL.
YOUR GREED MADE YOU CORRUPT...
...POISONOUS...
...AND BROKEN!
THE AMULET MUST HAVE BALANCE!
IT'S MUCH TOO STRONG FOR A SINGLE SOUL TO POSSESS!!

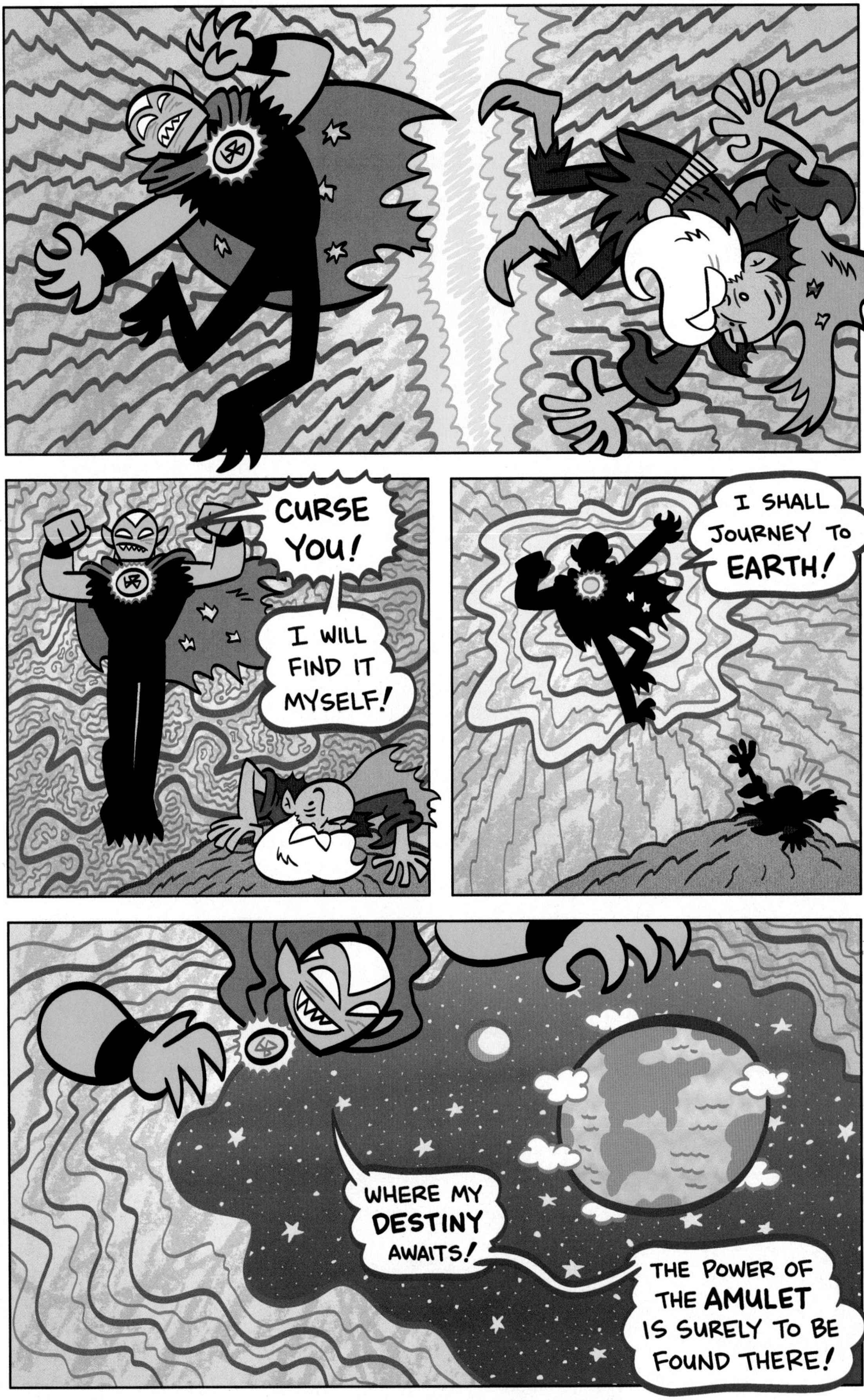
CURSE YOU!
I WILL FIND IT MYSELF!
I SHALL JOURNEY TO EARTH!
WHERE MY DESTINY AWAITS!
THE POWER OF THE AMULET IS SURELY TO BE FOUND THERE!

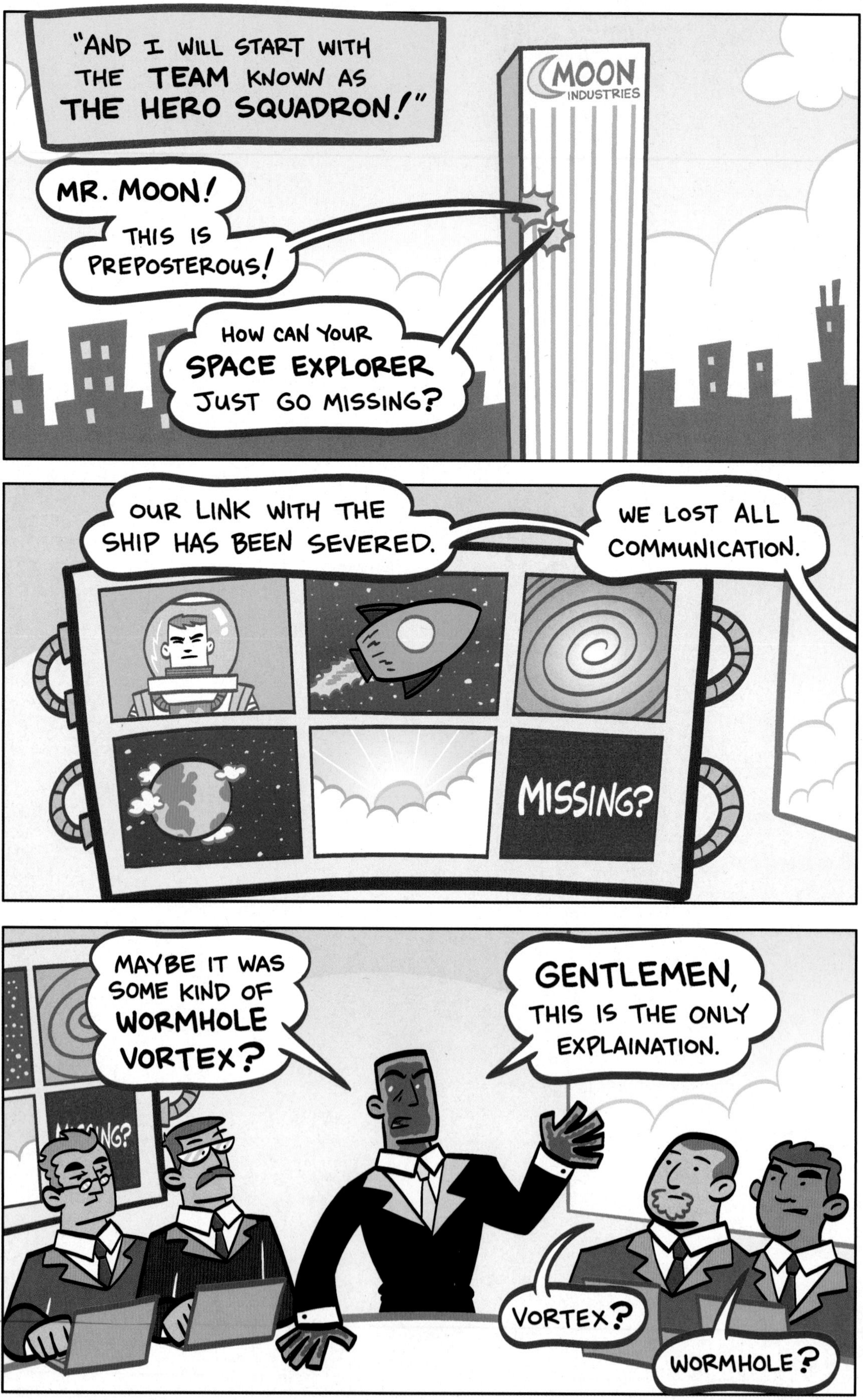
"AND I WILL START WITH THE TEAM KNOWN AS THE HERO SQUADRON!"
MOON INDUSTRIES
MR. MOON!
THIS IS PREPOSTEROUS!
HOW CAN YOUR SPACE EXPLORER JUST GO MISSING?
OUR LINK WITH THE SHIP HAS BEEN SEVERED.
WE LOST ALL COMMUNICATION.
MISSING?
MAYBE IT WAS SOME KIND OF WORMHOLE VORTEX?
GENTLEMEN, THIS IS THE ONLY EXPLAINATION.
VORTEX?
WORMHOLE?

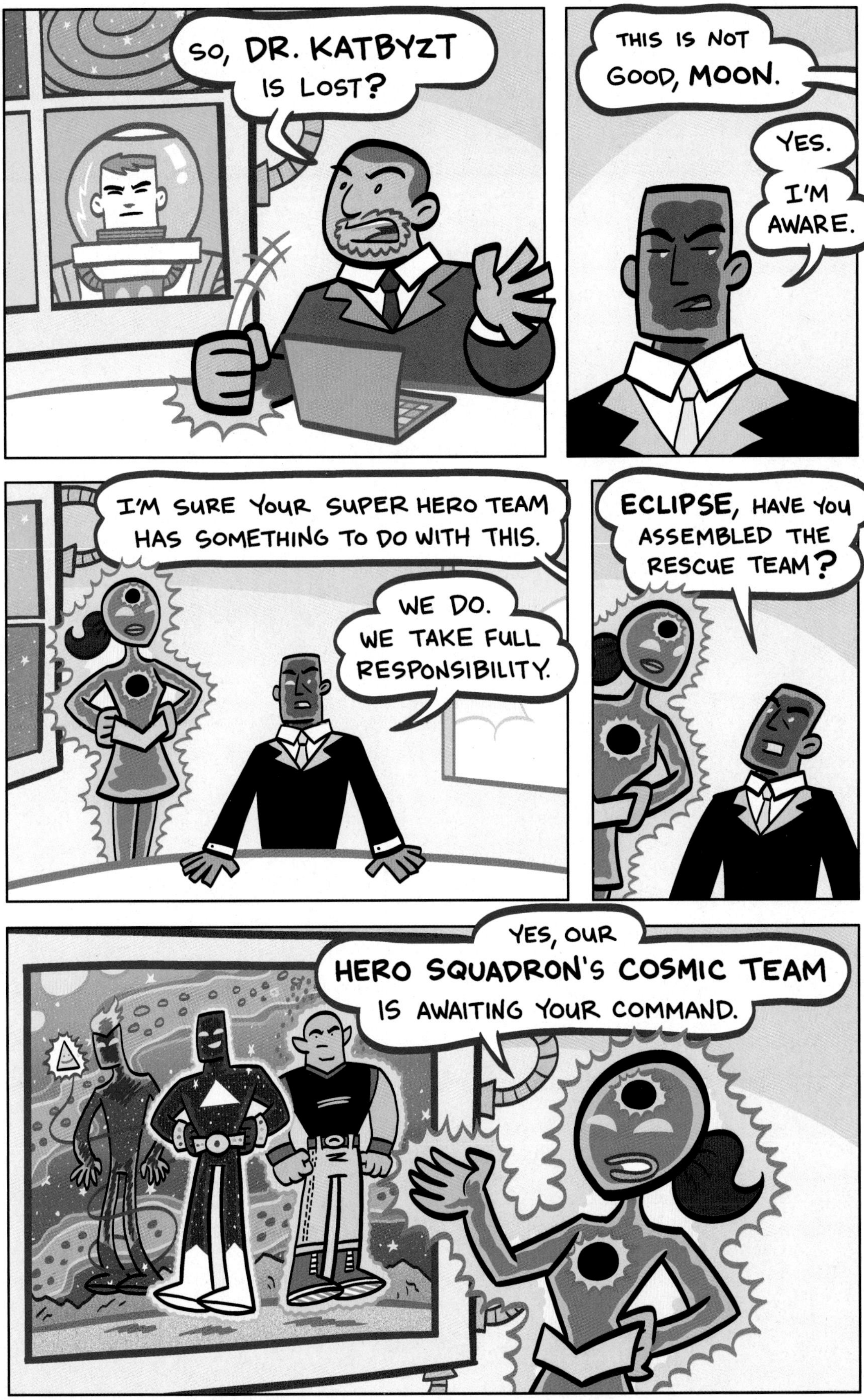
SO, DR. KATBYZT IS LOST?
THIS IS NOT GOOD, MOON.
YES.
I'M AWARE.
I'M SURE YOUR SUPER HERO TEAM HAS SOMETHING TO DO WITH THIS.
WE DO. WE TAKE FULL RESPONSIBILITY.
ECLIPSE, HAVE YOU ASSEMBLED THE RESCUE TEAM?
YES, OUR HERO SQUADRON'S COSMIC TEAM IS AWAITING YOUR COMMAND.

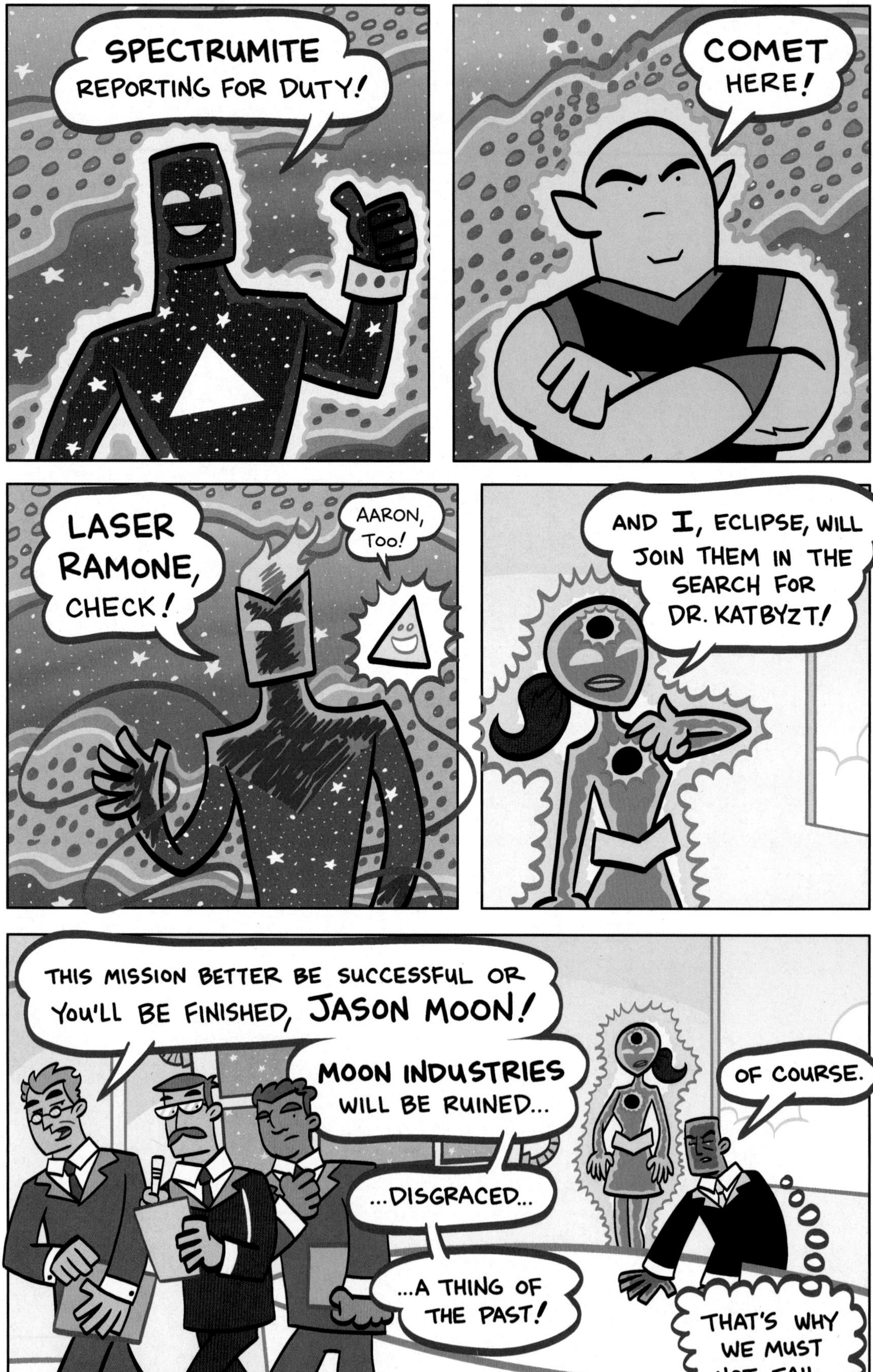
SPECTRUMITE REPORTING FOR DUTY!
COMET HERE!
LASER RAMONE, CHECK!
AARON, TOO!
AND I, ECLIPSE, WILL JOIN THEM IN THE SEARCH FOR DR. KATBYZT!
THIS MISSION BETTER BE SUCCESSFUL OR YOU'LL BE FINISHED, JASON MOON!
MOON INDUSTRIES WILL BE RUINED...
...DISGRACED...
...A THING OF THE PAST!
OF COURSE.
THAT'S WHY WE MUST NOT FAIL.

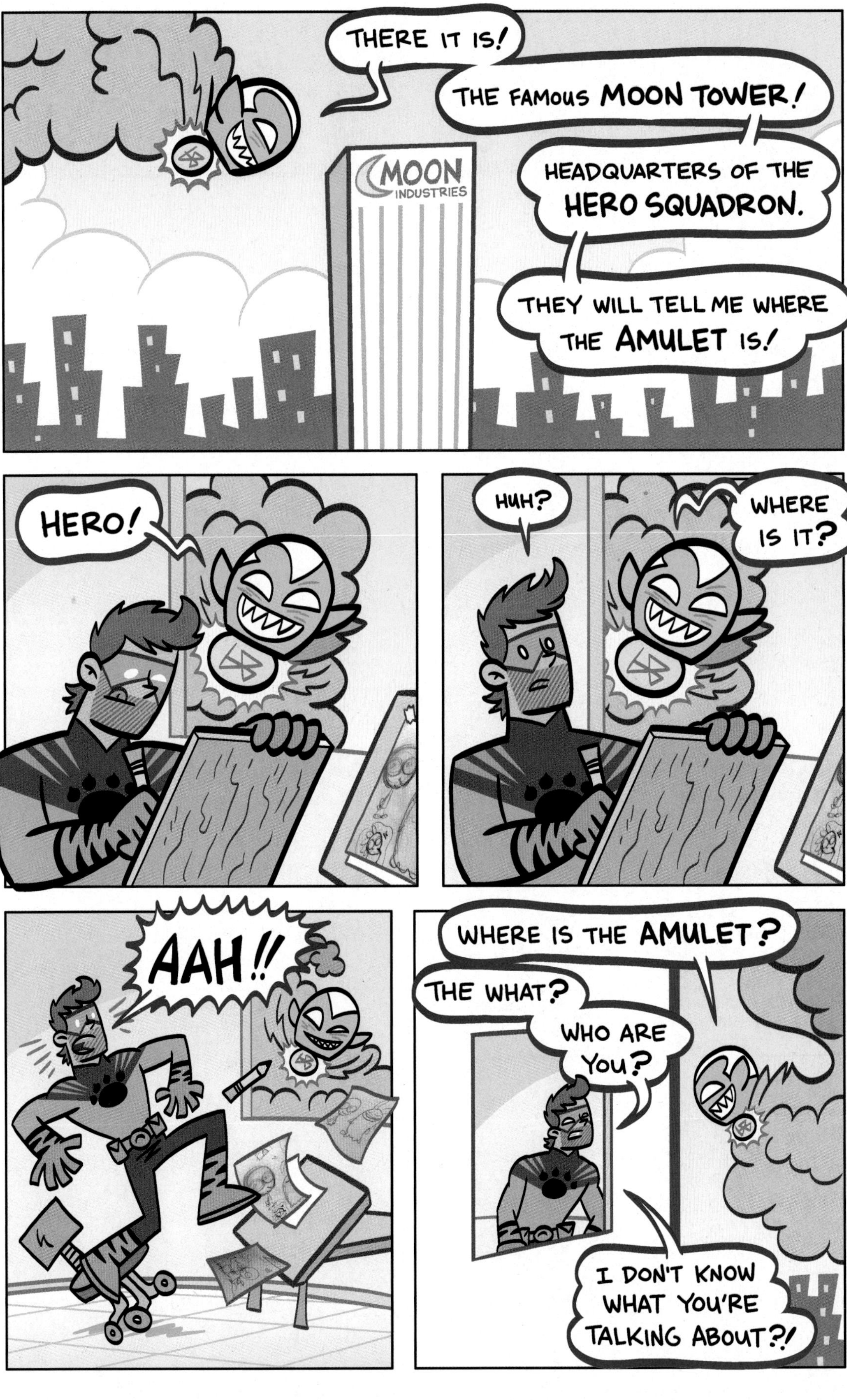
THERE IT IS!
THE FAMOUS MOON TOWER!
HEADQUARTERS OF THE HERO SQUADRON.
THEY WILL TELL ME WHERE THE AMULET IS!
MOON INDUSTRIES
HERO!
HUH?
WHERE IS IT?
AAH!!
WHERE IS THE AMULET?
THE WHAT?
WHO ARE YOU?
I DON'T KNOW WHAT YOU'RE TALKING ABOUT?!

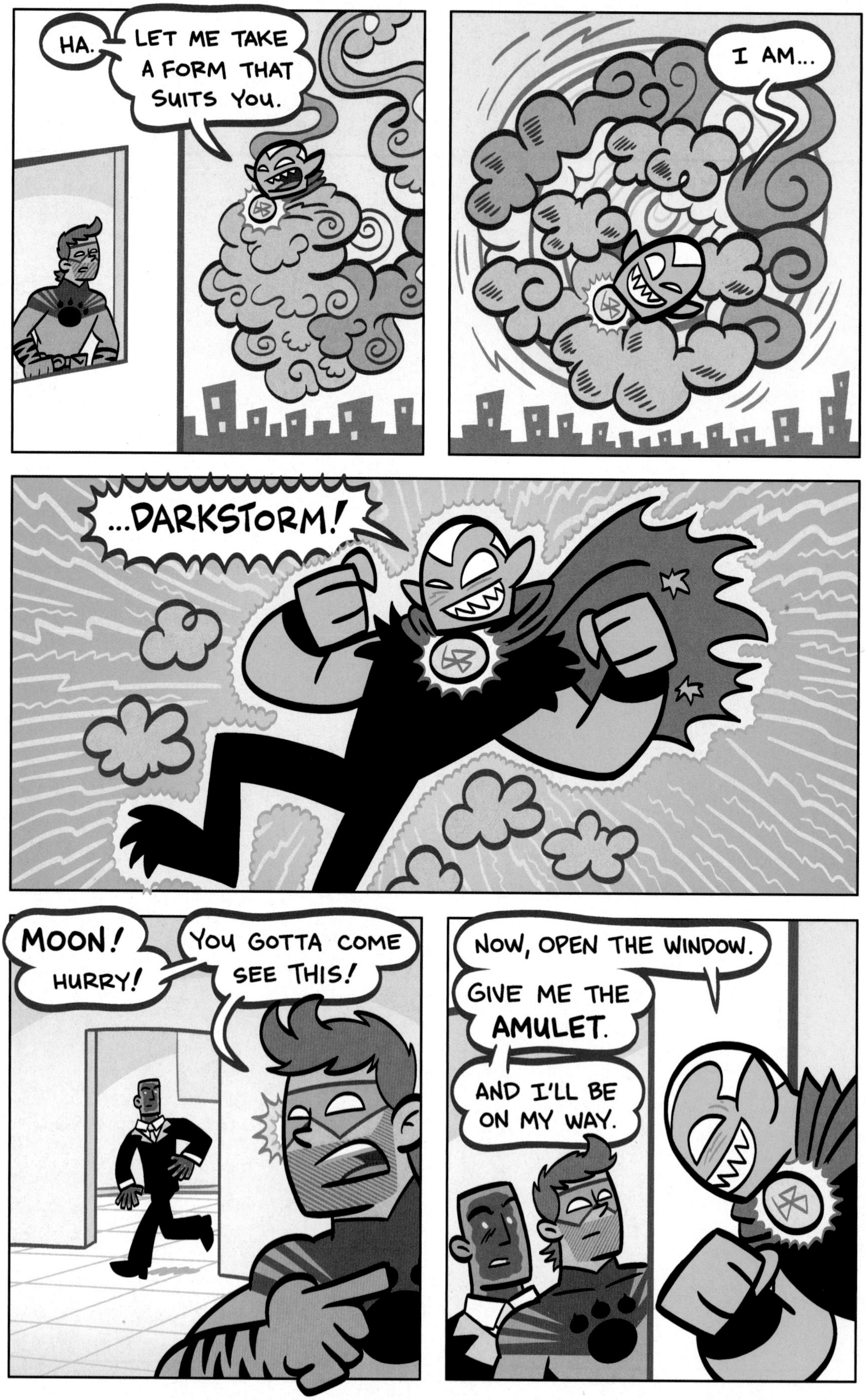
HA.
LET ME TAKE A FORM THAT SUITS YOU.
I AM...
...DARKSTORM!
MOON! HURRY!
YOU GOTTA COME SEE THIS!
NOW, OPEN THE WINDOW.
GIVE ME THE AMULET.
AND I'LL BE ON MY WAY.

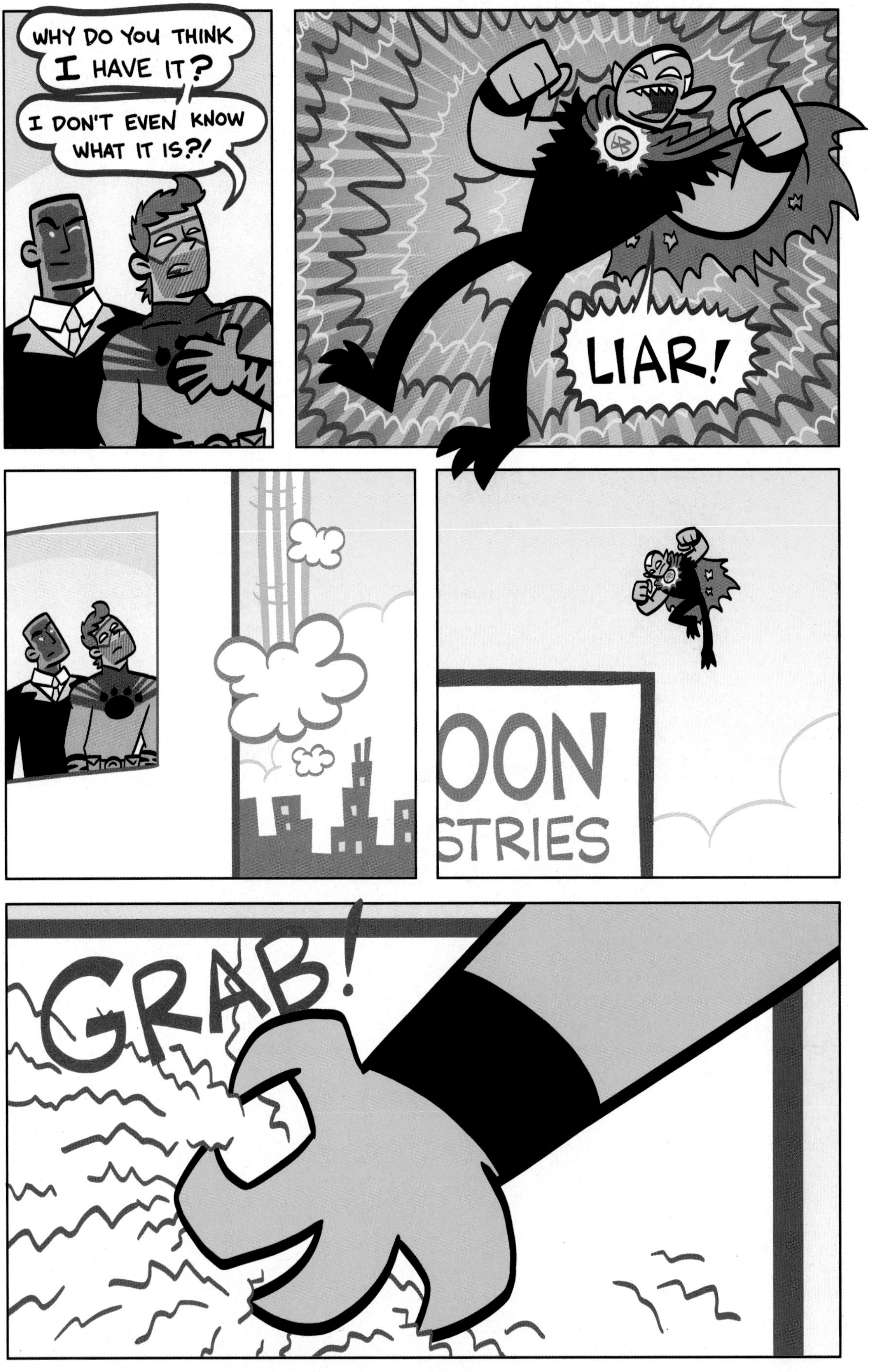
WHY DO YOU THINK I HAVE IT?
I DON'T EVEN KNOW WHAT IT IS?!
LIAR!
OON
STRIES
GRAB!

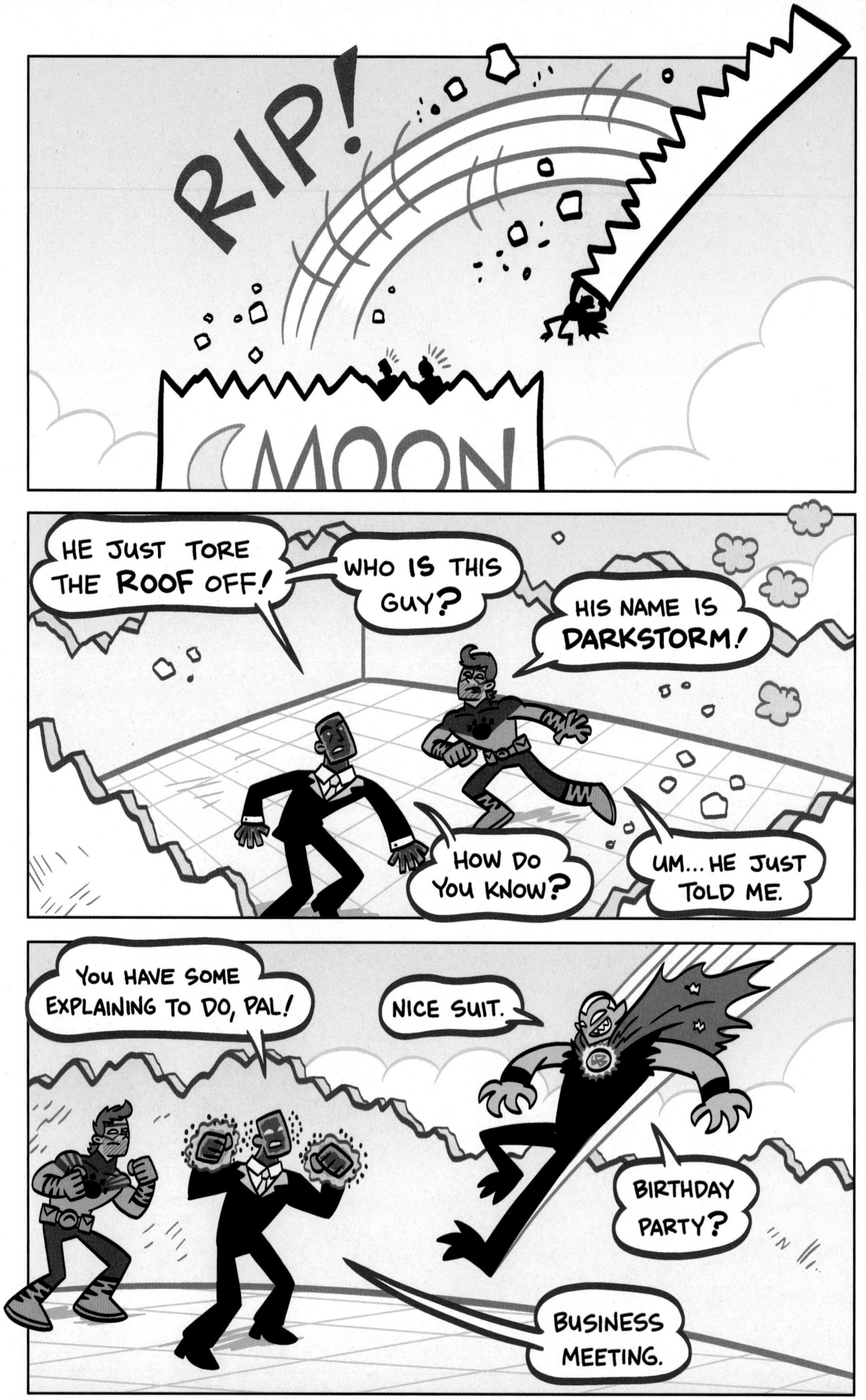
RIP!
MOON
HE JUST TORE THE ROOF OFF!
WHO IS THIS GUY?
HIS NAME IS DARKSTORM!
HOW DO YOU KNOW?
UM... HE JUST TOLD ME.
YOU HAVE SOME EXPLAINING TO DO, PAL!
NICE SUIT.
BIRTHDAY PARTY?
BUSINESS MEETING.

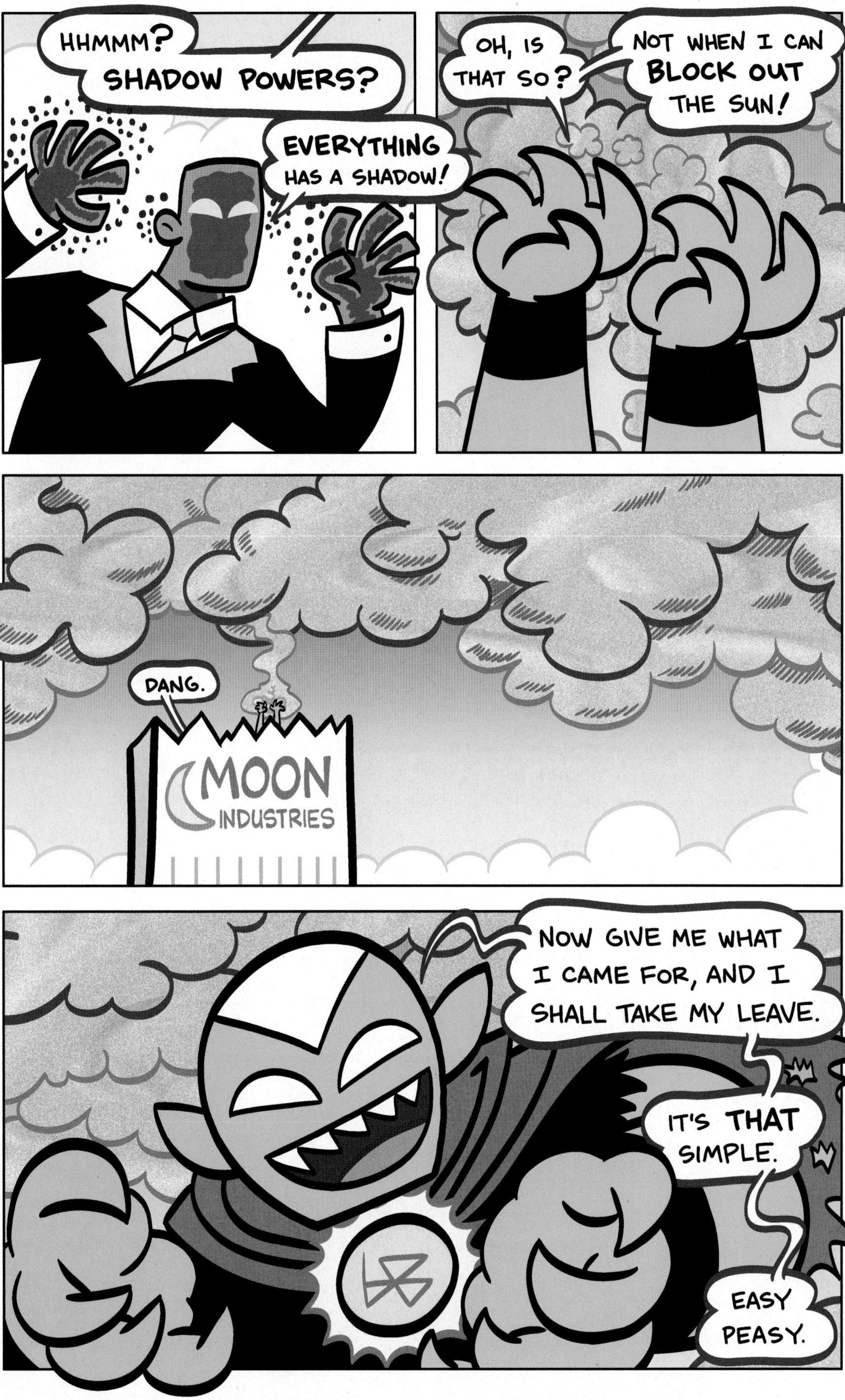
HHMMM?
SHADOW POWERS?
EVERYTHING HAS A SHADOW!
OH, IS THAT SO?
NOT WHEN I CAN BLOCK OUT THE SUN!
DANG.
MOON INDUSTRIES
NOW GIVE ME WHAT I CAME FOR, AND I SHALL TAKE MY LEAVE.
IT'S THAT SIMPLE.
EASY PEASY.

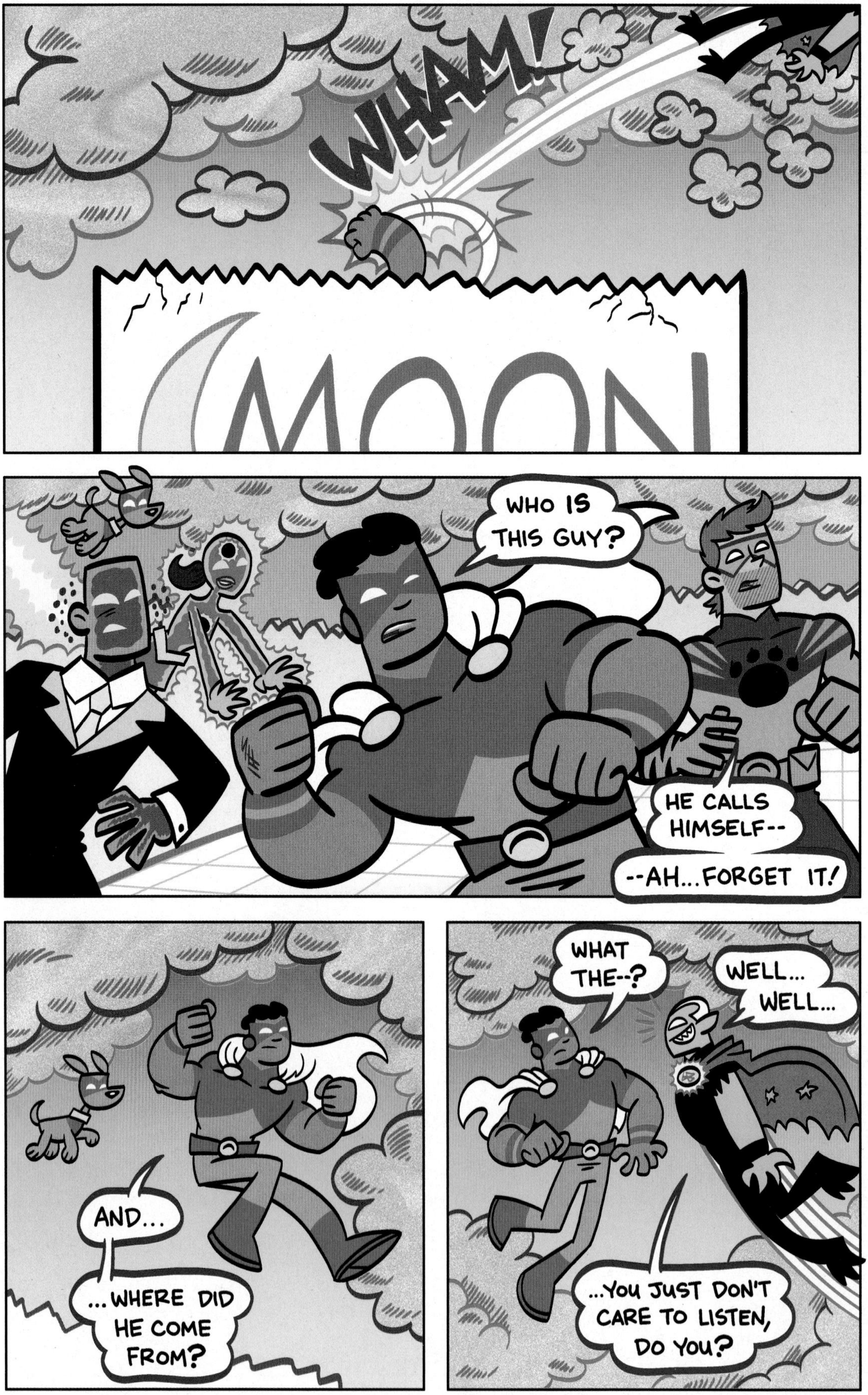
WHAM!
MOON
WHO IS THIS GUY?
HE CALLS HIMSELF--
--AH...FORGET IT!
AND...
...WHERE DID HE COME FROM?
WHAT THE--?
WELL... WELL...
...YOU JUST DON'T CARE TO LISTEN, DO YOU?

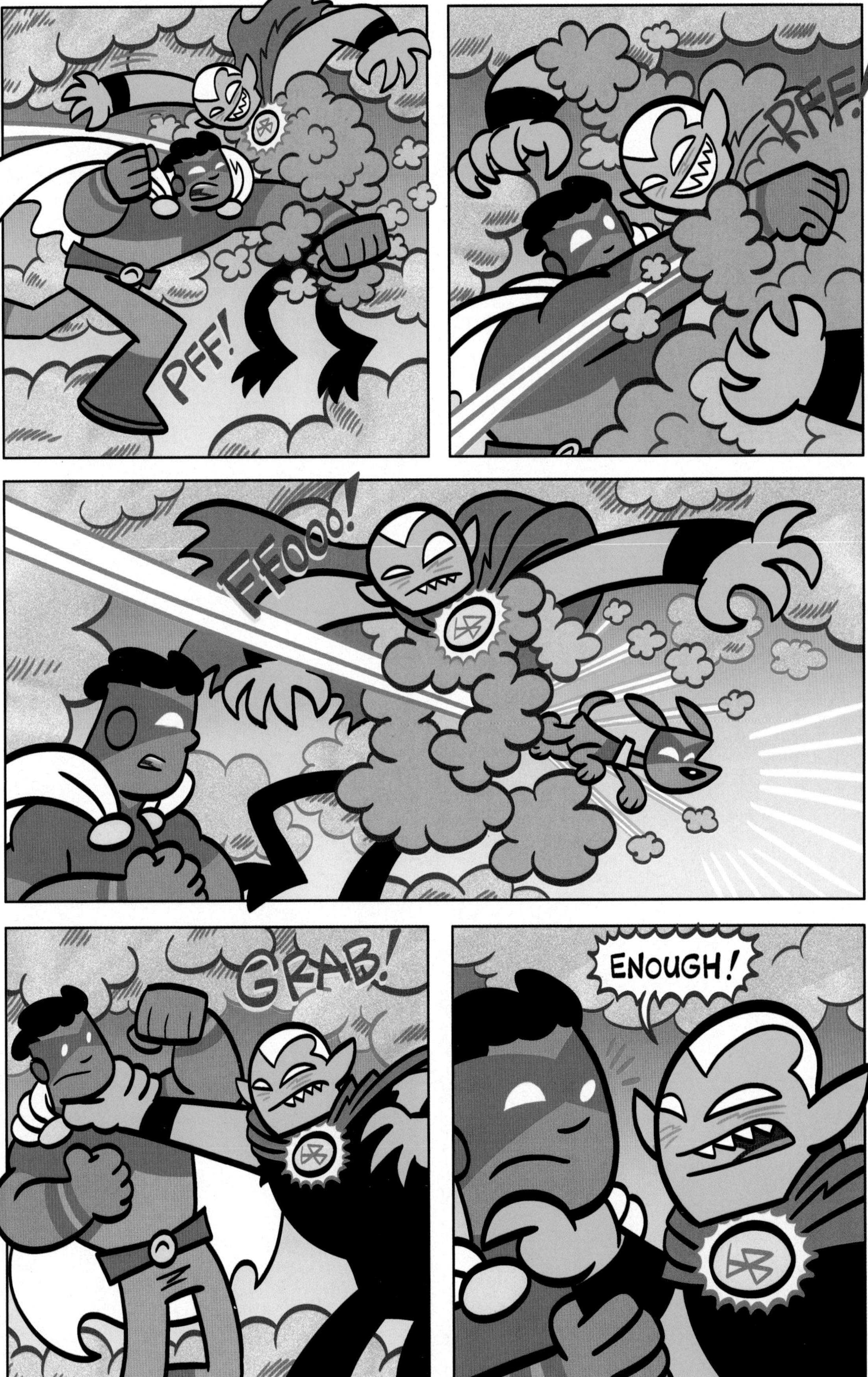
PFF!
PFF!
FFOOO!
GRAB!
ENOUGH!

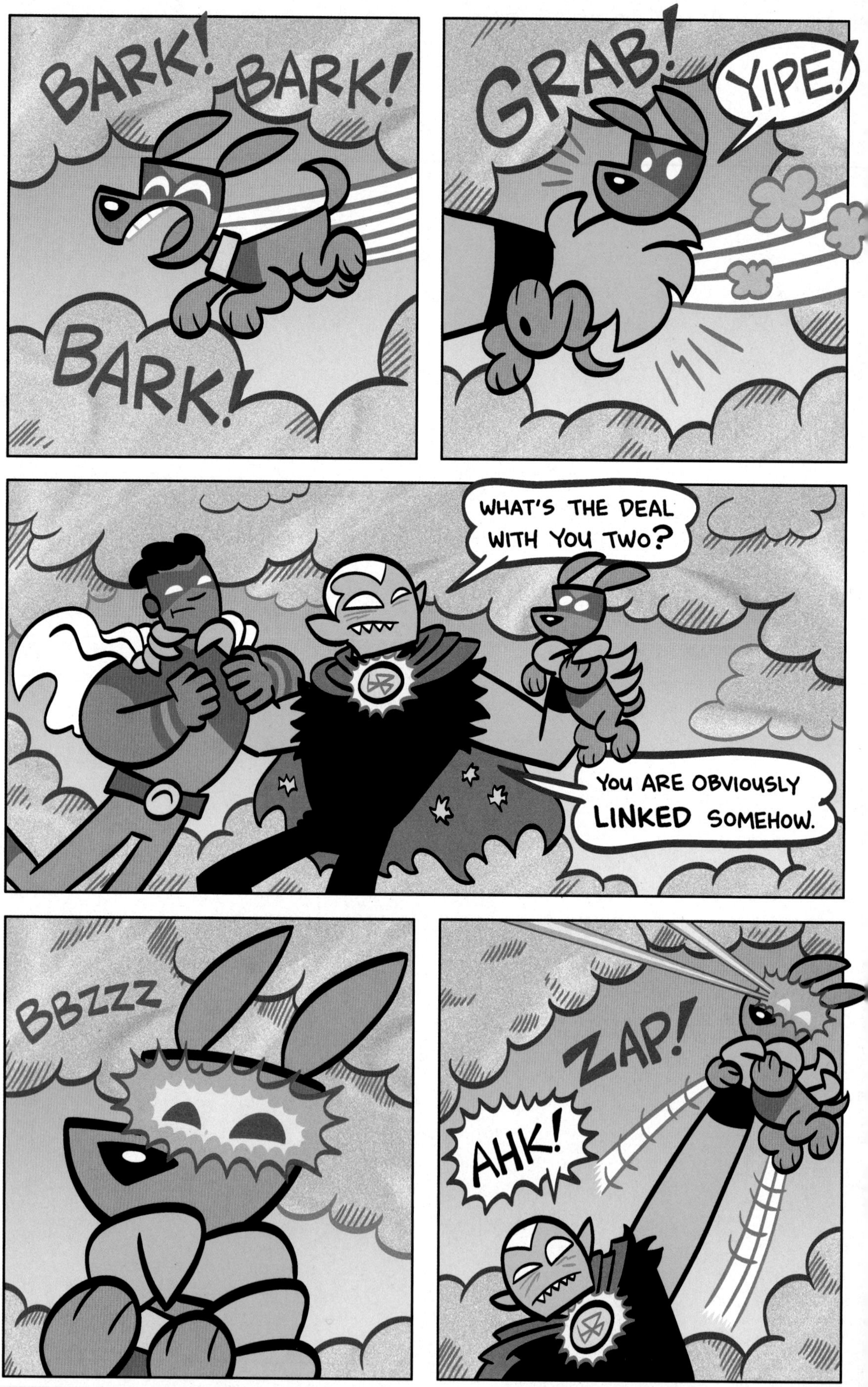
BARK! BARK!
BARK!
GRAB!
YIPE!
WHAT'S THE DEAL WITH YOU TWO?
YOU ARE OBVIOUSLY LINKED SOMEHOW.
BBZZZ
ZAP!
AHK!

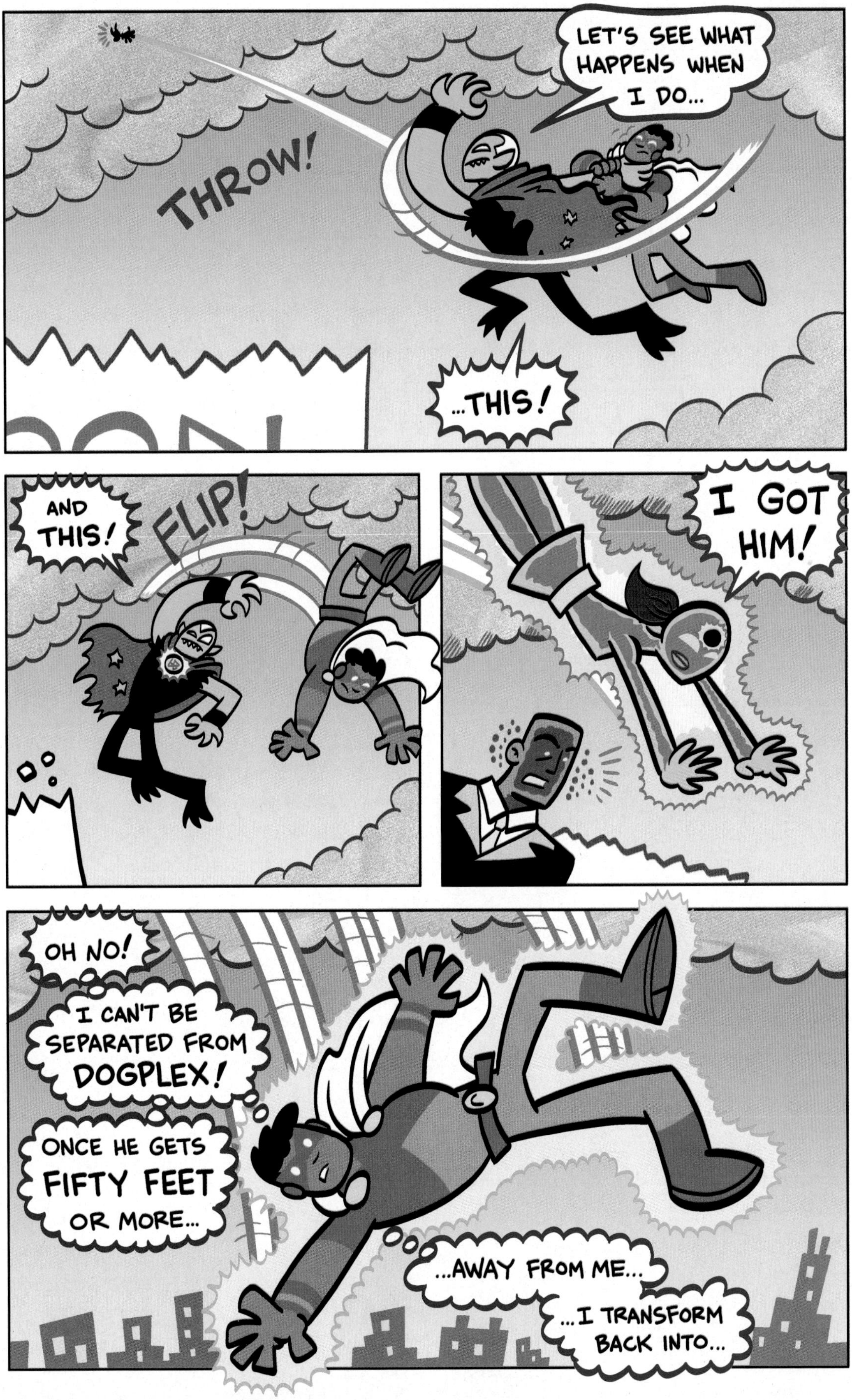
LET'S SEE WHAT HAPPENS WHEN I DO...
THROW!
...THIS!
AND THIS!
FLIP!
I GOT HIM!
OH NO!
I CAN'T BE SEPARATED FROM DOGPLEX!
ONCE HE GETS FIFTY FEET OR MORE...
...AWAY FROM ME...
...I TRANSFORM BACK INTO...

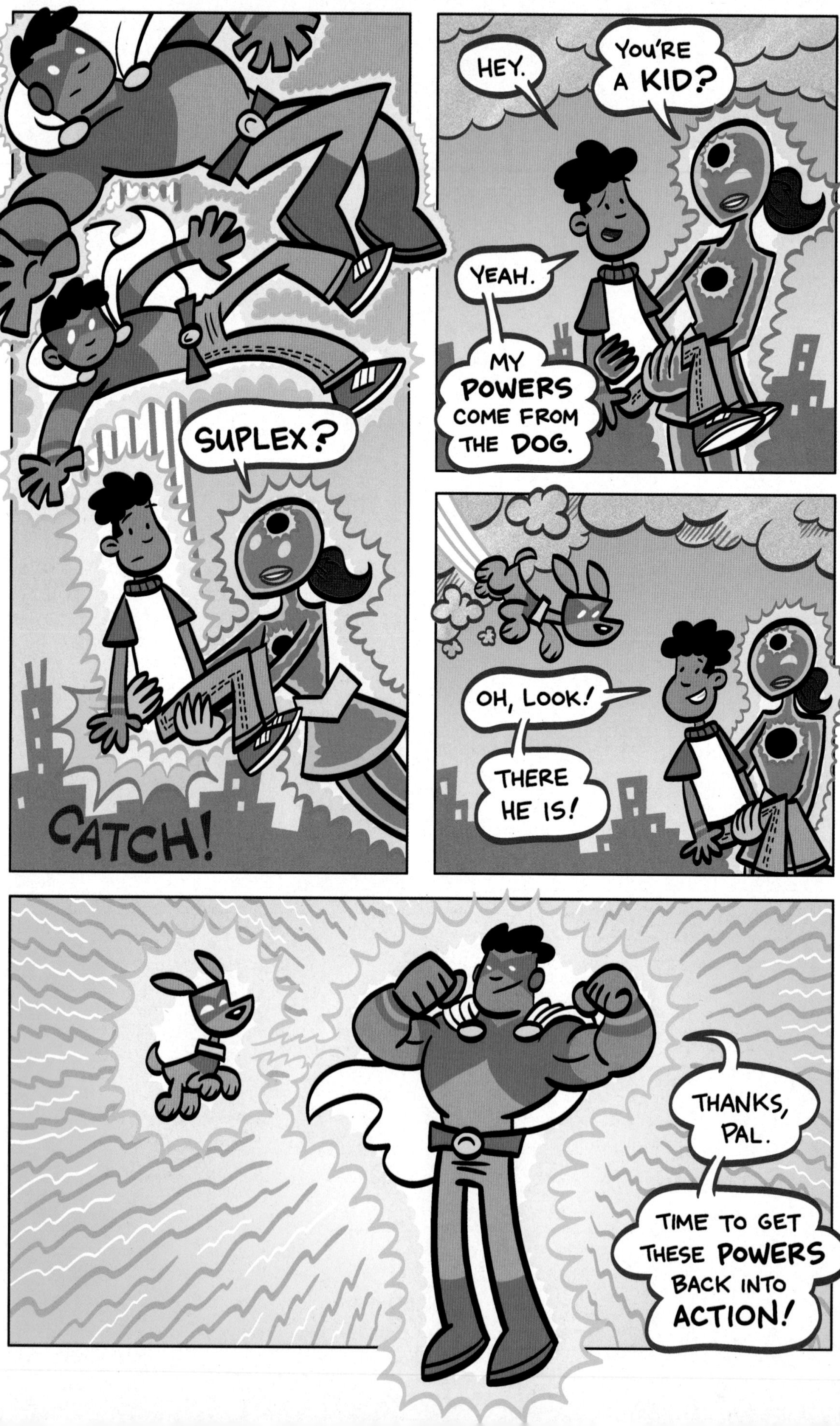
SUPLEX?
CATCH!
HEY.
YOU'RE A KID?
YEAH.
MY POWERS COME FROM THE DOG.
OH, LOOK!
THERE HE IS!
THANKS, PAL.
TIME TO GET THESE POWERS BACK INTO ACTION!

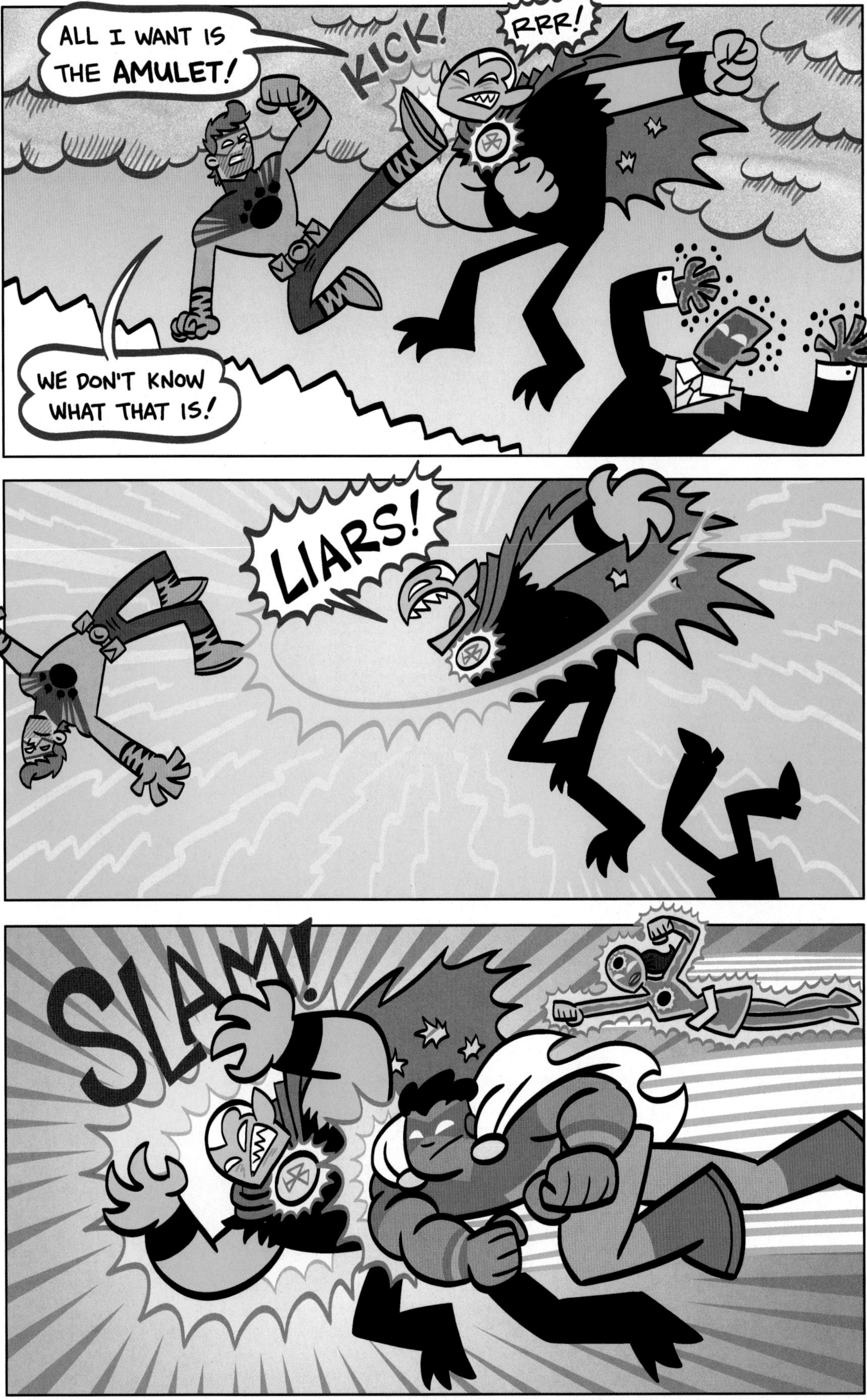
ALL I WANT IS THE AMULET!
KICK!
RRR!
WE DON'T KNOW WHAT THAT IS!
LIARS!
SLAM!

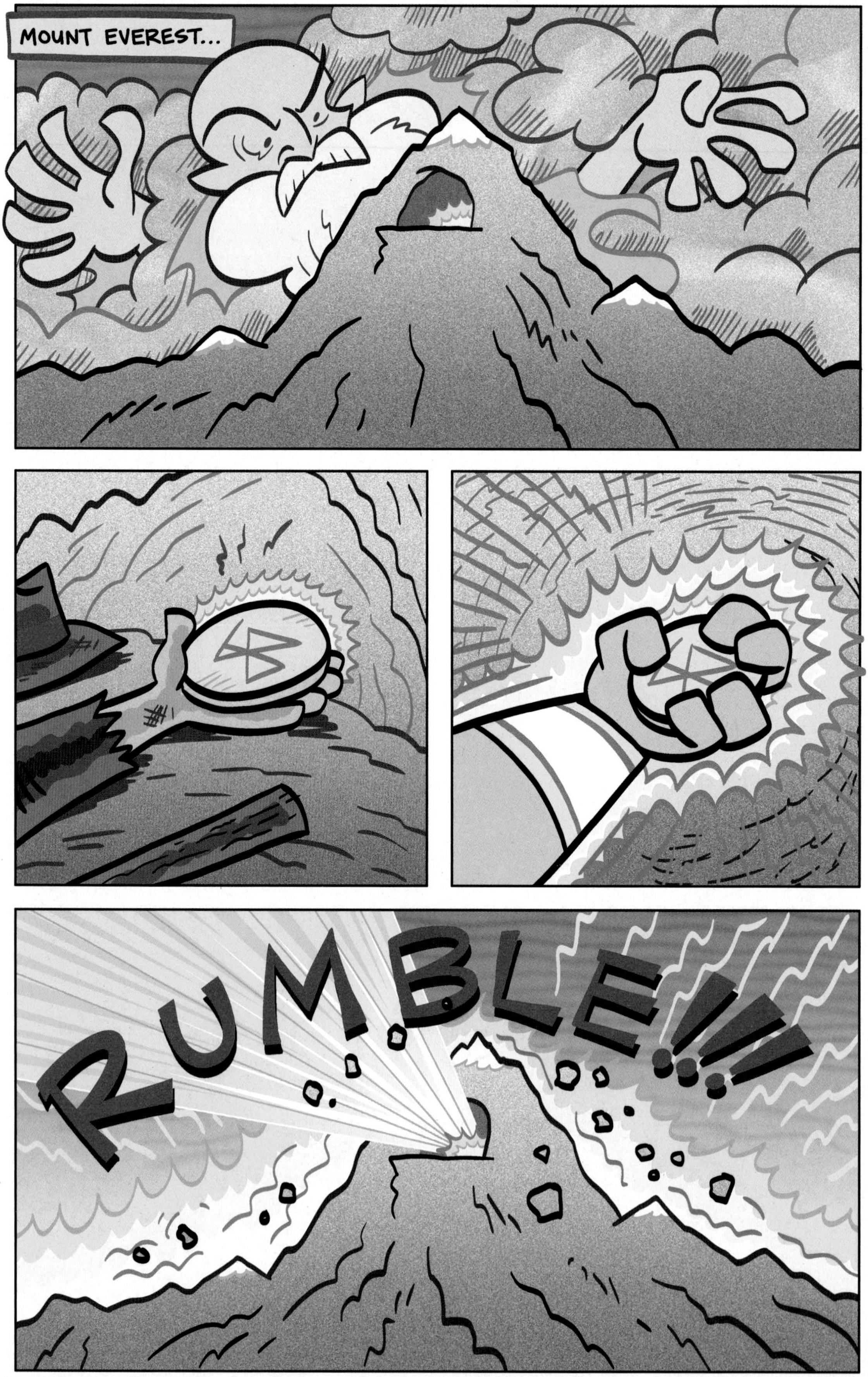
MOUNT EVEREST...
RUMBLE!!!!

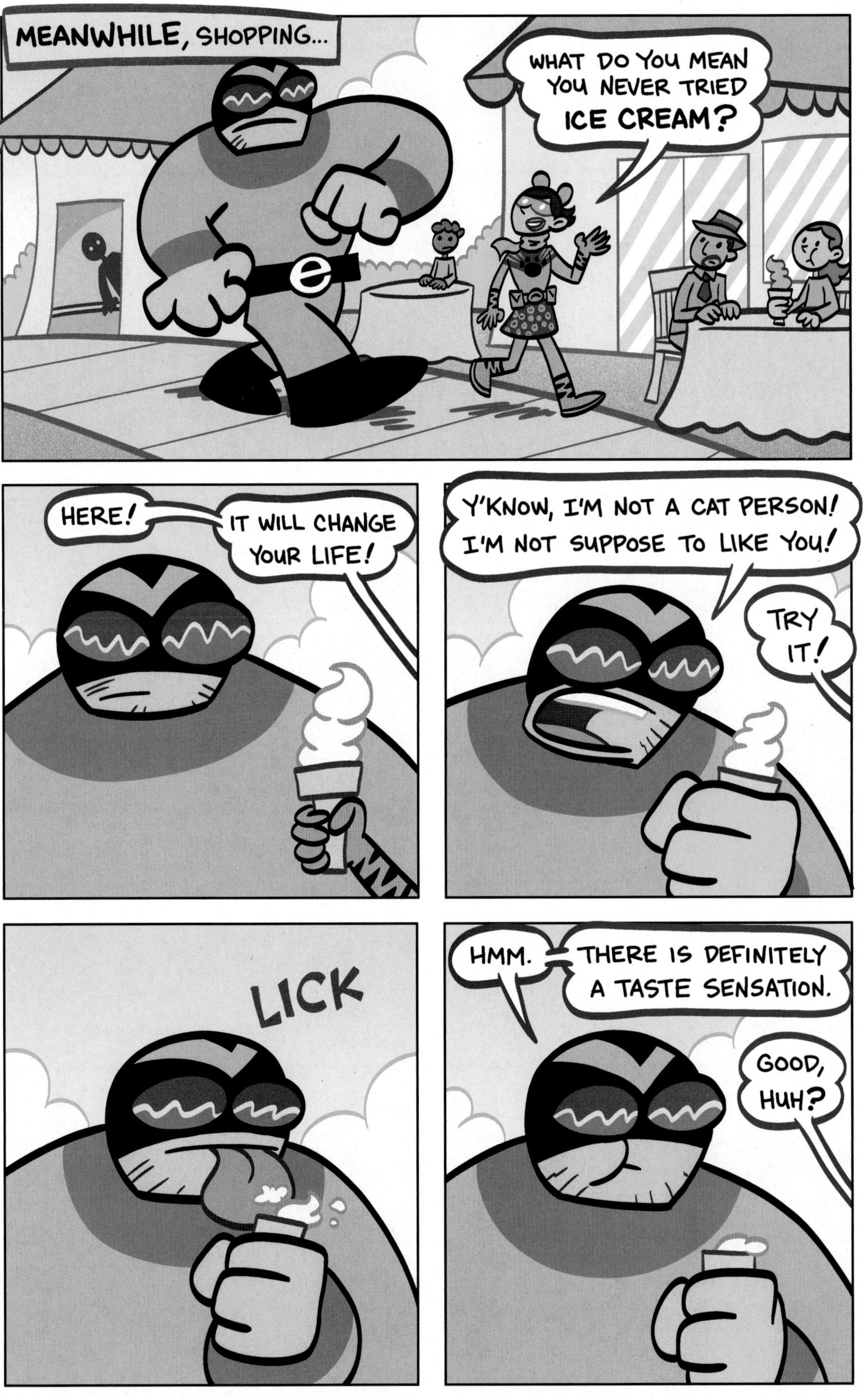

MEANWHILE, SHOPPING...
WHAT DO YOU MEAN YOU NEVER TRIED ICE CREAM?
HERE!
IT WILL CHANGE YOUR LIFE!
Y'KNOW, I'M NOT A CAT PERSON! I'M NOT SUPPOSE TO LIKE YOU!
TRY IT!
LICK
HMM.
THERE IS DEFINITELY A TASTE SENSATION.
GOOD, HUH?

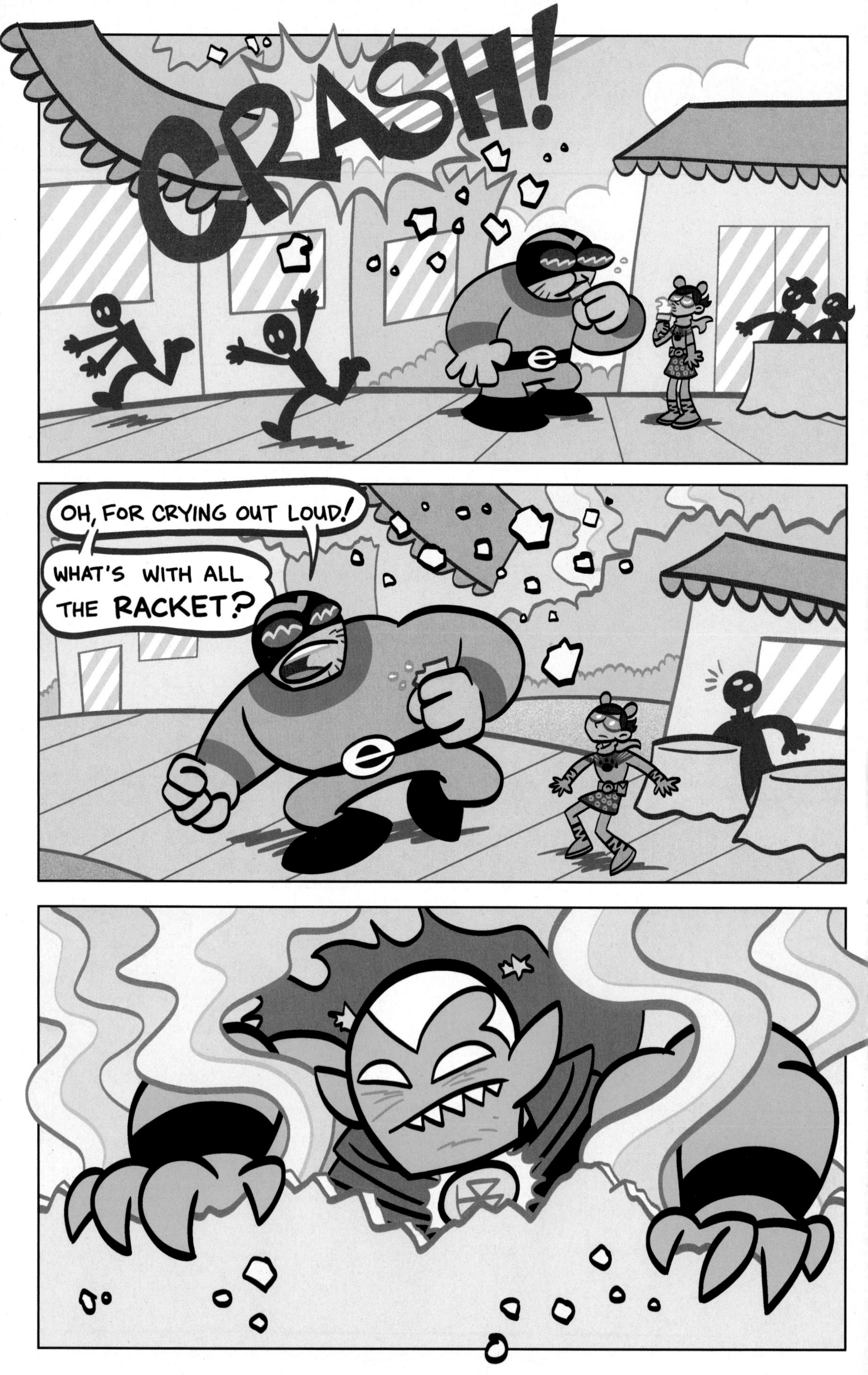
CRASH!
OH, FOR CRYING OUT LOUD!
WHAT'S WITH ALL THE RACKET?

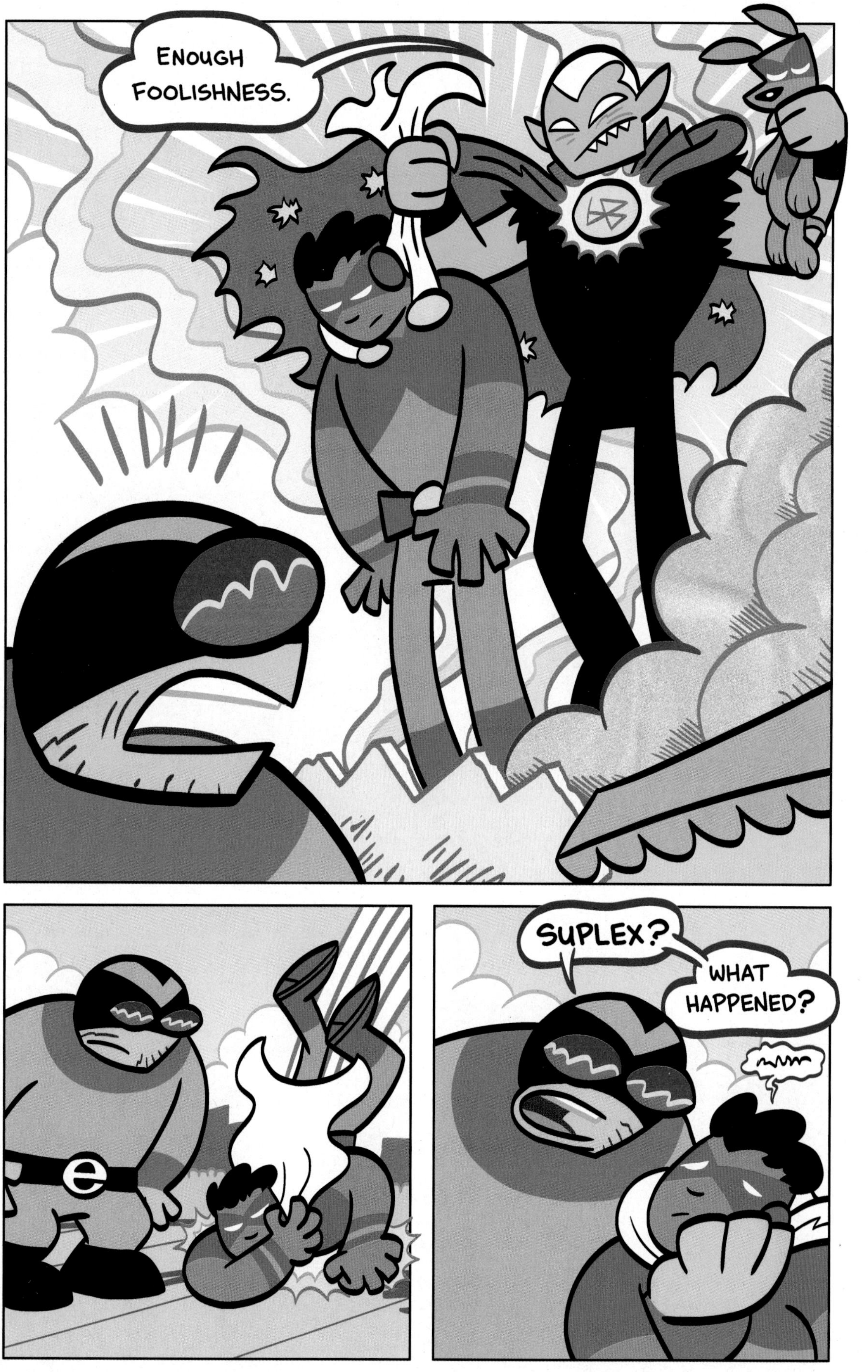
ENOUGH FOOLISHNESS.
SUPLEX?
WHAT HAPPENED?

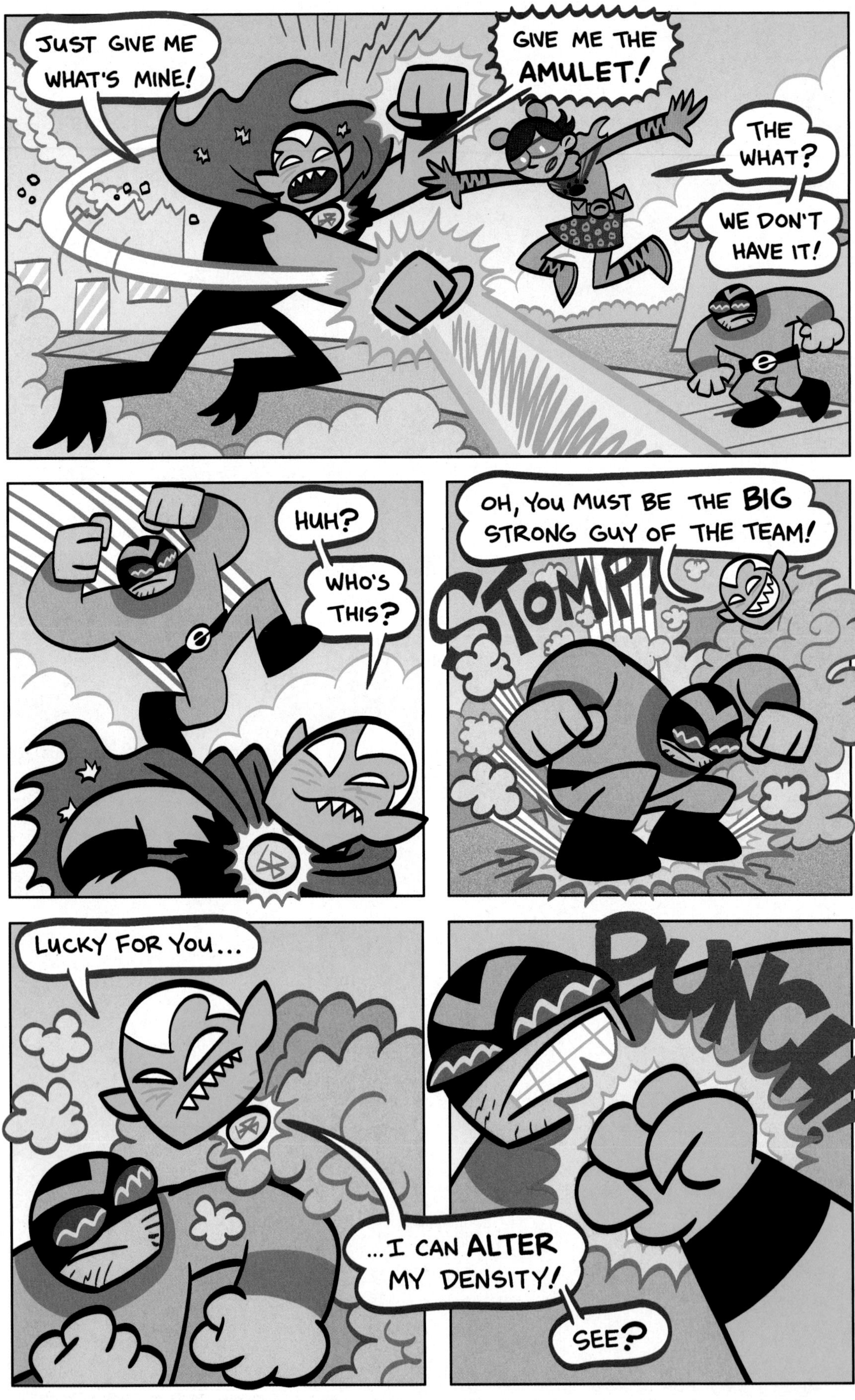

JUST GIVE ME WHAT'S MINE!
GIVE ME THE AMULET!
THE WHAT?
WE DON'T HAVE IT!
HUH?
WHO'S THIS?
OH, YOU MUST BE THE BIG STRONG GUY OF THE TEAM!
STOMP!
LUCKY FOR YOU...
...I CAN ALTER MY DENSITY!
PUNCH!!
SEE?

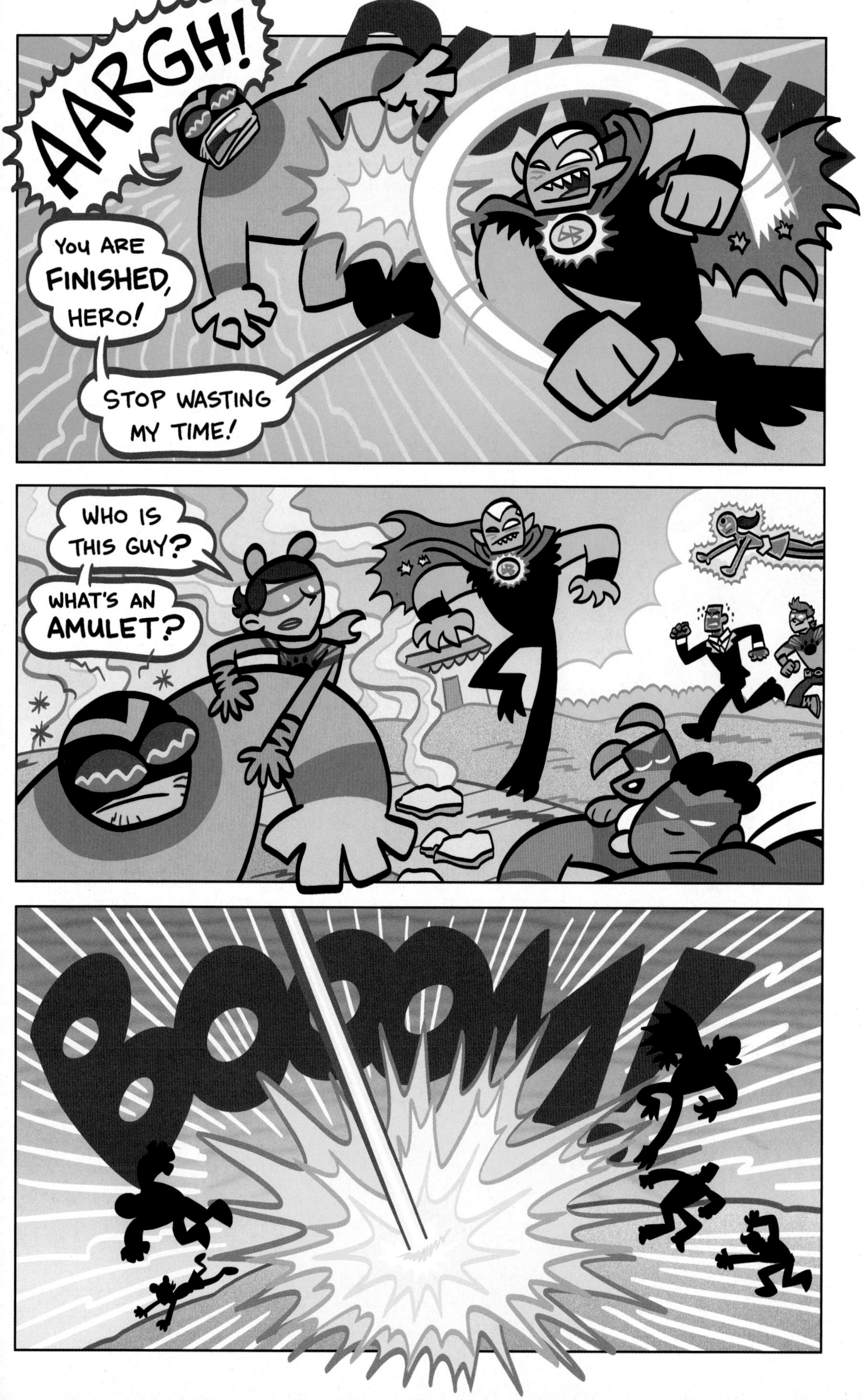
AARGH!
You are FINISHED, HERO!
STOP WASTING MY TIME!
WHO IS THIS GUY?
WHAT'S AN AMULET?

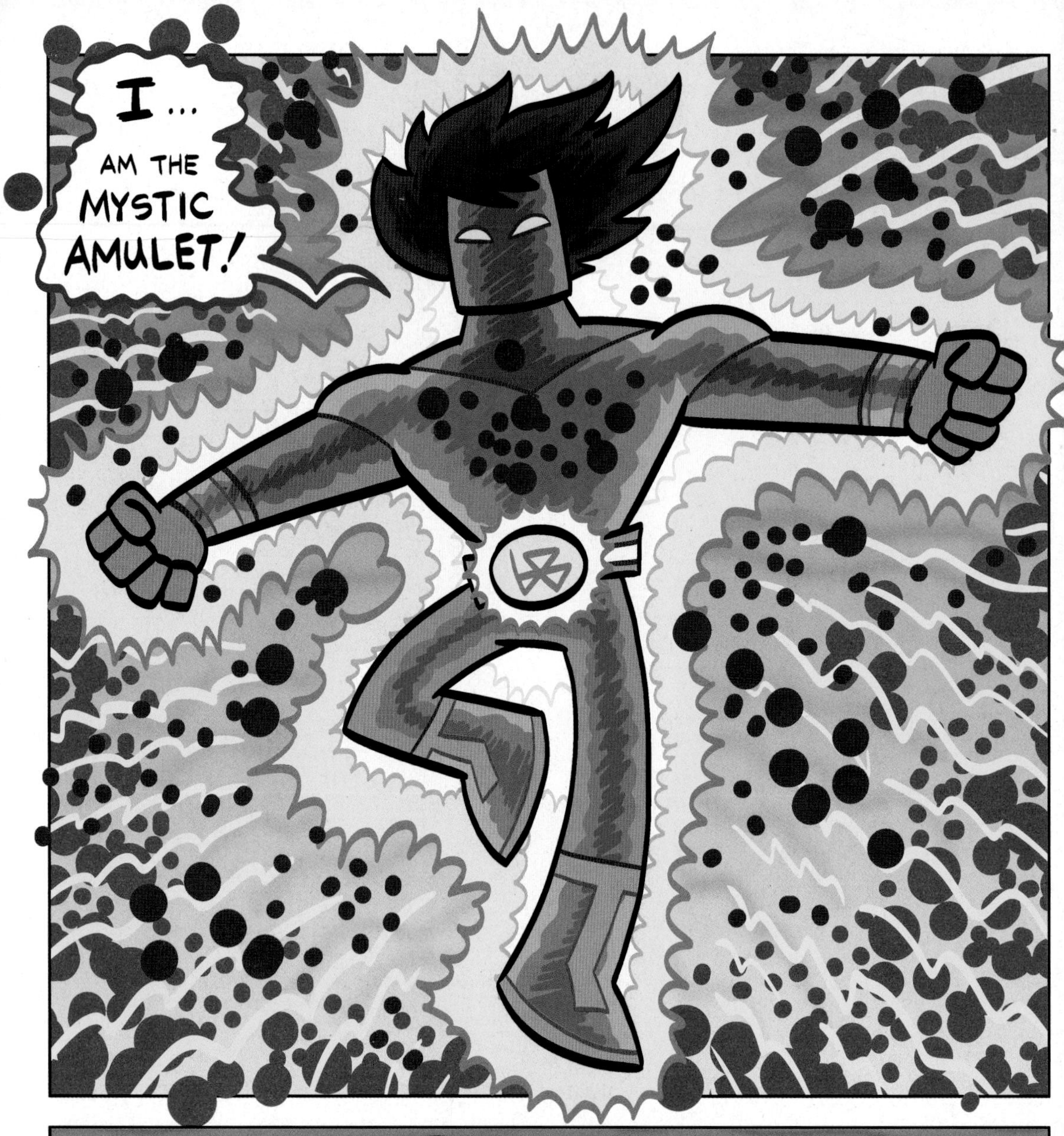
I... AM THE MYSTIC AMULET!

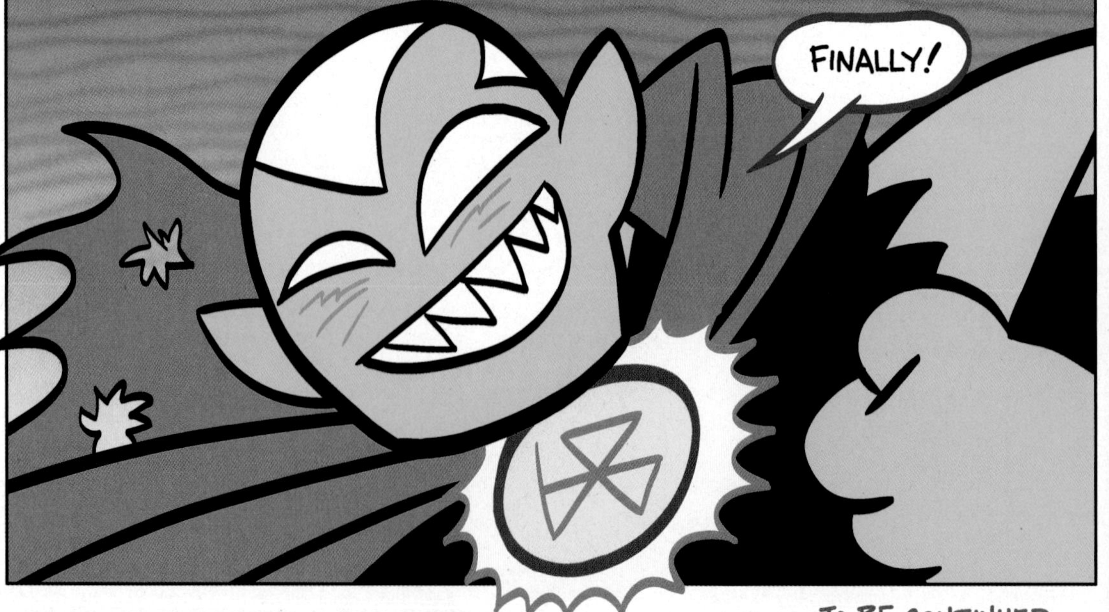
FINALLY!

-TO BE CONTINUED...

Before...

ART BALTAZAR's POWERS IN ACTION

...there was...

IMAGES OF ART COMICS!

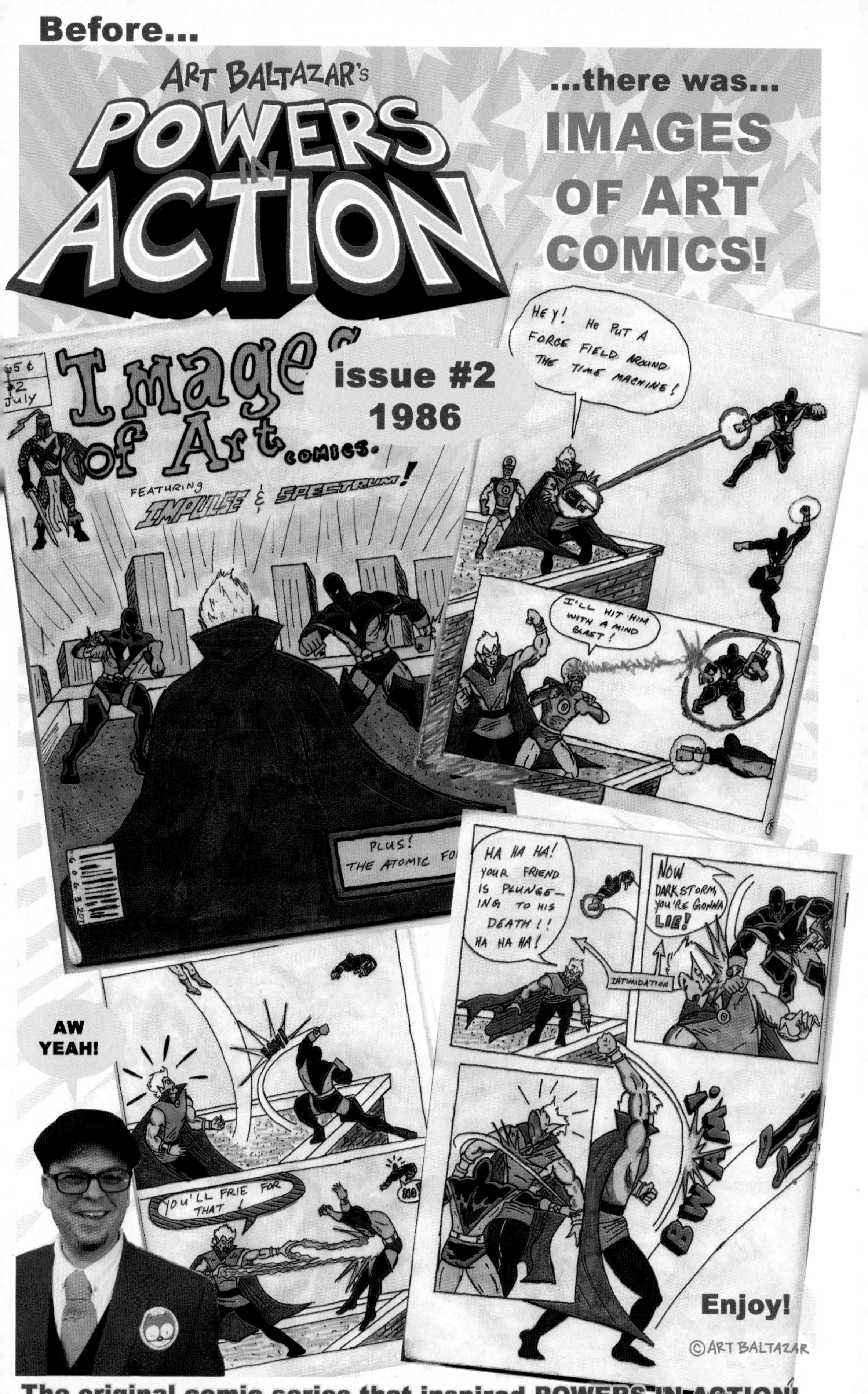

65¢
#2
July
Images of Art comics.
issue #2
1986
FEATURING IMPULSE & SPECTRUM!
PLUS! THE ATOMIC FO
HEY! HE PUT A FORCE FIELD AROUND THE TIME MACHINE!
I'LL HIT HIM WITH A MIND BLAST!
HA HA HA! YOUR FRIEND IS PLUNGE-ING TO HIS DEATH!! HA HA HA!
INTIMIDATION
NOW DARKSTORM, YOU'RE GONNA LIE!
YOU'LL FRIE FOR THAT!
NO!
BWAM!
AW YEAH!
Enjoy!
©ART BALTAZAR

The original comic series that inspired POWERS IN ACTION!

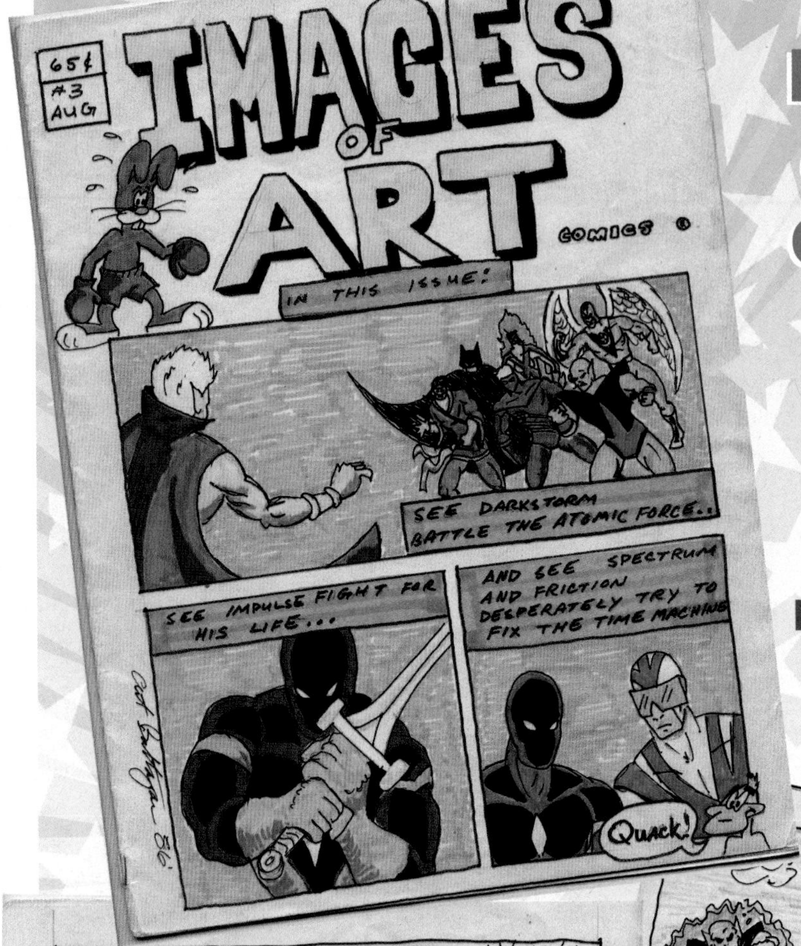
65¢
#3
AUG
IMAGES OF ART
COMICS ®
IN THIS ISSUE!
SEE DARKSTORM BATTLE THE ATOMIC FORCE..
SEE IMPULSE FIGHT FOR HIS LIFE...
AND SEE SPECTRUM AND FRICTION DESPERATELY TRY TO FIX THE TIME MACHINE
QUACK!

IMAGES OF ART COMICS!

issue #3 1986

Featuring... THE EVIL DARKSTORM!

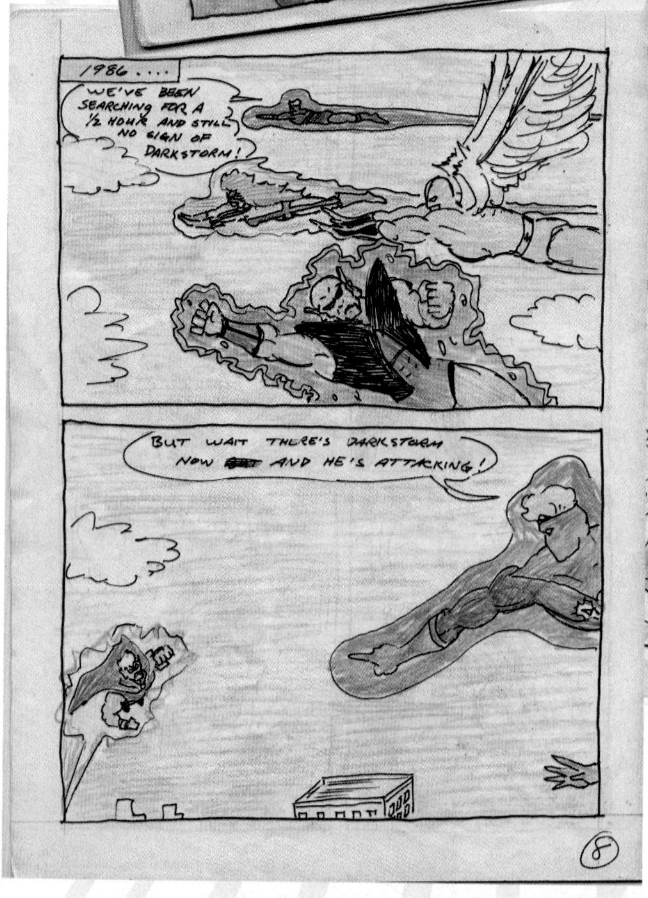
1986....
WE'VE BEEN SEARCHING FOR A 1/2 HOUR AND STILL NO SIGN OF DARKSTORM!
BUT WAIT THERE'S DARKSTORM NOW AND HE'S ATTACKING!
8

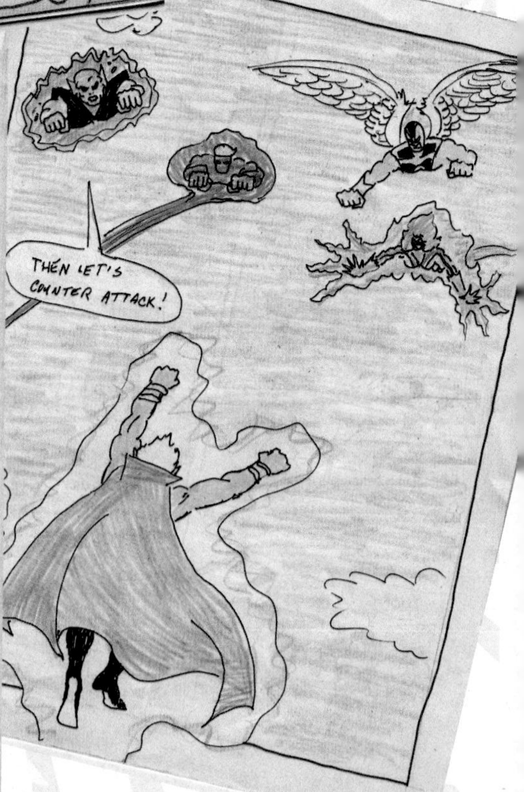
THEN LET'S COUNTER ATTACK!
9

The original comic series that inspired POWERS IN ACTION!

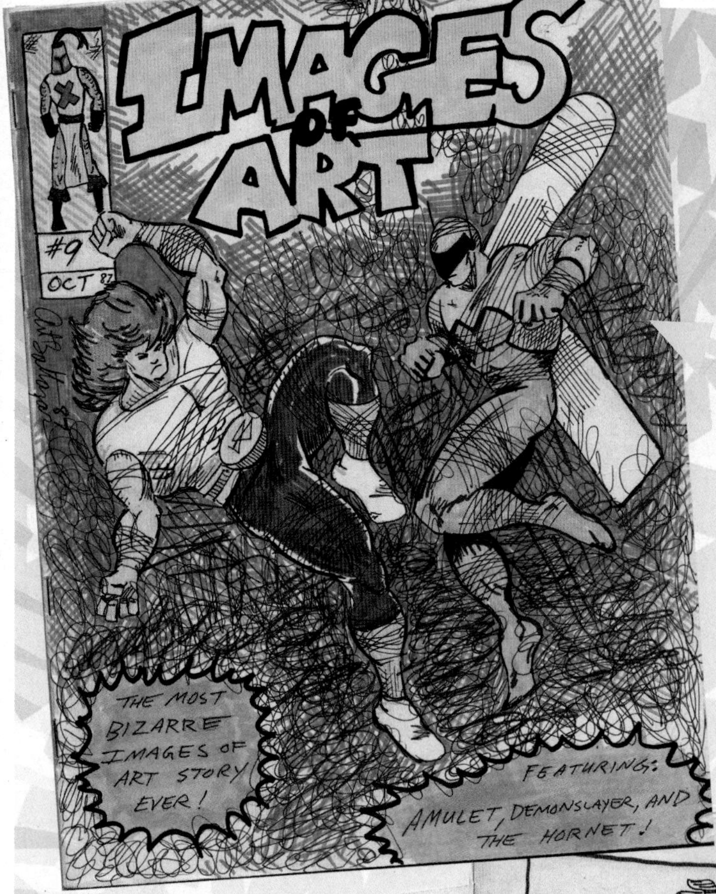
IMAGES OF ART
#9
OCT 87
THE MOST BIZARRE IMAGES OF ART STORY EVER!
FEATURING: AMULET, DEMONSLAYER, AND THE HORNET!

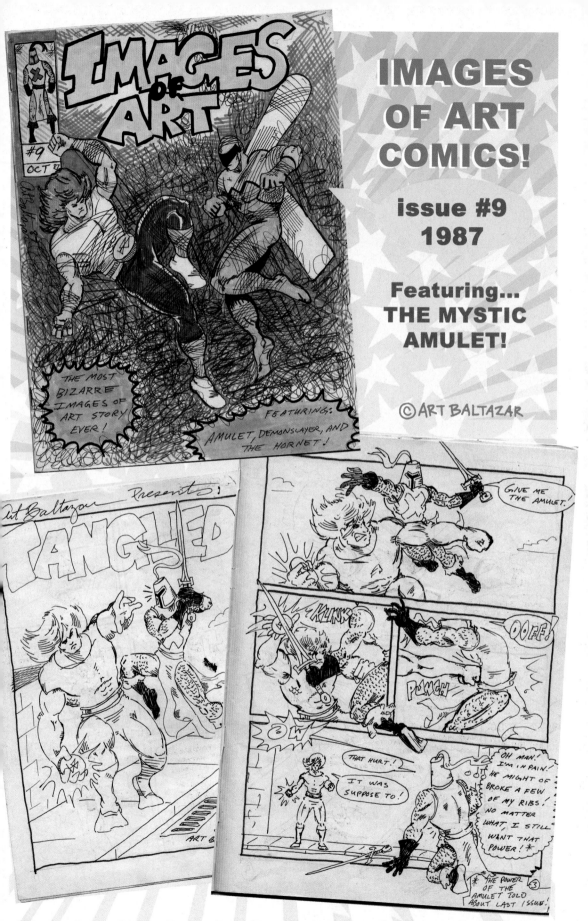

IMAGES OF ART COMICS!

issue #9
1987

Featuring...
THE MYSTIC AMULET!

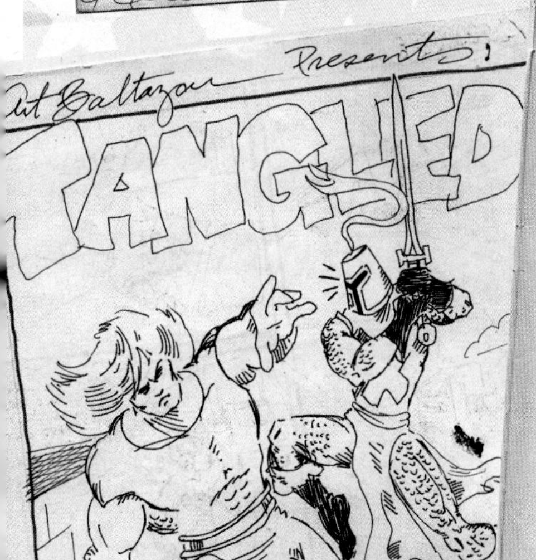
Art Baltazar Presents:

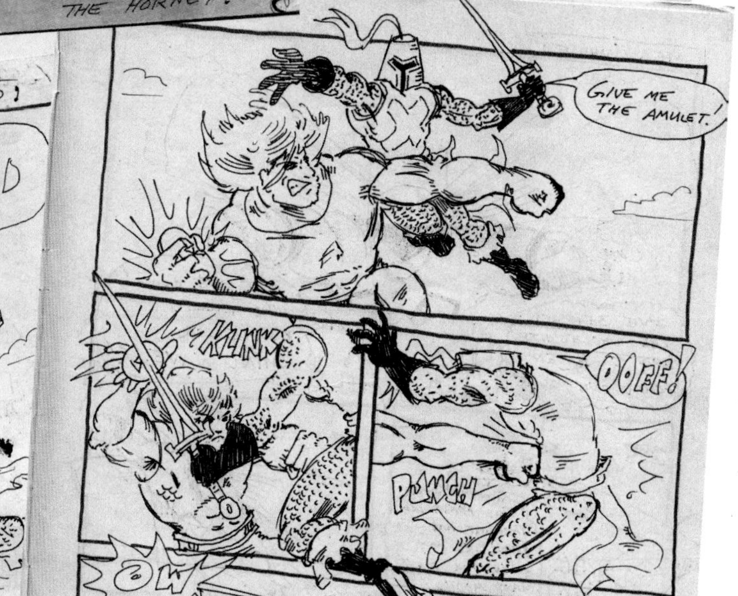
GIVE ME THE AMULET!
KLUNK
OOFF!
PUNCH
OW
THAT HURT!
IT WAS SUPPOSE TO!
OH MAN! I'M IN PAIN! HE MIGHT OF BROKE A FEW OF MY RIBS! NO MATTER WHAT, I STILL WANT THAT POWER! *
3
* THE POWER OF THE AMULET TOLD ABOUT LAST ISSUE!

The original comic series that inspired POWERS IN ACTION!

"MOON"

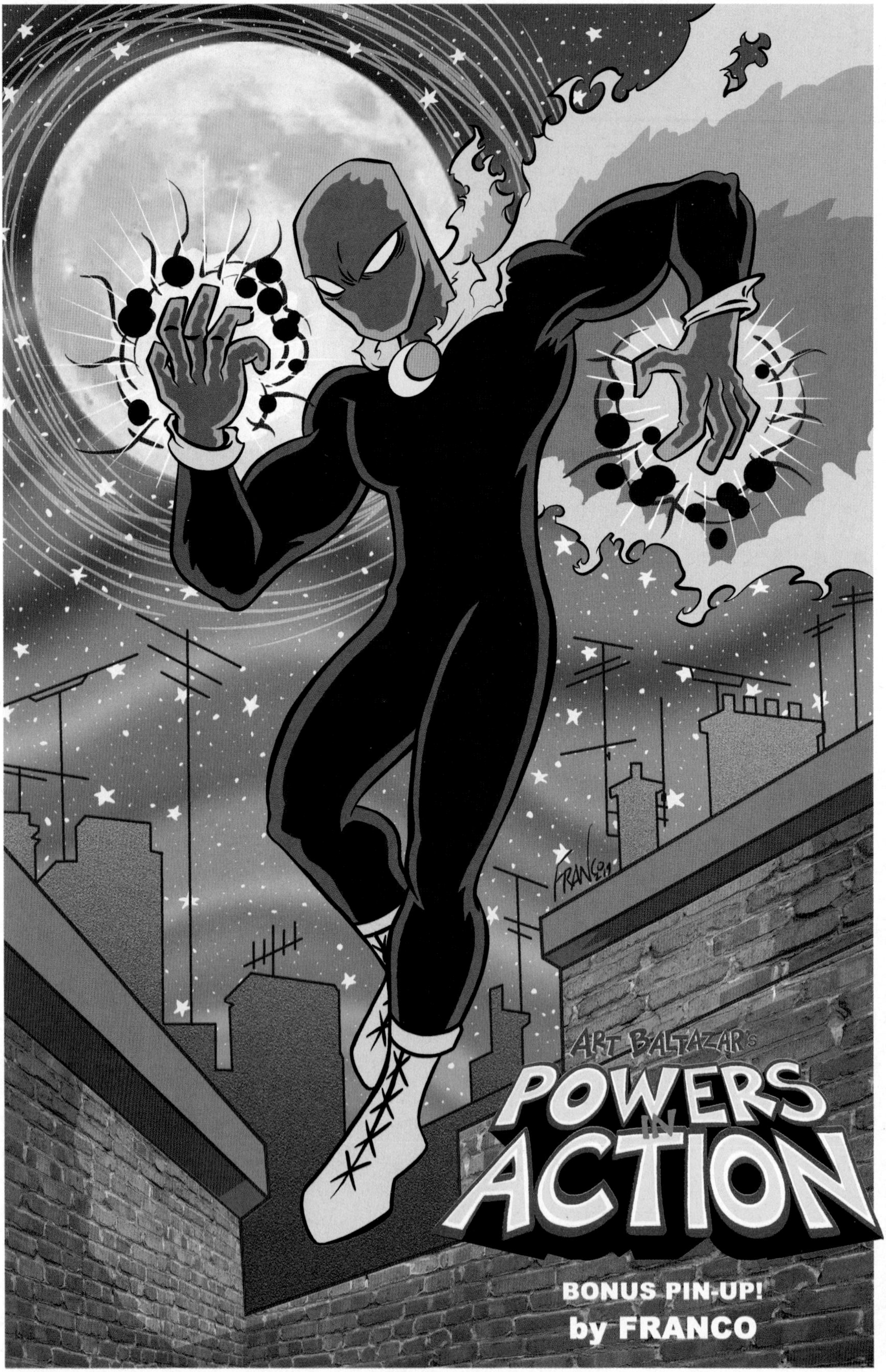
FRANCO
ART BALTAZAR'S
POWERS IN ACTION
BONUS PIN-UP!
by FRANCO

AW YEAH COMICS & ACTION LAB PRESENTS...

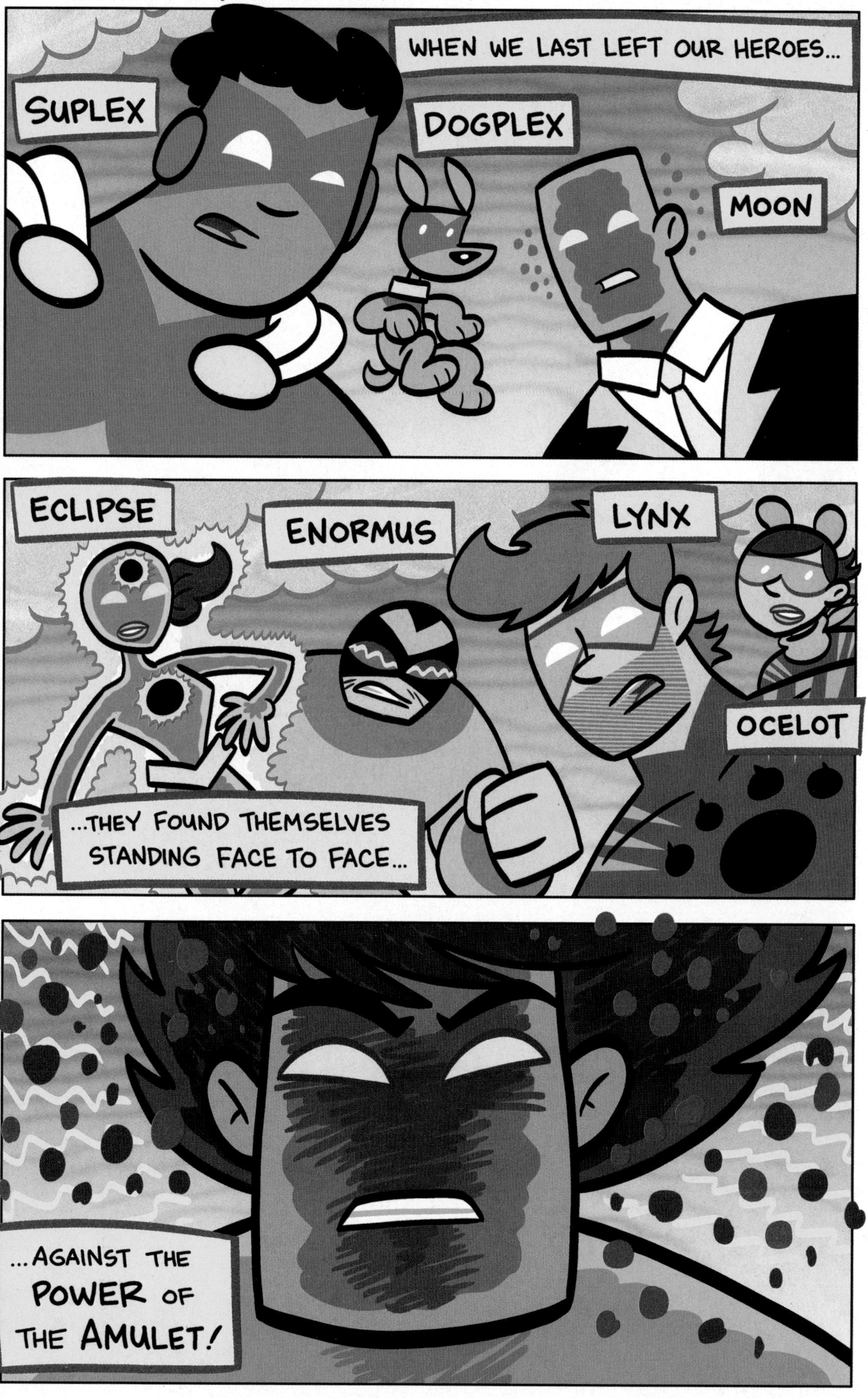

WHEN WE LAST LEFT OUR HEROES...
SUPLEX
DOGPLEX
MOON
ECLIPSE
ENORMUS
LYNX
OCELOT
...THEY FOUND THEMSELVES STANDING FACE TO FACE...
...AGAINST THE POWER OF THE AMULET!

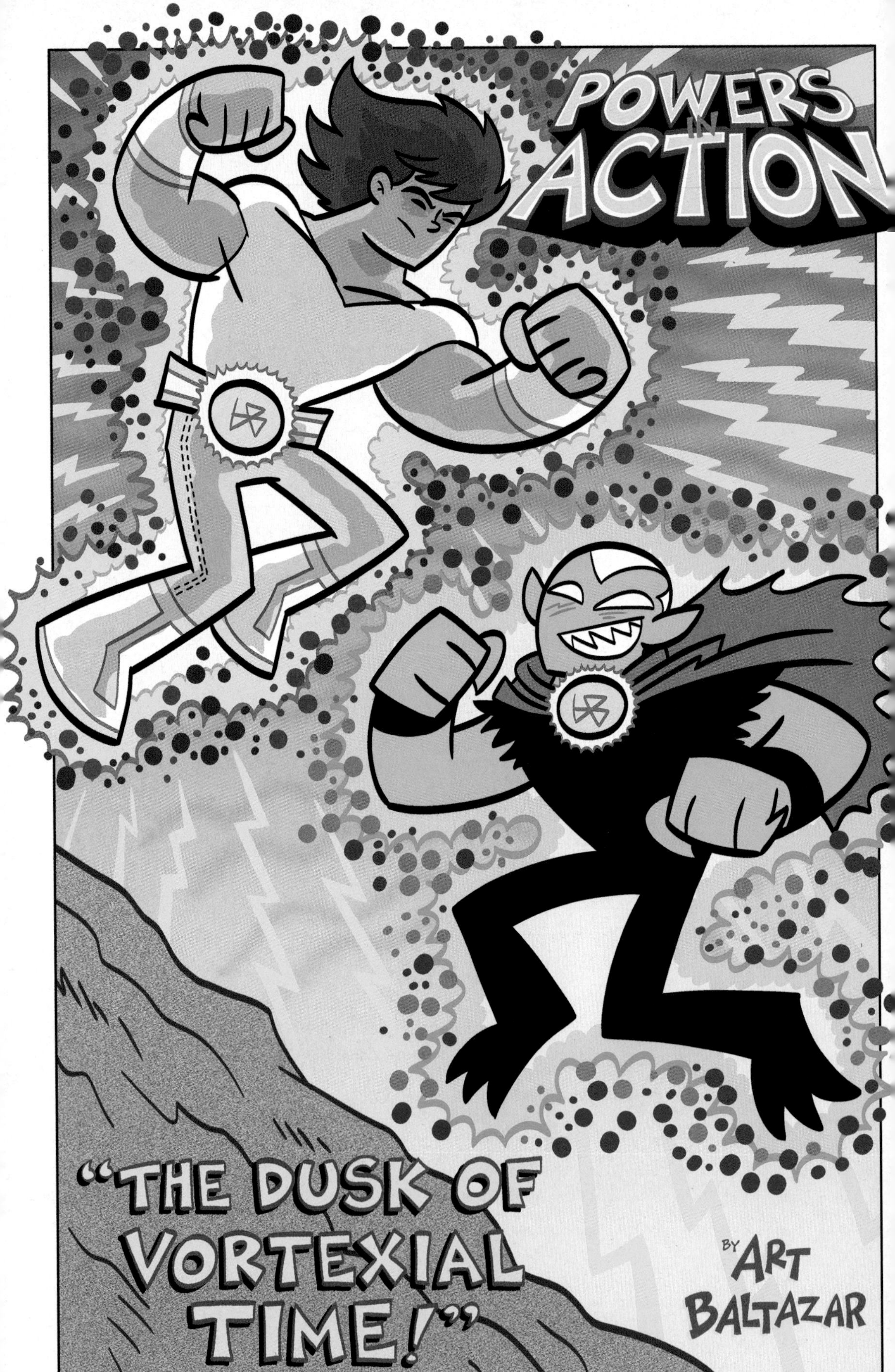
POWERS IN ACTION
"THE DUSK OF VORTEXIAL TIME!"
BY ART BALTAZAR

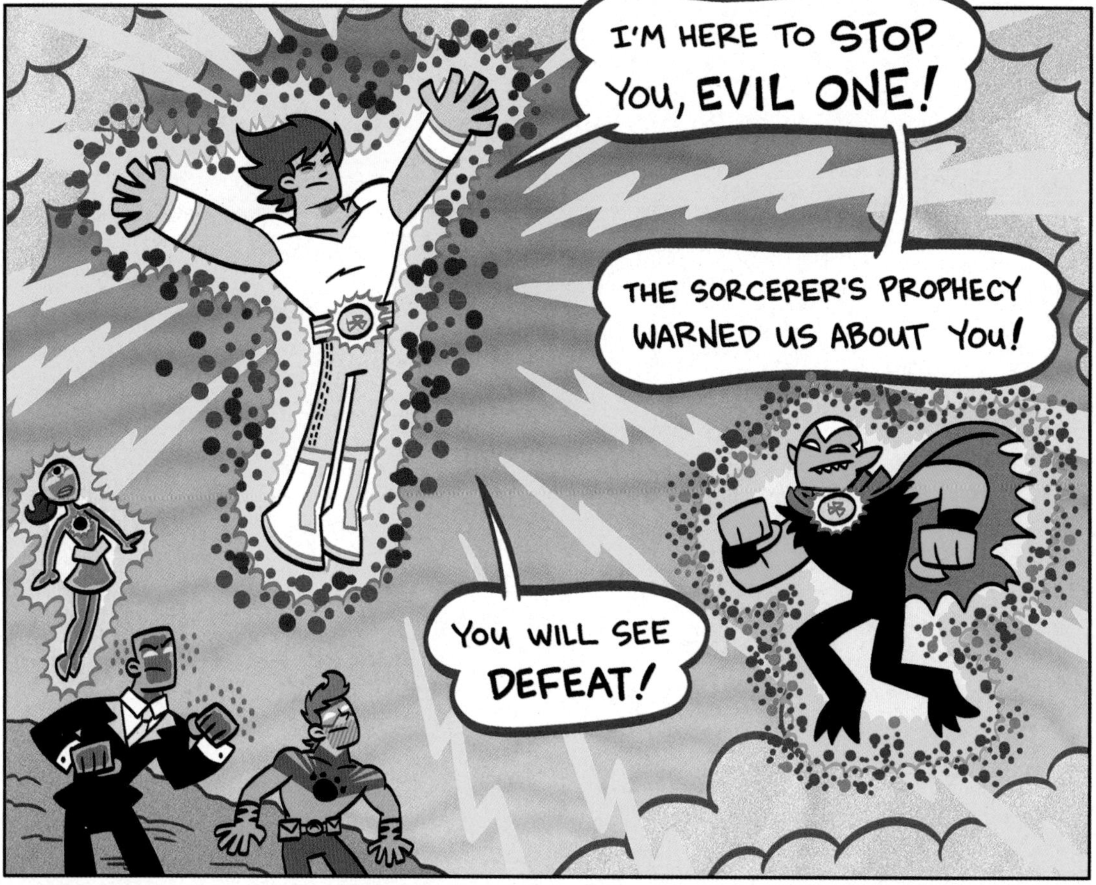
I'M HERE TO STOP YOU, EVIL ONE!
THE SORCERER'S PROPHECY WARNED US ABOUT YOU!
YOU WILL SEE DEFEAT!

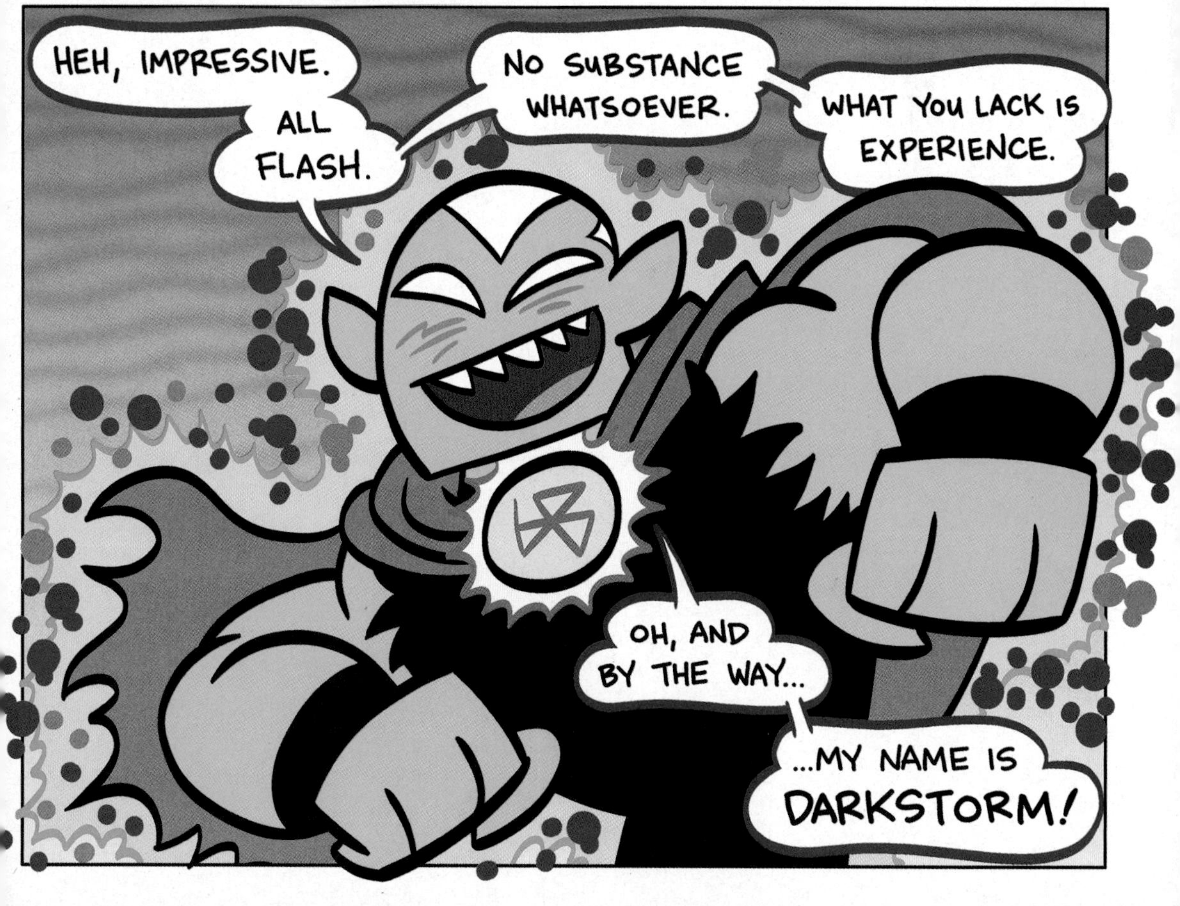
HEH, IMPRESSIVE.
ALL FLASH.
NO SUBSTANCE WHATSOEVER.
WHAT YOU LACK IS EXPERIENCE.
OH, AND BY THE WAY...
...MY NAME IS DARKSTORM!

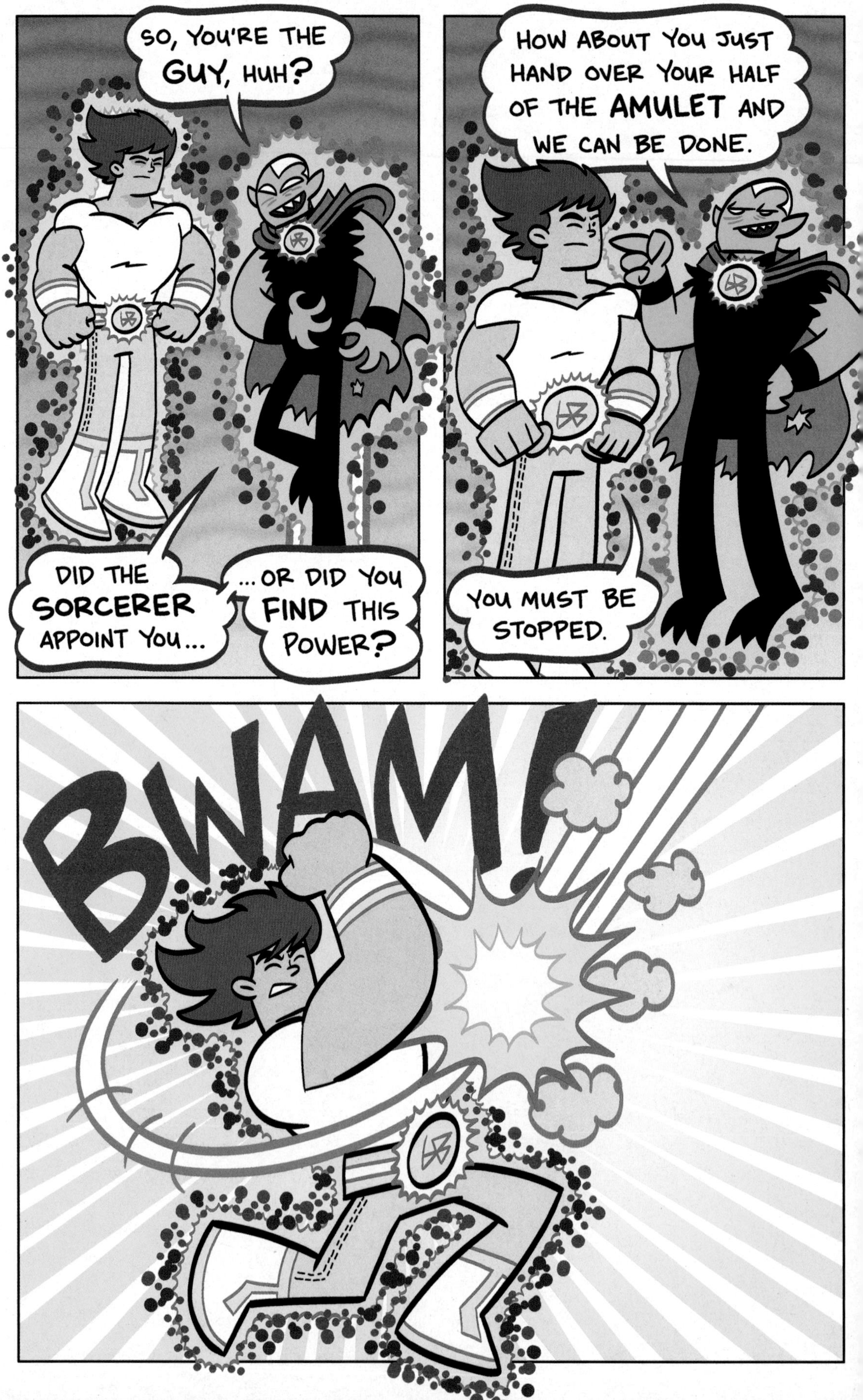

SO, YOU'RE THE GUY, HUH?
DID THE SORCERER APPOINT YOU...
...OR DID YOU FIND THIS POWER?
HOW ABOUT YOU JUST HAND OVER YOUR HALF OF THE AMULET AND WE CAN BE DONE.
YOU MUST BE STOPPED.
BWAM!

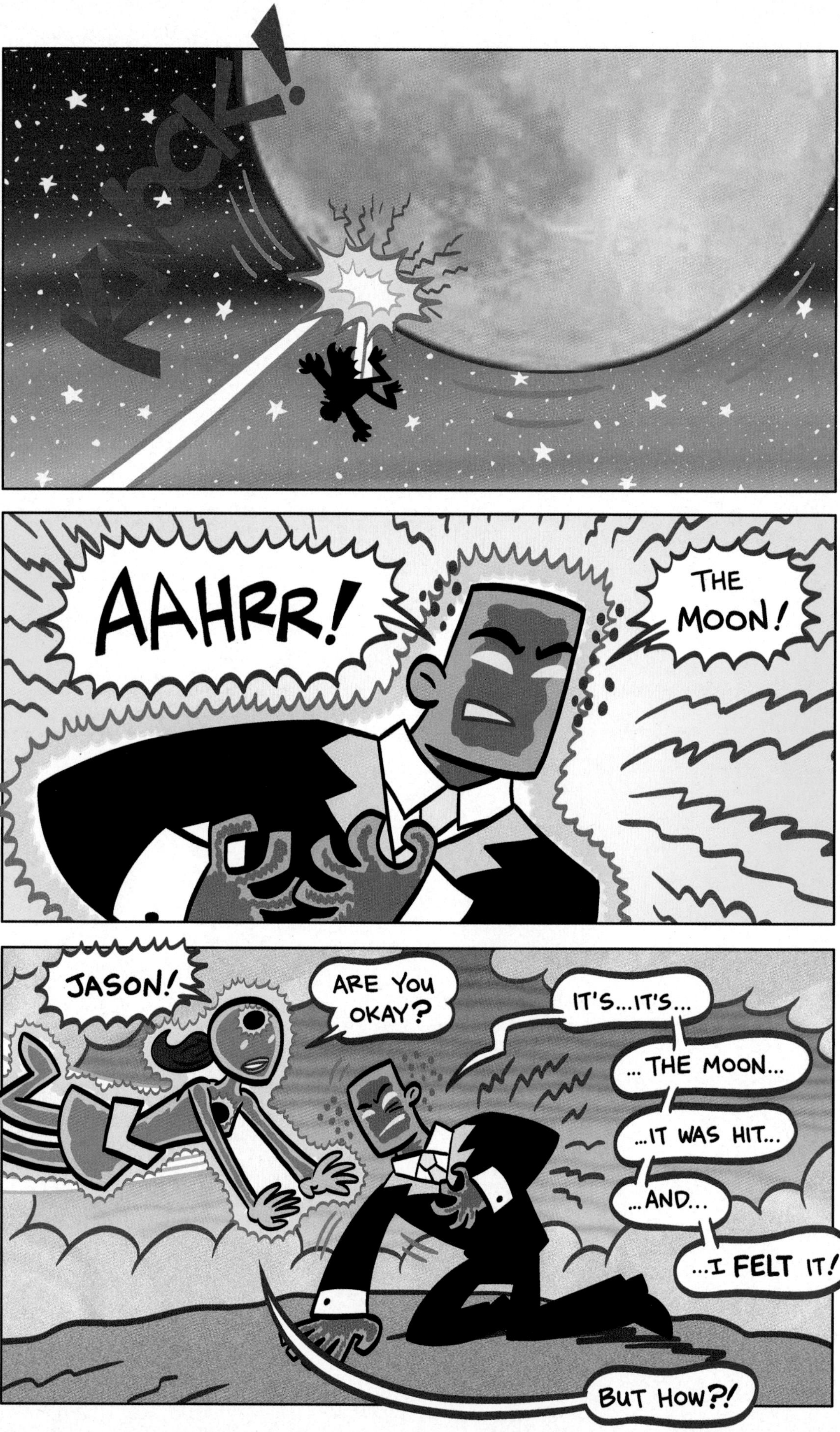
KRACK!
AAHRR!
THE MOON!
JASON!
ARE YOU OKAY?
IT'S...IT'S...
...THE MOON...
...IT WAS HIT...
...AND...
...I FELT IT!
BUT HOW?!

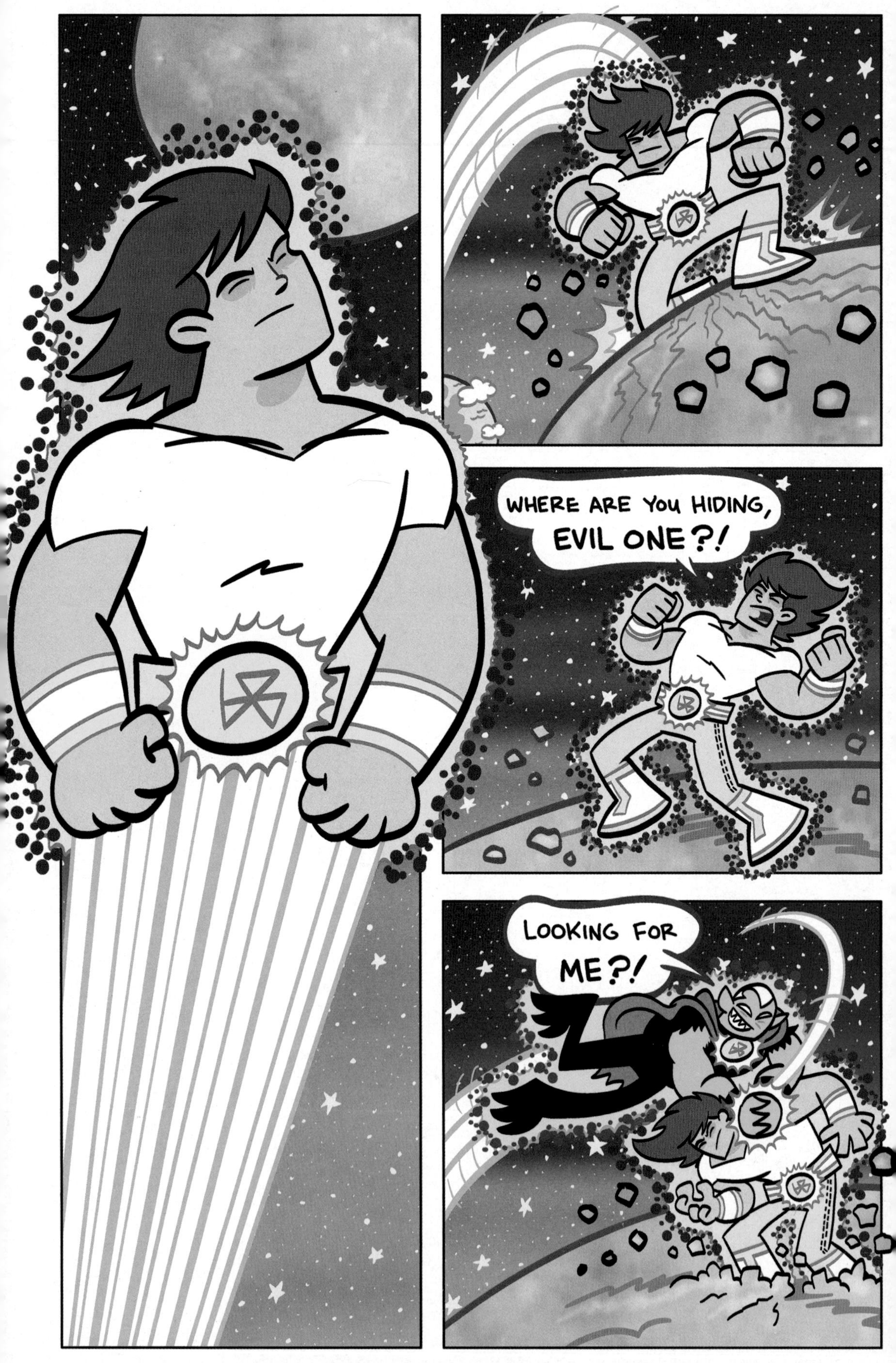
WHERE ARE YOU HIDING, EVIL ONE?!
LOOKING FOR ME?!

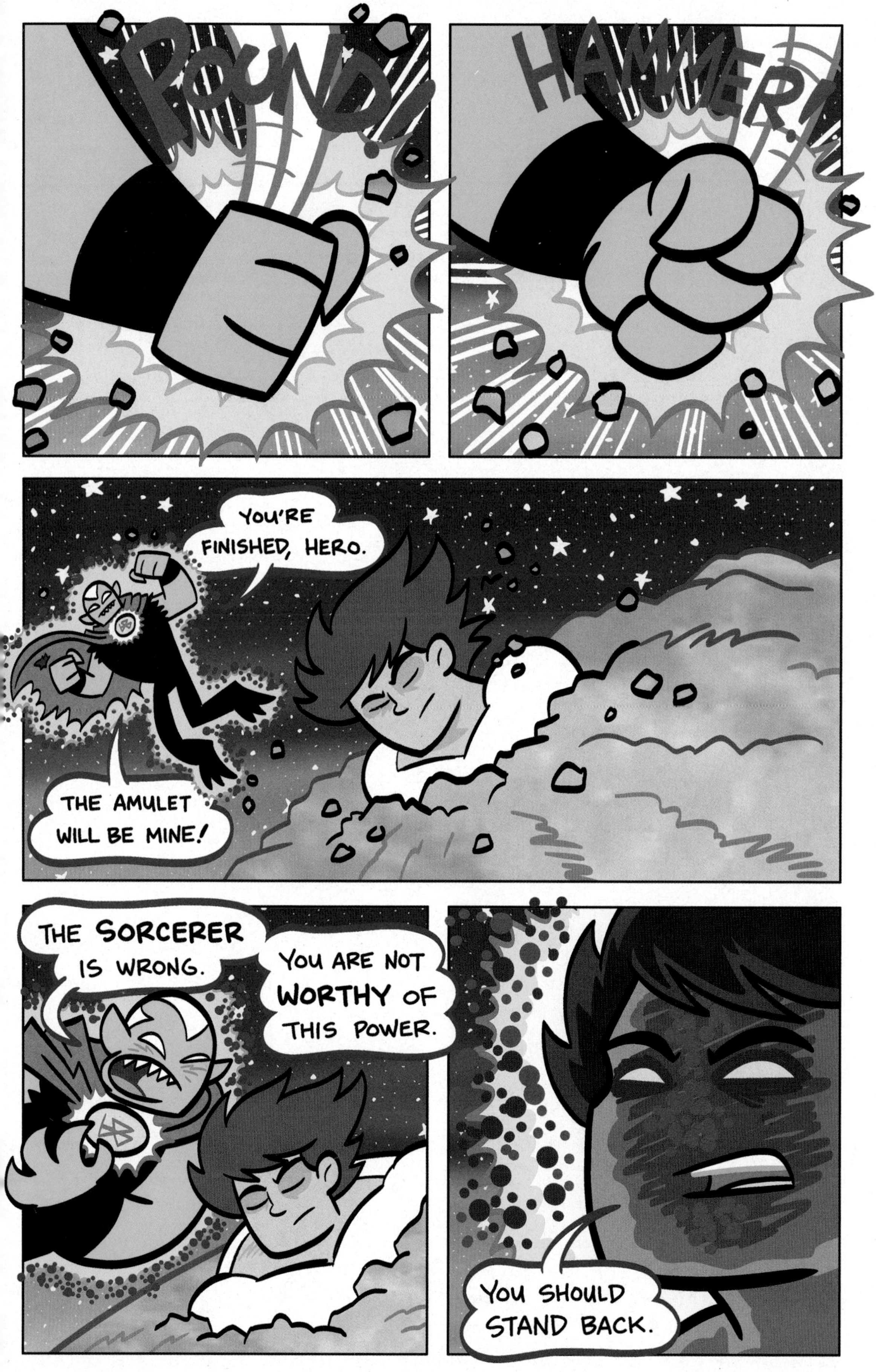
POUND!!
HAMMER!!
YOU'RE FINISHED, HERO.
THE AMULET WILL BE MINE!
THE SORCERER IS WRONG.
YOU ARE NOT WORTHY OF THIS POWER.
YOU SHOULD STAND BACK.

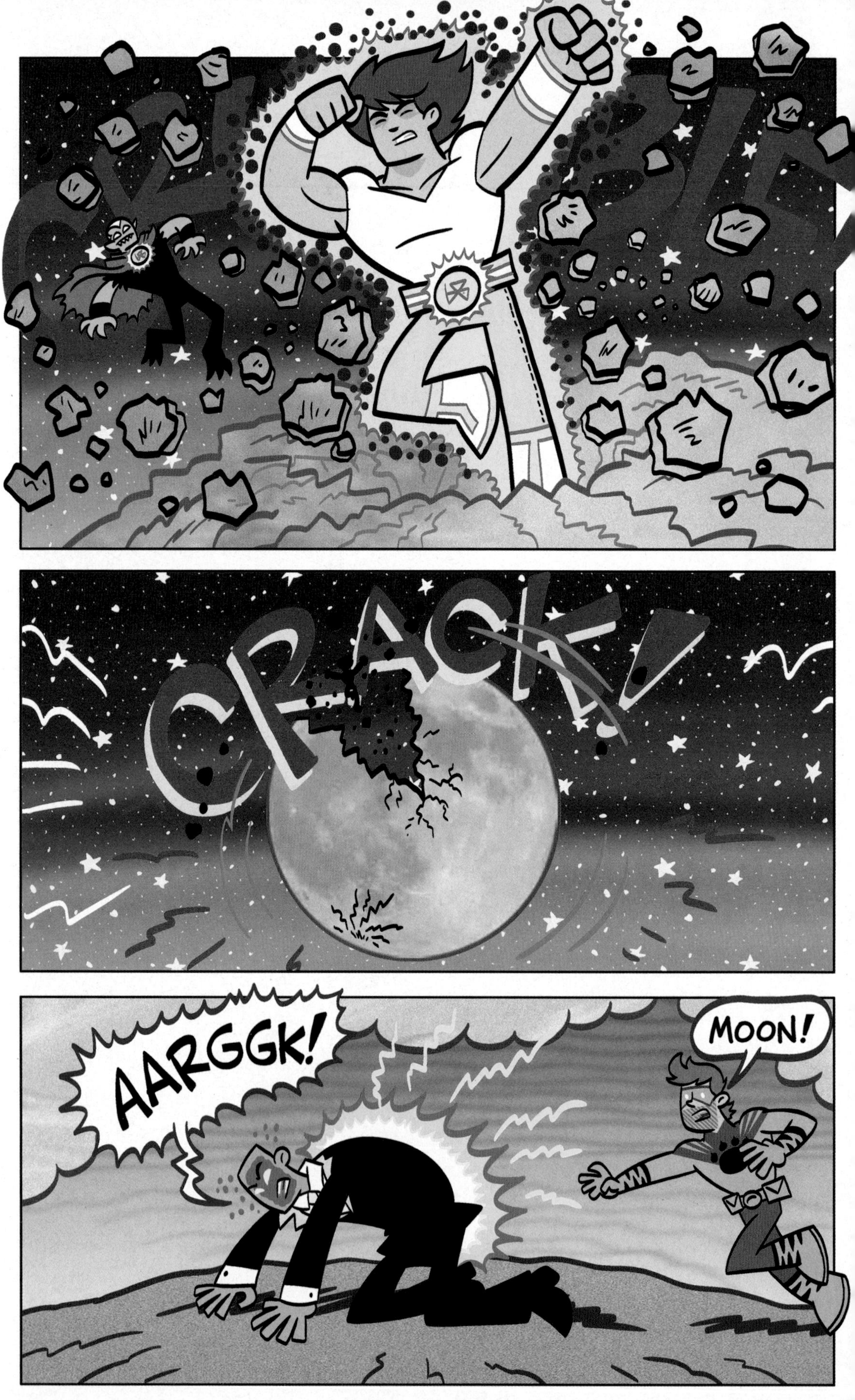
CRACK!
AARGGK!
MOON!

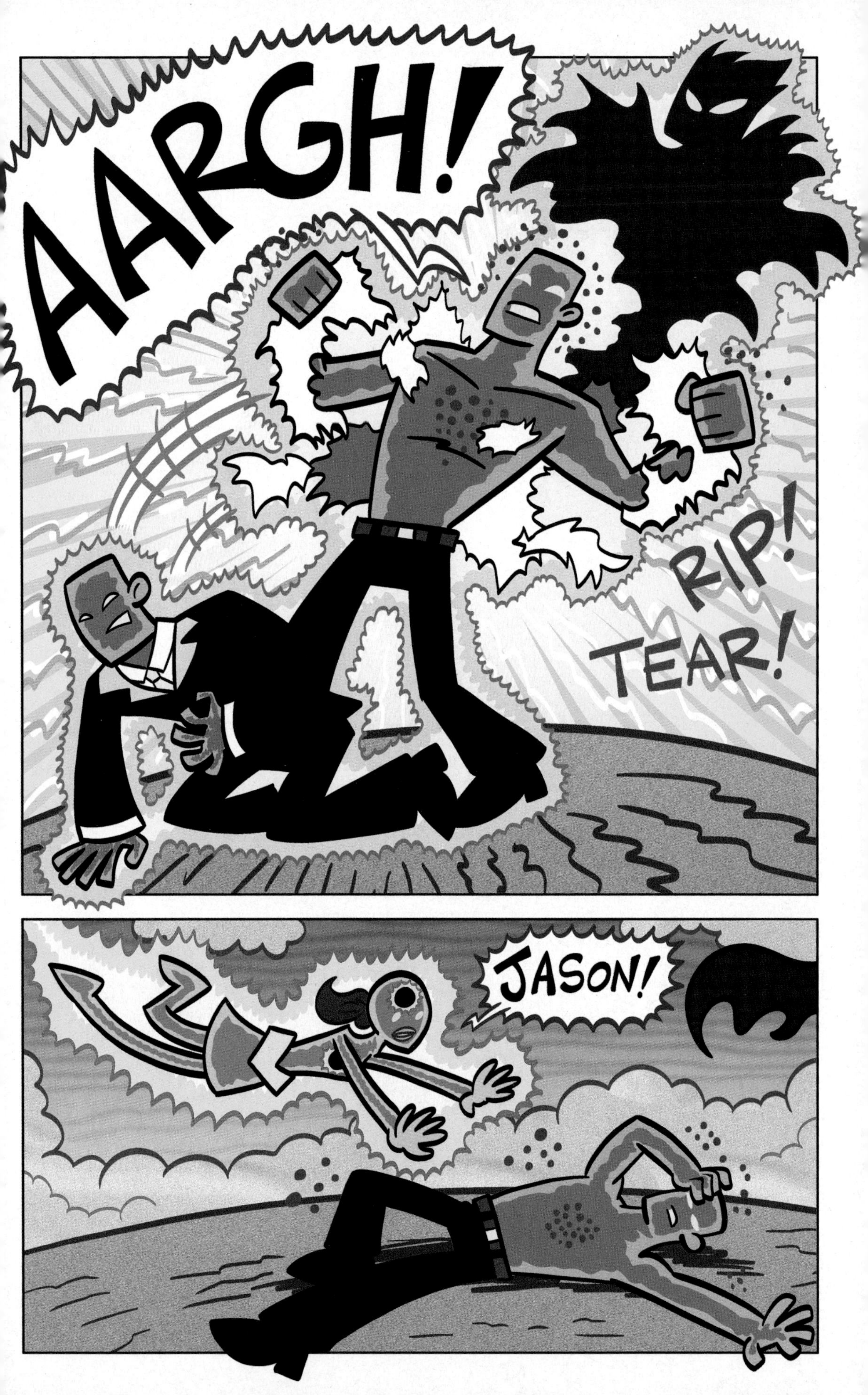
AARGH!
RIP!
TEAR!
JASON!

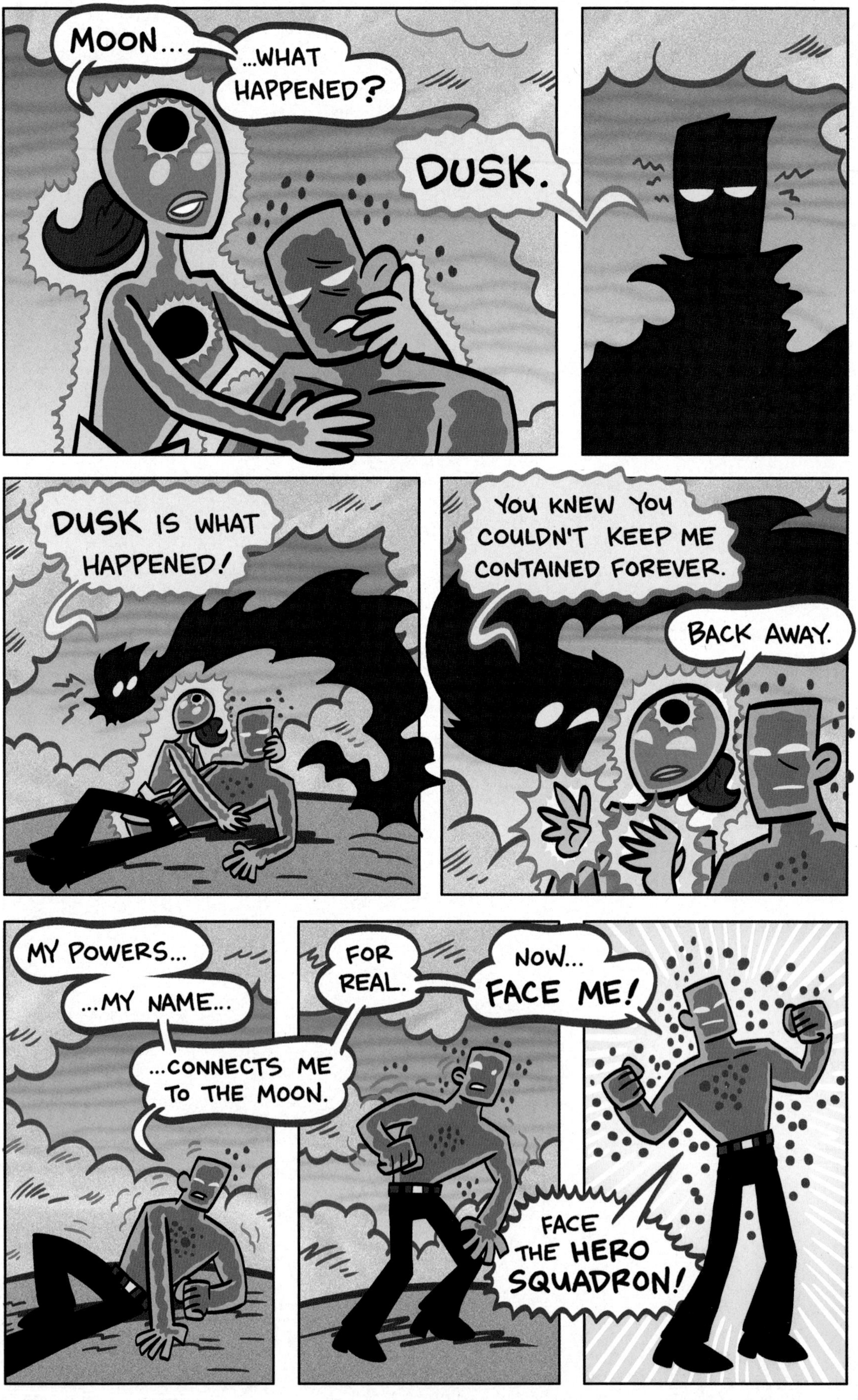
MOON...
...WHAT HAPPENED?
DUSK.
DUSK IS WHAT HAPPENED!
YOU KNEW YOU COULDN'T KEEP ME CONTAINED FOREVER.
BACK AWAY.
MY POWERS...
...MY NAME...
...CONNECTS ME TO THE MOON.
FOR REAL.
NOW... FACE ME!
FACE THE HERO SQUADRON!

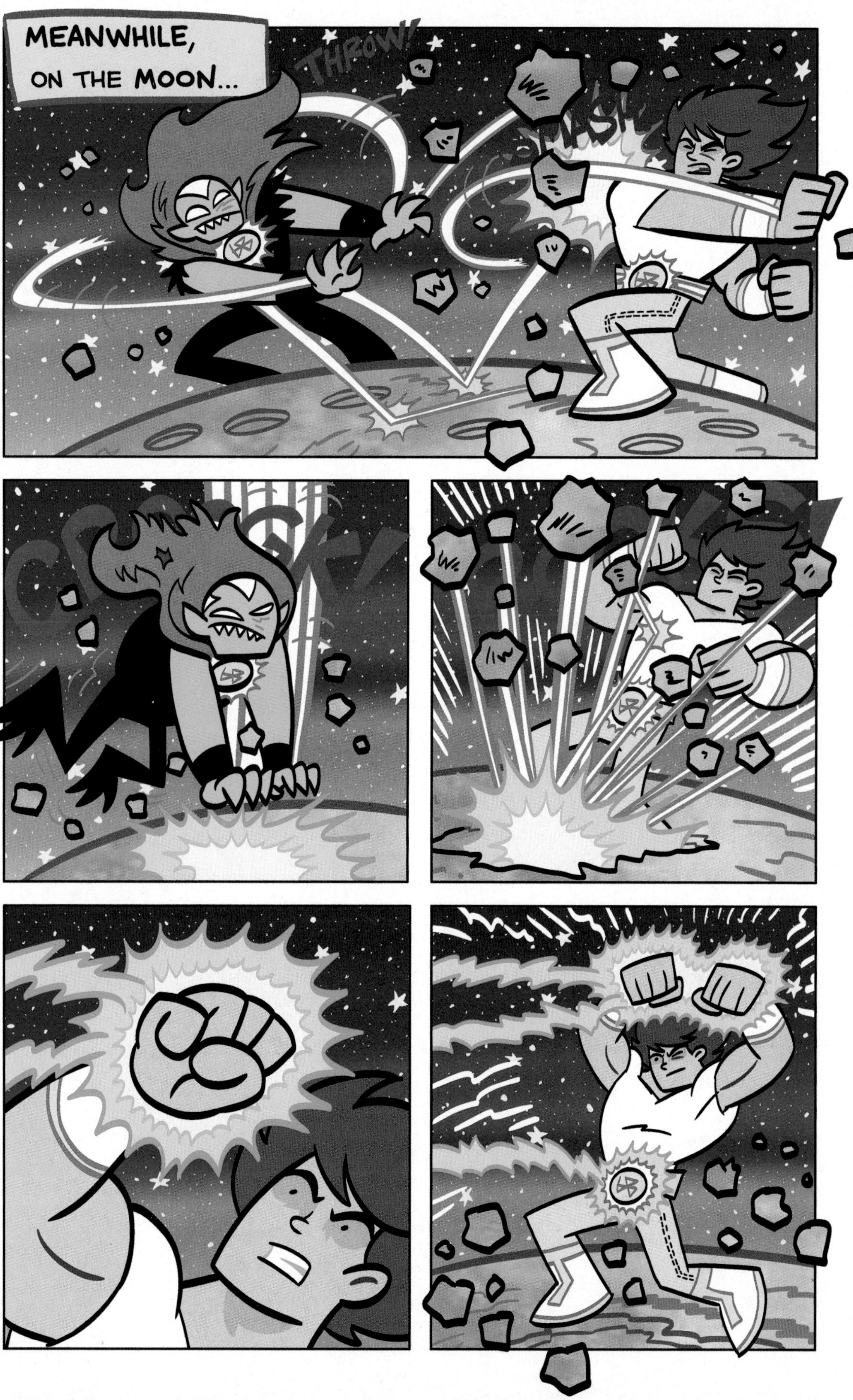
MEANWHILE, ON THE MOON...
THROW!

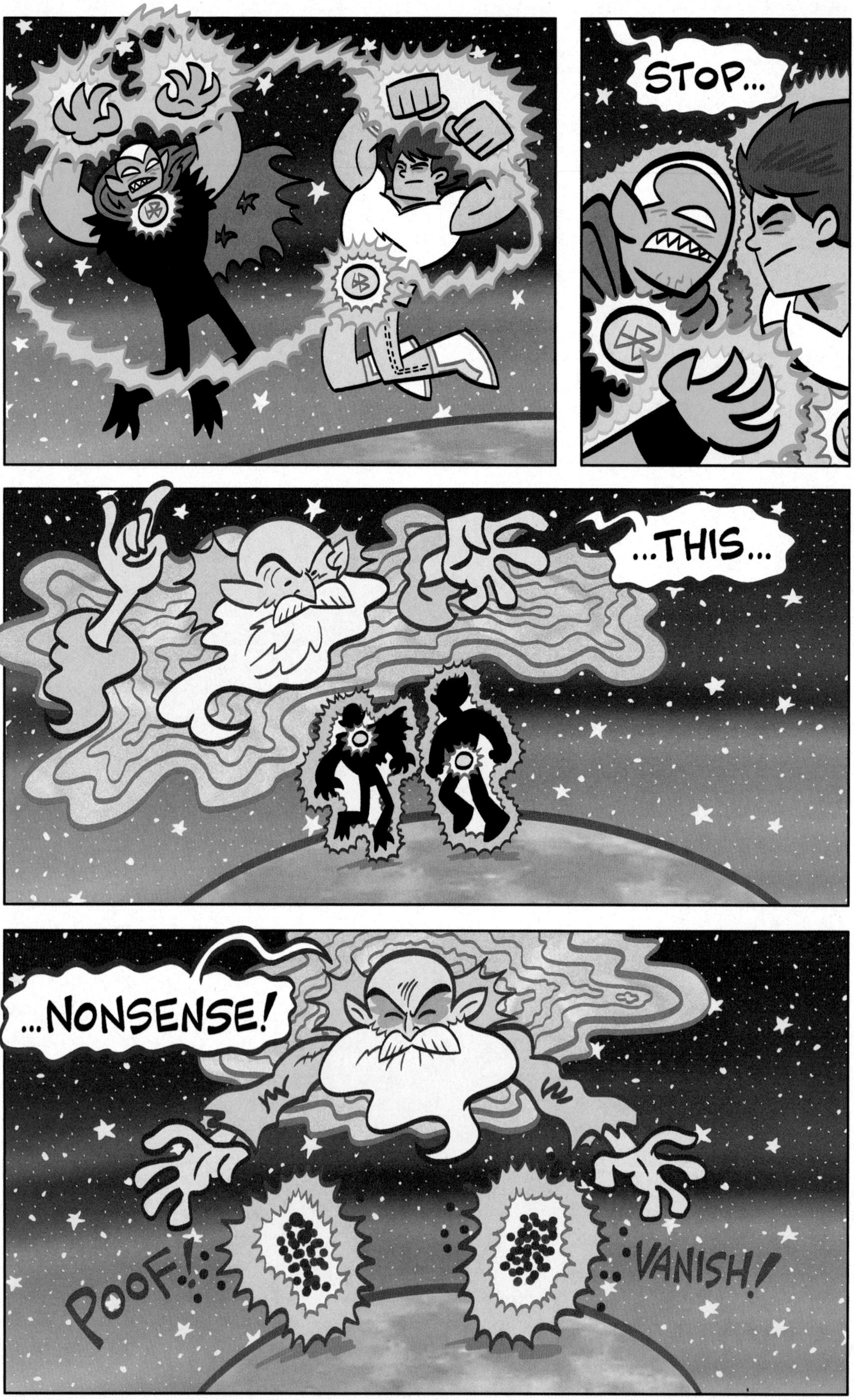
STOP...
...THIS...
...NONSENSE!
POOF!
VANISH!

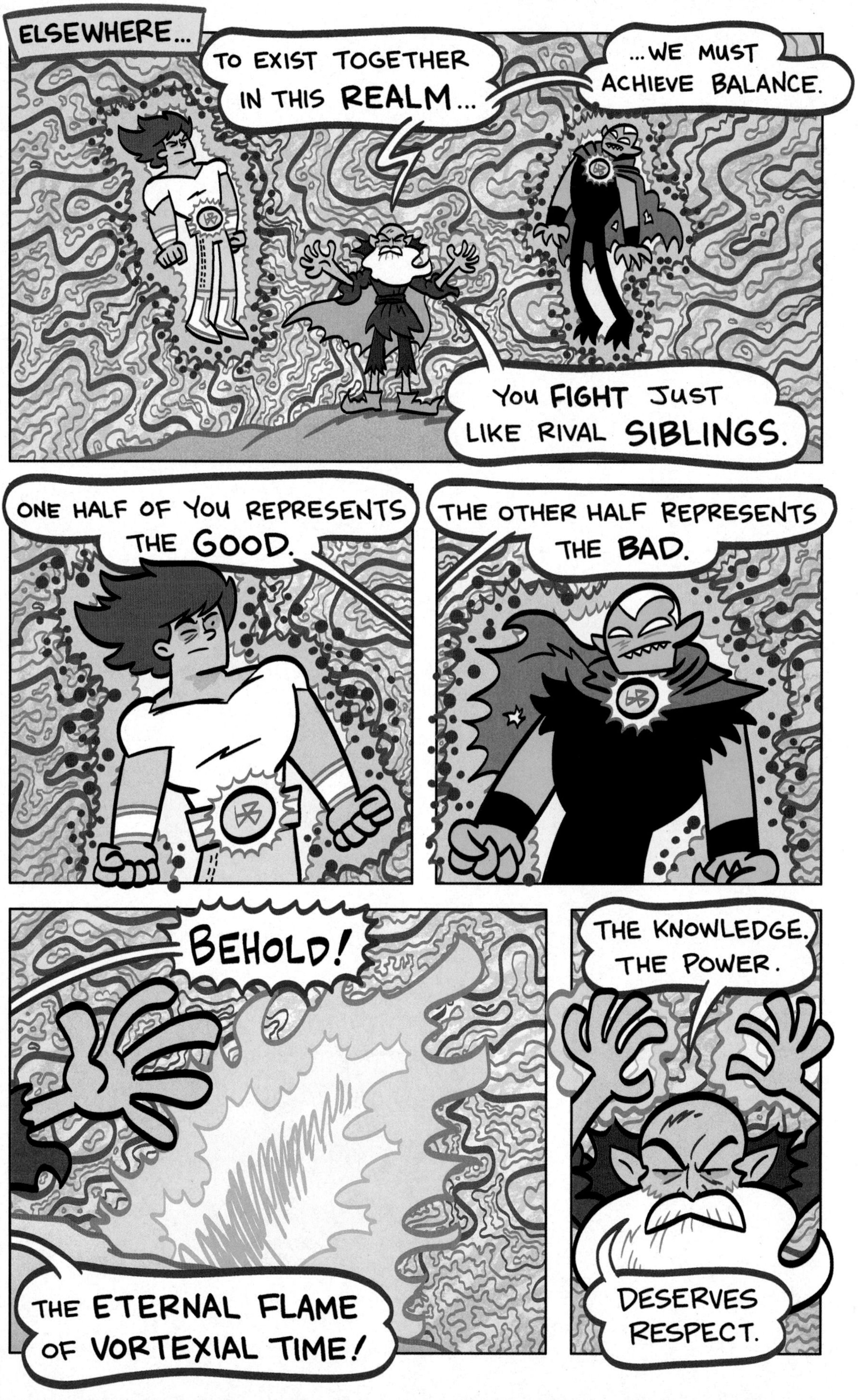
ELSEWHERE...
TO EXIST TOGETHER IN THIS REALM...
...WE MUST ACHIEVE BALANCE.
YOU FIGHT JUST LIKE RIVAL SIBLINGS.
ONE HALF OF YOU REPRESENTS THE GOOD.
THE OTHER HALF REPRESENTS THE BAD.
BEHOLD!
THE ETERNAL FLAME OF VORTEXIAL TIME!
THE KNOWLEDGE. THE POWER.
DESERVES RESPECT.

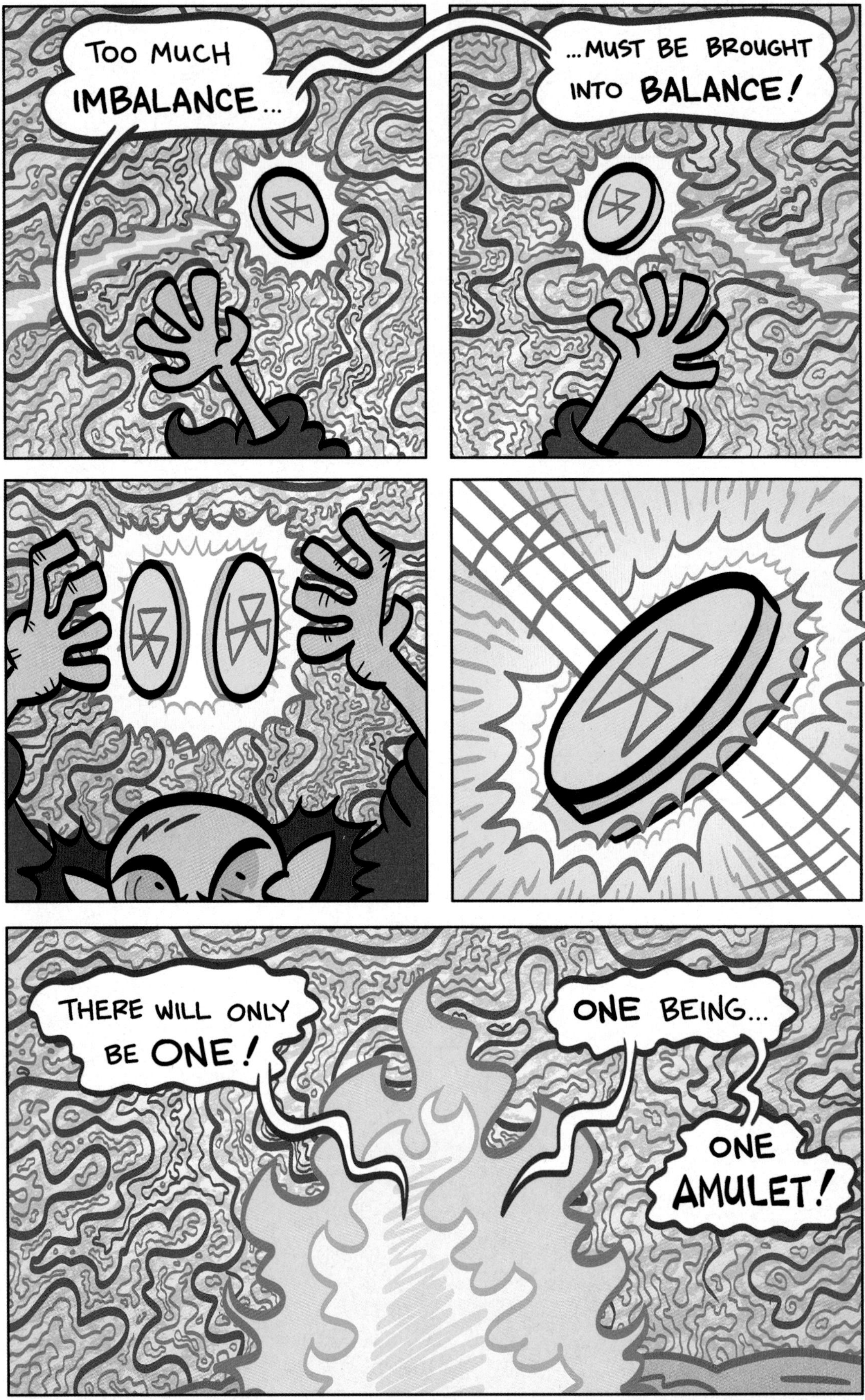
TOO MUCH IMBALANCE...
...MUST BE BROUGHT INTO BALANCE!
THERE WILL ONLY BE ONE!
ONE BEING...
ONE AMULET!

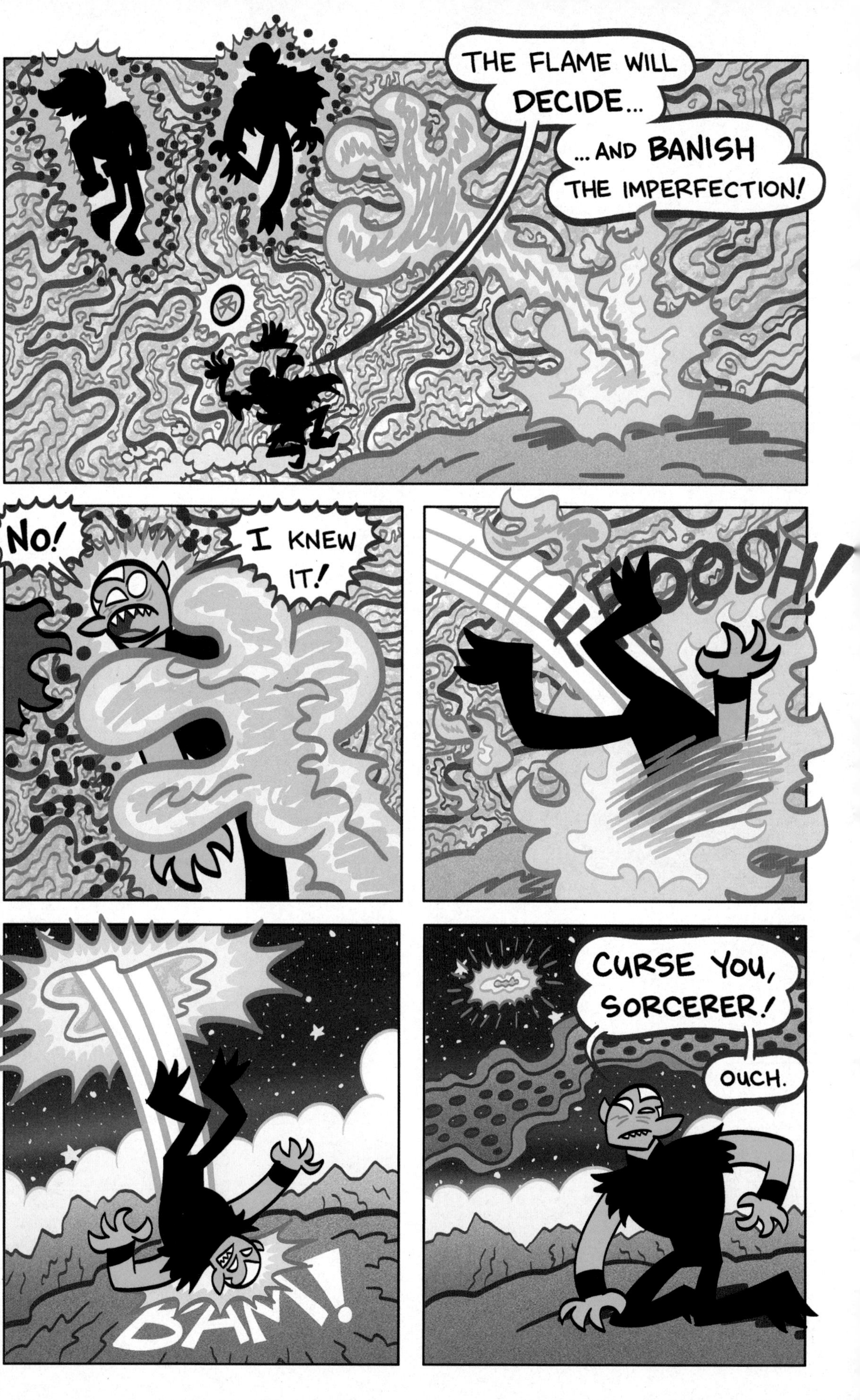
THE FLAME WILL DECIDE...
...AND BANISH THE IMPERFECTION!
No!
I KNEW IT!
FFOOSH!
BAM!
CURSE YOU, SORCERER!
OUCH.

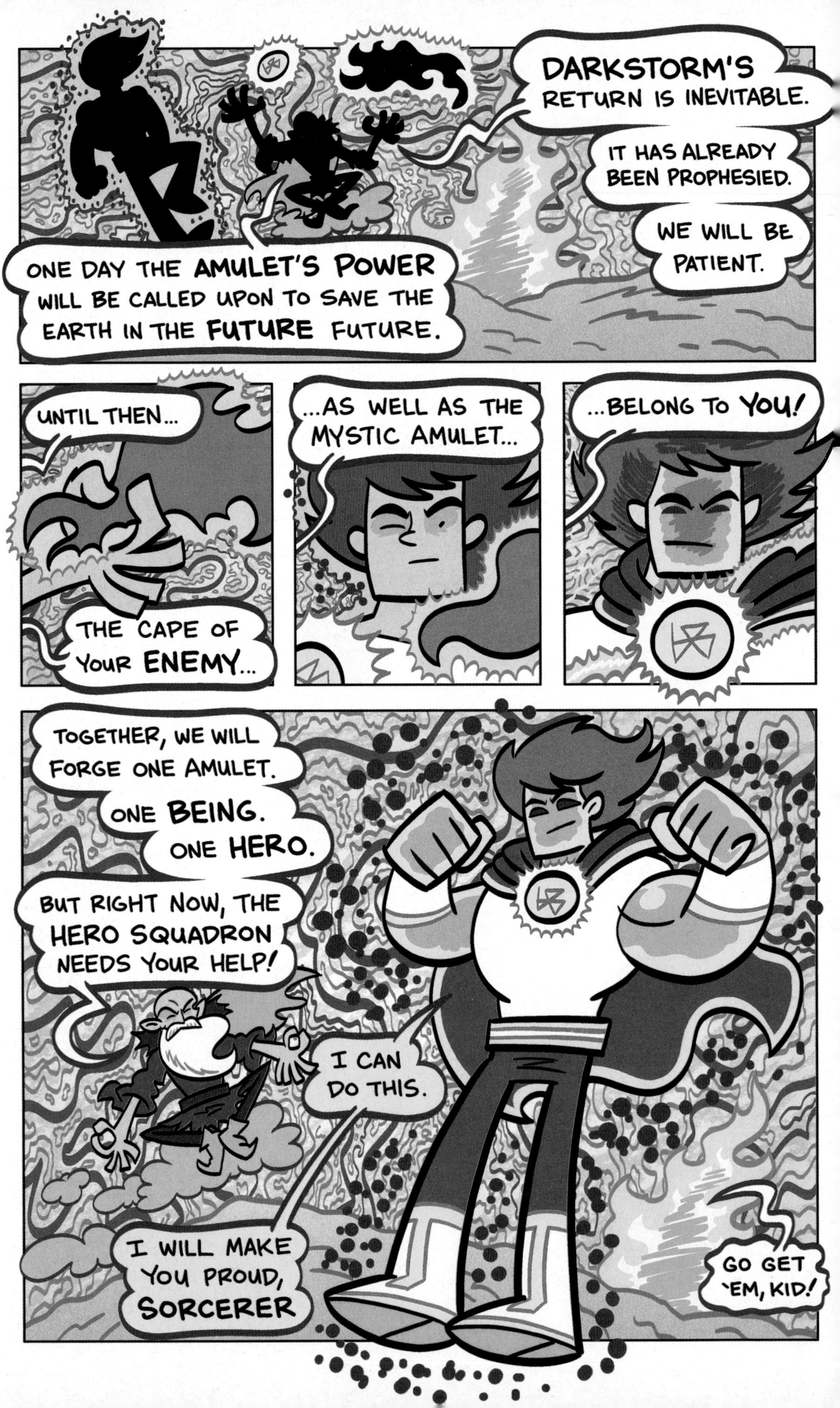
DARKSTORM'S RETURN IS INEVITABLE.
IT HAS ALREADY BEEN PROPHESIED.
WE WILL BE PATIENT.
ONE DAY THE AMULET'S POWER WILL BE CALLED UPON TO SAVE THE EARTH IN THE FUTURE FUTURE.
UNTIL THEN...
THE CAPE OF YOUR ENEMY...
...AS WELL AS THE MYSTIC AMULET...
...BELONG TO YOU!
TOGETHER, WE WILL FORGE ONE AMULET.
ONE BEING. ONE HERO.
BUT RIGHT NOW, THE HERO SQUADRON NEEDS YOUR HELP!
I CAN DO THIS.
I WILL MAKE YOU PROUD, SORCERER
GO GET 'EM, KID!

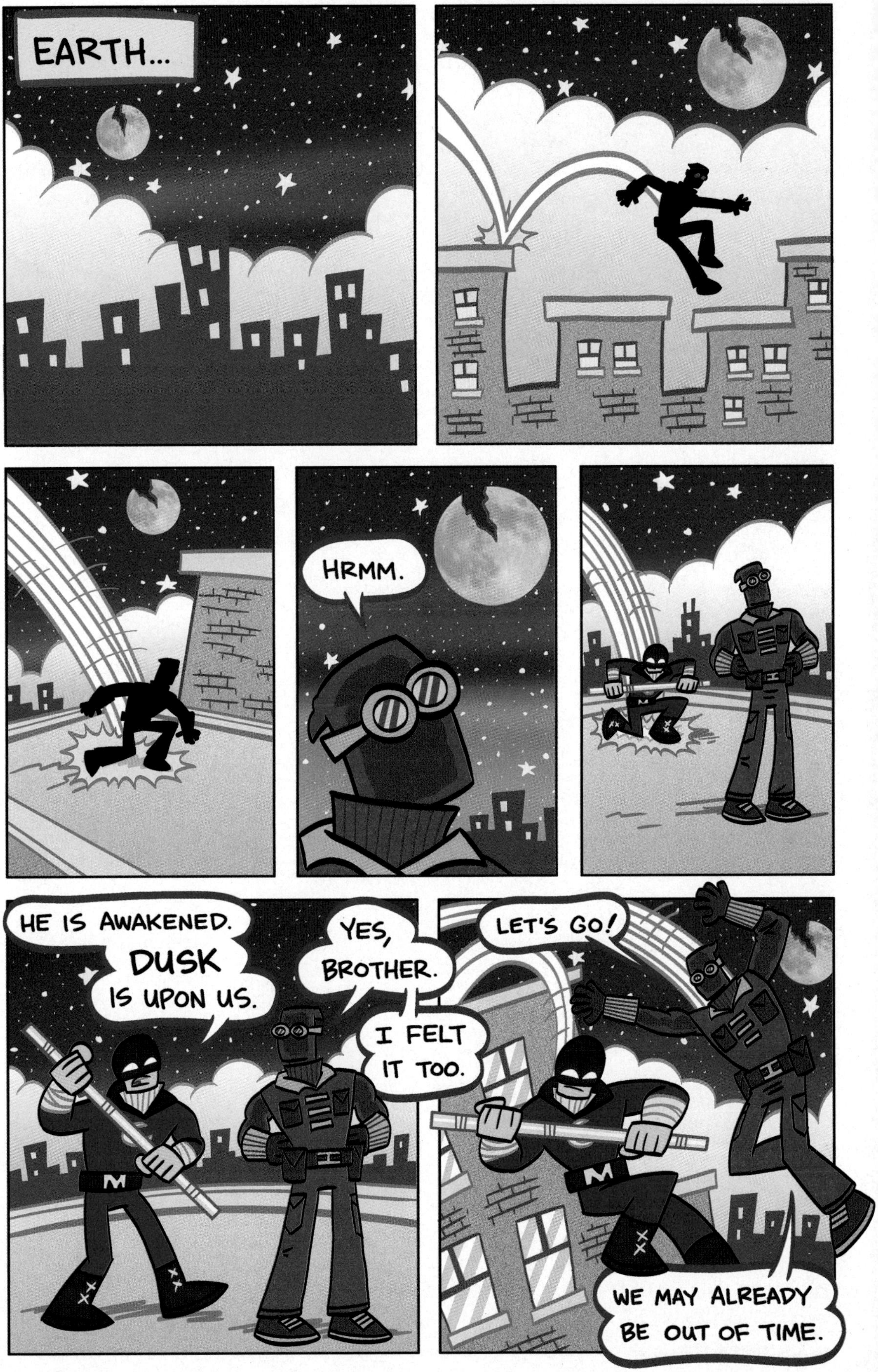
EARTH...
HRMM.
HE IS AWAKENED. DUSK IS UPON US.
YES, BROTHER.
I FELT IT TOO.
LET'S GO!
WE MAY ALREADY BE OUT OF TIME.

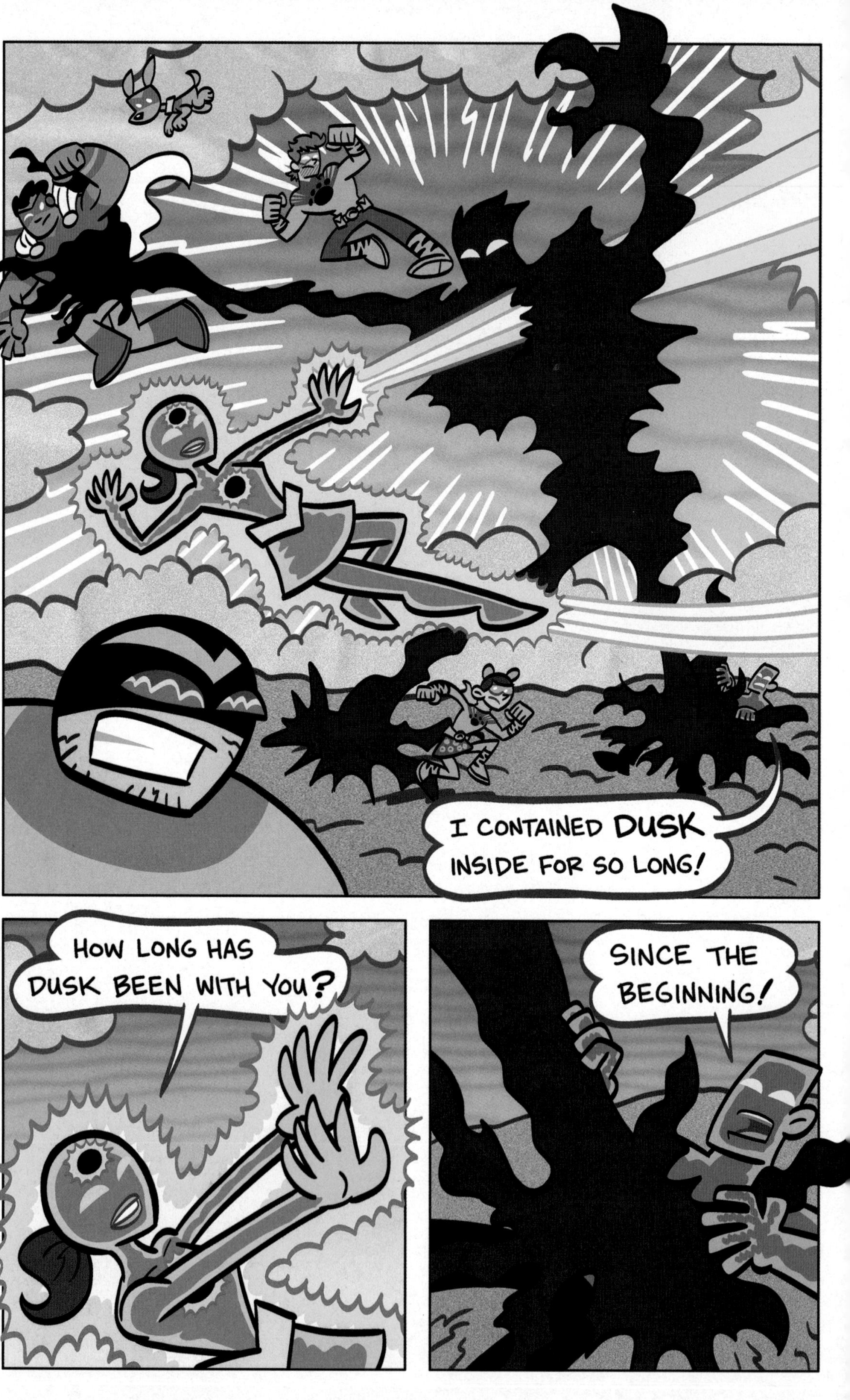
I CONTAINED DUSK INSIDE FOR SO LONG!
HOW LONG HAS DUSK BEEN WITH YOU?
SINCE THE BEGINNING!

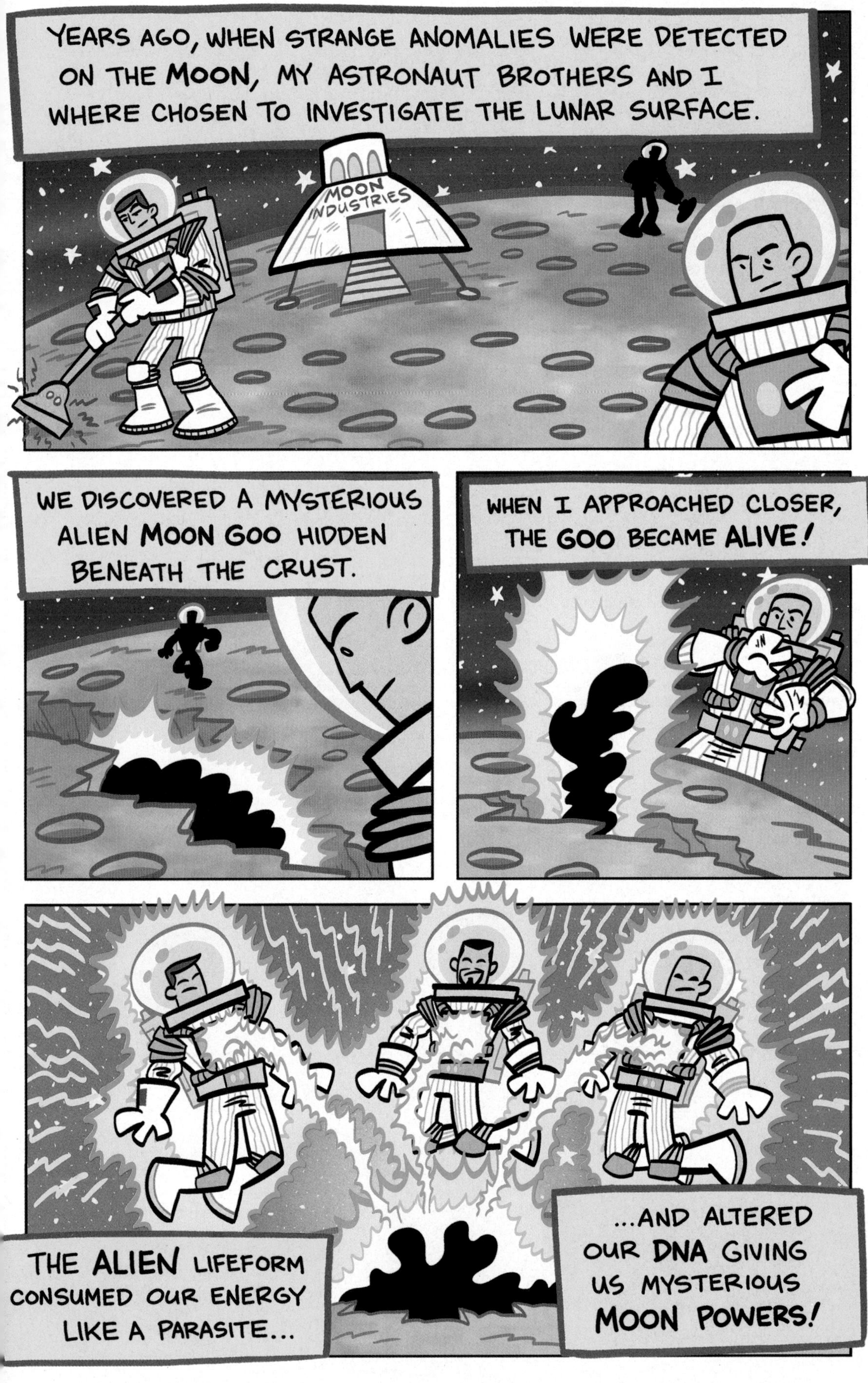
YEARS AGO, WHEN STRANGE ANOMALIES WERE DETECTED ON THE MOON, MY ASTRONAUT BROTHERS AND I WHERE CHOSEN TO INVESTIGATE THE LUNAR SURFACE.
MOON INDUSTRIES
WE DISCOVERED A MYSTERIOUS ALIEN MOON GOO HIDDEN BENEATH THE CRUST.
WHEN I APPROACHED CLOSER, THE GOO BECAME ALIVE!
THE ALIEN LIFEFORM CONSUMED OUR ENERGY LIKE A PARASITE...
...AND ALTERED OUR DNA GIVING US MYSTERIOUS MOON POWERS!

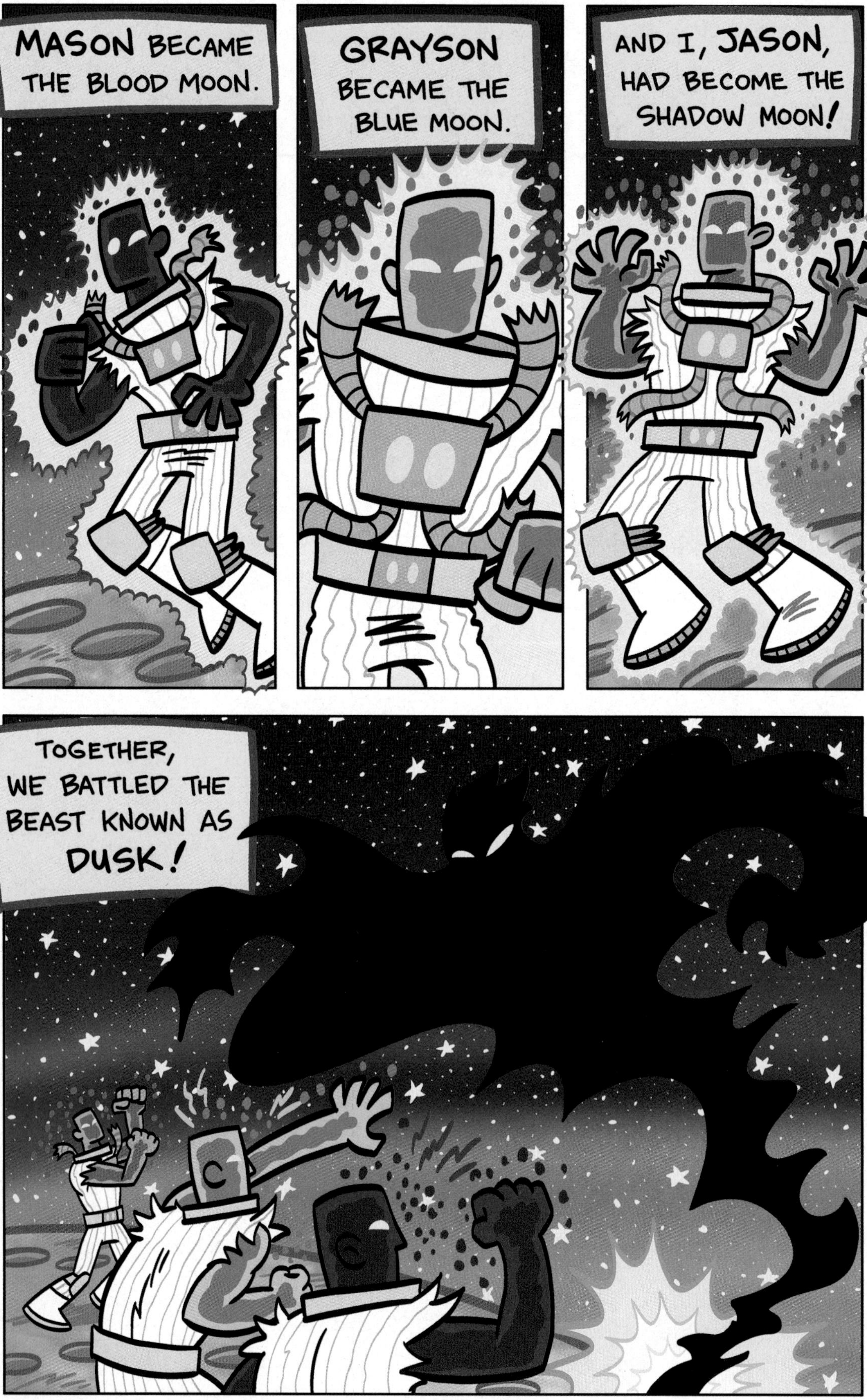
MASON BECAME THE BLOOD MOON.
GRAYSON BECAME THE BLUE MOON.
AND I, JASON, HAD BECOME THE SHADOW MOON!
TOGETHER, WE BATTLED THE BEAST KNOWN AS DUSK!

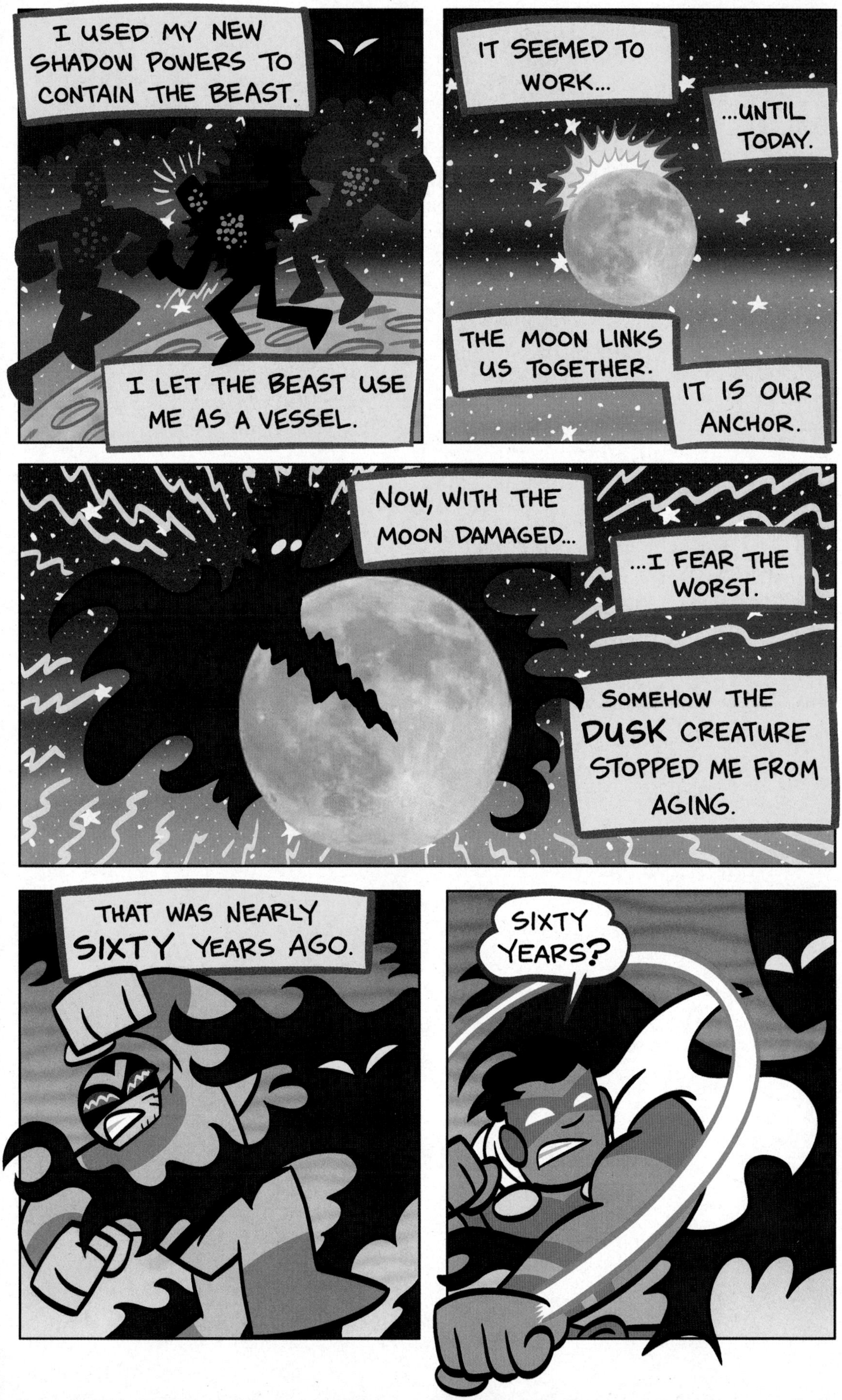
I USED MY NEW SHADOW POWERS TO CONTAIN THE BEAST.
I LET THE BEAST USE ME AS A VESSEL.
IT SEEMED TO WORK...
...UNTIL TODAY.
THE MOON LINKS US TOGETHER.
IT IS OUR ANCHOR.
NOW, WITH THE MOON DAMAGED...
...I FEAR THE WORST.
SOMEHOW THE DUSK CREATURE STOPPED ME FROM AGING.
THAT WAS NEARLY SIXTY YEARS AGO.
SIXTY YEARS?

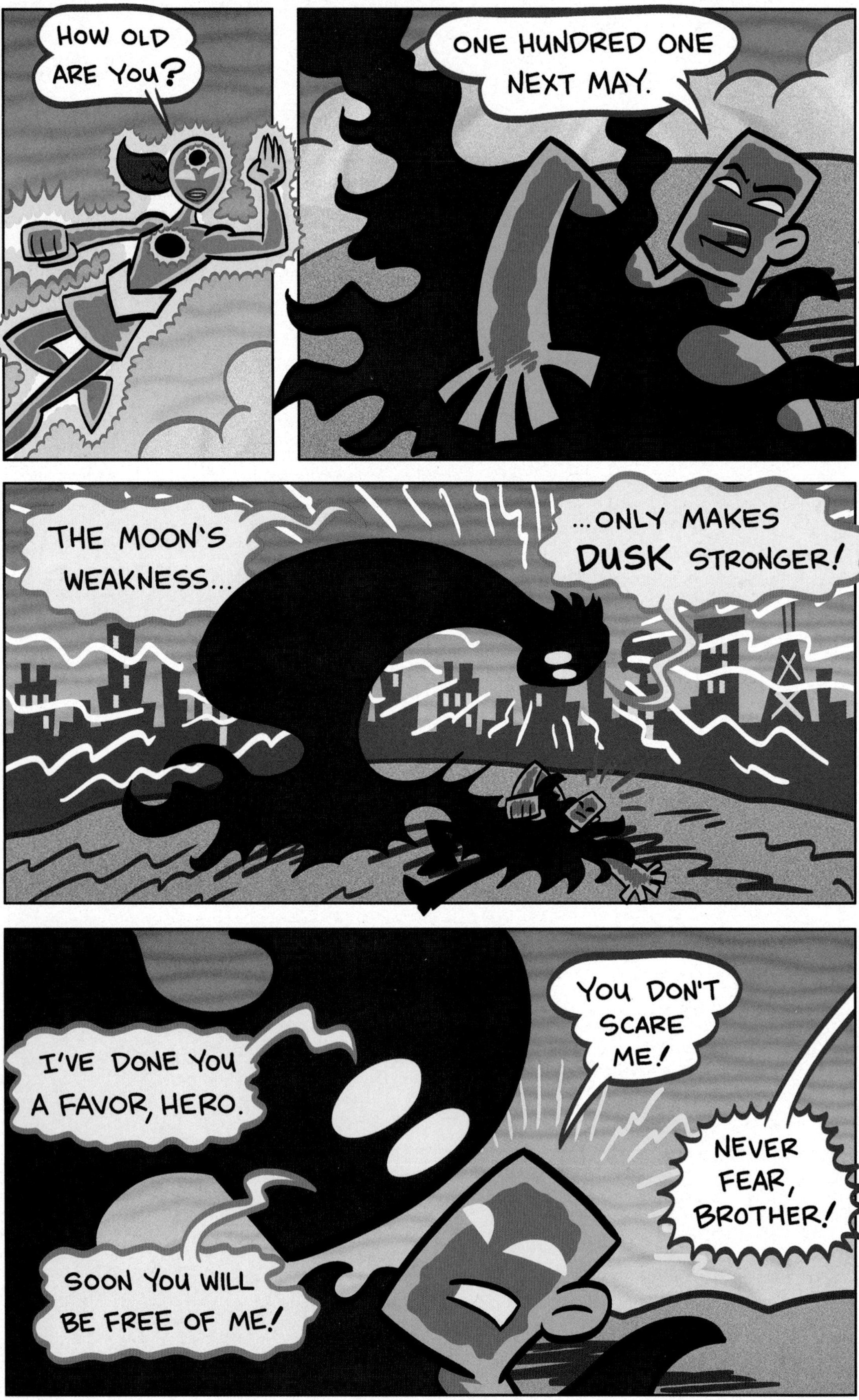
HOW OLD ARE YOU?
ONE HUNDRED ONE NEXT MAY.
THE MOON'S WEAKNESS...
...ONLY MAKES DUSK STRONGER!
I'VE DONE YOU A FAVOR, HERO.
SOON YOU WILL BE FREE OF ME!
YOU DON'T SCARE ME!
NEVER FEAR, BROTHER!

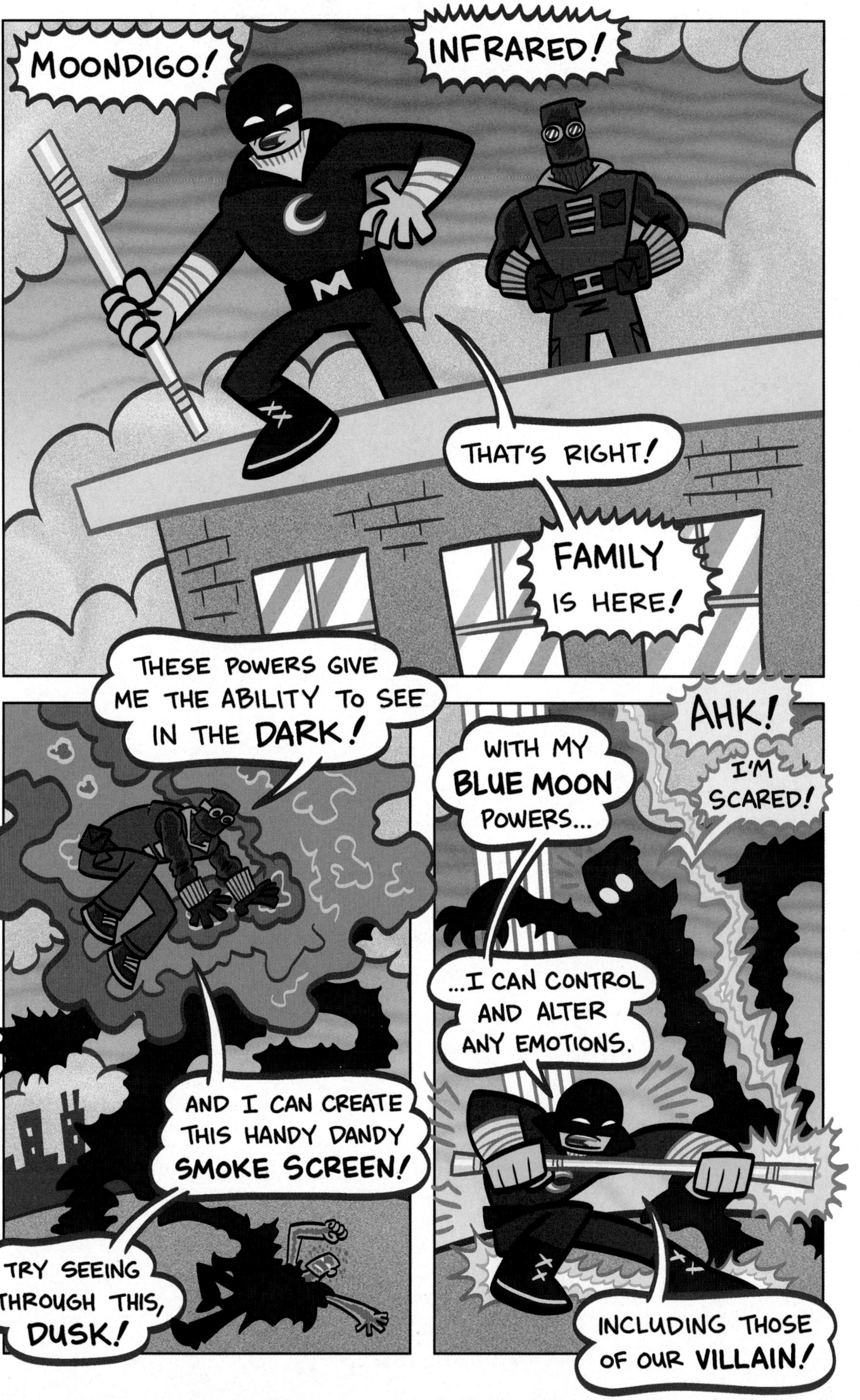
MOONDIGO!
INFRARED!
THAT'S RIGHT!
FAMILY IS HERE!
THESE POWERS GIVE ME THE ABILITY TO SEE IN THE DARK!
AND I CAN CREATE THIS HANDY DANDY SMOKE SCREEN!
TRY SEEING THROUGH THIS, DUSK!
WITH MY BLUE MOON POWERS...
AHK! I'M SCARED!
...I CAN CONTROL AND ALTER ANY EMOTIONS.
INCLUDING THOSE OF OUR VILLAIN!

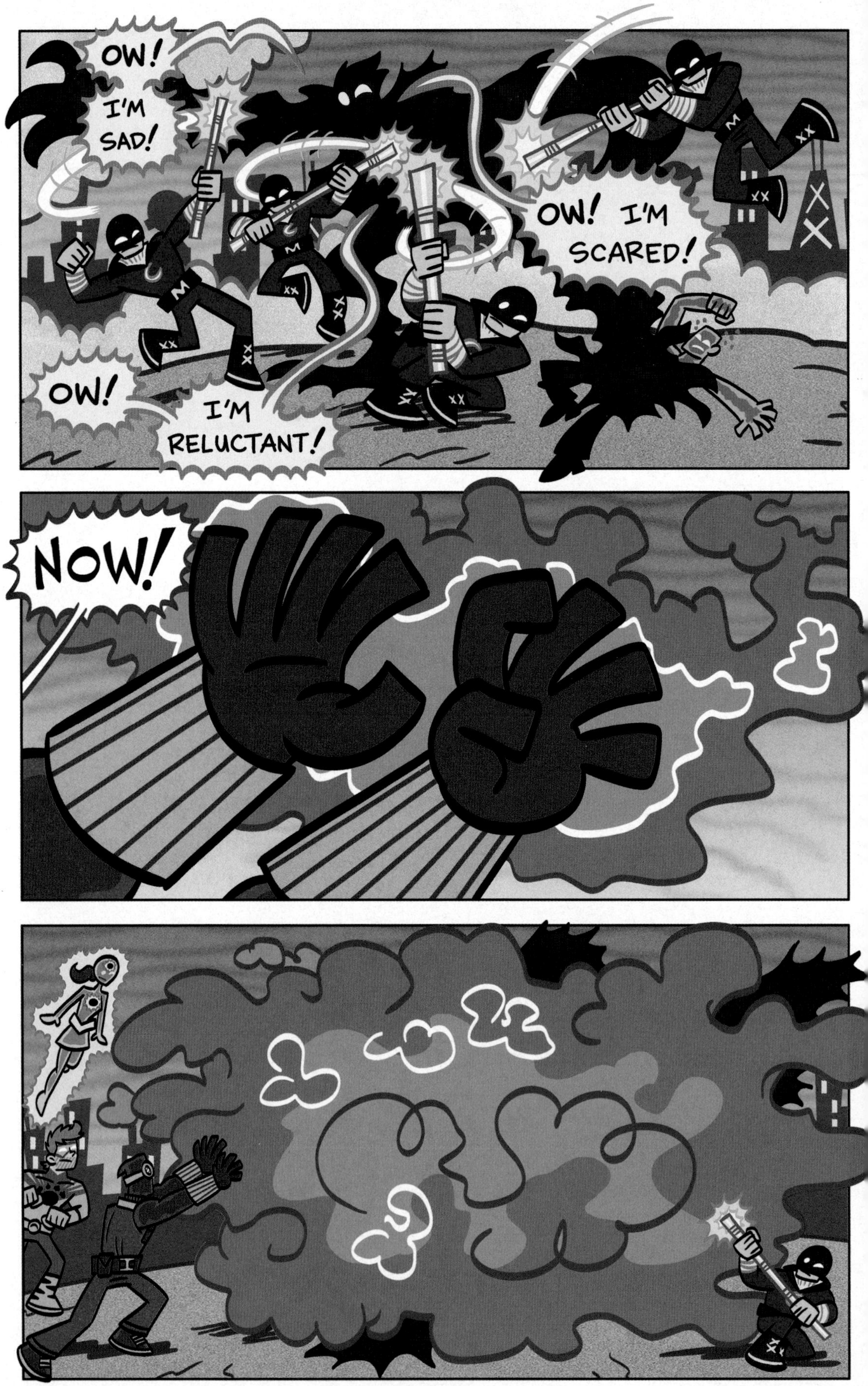
OW! I'M SAD!
OW! I'M SCARED!
OW!
I'M RELUCTANT!
NOW!

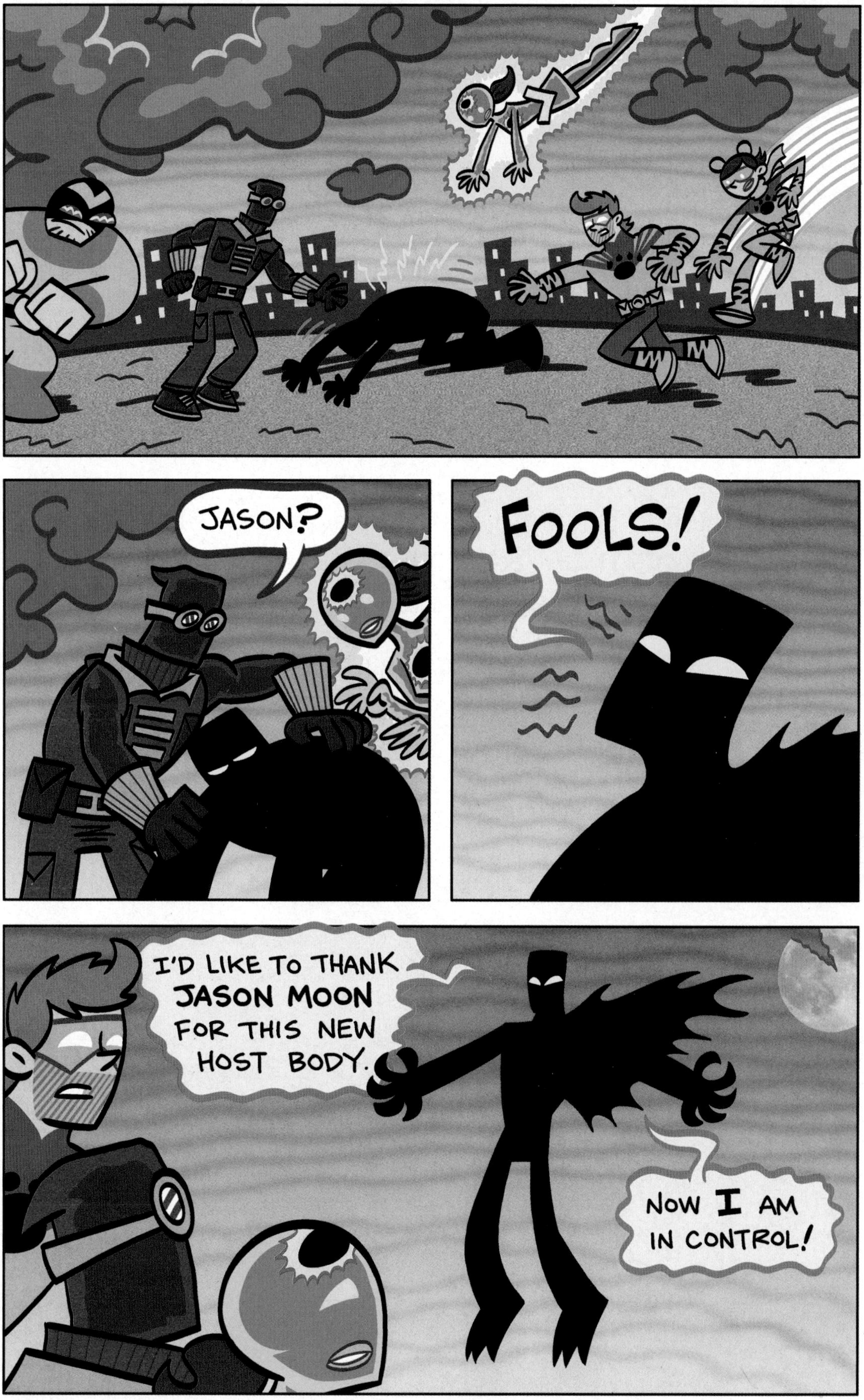
JASON?
FOOLS!
I'D LIKE TO THANK JASON MOON FOR THIS NEW HOST BODY.
NOW I AM IN CONTROL!

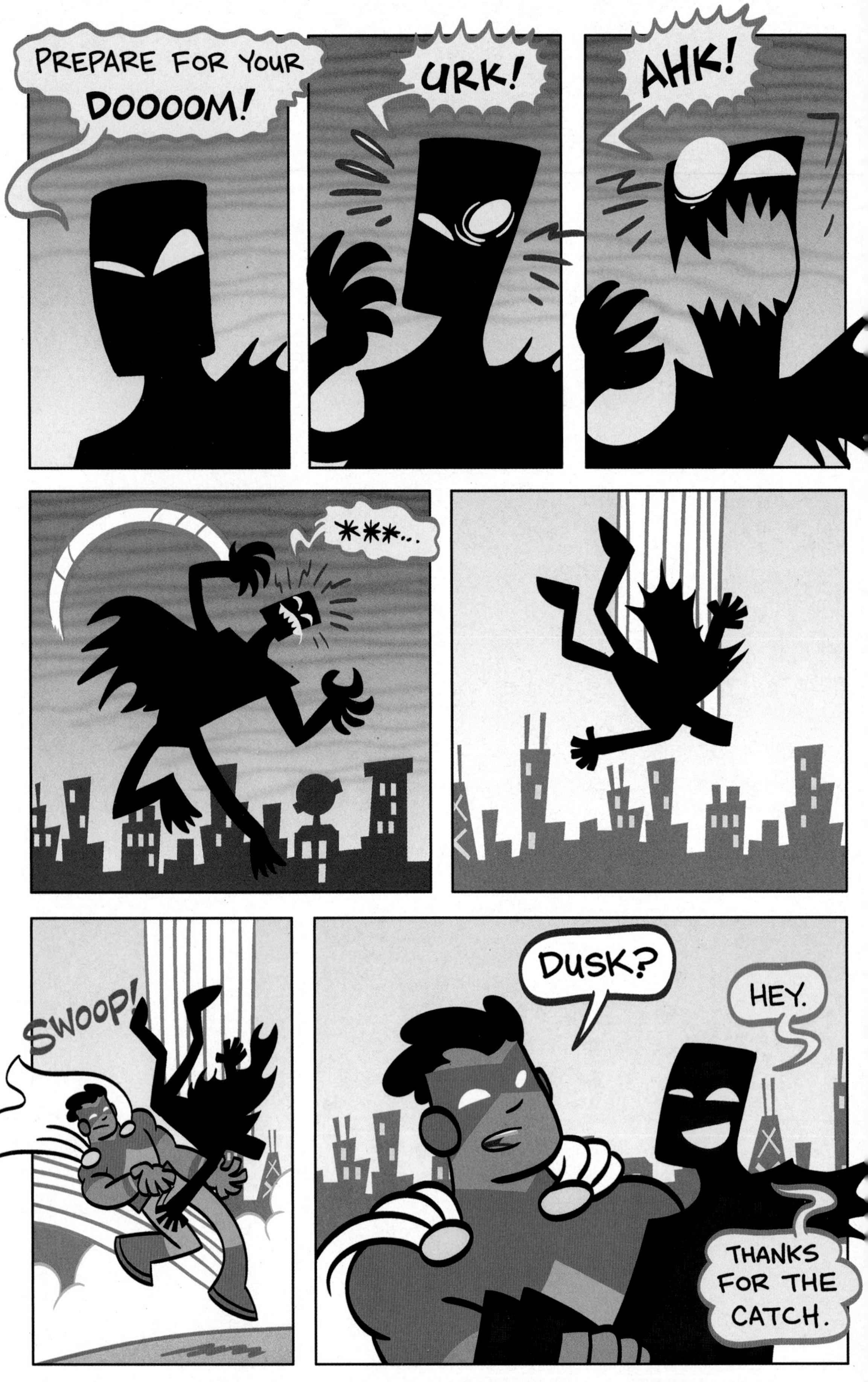
PREPARE FOR YOUR DOOOOM!
URK!
AHK!
***...
SWOOP!
DUSK?
HEY.
THANKS FOR THE CATCH.

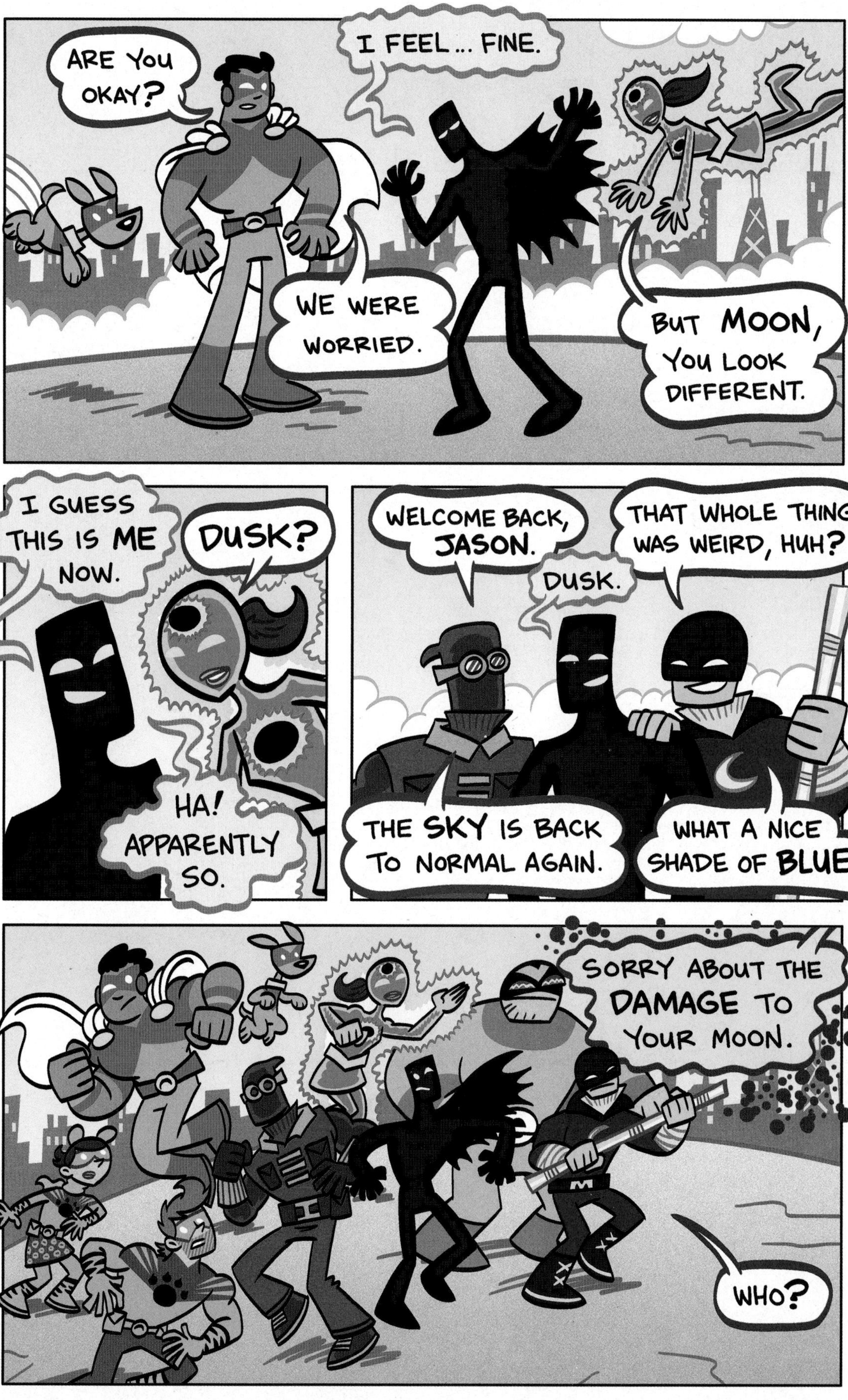
ARE YOU OKAY?
I FEEL... FINE.
WE WERE WORRIED.
BUT MOON, YOU LOOK DIFFERENT.
I GUESS THIS IS ME NOW.
DUSK?
HA! APPARENTLY SO.
WELCOME BACK, JASON.
DUSK.
THAT WHOLE THING WAS WEIRD, HUH?
THE SKY IS BACK TO NORMAL AGAIN.
WHAT A NICE SHADE OF BLUE.
SORRY ABOUT THE DAMAGE TO YOUR MOON.
WHO?

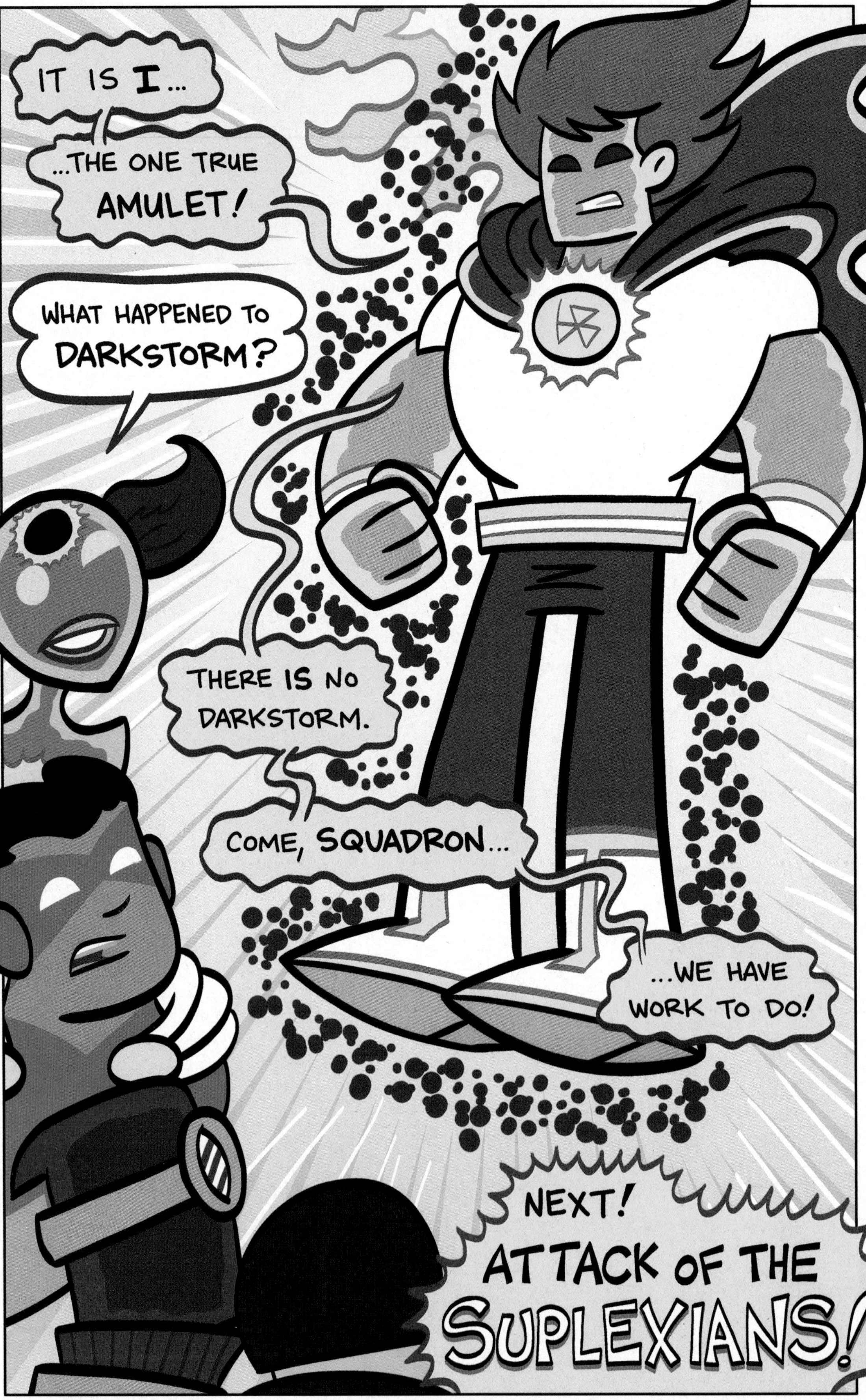
IT IS I...
...THE ONE TRUE AMULET!
WHAT HAPPENED TO DARKSTORM?
THERE IS NO DARKSTORM.
COME, SQUADRON...
...WE HAVE WORK TO DO!
NEXT!
ATTACK OF THE SUPLEXIANS!

Before...

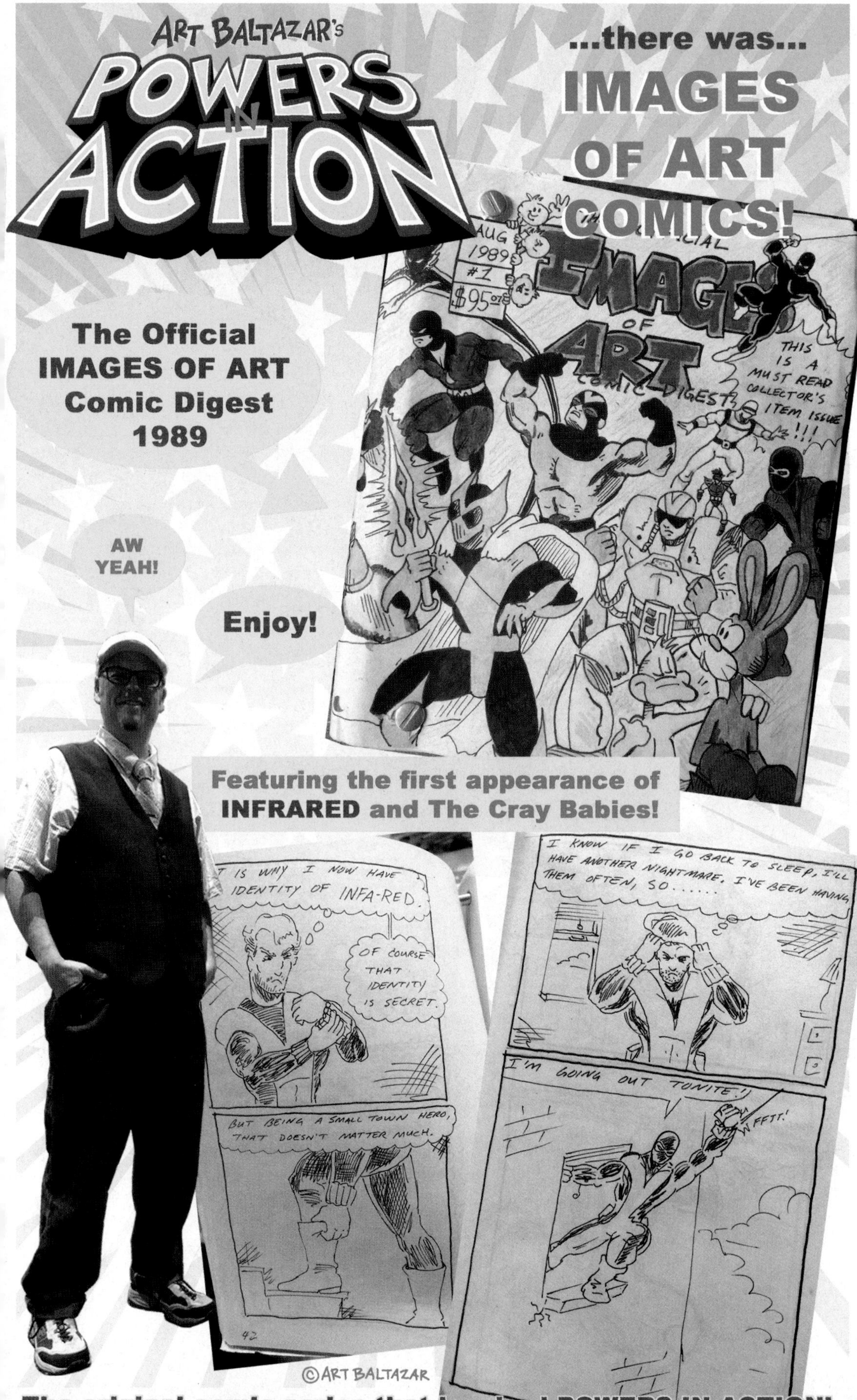

ART BALTAZAR's
POWERS IN ACTION
...there was...
IMAGES OF ART COMICS!
The Official IMAGES OF ART Comic Digest 1989
AW YEAH!
Enjoy!
AUG 1989
#1
$95.07
THE OFFICIAL IMAGES OF ART COMIC DIGEST
THIS IS A MUST READ COLLECTOR'S ITEM ISSUE!!!
Featuring the first appearance of INFRARED and The Cray Babies!
IDENTITY OF INFA-RED.
OF COURSE THAT IDENTITY IS SECRET.
BUT BEING A SMALL TOWN HERO, THAT DOESN'T MATTER MUCH.
42
I KNOW IF I GO BACK TO SLEEP, I'LL HAVE ANOTHER NIGHTMARE. I'VE BEEN HAVING THEM OFTEN, SO......
I'M GOING OUT TONITE!!
FFTT!

The original comic series that inspired POWERS IN ACTION!

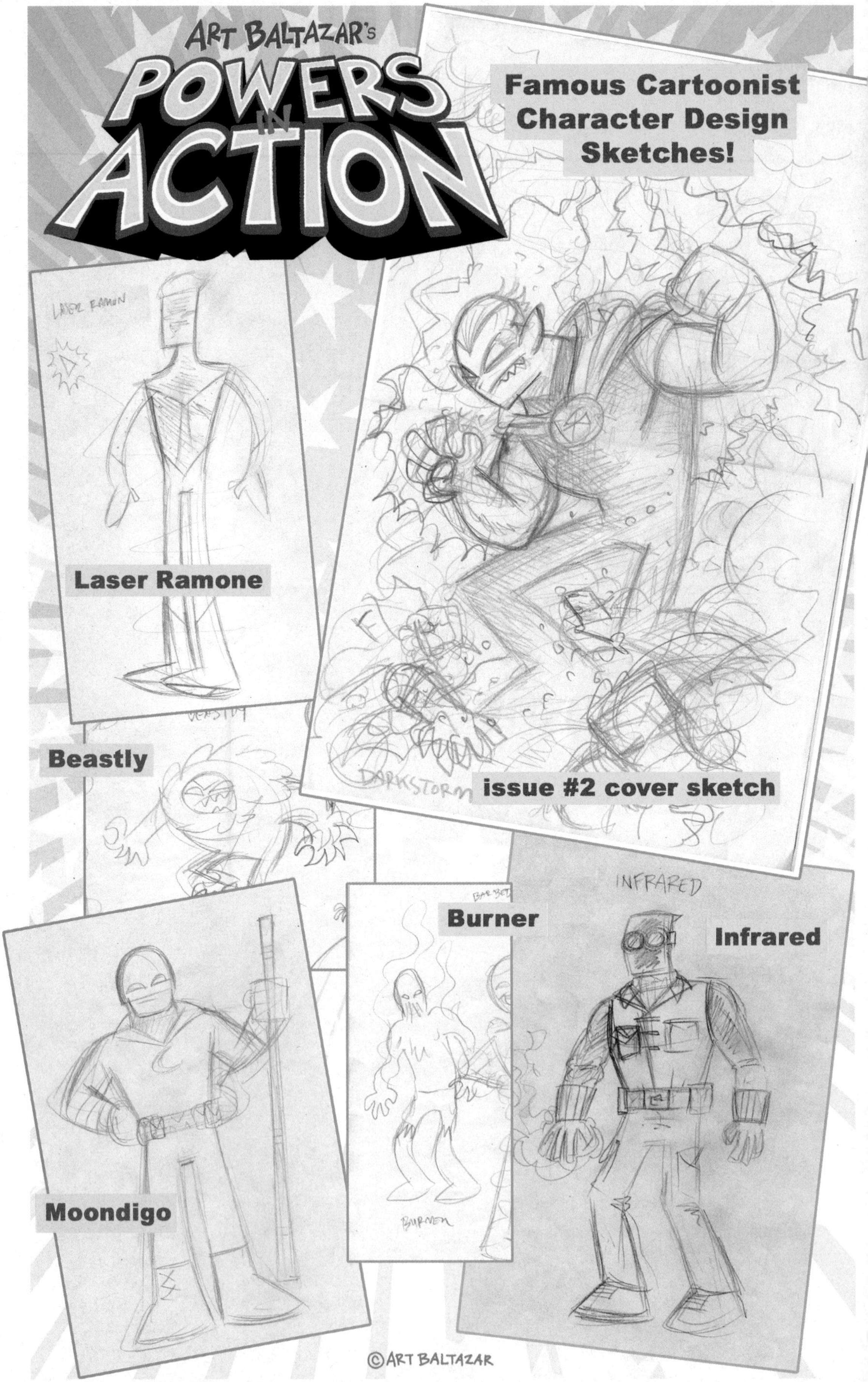
ART BALTAZAR's
POWERS IN ACTION
Famous Cartoonist Character Design Sketches!
Laser Ramone
issue #2 cover sketch
Beastly
Burner
Infrared
Moondigo
DARKSTORM
INFRARED

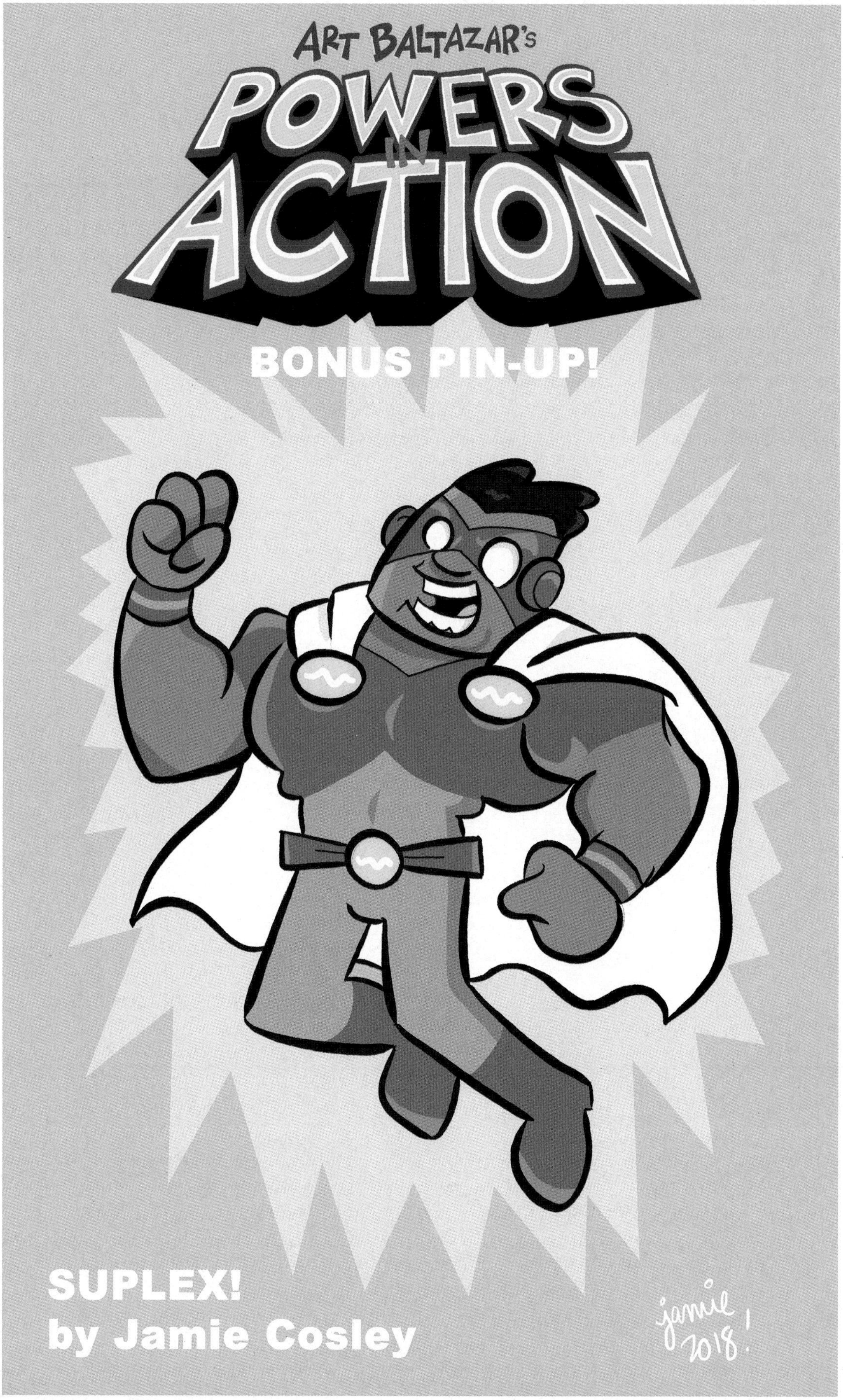
ART BALTAZAR'S
POWERS IN ACTION
BONUS PIN-UP!
SUPLEX!
by Jamie Cosley
jamie 2018!

BONUS BONUS ARTIST PIN-UP!!

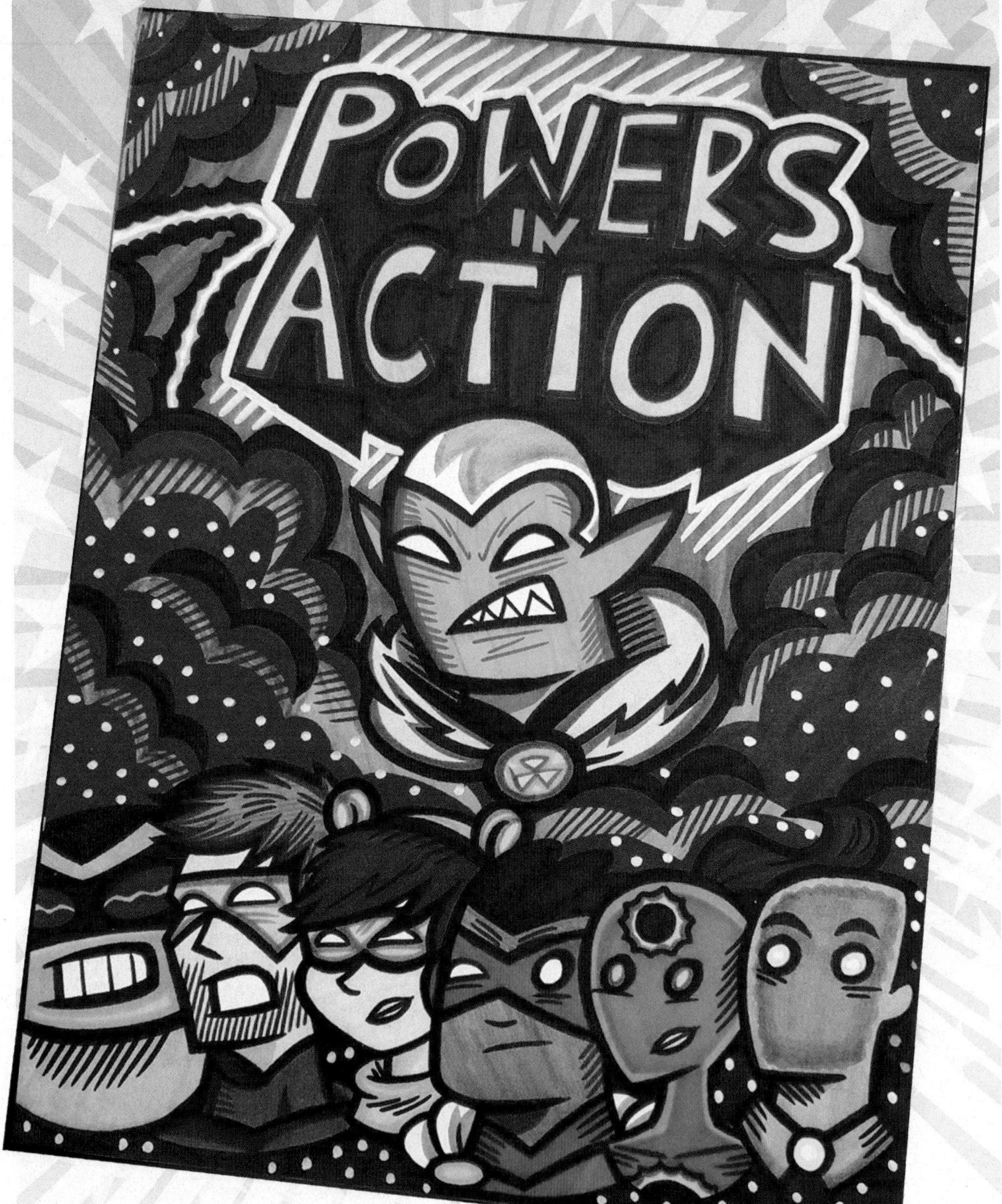
POWERS IN ACTION

THE HERO SQUADRON
by Chris Sandoval

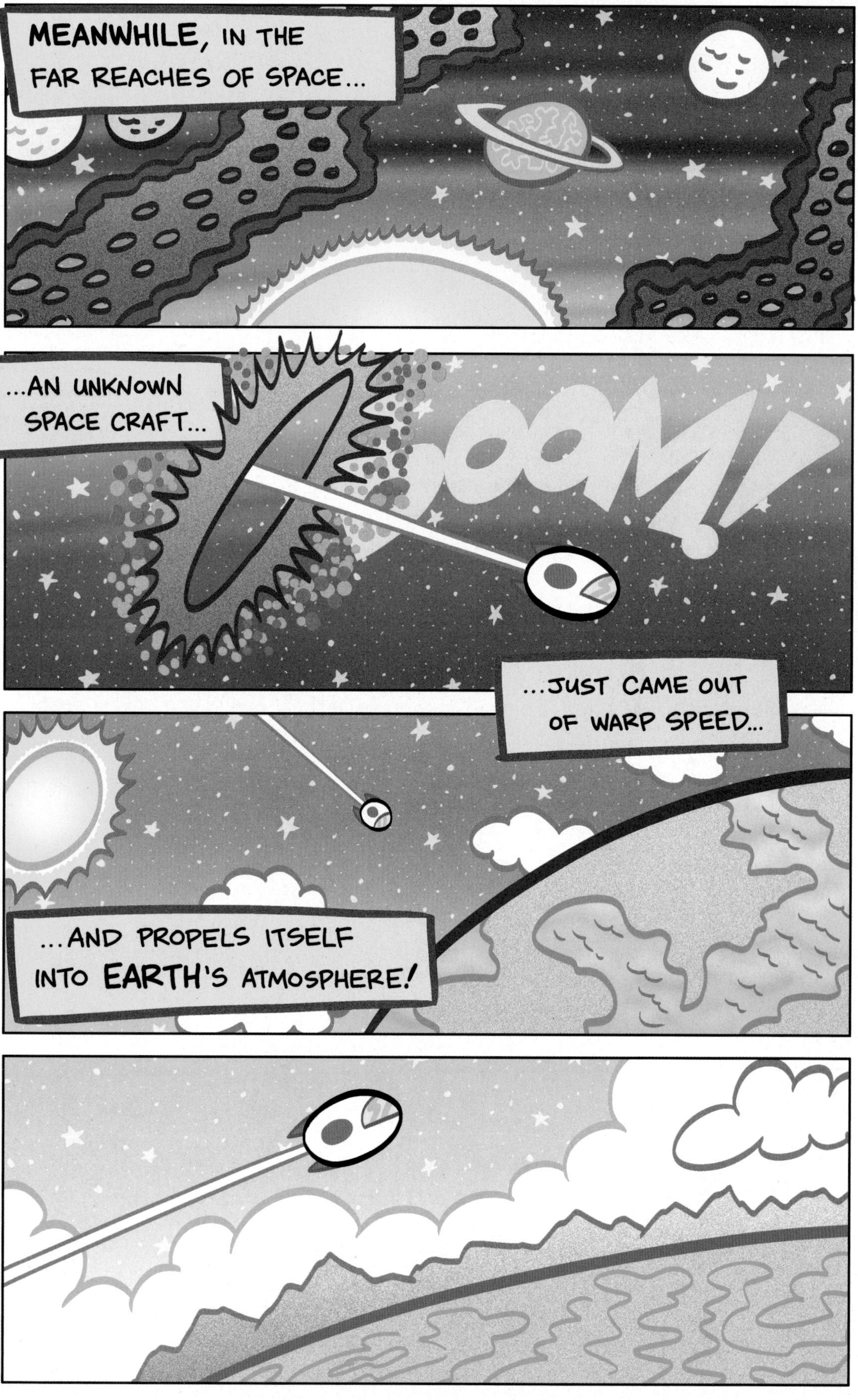
MEANWHILE, IN THE FAR REACHES OF SPACE...
...AN UNKNOWN SPACE CRAFT...
OOM!
...JUST CAME OUT OF WARP SPEED...
...AND PROPELS ITSELF INTO EARTH'S ATMOSPHERE!

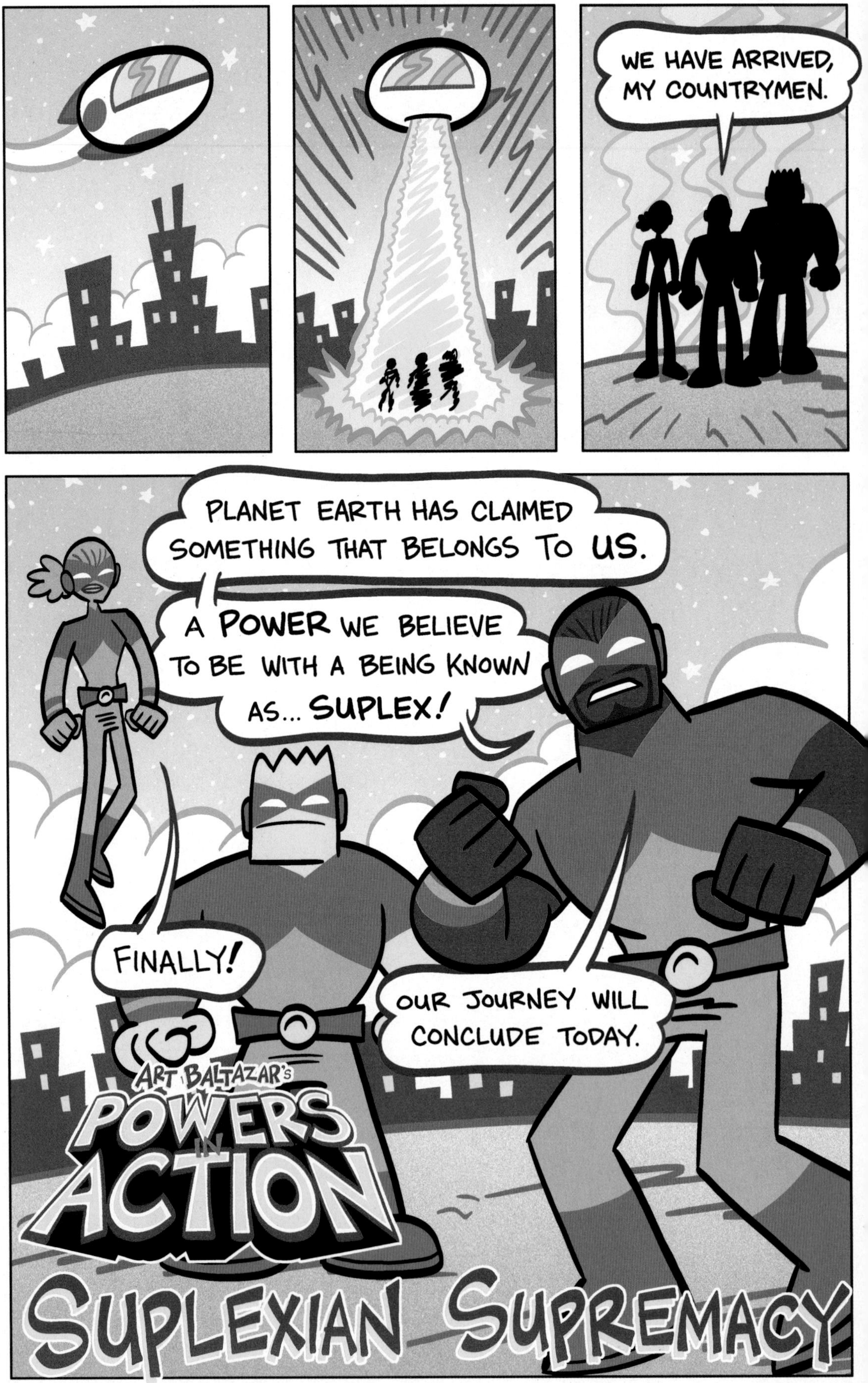
WE HAVE ARRIVED, MY COUNTRYMEN.
PLANET EARTH HAS CLAIMED SOMETHING THAT BELONGS TO US.
A POWER WE BELIEVE TO BE WITH A BEING KNOWN AS... SUPLEX!
FINALLY!
OUR JOURNEY WILL CONCLUDE TODAY.
ART BALTAZAR'S POWERS IN ACTION
SUPLEXIAN SUPREMACY

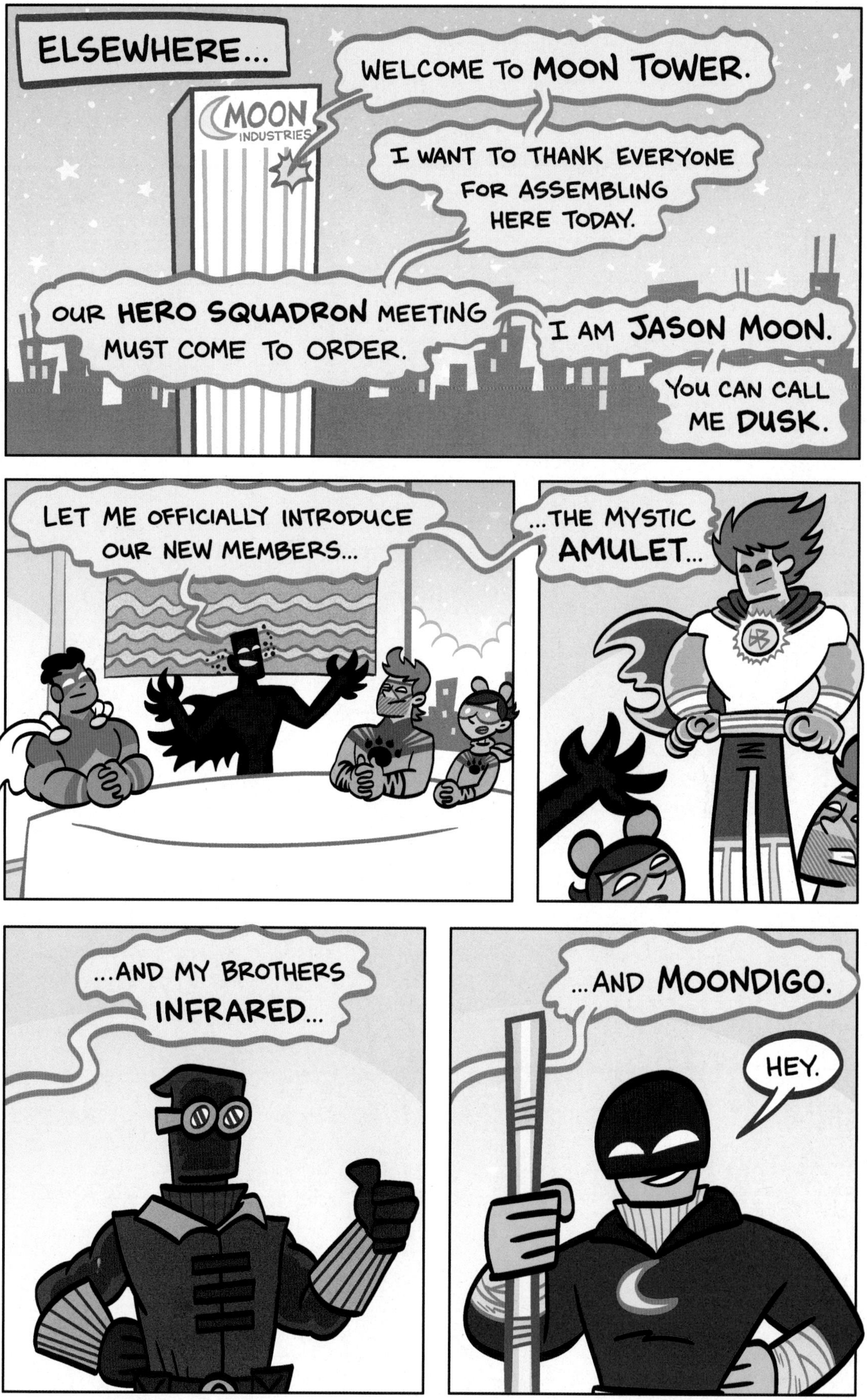
ELSEWHERE...
MOON INDUSTRIES
WELCOME TO MOON TOWER.
I WANT TO THANK EVERYONE FOR ASSEMBLING HERE TODAY.
OUR HERO SQUADRON MEETING MUST COME TO ORDER.
I AM JASON MOON.
YOU CAN CALL ME DUSK.
LET ME OFFICIALLY INTRODUCE OUR NEW MEMBERS...
...THE MYSTIC AMULET...
...AND MY BROTHERS INFRARED...
...AND MOONDIGO.
HEY.

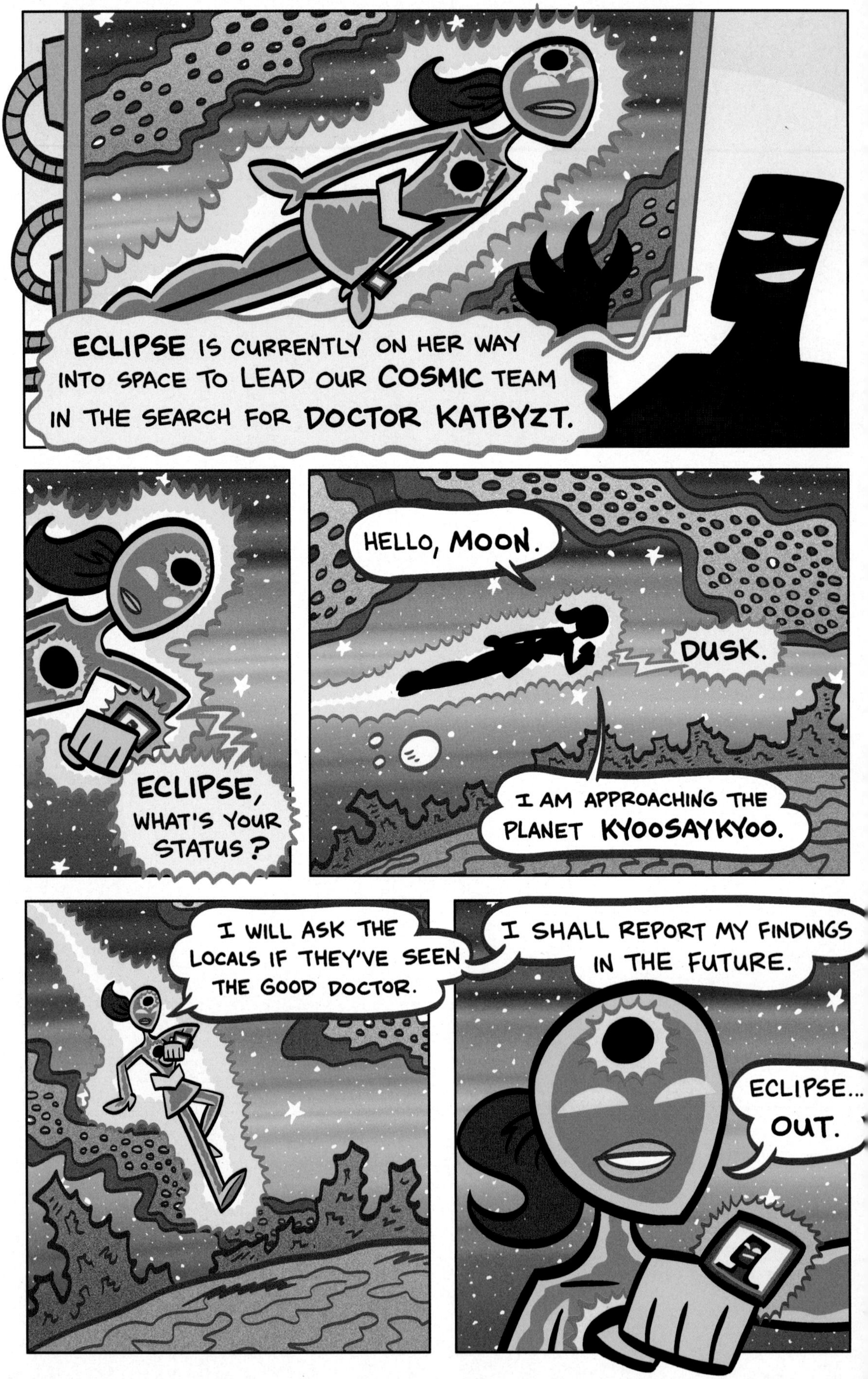
ECLIPSE IS CURRENTLY ON HER WAY INTO SPACE TO LEAD OUR COSMIC TEAM IN THE SEARCH FOR DOCTOR KATBYZT.
ECLIPSE, WHAT'S YOUR STATUS?
HELLO, MOON.
DUSK.
I AM APPROACHING THE PLANET KYOOSAYKYOO.
I WILL ASK THE LOCALS IF THEY'VE SEEN THE GOOD DOCTOR.
I SHALL REPORT MY FINDINGS IN THE FUTURE.
ECLIPSE... OUT.

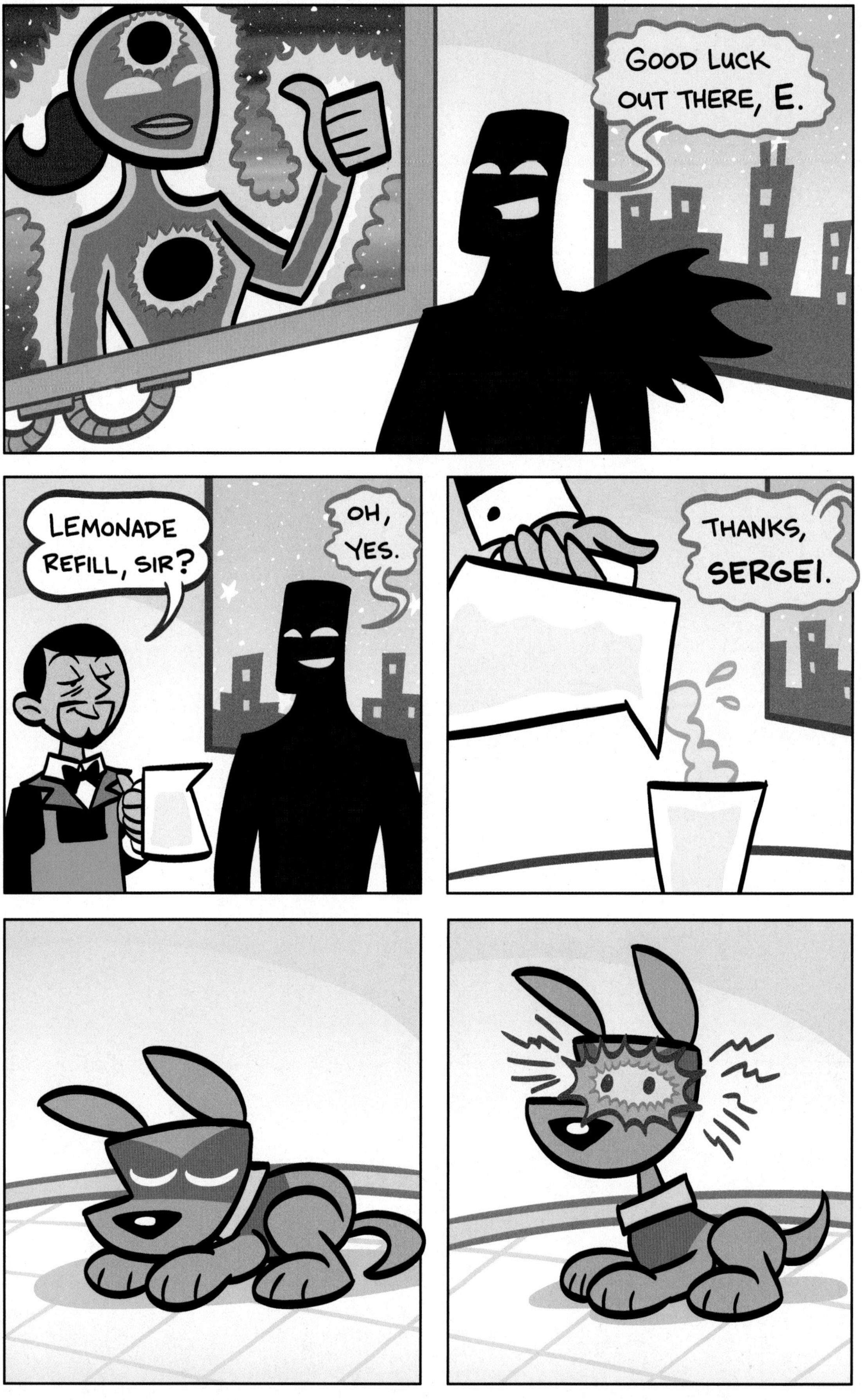
GOOD LUCK
OUT THERE, E.
LEMONADE
REFILL, SIR?
OH,
YES.
THANKS,
SERGEI.

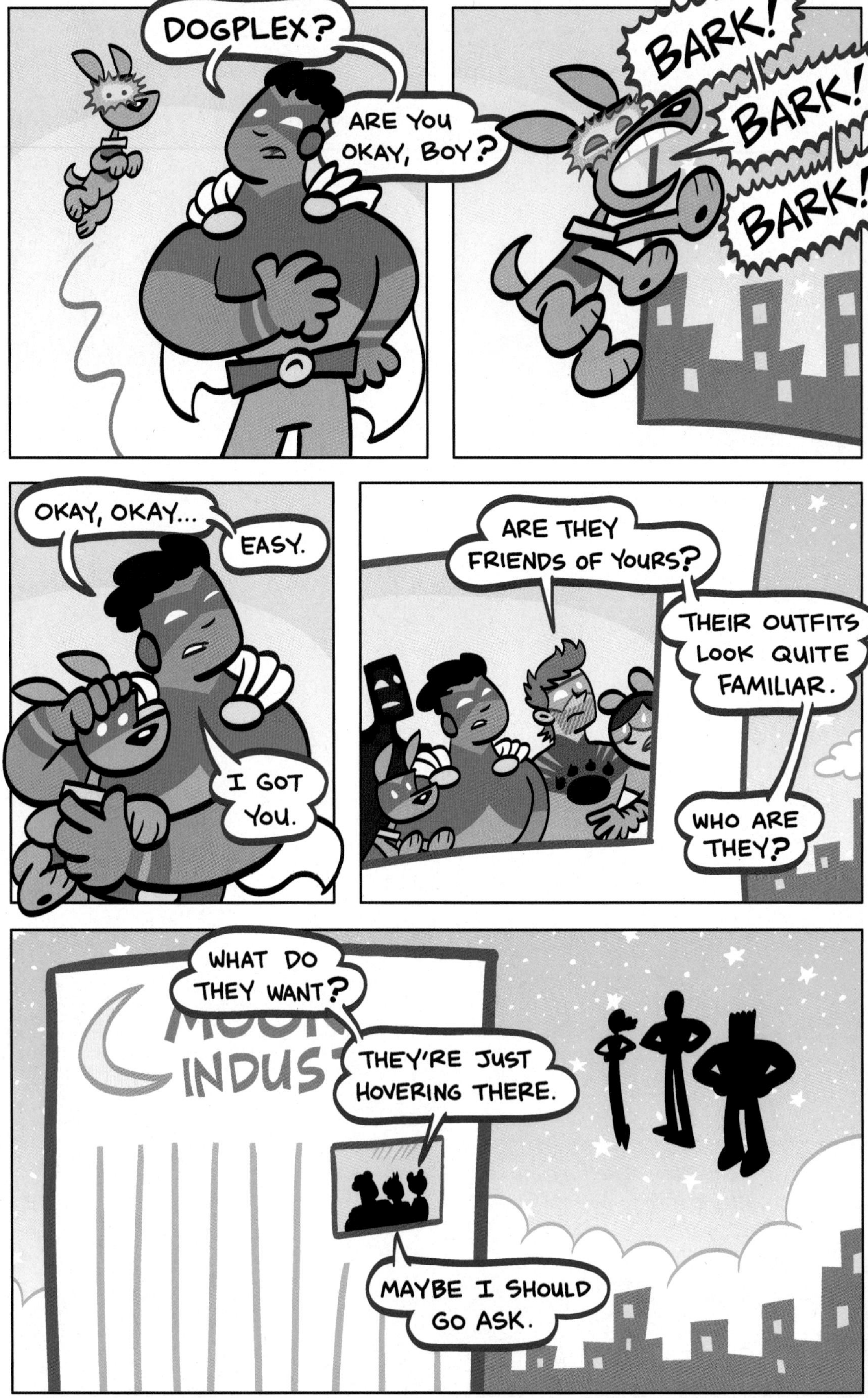
DOGPLEX?
ARE YOU OKAY, BOY?
BARK!
BARK!
BARK!
OKAY, OKAY...
EASY.
I GOT YOU.
ARE THEY FRIENDS OF YOURS?
THEIR OUTFITS LOOK QUITE FAMILIAR.
WHO ARE THEY?
WHAT DO THEY WANT?
THEY'RE JUST HOVERING THERE.
MAYBE I SHOULD GO ASK.

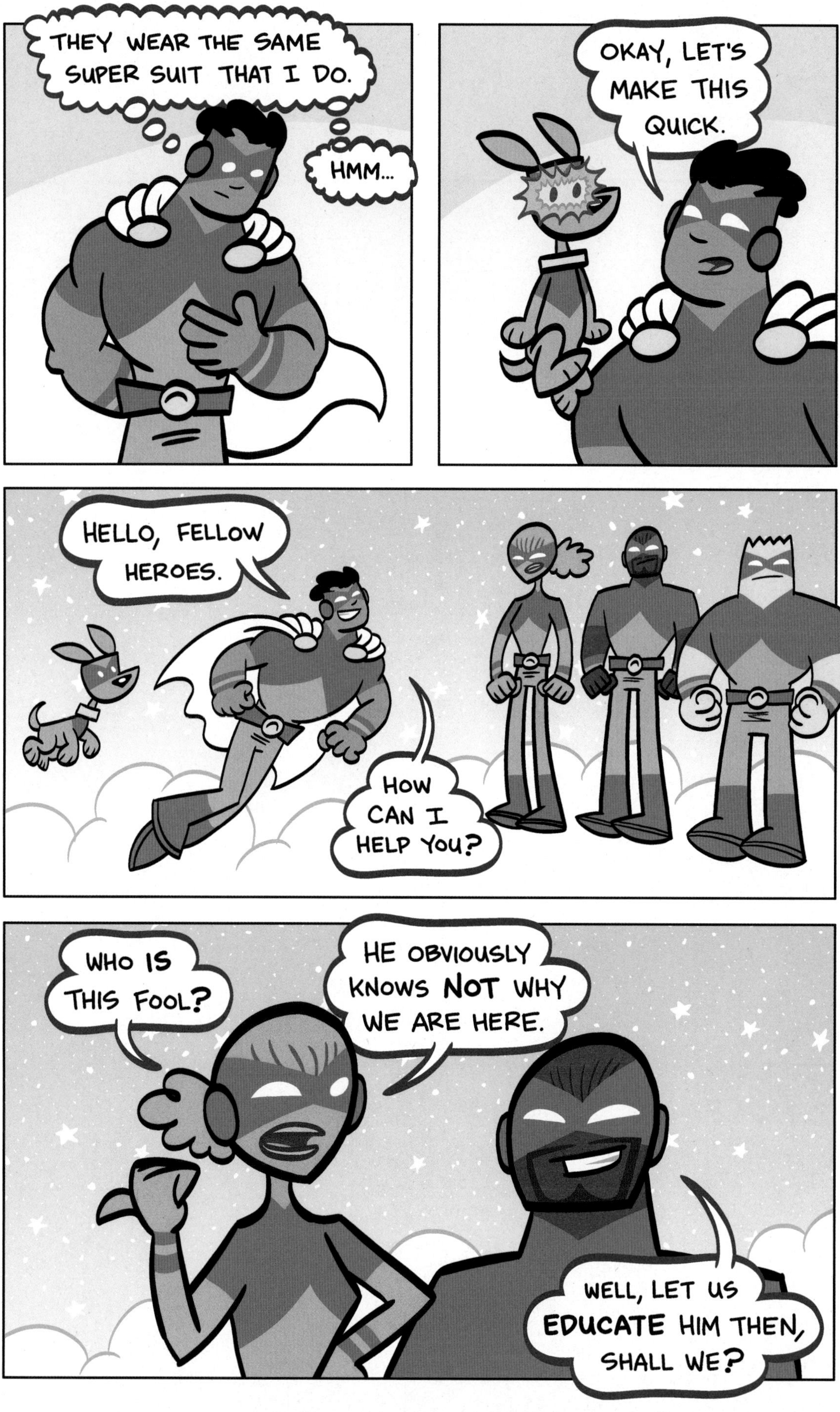
THEY WEAR THE SAME SUPER SUIT THAT I DO.
HMM...
OKAY, LET'S MAKE THIS QUICK.
HELLO, FELLOW HEROES.
HOW CAN I HELP YOU?
WHO IS THIS FOOL?
HE OBVIOUSLY KNOWS NOT WHY WE ARE HERE.
WELL, LET US EDUCATE HIM THEN, SHALL WE?

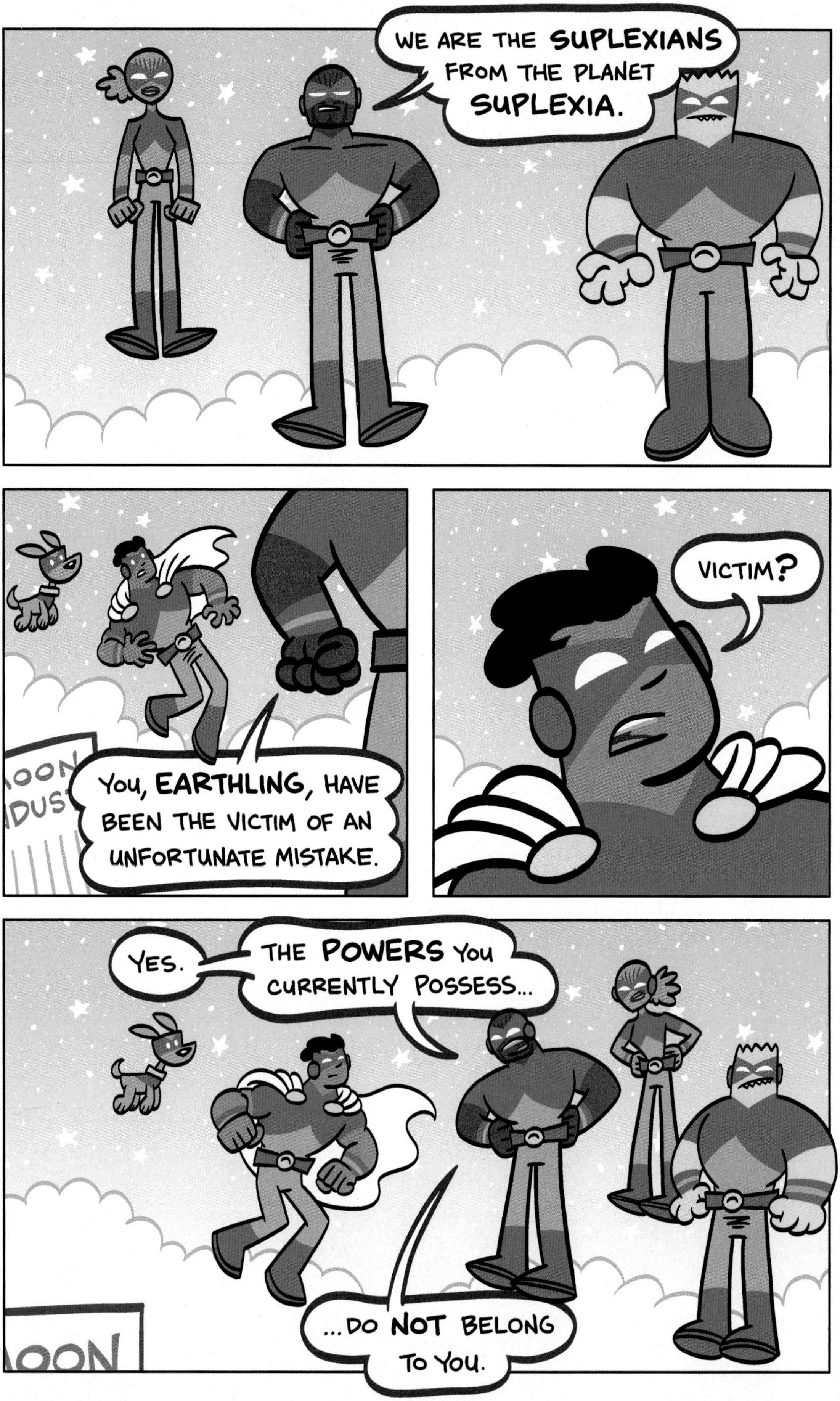
WE ARE THE SUPLEXIANS FROM THE PLANET SUPLEXIA.
You, EARTHLING, HAVE BEEN THE VICTIM OF AN UNFORTUNATE MISTAKE.
VICTIM?
YES.
THE POWERS YOU CURRENTLY POSSESS...
...DO NOT BELONG TO YOU.

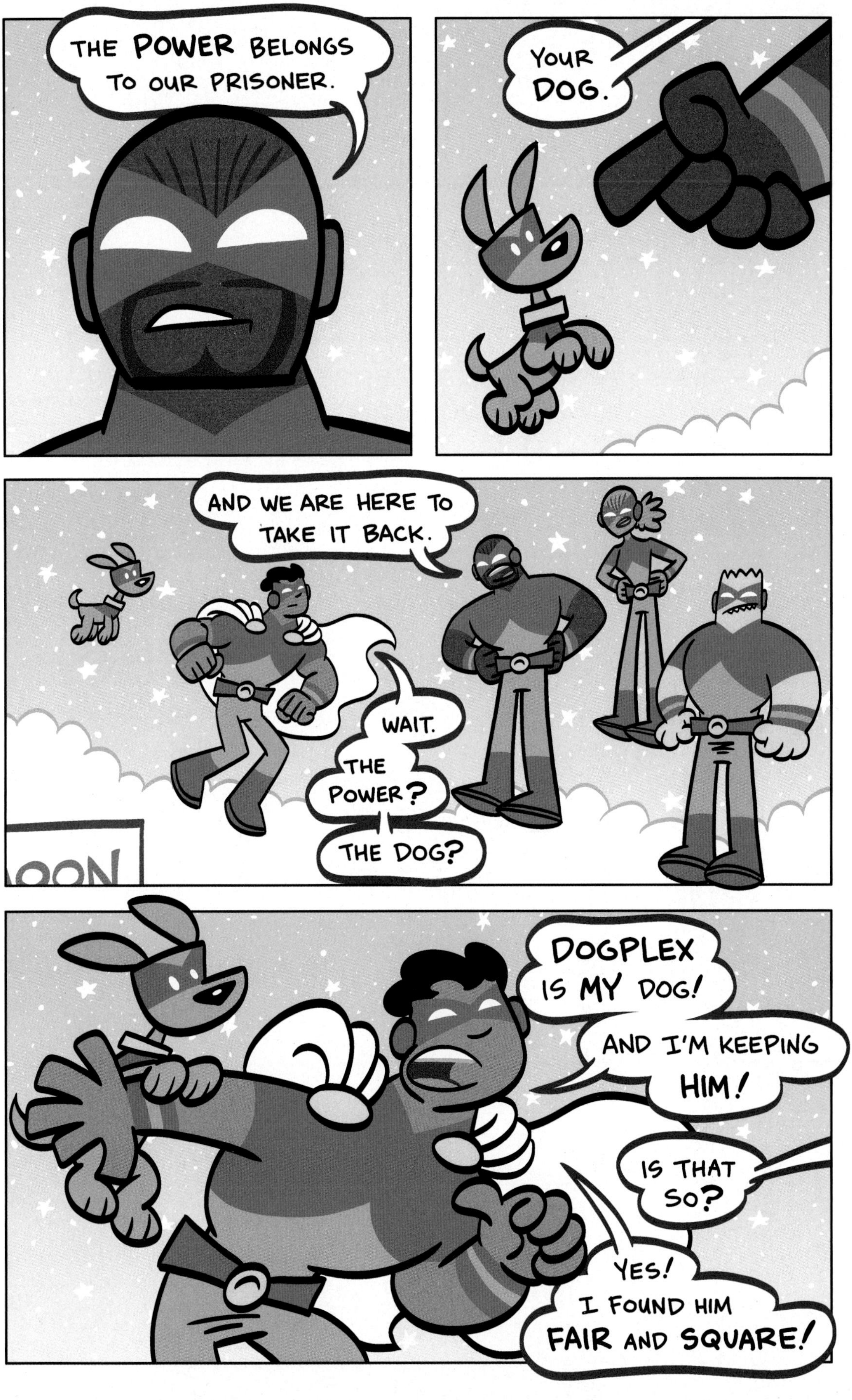

THE POWER BELONGS TO OUR PRISONER.
YOUR DOG.
AND WE ARE HERE TO TAKE IT BACK.
WAIT.
THE POWER?
THE DOG?
OON
DOGPLEX IS MY DOG!
AND I'M KEEPING HIM!
IS THAT SO?
YES!
I FOUND HIM FAIR AND SQUARE!

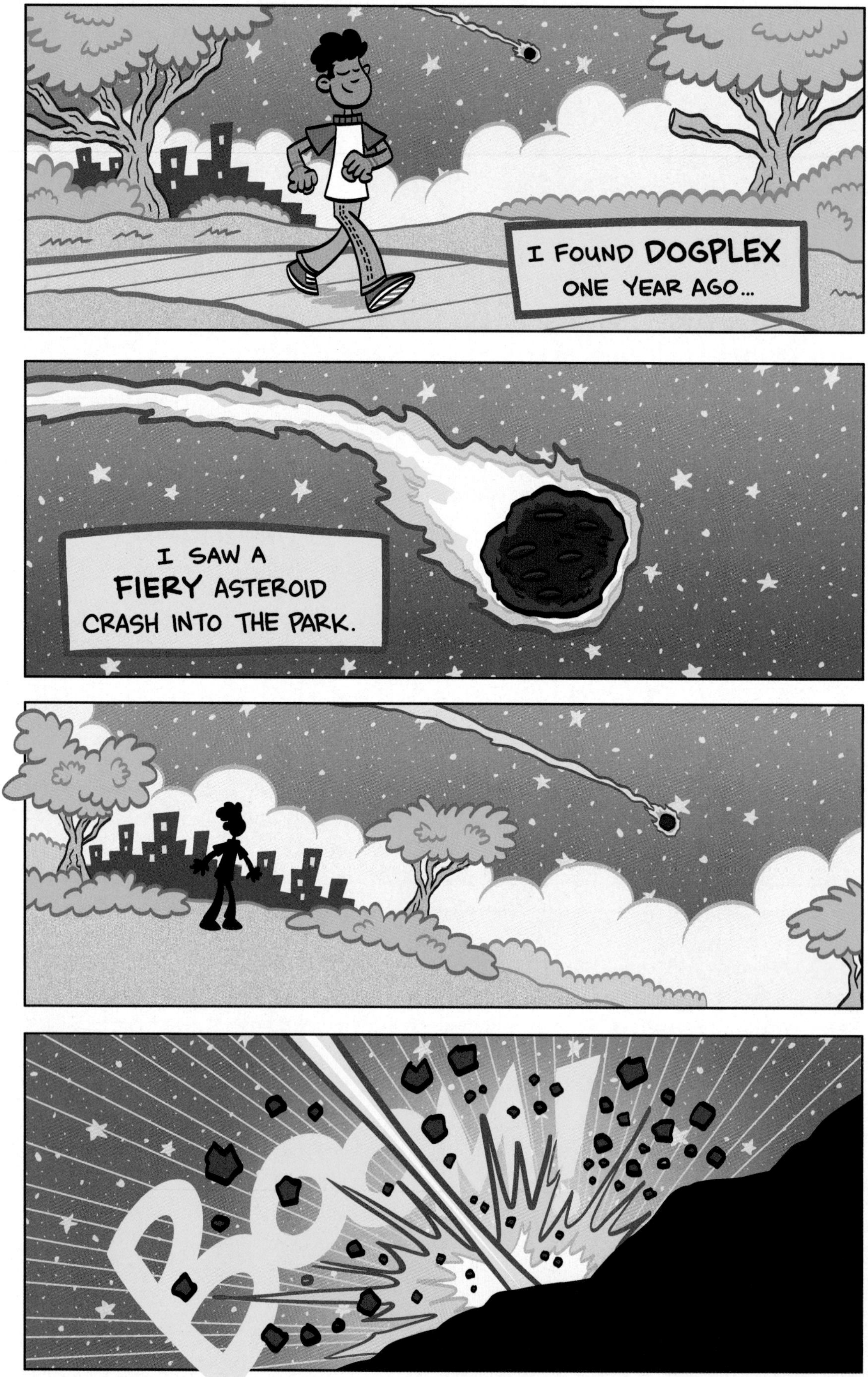
I FOUND DOGPLEX ONE YEAR AGO...
I SAW A FIERY ASTEROID CRASH INTO THE PARK.

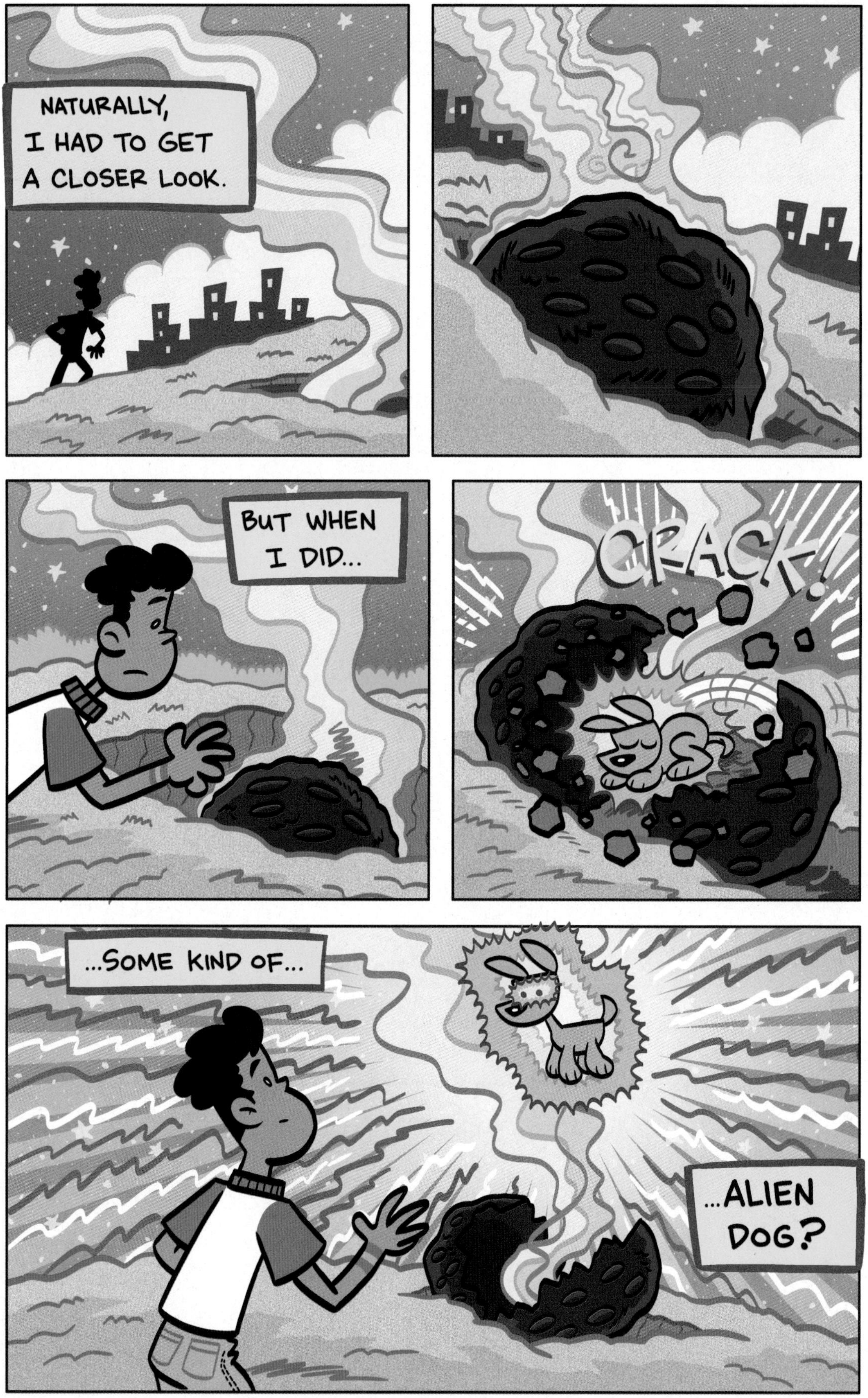
NATURALLY, I HAD TO GET A CLOSER LOOK.
BUT WHEN I DID...
CRACK!
...SOME KIND OF...
...ALIEN DOG?

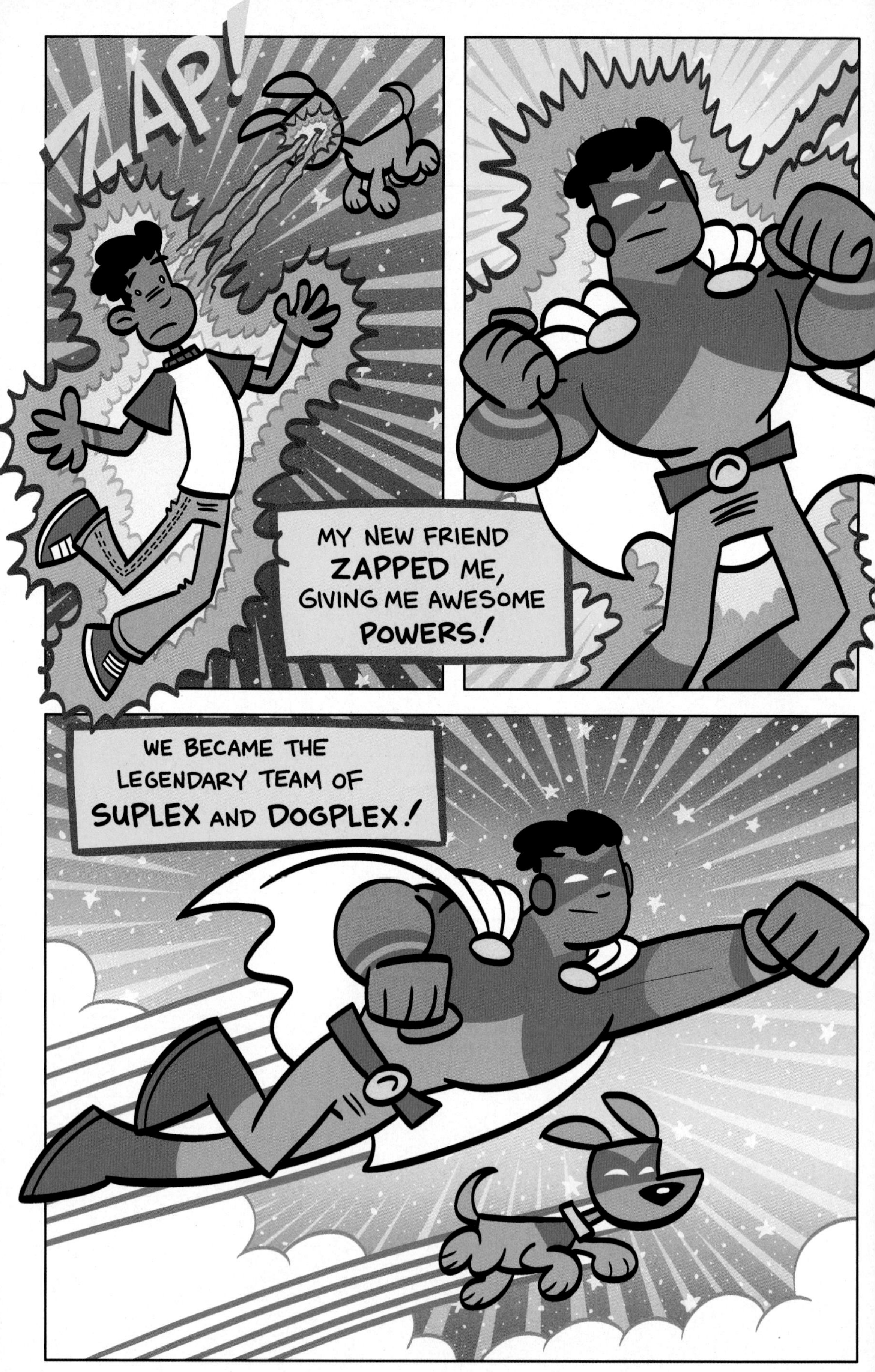
ZAP!
MY NEW FRIEND ZAPPED ME, GIVING ME AWESOME POWERS!
WE BECAME THE LEGENDARY TEAM OF SUPLEX AND DOGPLEX!

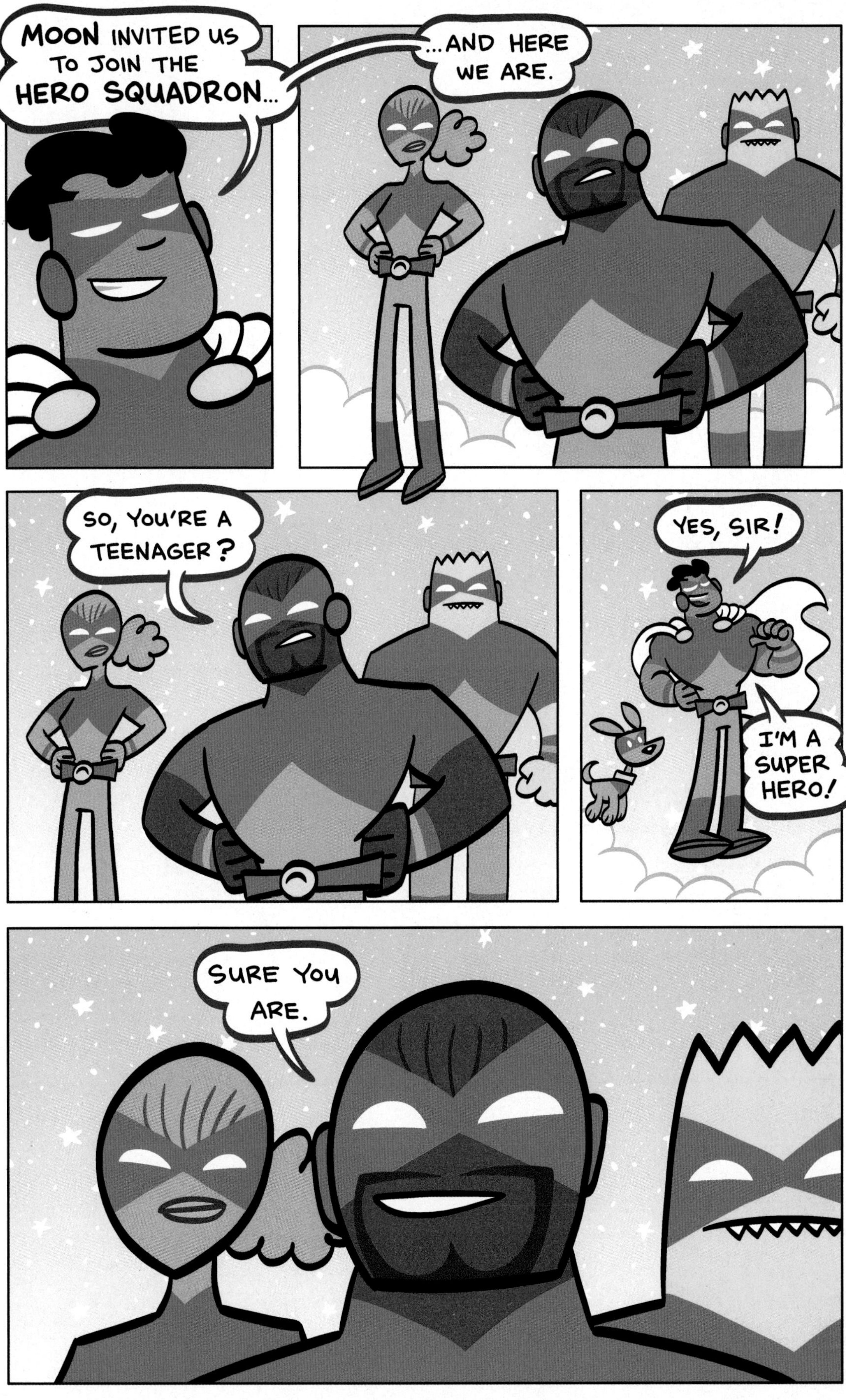
MOON INVITED US TO JOIN THE HERO SQUADRON...
...AND HERE WE ARE.
SO, YOU'RE A TEENAGER?
YES, SIR!
I'M A SUPER HERO!
SURE YOU ARE.

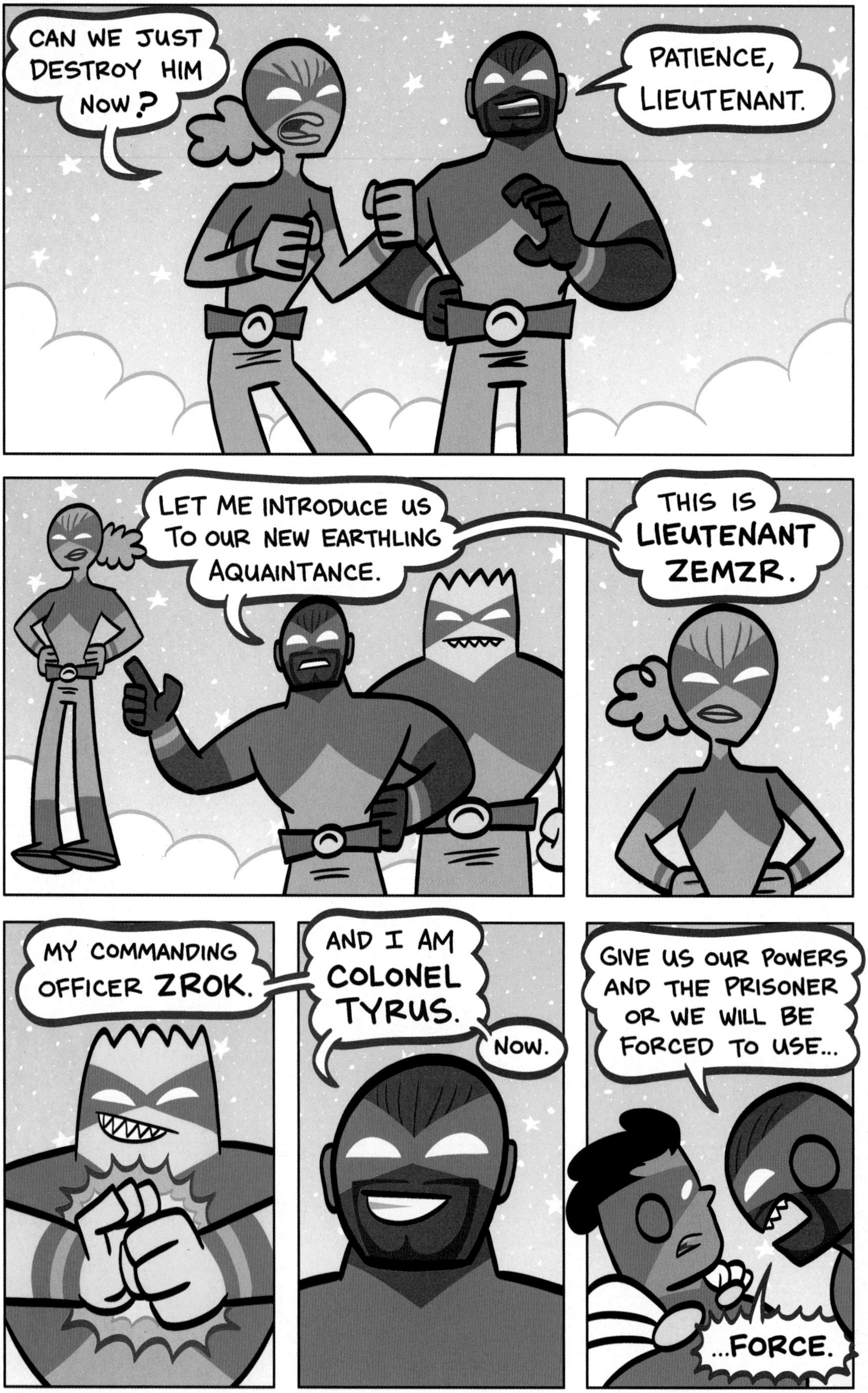
CAN WE JUST DESTROY HIM NOW?
PATIENCE, LIEUTENANT.
LET ME INTRODUCE US TO OUR NEW EARTHLING AQUAINTANCE.
THIS IS LIEUTENANT ZEMZR.
MY COMMANDING OFFICER ZROK.
AND I AM COLONEL TYRUS.
NOW.
GIVE US OUR POWERS AND THE PRISONER OR WE WILL BE FORCED TO USE...
...FORCE.

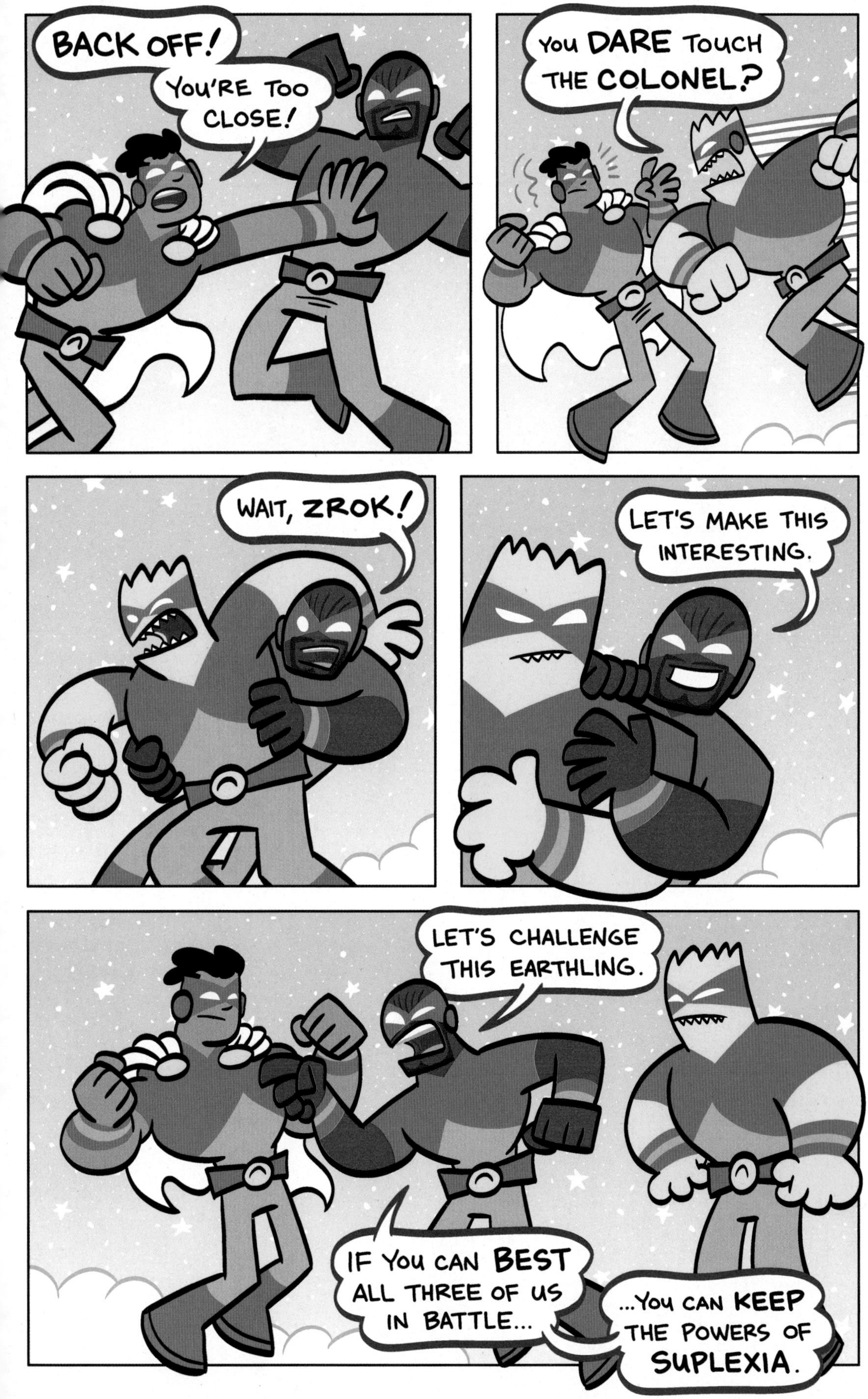
BACK OFF!
YOU'RE TOO CLOSE!
YOU DARE TOUCH THE COLONEL?
WAIT, ZROK!
LET'S MAKE THIS INTERESTING.
LET'S CHALLENGE THIS EARTHLING.
IF YOU CAN BEST ALL THREE OF US IN BATTLE...
...YOU CAN KEEP THE POWERS OF SUPLEXIA.

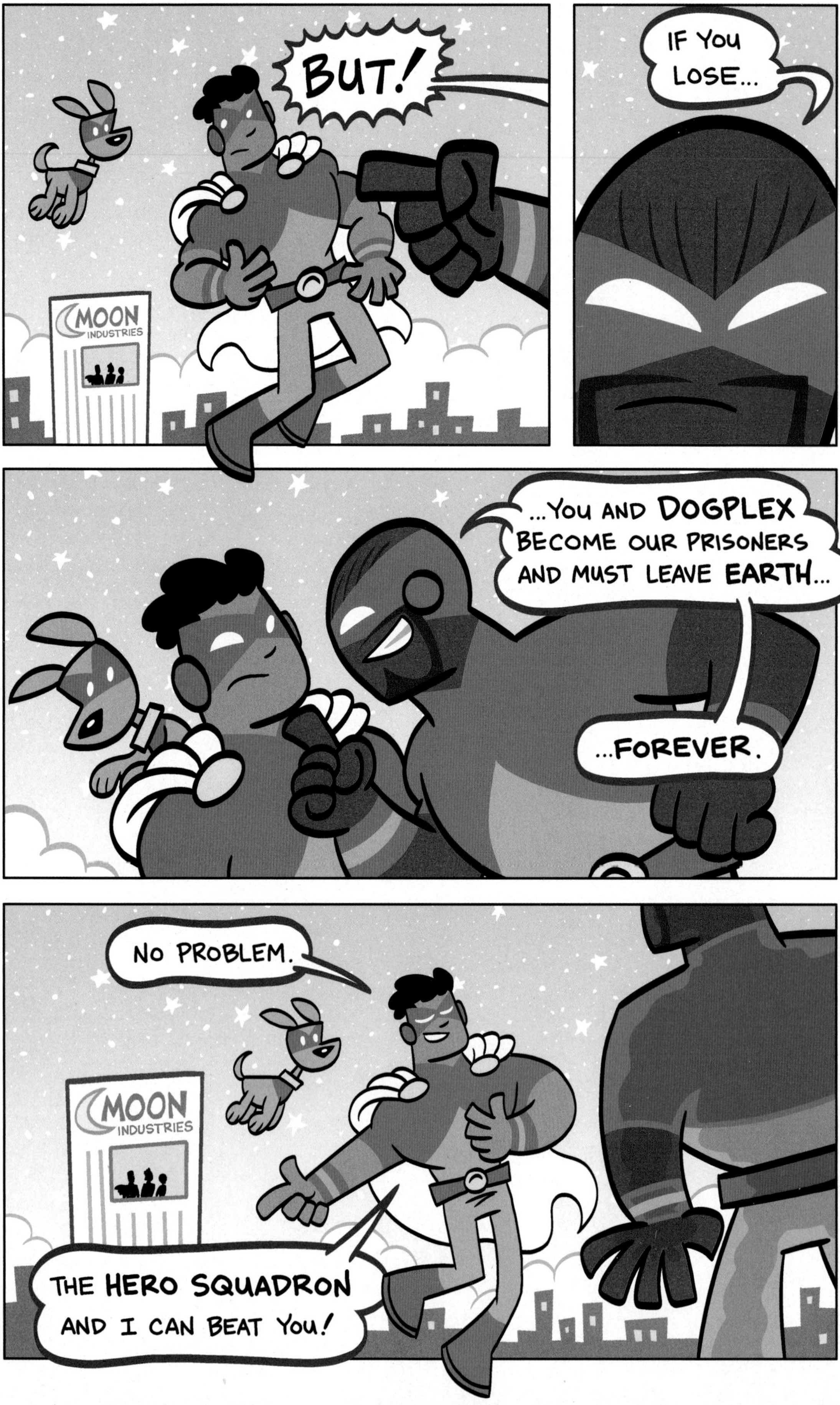
BUT!
IF YOU LOSE...
...YOU AND DOGPLEX BECOME OUR PRISONERS AND MUST LEAVE EARTH...
...FOREVER.
MOON INDUSTRIES
NO PROBLEM.
THE HERO SQUADRON AND I CAN BEAT YOU!

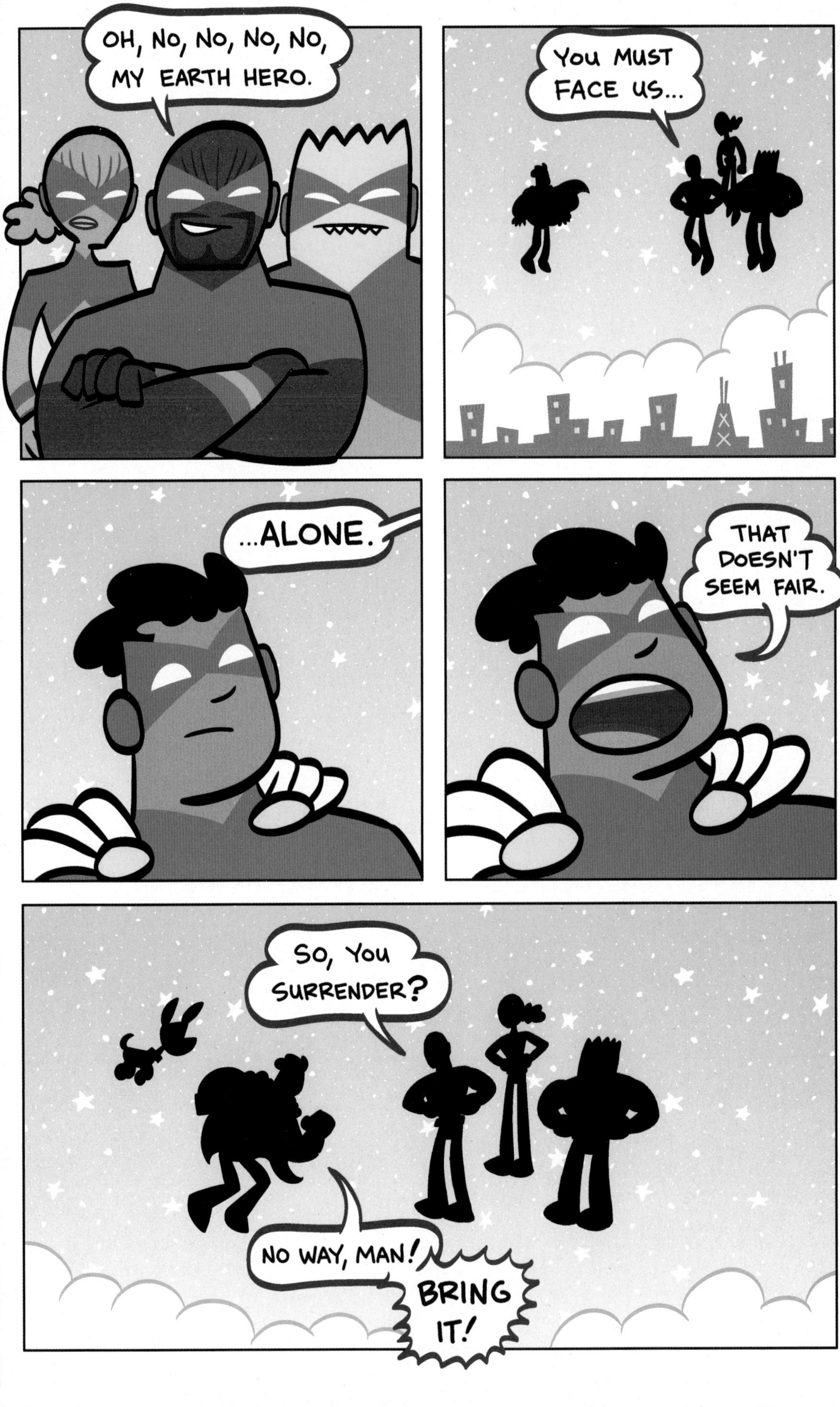
OH, NO, NO, NO, NO, MY EARTH HERO.
YOU MUST FACE US...
...ALONE.
THAT DOESN'T SEEM FAIR.
SO, YOU SURRENDER?
NO WAY, MAN!
BRING IT!

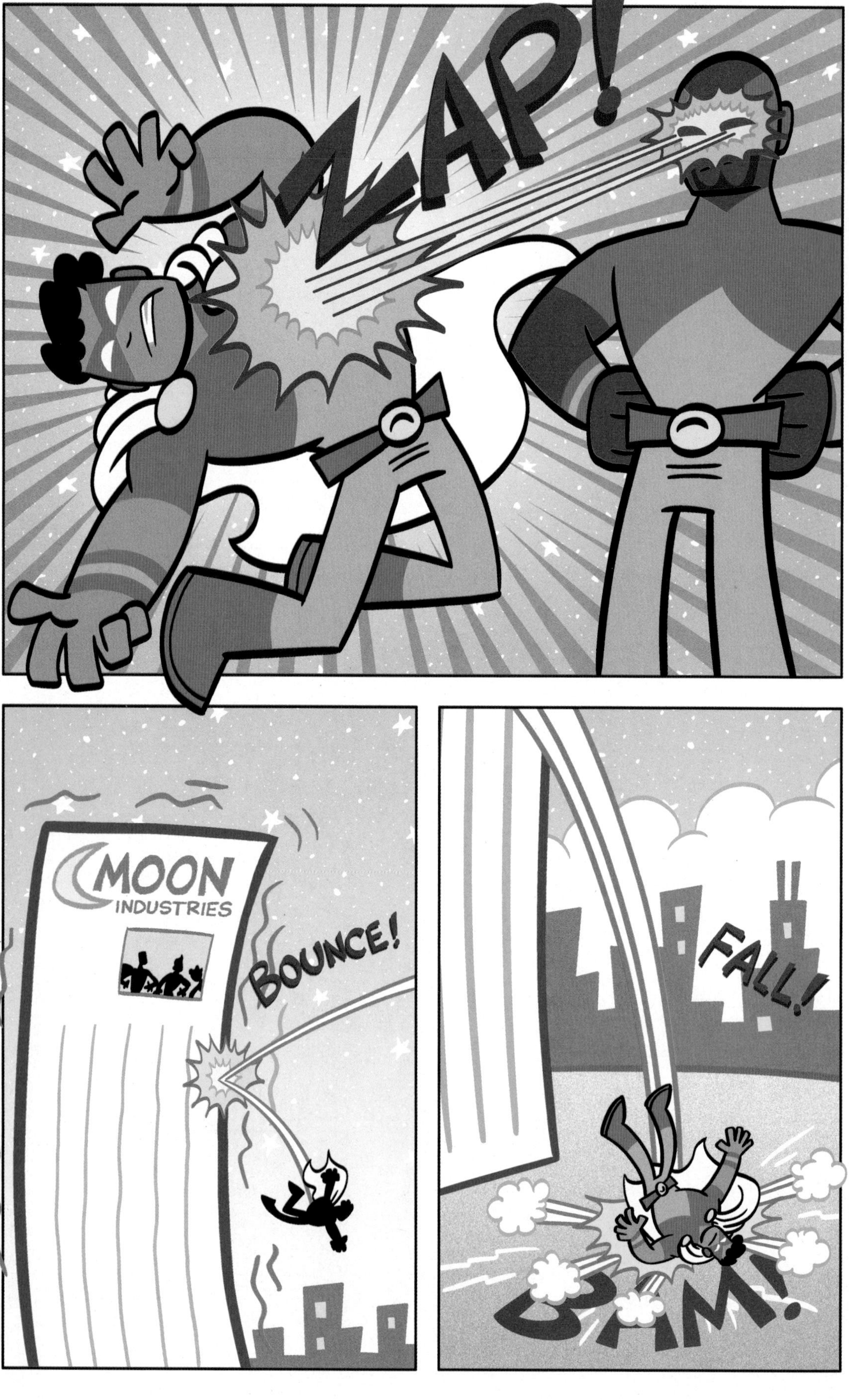
ZAP!
MOON
INDUSTRIES
BOUNCE!
FALL!

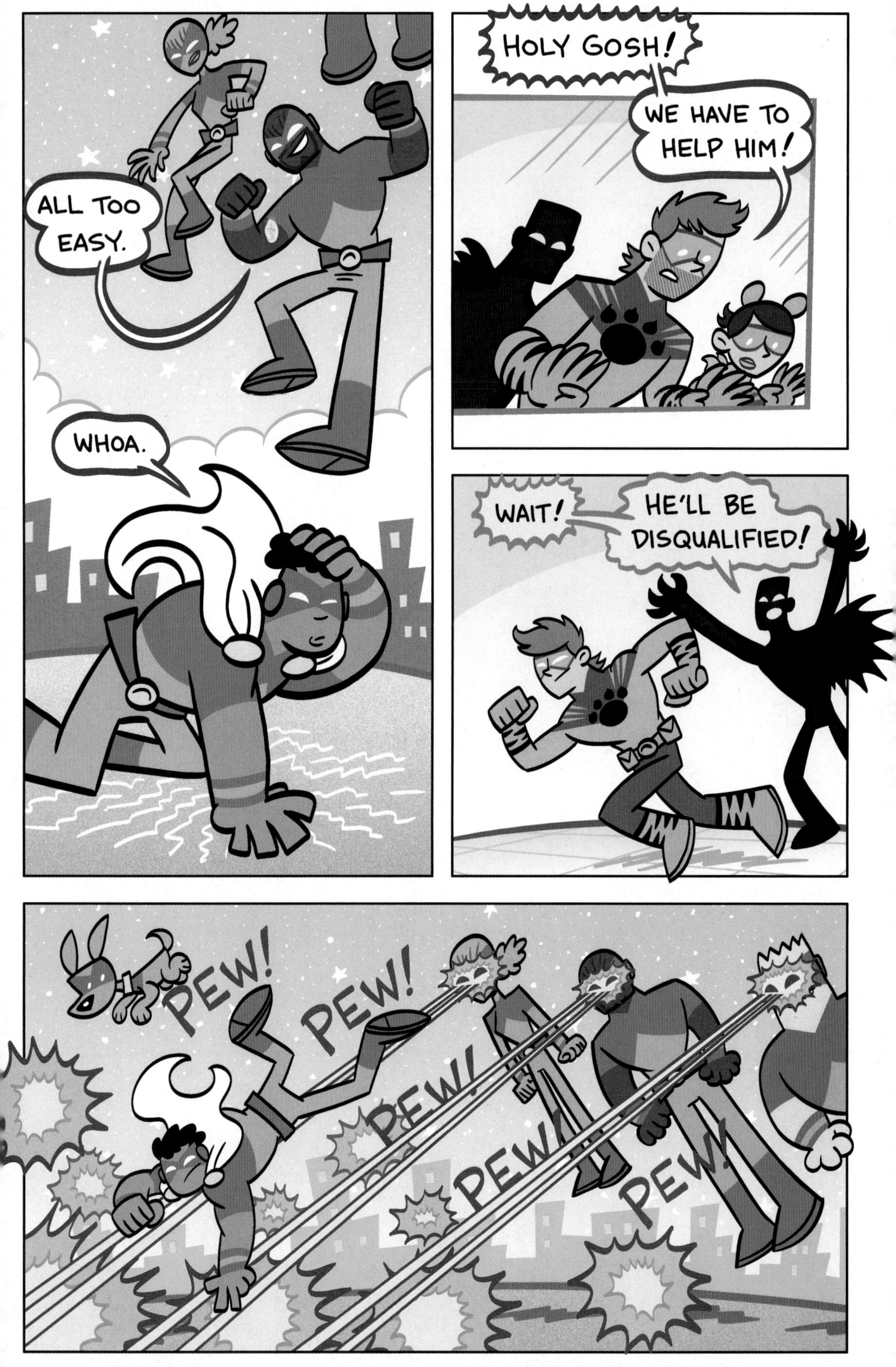
ALL TOO EASY.
WHOA.
HOLY GOSH!
WE HAVE TO HELP HIM!
WAIT!
HE'LL BE DISQUALIFIED!
PEW!
PEW!
PEW!
PEW!
PEW!

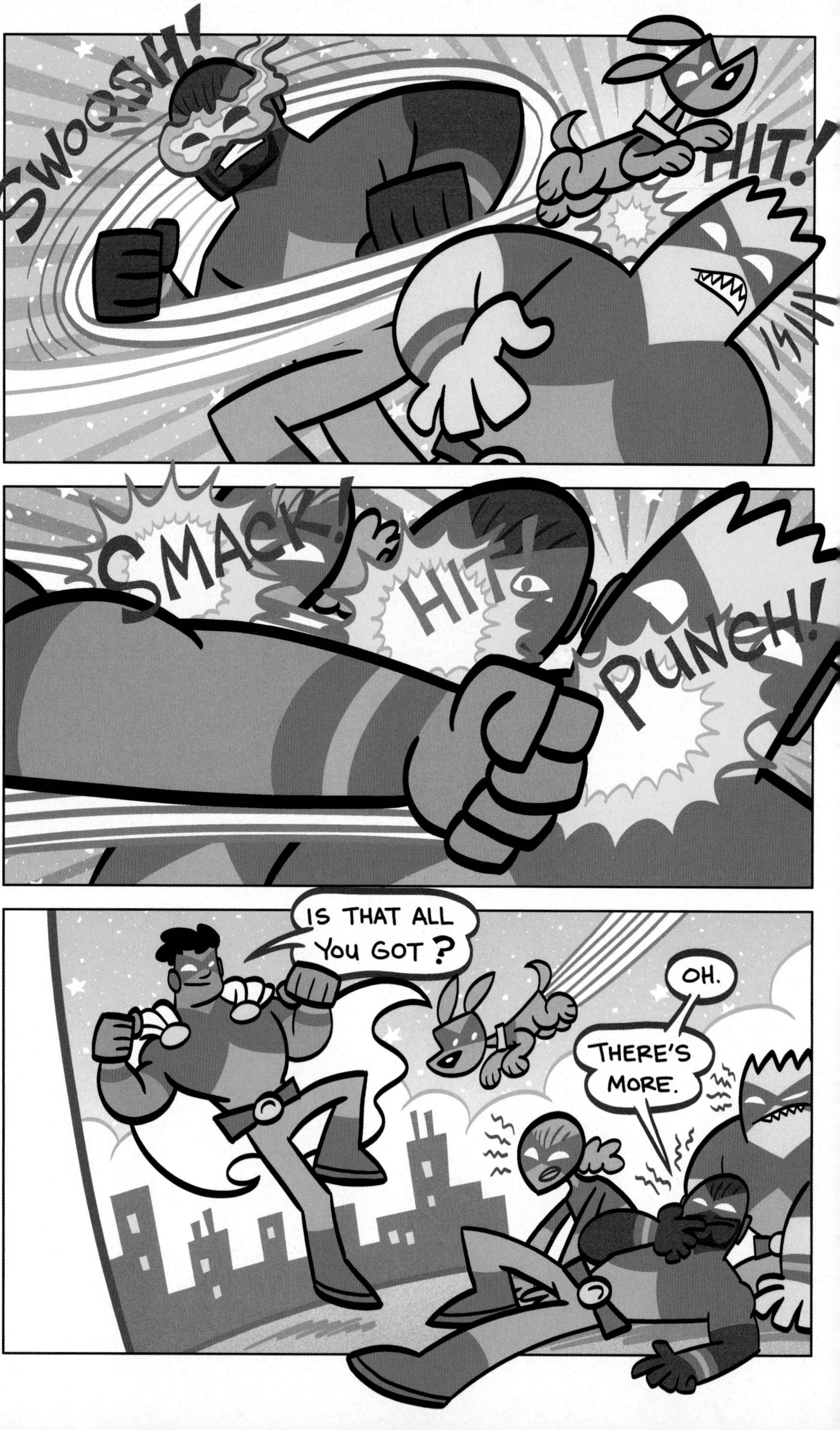
SWOOSH!
HIT!
SMACK!
HIT!
PUNCH!
IS THAT ALL YOU GOT?
OH.
THERE'S MORE.

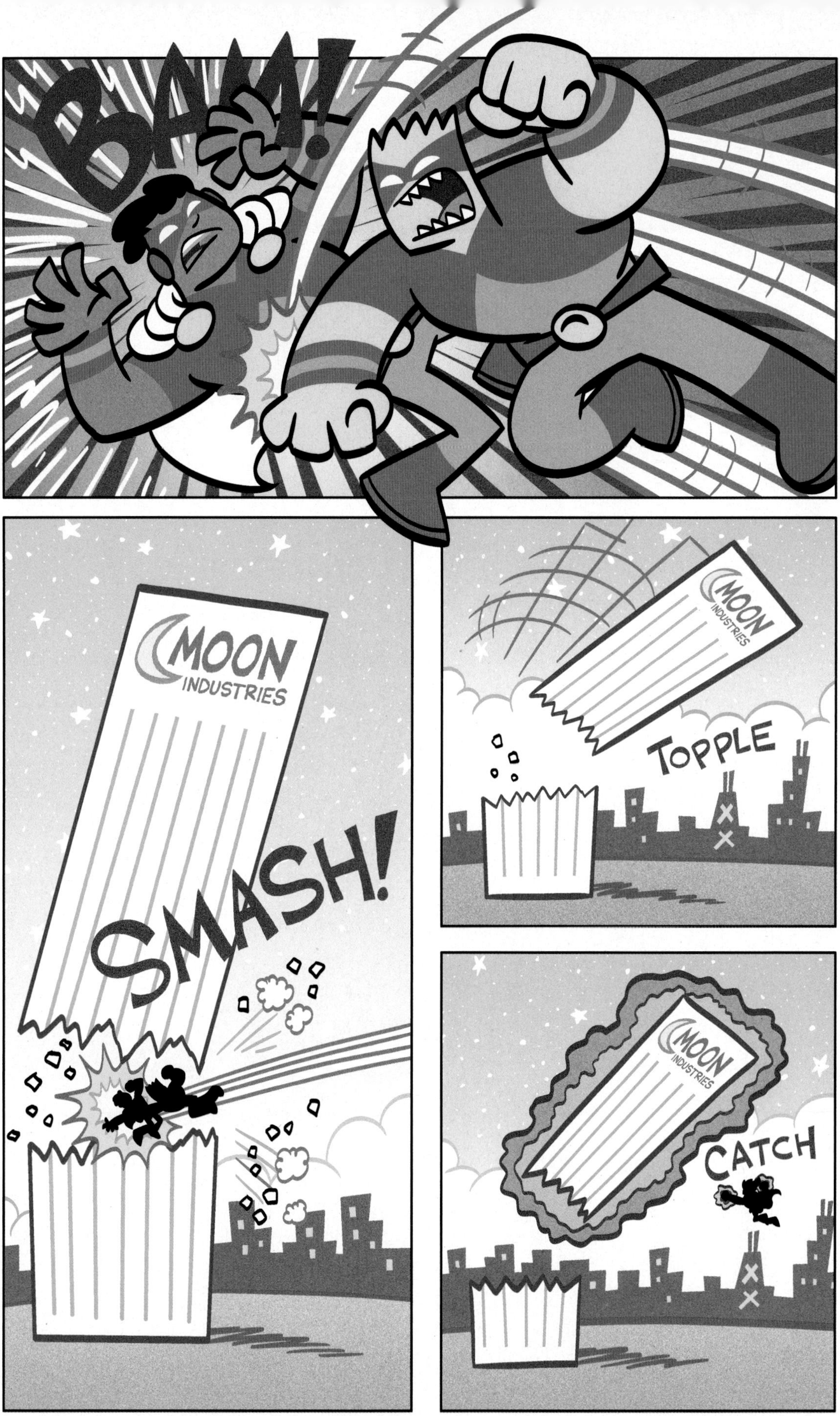
BAM!
MOON INDUSTRIES
SMASH!
MOON INDUSTRIES
TOPPLE
MOON INDUSTRIES
CATCH

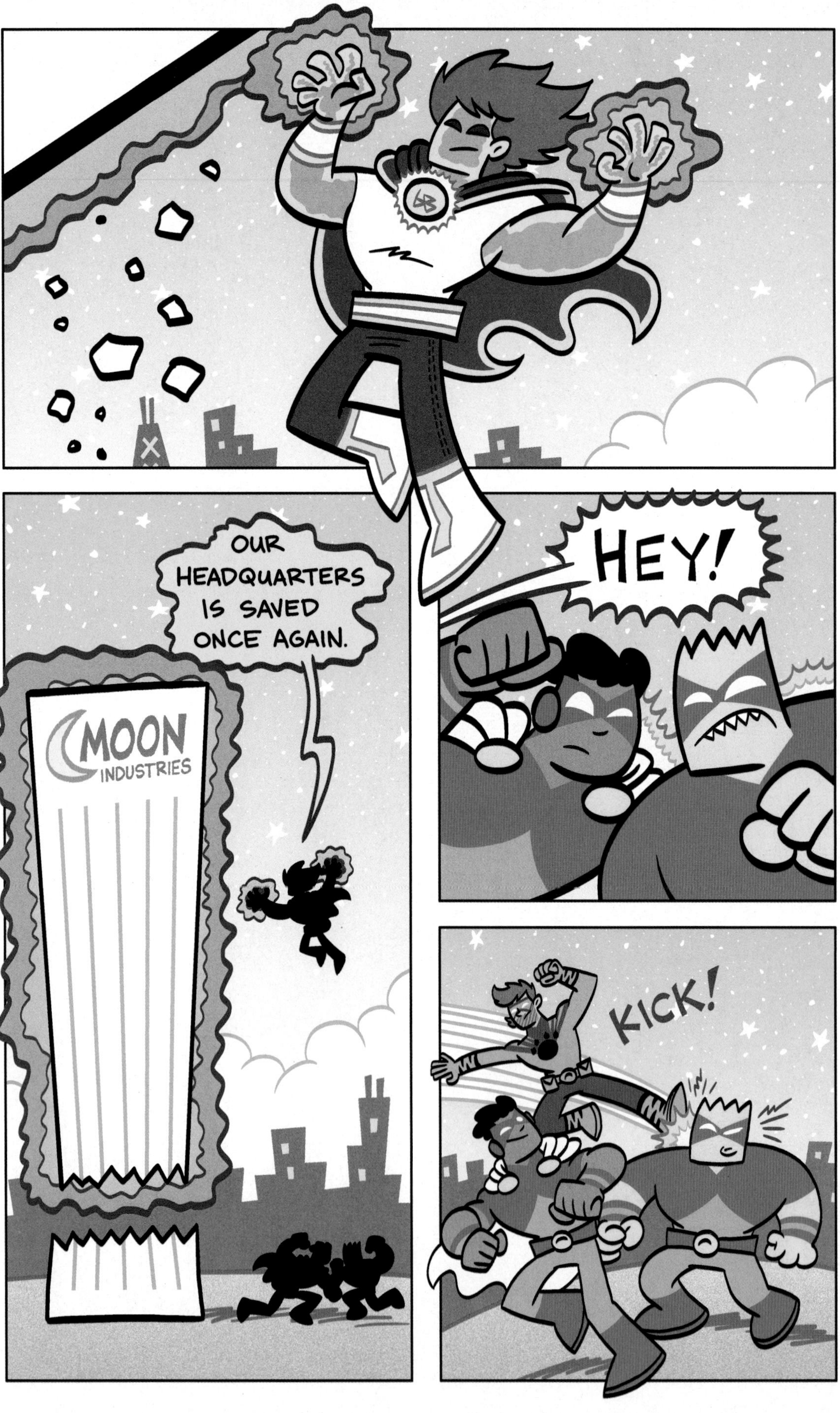
OUR HEADQUARTERS IS SAVED ONCE AGAIN.
MOON INDUSTRIES
HEY!
KICK!

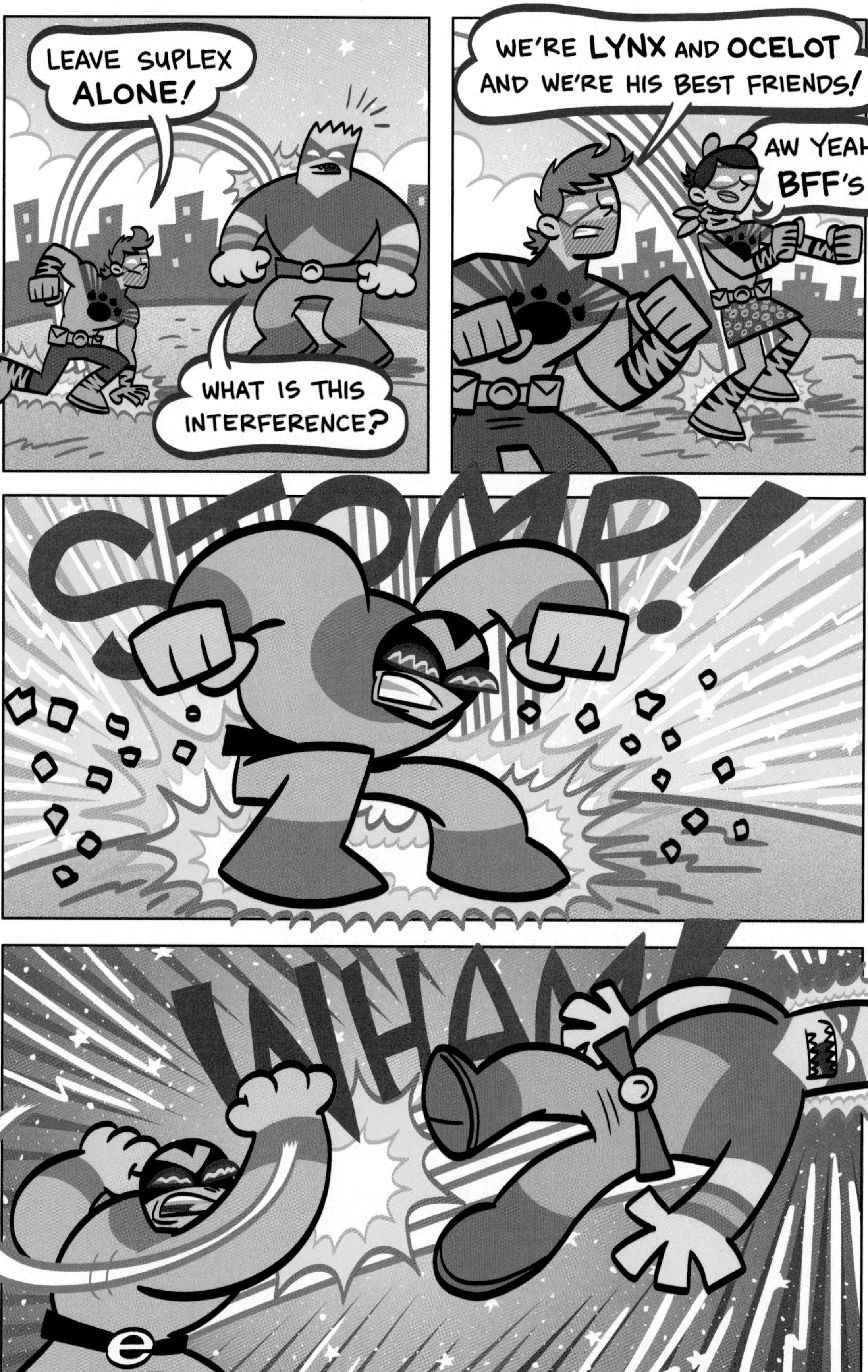
LEAVE SUPLEX ALONE!
WHAT IS THIS INTERFERENCE?
WE'RE LYNX AND OCELOT AND WE'RE HIS BEST FRIENDS!
AW YEAH, BFF's!

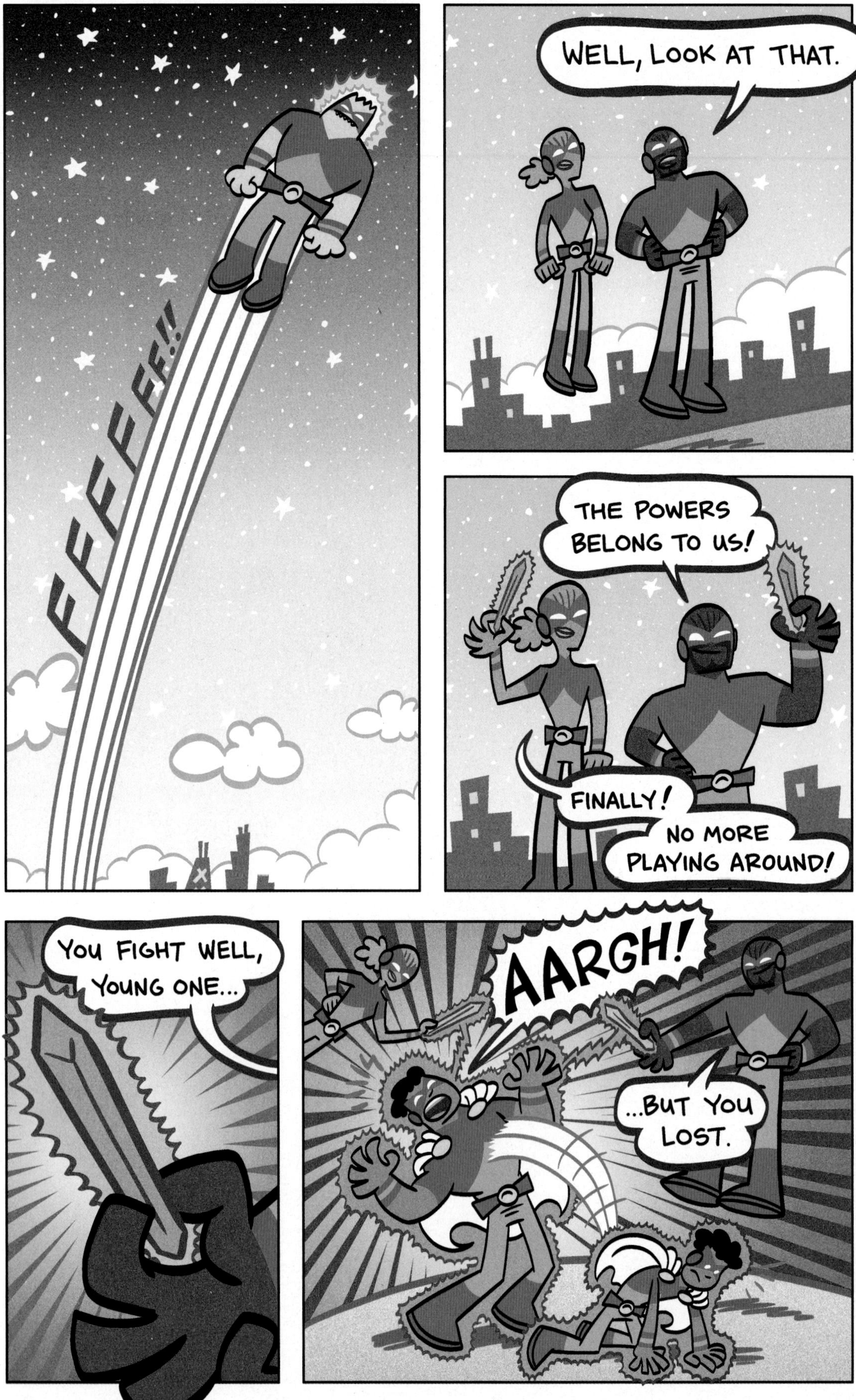
FFFFFFF!!
WELL, LOOK AT THAT.
THE POWERS BELONG TO US!
FINALLY!
NO MORE PLAYING AROUND!
YOU FIGHT WELL, YOUNG ONE...
AARGH!
...BUT YOU LOST.

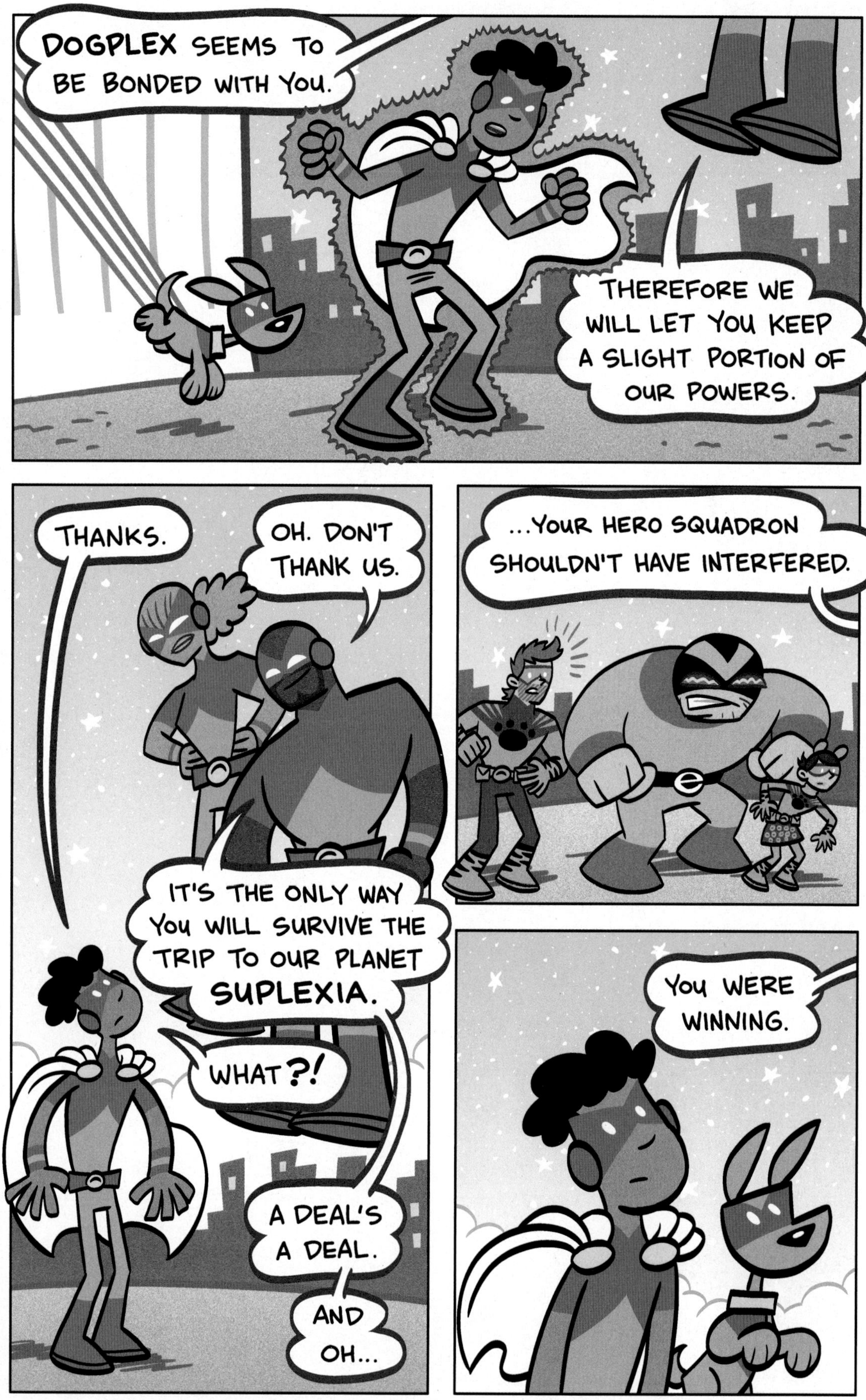
DOGPLEX SEEMS TO BE BONDED WITH YOU.
THEREFORE WE WILL LET YOU KEEP A SLIGHT PORTION OF OUR POWERS.
THANKS.
OH. DON'T THANK US.
IT'S THE ONLY WAY YOU WILL SURVIVE THE TRIP TO OUR PLANET SUPLEXIA.
WHAT?!
A DEAL'S A DEAL.
AND OH...
...YOUR HERO SQUADRON SHOULDN'T HAVE INTERFERED.
YOU WERE WINNING.

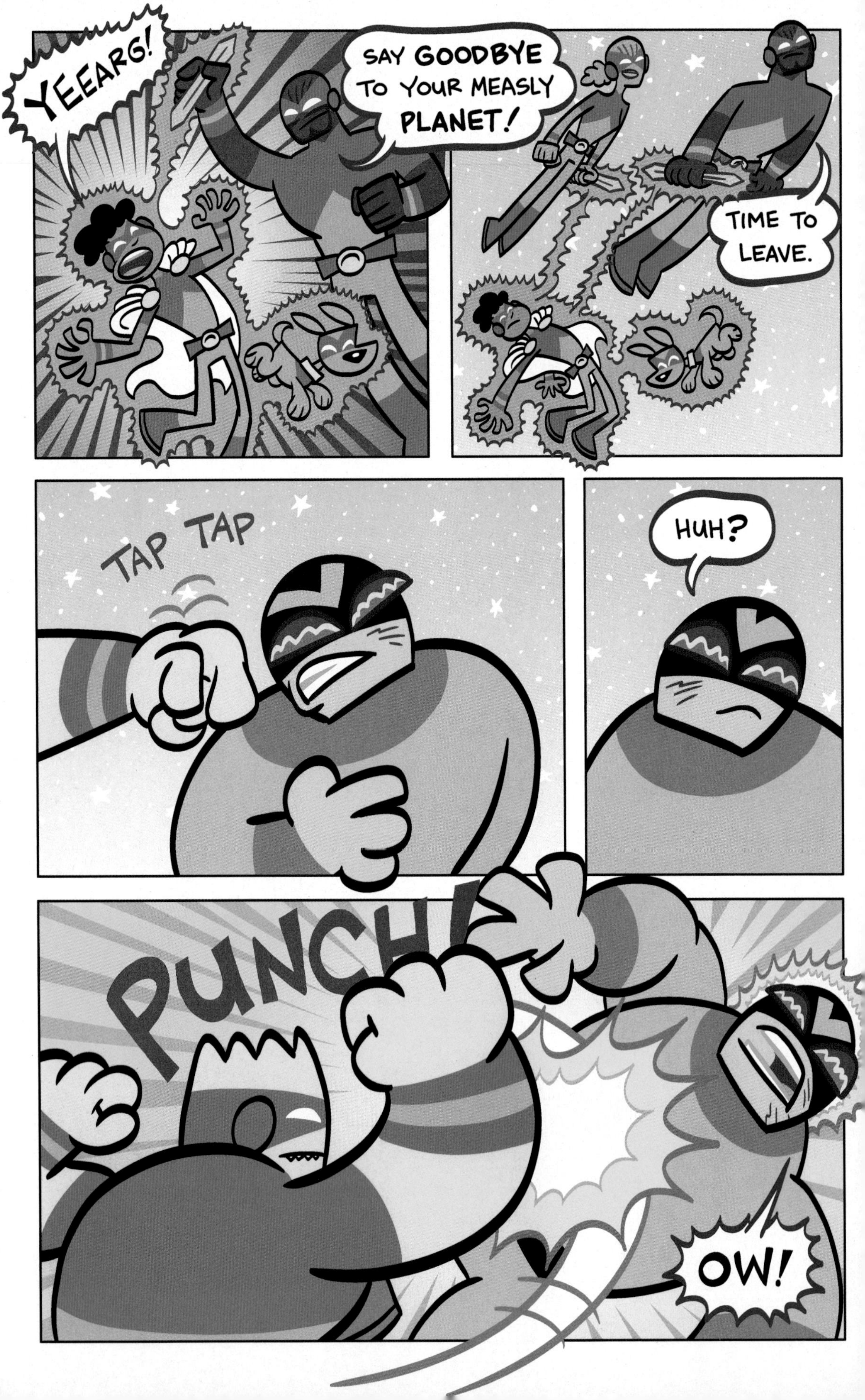
YEEARG!
SAY GOODBYE TO YOUR MEASLY PLANET!
TIME TO LEAVE.
TAP TAP
HUH?
PUNCH!
OW!

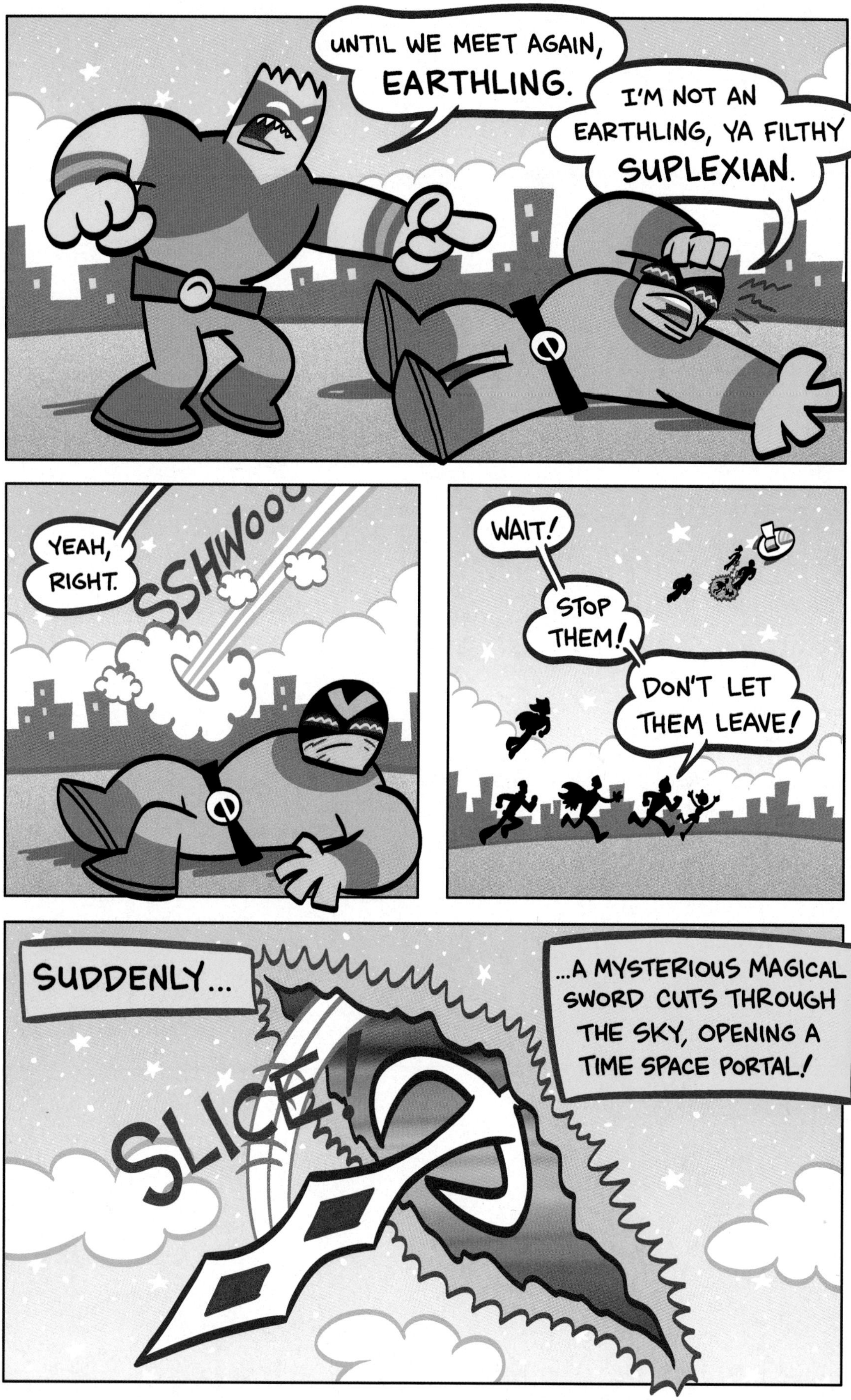
UNTIL WE MEET AGAIN, EARTHLING.
I'M NOT AN EARTHLING, YA FILTHY SUPLEXIAN.
YEAH, RIGHT.
SSHWOOO
WAIT!
STOP THEM!
DON'T LET THEM LEAVE!
SUDDENLY...
...A MYSTERIOUS MAGICAL SWORD CUTS THROUGH THE SKY, OPENING A TIME SPACE PORTAL!
SLICE!

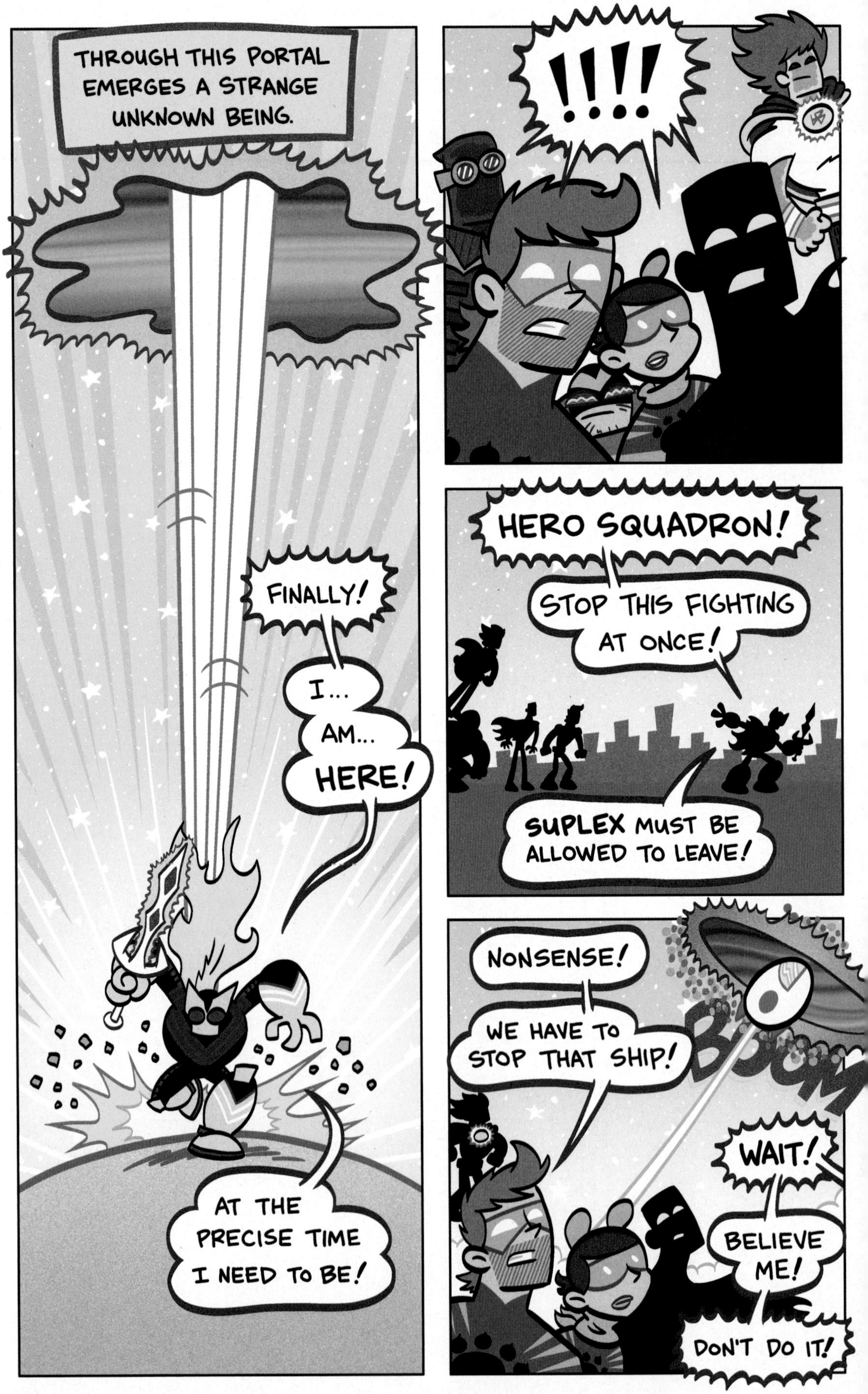
THROUGH THIS PORTAL EMERGES A STRANGE UNKNOWN BEING.
FINALLY!
I...
AM...
HERE!
AT THE PRECISE TIME I NEED TO BE!
!!!!
HERO SQUADRON!
STOP THIS FIGHTING AT ONCE!
SUPLEX MUST BE ALLOWED TO LEAVE!
NONSENSE!
WE HAVE TO STOP THAT SHIP!
BOOM
WAIT!
BELIEVE ME!
DON'T DO IT!

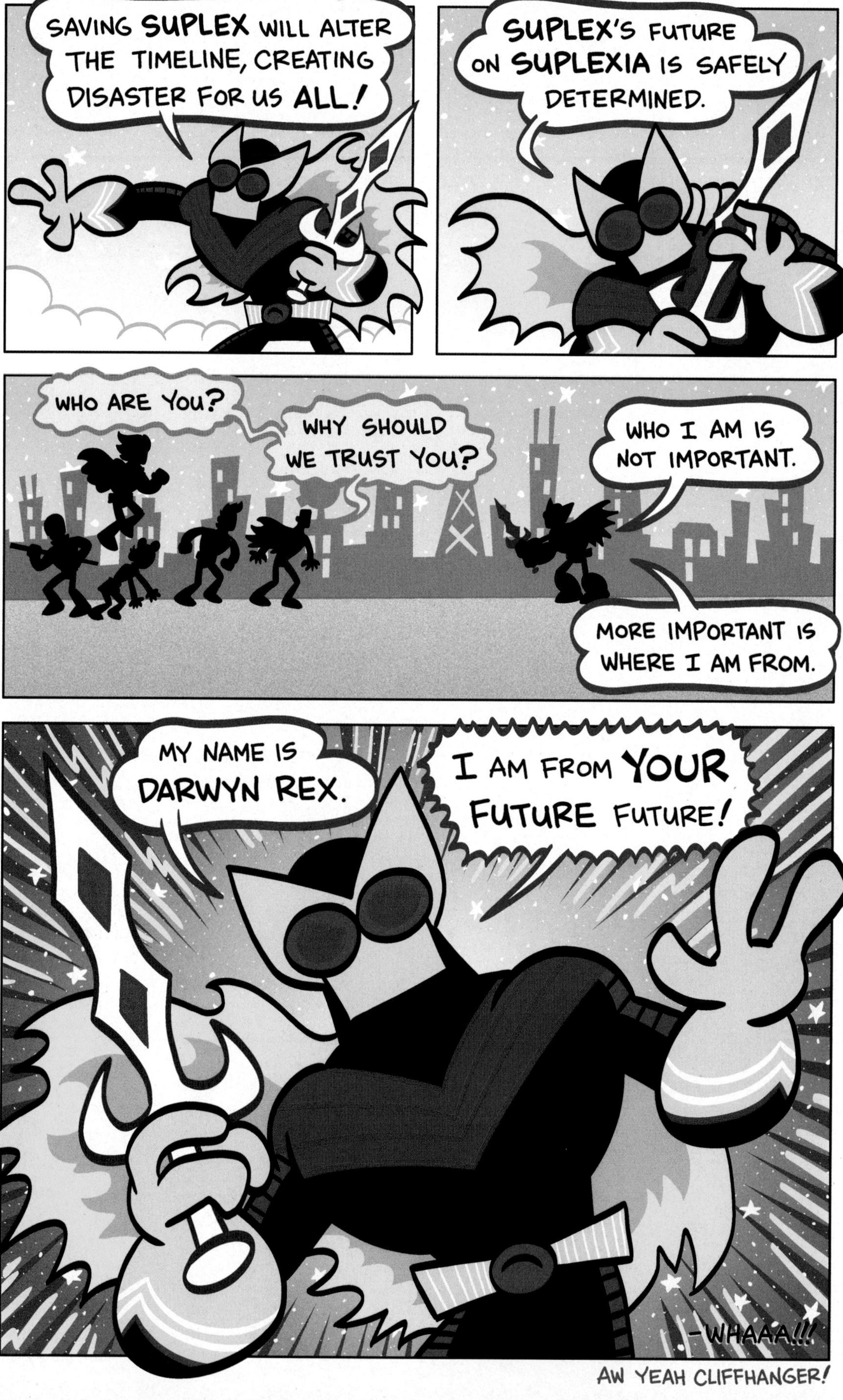

SAVING SUPLEX WILL ALTER THE TIMELINE, CREATING DISASTER FOR US ALL!
SUPLEX'S FUTURE ON SUPLEXIA IS SAFELY DETERMINED.
WHO ARE YOU?
WHY SHOULD WE TRUST YOU?
WHO I AM IS NOT IMPORTANT.
MORE IMPORTANT IS WHERE I AM FROM.
MY NAME IS DARWYN REX.
I AM FROM YOUR FUTURE FUTURE!
-WHAAA!!!
AW YEAH CLIFFHANGER!

Before...

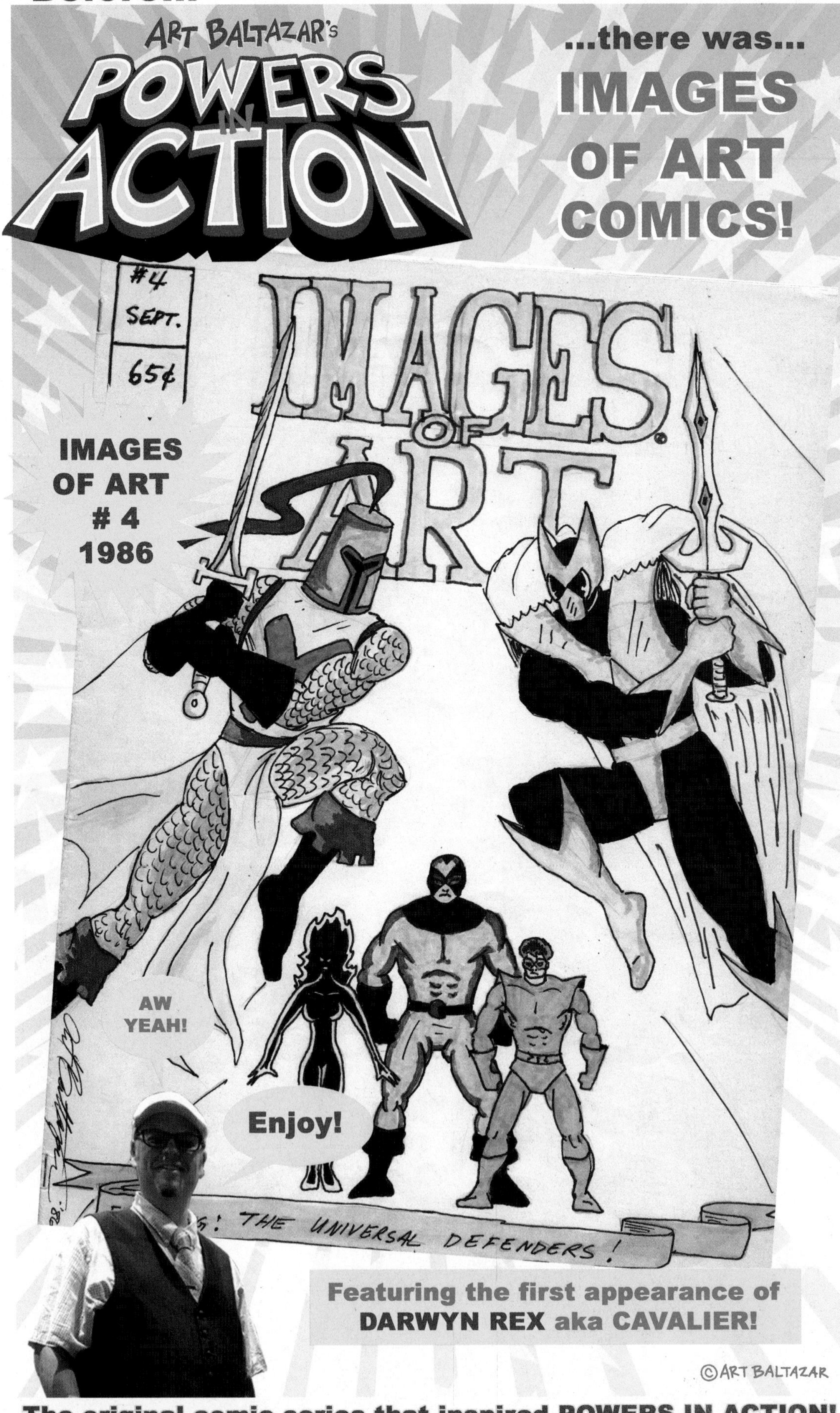

ART BALTAZAR's
POWERS IN ACTION
...there was...
IMAGES OF ART COMICS!
#4 SEPT. 65¢
IMAGES OF ART
IMAGES OF ART # 4 1986
AW YEAH!
Enjoy!
THE UNIVERSAL DEFENDERS!
Featuring the first appearance of DARWYN REX aka CAVALIER!
©ART BALTAZAR

The original comic series that inspired POWERS IN ACTION!

Before...

ART BALTAZAR's POWERS IN ACTION

...there was...

IMAGES OF ART COMICS!

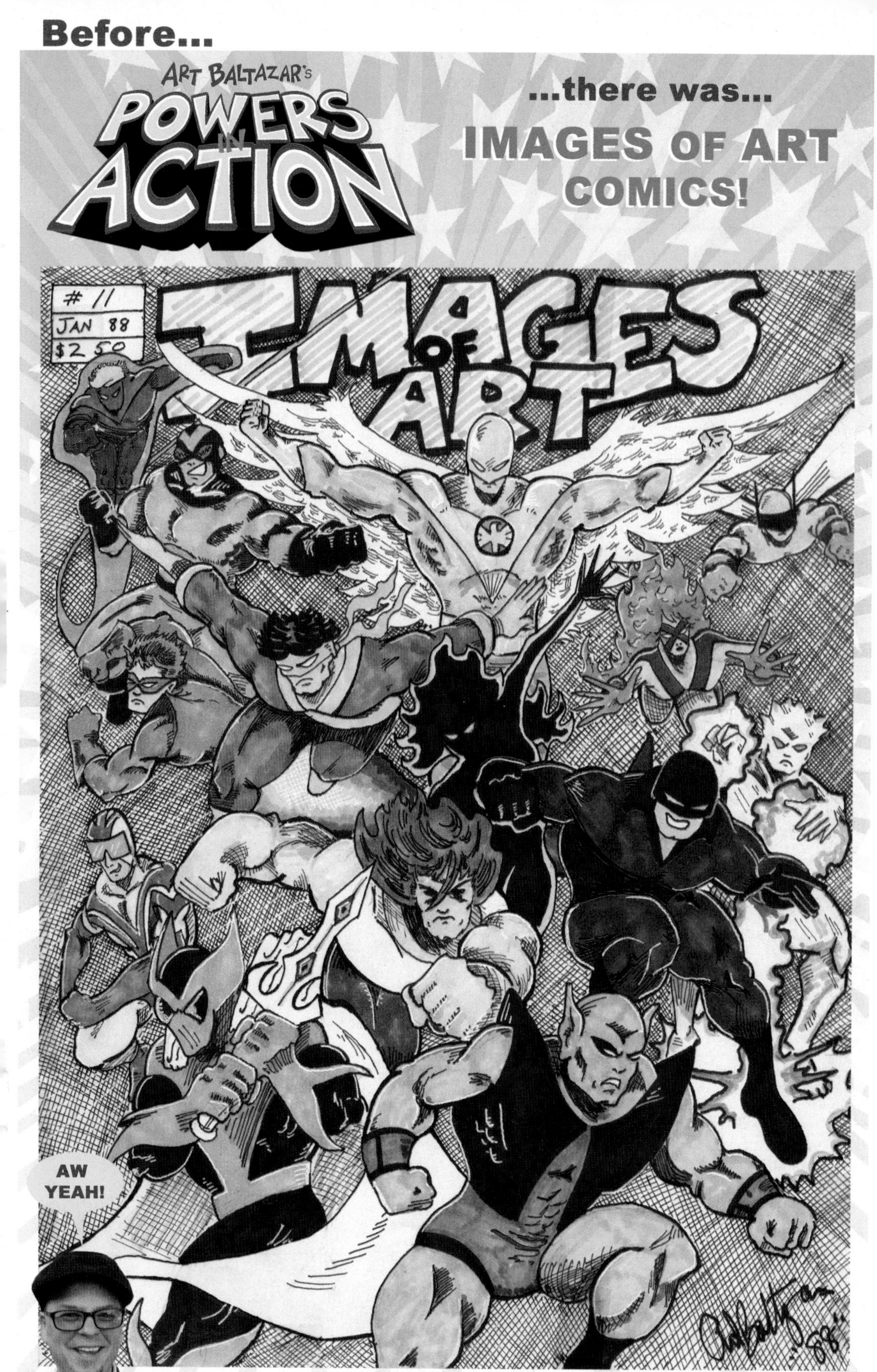
#11
JAN 88
$2.50
IMAGES OF ART
AW YEAH!

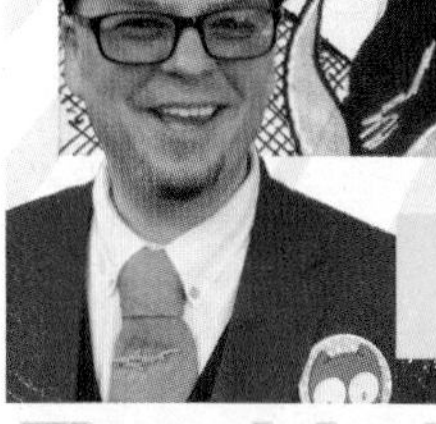

IMAGES OF ART #11 from 1988

The original comic series that inspired POWERS IN ACTION!

BONUS BONUS ARTIST PIN-UP!!

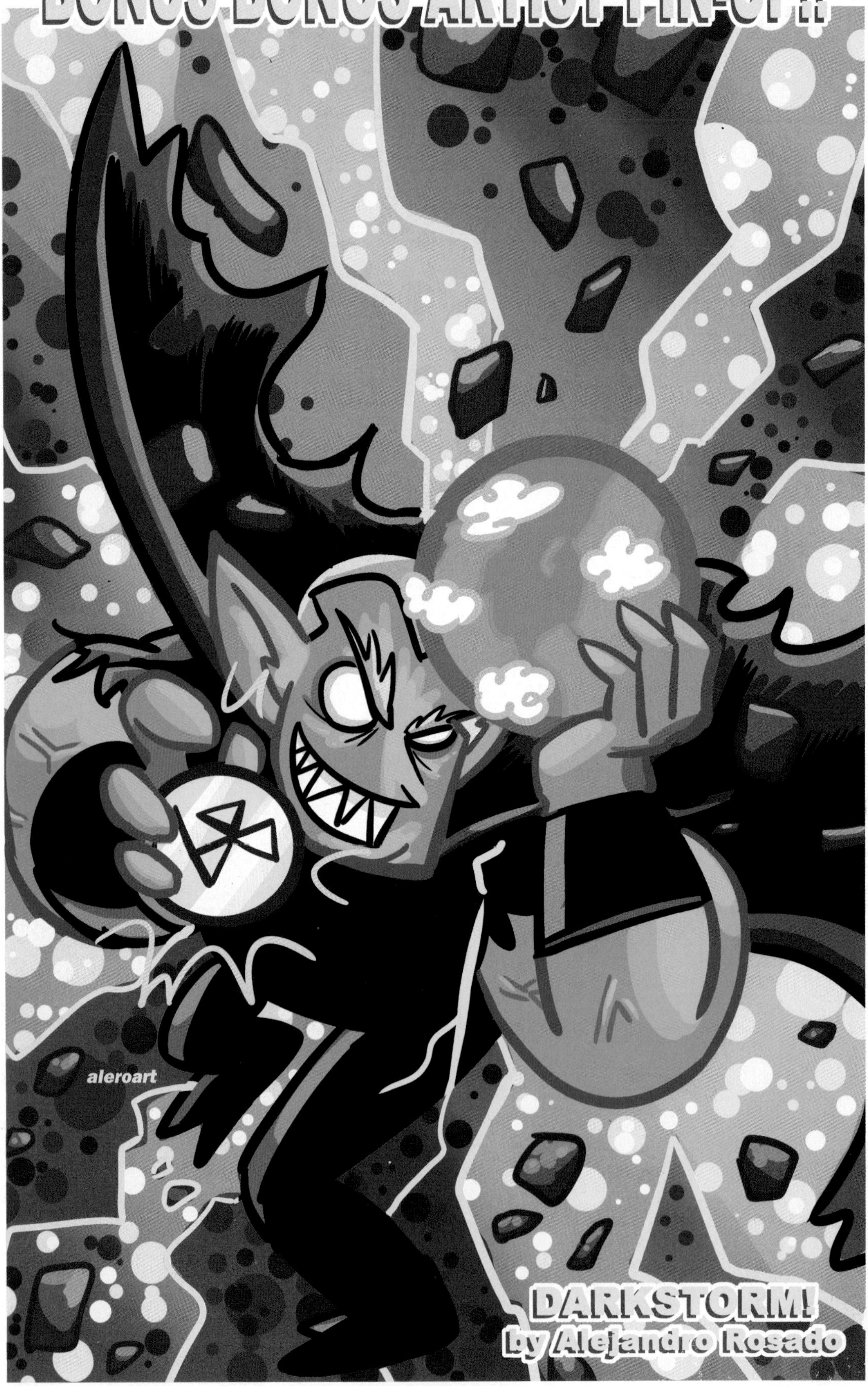
aleroart
DARKSTORM!
by Alejandro Rosado